Shadow Lane
Volume 10

The Spanking Adventures of Amanda Sands

by
Eve Howard

CCB Publishing
British Columbia, Canada

Shadow Lane Volume 10: The Spanking Adventures of Amanda Sands

Copyright ©2010 by Eve Howard
ISBN-13   978-1-926585-79-6
First Edition

Library and Archives Canada Cataloguing in Publication
Howard, Eve, 1953-
Shadow lane : volume 10 : the spanking adventures of Amanda Sands /
written by Eve Howard – 1st ed.
ISBN 978-1-926585-79-6
Also available in electronic format.
I. Title.
PS3608.O82S54 2010   813'.6   C2010-902370-6

Cover and interior artwork by Tarsis: www.briantarsis.com

Publisher: CCB Publishing
             British Columbia, Canada
             www.ccbpublishing.com

Dedicated to the real life Thalia and the real life Marguerite,
my beautiful, decadent muses

Shadow Lane

Volume 10

The Spanking Adventures of Amanda Sands

Contents

Amanda Sands and Marty Patmore

Chapter One

Marriage Proposal

Hugo Sands had seldom, if ever, been interrupted while spanking a girl in his shop, but that autumn afternoon the bell tinkled at the very moment he had impulsively seized Laura Random and thrust her down across his immaculately trousered lap.

"You're really lucky," he told his beloved, releasing her and getting to his feet. "The first time I bother to propose to you in all these years and you turn me down? This interview is not over!"

"I just said I wanted to think it over," Laura protested weakly as he strode out of the lounge and onto the floor of his antiques shop to greet the very interesting looking young lady who had just walked in. She was a willowy ash blonde in a flawlessly tailored navy suit with a pencil skirt, narrow lapels and a crisp white shirt. She wore navy spectator pumps and carried a matching envelope clutch. Her long, straight, fair hair framed a charming face, aglow with health and intelligence.

"Hello!" said Hugo warmly.

"Hello!" she replied, with ill-suppressed excitement, "Are you Hugo Sands?

"Yes! You must be the model from Boston?"

The girl stared at him for just a moment in perplexity before nodding in smiling agreement with his conclusion.

"I thought your train wasn't getting in until two. Oh well, no matter. You photo didn't do you justice, Margot," said Hugo, shaking her slender hand.

"Oh, Margot couldn't make it. She got sick. They sent me instead. I hope that's okay. My name is Amanda," said the girl with a smile that crinkled her light blue eyes in a childlike fashion.

"It's fine," he said, looking her over again. "You are over eighteen though, right? I mean, you have photo id?"

"Oh, certainly. I have a passport and a driver's license."

"Perfect! Well, come on back to the office and I'll show you the set and where you can get ready. Though you won't have to do much. That's a honey of an outfit you have on."

"Thank you! I bought it just to meet you."

"Really?"

"Believe me, this is the most exciting day of my life!"

"So, you're really in the scene, then?" Hugo led her back to his office where Laura was checking the battery on her camera. "Laura, this is Amanda. She came instead of Margot, who's apparently sick."

"Hi Amanda. I'll be taking the photos," said Laura, shaking Amanda's hand. "God, you're gorgeous," Laura added, delighted by the beauty of her subject.

"And I'll be spanking you," said Hugo.

"I'm both thrilled and terrified," Amanda replied with her hand to her heart.

"Seriously, though, you look incredibly young," Hugo said. "Just how old are you?"

"I'm 18."

"And, have you played before?"

"With my boyfriend I have!"

"So you're saying you were into spanking before you started modeling?"

"Oh, definitely. I think it's in my blood!"

"Why?" Laura asked, interested because an enthusiasm for spanking seemed to run in her own family as well.

"Well, because I know for a fact that my father spanked my mother on the night I was conceived."

"How do you know that?" Laura asked.

"Because she told me that he always spanked her before they had sex."

"Wow," said Hugo. "Well, you'll do very nicely, I think. Why don't we go back to the studio and get started?"

Laura showed Amanda to a small room fitted up as a dressing room where Amanda sat at an ebony vanity and touched up her lipstick. The adjoining photographic studio featured a set that had been furnished as an old fashioned executive office, with a large mahogany desk and matching bookcase, brass-riveted leather chairs and a matching sofa.

Hugo and Laura had posed for and shot so many spanking photo sets over the years that the positioning and action flowed effortlessly, with a minimal exchange of verbal direction.

"Now listen honey, since this is only for stills, I'm not going to really spank you until we get to the bare bottom part, when you need to be pink," said Hugo, once the initial pull over and surprised reaction shots had been taken by Laura.

"But, I won't be able to produce the proper expression unless I'm really feeling it!" Amanda protested, looking back at him.

"You want me to really spank you?" he grinned at the agreeable girl.

"Yes! I need something to write in my diary tonight!"

Hugo shrugged at Laura, then slowly and methodically began to enact all the stages of a spanking that would go into making up an exciting photoset for an elegant spanking magazine. He'd been publishing his New Rod Quarterly since before Amanda was born and had a reputation for posing the most refined spanking photos in the scene. This Amanda would be the newest jewel in The New Rod's crown. For a slim girl, she had a remarkably shapely, jutting bottom, which Hugo began to warm through the fine wool suit skirt with the palm of his hand.

"Oh," she interrupted him. "I can take it much harder than that."

Hugo grinned at Laura, tucking his hand around Amanda's waist and pausing while Laura lined up the shot.

"Amanda, cheat your eyes up like you're looking back at Hugo but keep your face turned towards me," said Laura. "Hugo, look at her, in my direction. Okay, give her about six swats, but slowly."

Hugo administered six hard swats, spaced ten or so seconds apart, each one eliciting a sharp intake of breath, a leggy kick and a vigorous flip of a curtain of silken sandy blonde hair.

"You two almost look alike," Laura commented, snapping photos every couple of seconds. "You have identical coloring and the shape of your eyes...Hugo, we should make this a father-daughter scenario."

The comment caused a naughty smile to flit across Amanda's face, again crinkling her eyes in a manner that made her look years younger than eighteen. Laura snapped another face shot then paused.

"Hugo, could I talk to you for a minute?" Laura said.

"Why? What's going on?"

"Just a second," said Laura, marching out of the room.

Hugo put Amanda off his lap and told her to wait there then joined Laura in the dressing room.

"What is it?"

"We need to look at that girl's id before we lift her skirt. She looks so young to me!"

"Okay, okay, no problem."

They went back into the studio.

"Honey, let's get your id shot now, so we don't have to think about it later," said Hugo to Amanda.

"Sure," replied Amanda, digging her documents out of her purse and presenting them to Hugo.

"Go ahead and hold them so Laura can photograph them," said Hugo, "you know how."

Amanda looked momentarily puzzled then laughed and replied, "Well, I'm kind of new to this, I forgot how."

"Hold them under your chin," said Laura, positioning the opened passport and driver's license in Amanda's hands.

While Laura was focusing on Amanda's face and the identifying documents below she noticed that Amanda's last name was Sands.

"What a funny coincidence," said Laura, "Amanda's last name is Sands."

"That is funny," said Hugo. "Well? How's that birth date?"

"Oh, she's eighteen all right. Just," Laura replied.

Just then the phone rang. Laura picked it up, spoke for a few moments then turned to Hugo. "It's Margot. She's at the station."

"I thought you said Margot was sick?" Hugo said to Amanda.

"She must have felt better at the last minute and not realized they sent me," Amanda replied calmly.

"Laura, would you run and pick her up? We'll turn this into a double shoot."

"That will work," said Laura, leaving Hugo to stare at Amanda with a strange sensation.

"You're not... related to me, are you?" he asked, feeling as he looked into her pale blue eyes that he was looking into a mirror.

"Yes, I am. Haven't you figured it out yet?"

"I know I don't have any more nieces. Are you perhaps a second cousin?"

"You wish. I'm your daughter." A moment of silence passed as he stared at her intently, searching her face for a trick or a prank. It was impossible, unbelievable, for to his certain knowledge he had never impregnated any woman in the entire course of his life. And yet, she looked so much like him, it was almost impossible not to believe it at once. Even Laura had instantly noticed the resemblance.

"But..." Hugo hesitated as he groped for the right words, "...how is it I haven't heard about you before? Who's your mother?"

"Don't you remember who you were making love to eighteen years ago?"

"Cassandra," he replied at once, recalling his long lost love and a prophetic poem, which she had left behind, containing a cryptic, line about two becoming three. That line had haunted him since Laura had unearthed the scroll on the upper shelf of a closet in a room in his house occupied by Cassandra almost two decades before.

"Yes!"

For a moment they simply gazed at each other. Then he came out of his reverie, resisting the urge to embrace his newly sprung offspring as he remembered the event she had interrupted upon her arrival.

"Of all days you had to show up!" Hugo snapped, pacing with his hands in his pockets.

"Why? What's the matter with today?" Amanda queried, observing that he seemed more peeved than upset.

"I was proposing marriage to Laura after six years of being crazy about her and she was thinking about saying yes. How unsexy is a suitor with a grown daughter!"

"I think you're incredibly sexy," said Amanda, unfazed.

Then Hugo began to process the scandalous realization that he'd just spanked his own daughter. "So, what was with the prank?" he demanded.

"The posing as a model? That was a sudden inspiration. I've always wondered what a spanking from my daddy would feel like!" said Amanda, spontaneously hugging Hugo. He hugged her back briefly then thrust her away, exclaiming, "This is absurd. It can't be. It must be a practical joke. Why show up now? Why today? I'm confused. Let's get coffee."

They locked up the store and walked across the street to Marguerite Alexander's bookshop, where Hope Spencer Lawrence was presiding over an empty coffee bar.

"Hi Hope," said Hugo, leaving Amanda at one of the small tables by the hearth. "Bring us a couple of double caps, would you?"

"Who's the babe?" asked the resident blonde beauty of Random Point in all innocence, used to Hugo stuffing his models with chocolate chip muffins during photo shoots. Hope Spencer Lawrence would have shot regularly for Hugo herself, had her husband not been an instructor at the local prep school attempting to maintain a low profile about his wife's professional B&D past.

"My daughter, apparently," Hugo confided, too struck by the uncanny resemblance between himself and the girl to attempt to deny it. Anyway, the word Cassandra had more or less explained it all. Anything was possible when that laser-focused female was involved.

"She'll bring us coffee," said Hugo, sitting opposite Amanda, who folded her French manicured hands calmly on the small, round wooden table between them but grinned back at him, mirthful at the trick she had pulled off.

"I just don't understand your mother's behavior," Hugo said somewhat helplessly. "I was still completely enamored with her when she left me. She never said a word about a baby. Why? I would have married her."

"Yes, we always felt you would have. But Mother knew you didn't want children and didn't feel it was fair to thrust me on you."

"She might have let me know! Oh, am I going to thrash her for this!"

"She also said your aura was too powerful to expose an impressionable child to."

Hugo groaned and exclaimed, "That's the first thing you've said that doesn't surprise me. No doubt she traced the moment of your conception to a period during which mercury was in retrograde, and it gave her a foreboding of evil."

"She merely felt that a child should be reared by milder and less mercurial types than yourself."

"Oh, is that so? And who'd she fix you up with instead?"

"A wise and industrious vegan who married Mother when I was three and has furnished me with gentle guidance ever since. He owns yoga studios and health food stores in San Francisco."

"Well, what the hell did she think I would have done to you?" Hugo bristled.

"She just didn't want me growing up to be a spoiled daddy's girl."

"So? How did you turn out?"

"I'm a daddy's girl," she grinned. "But not spoiled. I worked in the store and taught yoga classes all through high school."

"So, when did you find out about me?" Hugo asked, thanking Hope for the large steaming cups of cappuccino she set down before them.

"Hello," said Hope, smiling at Amanda.

"Hello," Amanda replied.

"Later," said Hugo, shooing Hope back to the coffee bar.

"Well, I was twelve going on thirteen when I began to explore Mother's sizable collection of erotica, which included issues of your magazine going back many years. Enthralled, I worked my way backwards in time until I reached the issues that my mother actually had modeled for and worked on with you. Mother saw how much the New Rod Quarterly interested me and told me about the relationship she'd had with its editor, confiding that it had been the first great romance of her life. The magazines had publication dates so it was easy for me to figure out that she'd been sleeping with you when I was conceived. She didn't deny it.

Naturally I wanted to meet you at once, but she convinced me to develop myself into an independent person of whom you might be proud before inserting myself into your life. When I asked her what she thought I should do to make you proud of me, she suggested I get myself into Harvard. I'm starting my freshman year next week."

"You don't say so! Congratulations, honey!"

"Thank you. By the way, here's the bill for my first semester," she said, handing him an eye opener of an invoice.

"Oh my god, is that what college costs these days?"

"Mother didn't think you'd mind since she's handled everything else."

"Sure," Hugo said, folding the bill and slipping it into his jacket pocket. "It's the least I can do."

"Actually the least you could do would be to buy me this coffee. Paying for Harvard is handsome," smiled Amanda, sipping creamy foam.

Hugo kept looking at her, unable to stop himself from smiling. "I can't believe she kept this kind of secret from me. But she's certainly done a good job with you. Probably much better than I could have done."

"She'll be happy to hear that. She always told me that you were the only man she actually tried to please."

"What about your current dad?"

"He's easy to please. You just have to be perfect at all times."

"Is that why you're so together?"

"Thank you for noticing," she grinned.

"You seem like a happy girl. Are you happy?"

"I'm as happy today as I've ever been," Amanda replied, clasping one of his hands between both of her own for just an instant.

"I wish I didn't have the shoot scheduled, but Laura will be bringing back the real model any minute."

"Can't I continue to be in the shoot?" Amanda asked.

"You really WANT to be in a spanking magazine?" Hugo was astonished.

"I really WANT to be on the cover!"

Hugo laughed and shook his head.

"I'm serious, Mr. Sands," said Amanda.

"Is that what you plan to call me?"

"What would you like me to call you?"

"Hugo will do."

"I notice you've already acknowledged me as your daughter," said Amanda, nodding towards Hope, who was pretending to polish the counter. "That's charming."

"I'm still going to thrash your mother for keeping you a secret."

"We saved one ritual for you to take me through," Amanda said with a newer and even more naughty sparkle in her eyes.

"Really? Which one?" Hugo leaned his chin on his hand, fascinated by the well-mannered, beautifully spoken girl.

"I've waited to smoke weed all this time!" Amanda announced triumphantly.

"You did?"

"It's true. When I was around fourteen Mother suggested I save that one particular rite of passage to enjoy with you for the first time. She said you'd be the perfect guide and that you always had good bud. I think she was very clever, devising such an interesting way to keep me straight all during high school, don't you? I've always been into postponing pleasure. It's why I've been a good student."

"What a beautiful and appropriate sentiment," Hugo reflected, recalling that Cassandra's first gift to him was that of mushrooms. "I guarantee that the bud will be good," Hugo promised, briefly touching her velvety cheek. "And you being my daughter, I'm sure you've smoked enough by now to know the difference."

Amanda pinkened but only slightly.

"But about the photo shoot..." he began.

"You could call the photo spread Daddy's Girl," she persisted enthusiastically.

"It's very sweet of you to offer, but I can't exploit my own daughter."

"It isn't exploitation. What you do is art."

"Thank you," Hugo said, "I'm bowled over by your sophistication."

"Well, I grew up in San Francisco."

"Look, Amanda, even if it's not exploitation, me spanking you... isn't that ...I mean, doesn't that feel incestuous to you?"

"Why should it? To me, you're a glamorous stranger who came into my life through glossy photos and thrilling fiction, my mother's favorite lover from long ago."

"She said I was her favorite?"

"Can you doubt it?" Amanda teased, with a gleam in her eyes.

Hugo couldn't help but laugh, "I see you already know how to get a man in the palm of your hand."

"Mother thinks it would be fitting for me to appear in The New Rod Quarterly, as an example of things coming full circle. Besides, it would make me happy to be able to contribute, since you're taking on my college expenses."

"You seem very uninhibited."

"I am," Amanda agreed.

"That's a rare quality in one so young."

"My goal for freshman year is to become a Playboy centerfold."

"A...What???"

"Sounds crazy, doesn't it? But it's part of my strategy to take the world by storm." Amanda shrugged out of her jacket and draped it on the back of her chair, her fitted white blouse amply revealing how well suited she would be to pose for any centerfold on the planet.

"So, you're extremely uninhibited!" Hugo grinned. "I have to say, Cassandra certainly raised a more interesting child without me than she could have done with me." Then he happened to notice the clock on the wall. "Damn it, we have to get back. The girl will be there and I'll have to figure out what to do with you. Damn it!"

"Just let's finish the photo set," Amanda suggested brightly.

"No, I'm not laying another hand on you until I think this through and arrive at the same casual attitude you seem to have. Anyway, we already got enough photos for a cover and a profile spread."

"Oh, all right," she agreed, with resignation. "I'll work on you while you're getting me stoned tomorrow. I'll change your way of thinking."

"You are going to be a dangerous woman," Hugo predicted, leaving money on the table.

"I knew you'd get me," she said, jumping up to follow him out.

"Did you drive into Random Point?" Hugo asked as they walked out of the bookstore and back across cobbled Shadow Lane to his own shop.

"Yes, I left my rental car at the Inn."

"You've got yourself a room?"

"Of course. I didn't know if I'd be welcome to stay with you."

"Well, keep the room for tonight while I break the news to Laura. Did I mention I was in the middle of proposing to her when you walked in? And she was in the middle of putting me off, for some reason I can't understand. Tomorrow you can come and stay with me. Tonight I need to hash this out with her or it's going to preoccupy me. And I want to give you my full attention."

"She's beautiful. I hope she likes me."

"Oh, you'll be like a sister to her before you know it. In fact, I have a lot of friends who are going to make a very large fuss over you."

Amanda beamed. She had worked hard and been modest to please her stepfather, with the new one, she would merely have fun and in so doing, please him as well. She had one week before her freshman year commenced. After which there would be little time to spare. She saw that she was making a good impression. Her mother's predictions about Hugo had all come true. He was easily beguiled, pleasant, natural and more than willing to treat her as a mature adult. Mother had been wise to withhold her from Hugo. He would have turned her head.

She'd been perfectly serious in expressing her desire to pose for Playboy, for it was part of her master plan, to develop a glamorous persona as an arresting counterpoint to her serious academic one. She planned to double major in economics and Latin American studies, and was already fluent in Spanish. She envisioned herself at some future point, in a tight, white linen suit and four inch high, ankle-strap heels, devastating dark, hot-blooded men across board room tables in sultry climes, then being ravished by them under mosquito netting. She had a framed photograph of Benecio del Toro by her bedside and a scrapbook of the greatest Latin actors of the 20th century that she used to look at before going to sleep, choosing a different dark eyed face each night to fantasize about in her dreams.

The next afternoon, a shimmering one in late September, Laura was still thinking over Hugo's proposal as she peddled her bike down leaf-dappled Shadow Lane. The sky was exceptionally blue and the air sweet and balmy on this last golden day of summer. She'd unconsciously turned her wheels toward Michael Flagg's tavern. She might get a sandwich. Perhaps Marguerite would be there and they could discuss everything. When Laura discovered that it was only Michael there, in the empty pub, her pulse raced.

"Fate has decided the events to follow," Laura told herself, sliding onto a bar stool and smiling at her host. Michael stopped polishing glasses and clasped her hands in greeting.

"You're just in time for lunch," said Michael, opening the box of sandwiches that had just been delivered from the Ball and Feather Inn. "They sent chicken tarragon, roast lamb and pepper steak."

"I'll have a pinot grigio and the chicken," said Laura, then watched her fair haired, attractive and muscular 6'3" host open a bottle for her. "Where is everyone?" she asked, when he set the plate and glass before her.

"Carmen's not coming in until later."

"Where's Marguerite? I didn't see her at the gym this morning."

"She took the baby and the nanny to Boston for a few days to visit her family."

"This must be kismet," Laura thought to herself, taking a sip of the crisp, fruity wine. She said, "Hugo finally proposed to me."

"High time!" Michael smiled, well aware of Hugo's long pursuit of Laura, which had only resolved itself into a relationship in the last few years. "Have you said yes?"

"I'm still thinking it over. I still have one wild oat left to sow and I think I'd rather do that before than after I'm married."

"Really!" Michael leaned back against the counter behind him and folded his arms. The former detective immediately realized that hunger for something other than a fancy baguette sandwich had brought Laura to The Dutch that day. "And might this particular oat be the lawful wedded possession of your best friend?"

"I don't think Marguerite would mind. Especially since she's out of town anyway. She was Hugo's plaything for years. Why shouldn't I be yours for one hour?"

"That's all I get, one hour?"

"Maybe two?" Laura grinned.

"Is Hugo going to hear about this?"

"No. He'd find it disagreeable."

"In that case, Marguerite shouldn't hear about it either."

"Agreed."

"We don't want to risk her blurting it out to Hugo."

"Right."

"Well? Where should we do this thing?"

"The house in the woods, I think," said Laura, referring to Michael's residence, a handsomely fitted out cottage which together with Marguerite's white Cape Cod house in the village afforded the newlyweds just the right amount of living space. It was the place where he and Marguerite went to make love and play in complete privacy, a luxury worth an extra mortgage payment.

Laura bit delicately into the sandwich and drank some wine. Then she laughed.

"What?" Michael was looking at her, trying to figure out why it had taken her six years to ask him to play. He had always coveted the dark-eyed brunette, from the first day he met her, in Marguerite Alexander's shop.

"Hugo thinks I'm hesitating because I'm still brooding about that stupid caning he gave me years ago."

"Well, you didn't talk to him for two years," Michael pointed out.

"I know. It was the only way I could make sure he realized I don't like that kind of thing."

"I think you made your point."

"So, you'll never believe this, but guess who walked into the shop yesterday..."

Hugo and Amanda had spent the afternoon biking around Random Point, eating a picnic lunch on the beach and getting stoned in the woods.

He'd brought a blanket in his knapsack and they lay on their backs, looking up at the cottony clouds scudding across the deepest of blue skies through the latticed umbrella of turning leaves.

"This IS the best day of my life," she confided. "Everything is just so engaging."

"What I can't understand is," he leaned up on an elbow to look down at her, "why you didn't get in touch with me until now. I mean, I can understand you letting your thirteenth, maybe even fourteenth birthday go by, but you've known about this for how long, six years? Why didn't you at least write to me?"

"Mother convinced me to keep the secret."

"Well, I think it's the worst thing she's ever done in her otherwise morally spotless life," Hugo said with feeling.

"She didn't want you to regard me as a responsibility to contend with. And my stepfather thought you'd spoil me and distract me from my studies, like candy. Since I don't mind putting off treats, I didn't press to meet you."

"I suppose it's for the best," Hugo reflected, dropping back down to gaze up at the sky. "Your step dad sounds properly strict, not someone you can get around, like me."

Amanda rolled over on her stomach and leaned up on her elbows.

"I think it would have broken his heart if I'd defected to you any earlier," she admitted. "And, as you say, he did a lot for me."

"I just hope this isn't about her being afraid I'd actually spank a child."

"Oh no. Of course not. Everyone knows that spanking people don't do that sort of thing with their own children."

"So you got your first spanking from a boyfriend?"

"Who said that? My stepfather spanked me many times."

"Really?"

"Between three and five I would throw tantrums to get attention. My stepfather has a low tolerance for misbehavior and he's half Chinese. Corporal punishment is big in their culture. So I got spanked."

"Well, I don't suppose it did you any harm," said Hugo, lazily admiring his surprising progeny. That afternoon she looked the picture of autumn, in brown tweed leggings, brown knee boots, a white shirt and gold merino wool cardigan, her fair hair a mixture of natural pale shades, appearing even lighter in the dappled sunlight filtering down through the russet canopy above them.

"Can't we pick up where we left off yesterday in the studio?" she asked.

"You mean, me spank you again?" he stared at her in disbelief.

"Yes, you stopped just as I was getting into it."

"But... to what end?" he appeared genuinely puzzled, unable to comprehend her motivation.

"It will give me something to write in my diary."

"No," he pillowed his head on his hands, "it's too perverse, even for me."

"Why?"

"I'm sorry, honey, but to me this is too sexy a thing to do with my own daughter."

"Gee, it's not like I'm innocent," she protested. "I've already had six lovers."

"No kidding," he smiled. "I thought you were into postponing pleasure."

"Every kind but that. That I go for."

"Know what, Amanda? There are a half dozen decent, gentlemanly players right here in Random Point. Any one of them would be happy to furnish you with diary entries on a moment's notice. In fact, I'll take you to meet the hottest one of them on our way home. He wound up marrying one of my favorite submissives, but I happen to know that she's out of town."

"I think you're being very conventional," Amanda declared. "And anyway, I'm not trying to seduce you. I just want to play. It's so ridiculously innocent that I can't see what you're hesitating about."

"I see that you're determined to get your own way," Hugo observed, his concern about breaking taboos beginning to ebb. What harm could it really do if this was what she wanted? "Maybe I'll have to teach you a lesson about playing with fire."

This declaration, though mildly couched, caused an instant blush to mantle her cheeks. Hugo sat up with a sigh, saying, "Remember, you asked for this!" The next moment he had pulled the lithe girl across his lap.

A spanking over street clothes, with its spontaneity and insulated warmth, is a type of spanking relentlessly sought by romantics and purists alike. Amanda was thrilled to receive it and expressed her approbation by making practically no sound beyond the occasional gasp, pant or yip as Hugo's palm descended on her upturned seat. What followed was a series of rhythmic, medium hard smacks, administered briskly while continuously alternating cheeks, straight across the jutting centermost portion of her slim but well formed bottom. Then he spanked the upper middle portion of her bottom just as thoroughly, then the lower. Then he spanked her upper thighs and even bestowed a few smacks on her shapely calves through the backs of her leather boot shafts, which made her catch her breath and emit the faintest of moans. "Yes! I like it there!" she suddenly cried, pointing the index finger of one gloved hand towards her calves.

"Trust you to be different," he said, continuing the spanking as she liked it, by including her legs in his rotations.

"And, maybe, it could be harder," she murmured, almost inaudibly, before hiding her face in her hands.

Impressed by her serene tolerance, Hugo increased the force behind his swats but slowed the velocity, allowing every harder smack to penetrate through her layers of outer clothing before administering the next.

"Oh," she groaned, "please, harder still!"

"All right, twelve of the best. Right now. Are you ready?"

"Yes!"

"But you'd better think pure thoughts," he warned. "because if I get the slightest inkling that you're thinking the other kind, this is never going to happen again."

"I understand," she promised. "I'll be good."

Whether she was good or not, Hugo never knew and never asked. He finished the spanking with twelve hard smacks, the last four across her calves, each of which made her kick and then let her lay perfectly still across his lap while she composed herself. When he finally turned her around, she threw her arms around his neck and hugged him hard.

She looked at him and said, very slowly, "That...was...perfect!"

"Okay," Hugo thought to himself, "this is all past weird. I am obviously having a very perverse dream, from which I am about to awake. I'll find myself in my bed at the house, Laura will be beside me. It will be the morning of the day I planned to propose and the only one to show up for the shoot will be Margot, the legitimate model from Boston." Hugo closed his eyes hard, then opened them. But the only thing he saw when he did was Amanda jumping to her feet and brushing down her slightly rumpled clothes.

"I'm hungry, aren't you?" she asked with a grin.

As the day began to wane, they peddled homewards, passing close by Michael Flagg's cottage, off Shadow Lane.

"A friend of mine lives there," said Hugo, the next moment noticing a familiar bike banked against the porch rail. As they came closer to the cabin, the distinctively crisp sound of a paddling from within could be heard without. Hugo flushed with pique as he realized his almost-fiancée was inside Michael Flagg's house, being played with.

"It sounds like he's corporally punishing someone!" Amanda exclaimed.

"That's Laura's bike," Hugo revealed, already comfortable enough with Amanda to make her his confidante.

"Oh!"

They stopped their bikes and stared at the cottage.

"Do you want to go in and break it up?" Amanda asked conspiratorially.

"It would be fun to discompose them," Hugo mused.

"You have the perfect excuse for dropping in. Introducing me."

"So that's how she considers a marriage proposal from her lover," Hugo remarked.

"You're not really mad, are you?"

Hugo smiled. "How can I be mad on such a beautiful day?"

"But you're annoyed."

"I am annoyed," said Hugo.

"Come on, let's have some fun!" she urged him. "Imagine how irritated they'll be at having to stop playing."

"You're bad," Hugo grinned at her.

"I'm having so much fun today!" she exclaimed.

They dismounted, parked their bikes against a tree and climbed the porch.

"We should make them feed us, anyway," Hugo said. Before Amanda could reply, the front door swung open and Michael Flagg stuck his head out. Flushing as only one of Celtic ancestry can do, he nevertheless recovered quickly from the shock and emerged to greet his unexpected guests.

"Hugo! Well, and this must be Amanda? Laura was just telling me about your arrival." Michael extended his hand to shake Amanda's.

"Yes, we could hear you talking from here," Hugo said dryly.

"You're a little prankster, I hear," Michael said.

Laura emerged next, dressed in a beige wool dress, brown sweater and boots that laced up the back. Her long, chestnut brown hair was unrumpled but her color was high.

"Hi," she said, smiling at Amanda and avoiding Hugo's eyes.

"Come in. We'll have some coffee," said Michael, ushering them inside to a large, paneled room with a fireplace and a good deal of oversized oak furniture, upholstered in royal blue with cream and burgundy accents. There were no animals mounted on the walls, but the cottage had a lodge-like feel and scent.

"Any food to go with that coffee?" Hugo asked, casually falling into a chair.

"I have just the thing," Michael said, going to start the coffee and bring out some sandwiches he'd brought home from the tavern.

Laura slipped into a chair near Amanda and stretched out her hand to the younger woman, saying, "I have a younger sister you're going to like very much."

"I think I'm borrowing her bike today," Amanda said, squeezing Laura's hand warmly before letting it go.

"I'll introduce you on your next visit," said Laura.

"I haven't been invited back for a second visit so far," said Amanda, in a stage whisper, shooting a look at Hugo.

"Honey, it goes without saying that you should consider my home your own," he assured her. "Now, let Michael show you around the house, its got quite lot of features."

"All right!" Amanda followed the path her host had trod out of the room, leaving Hugo to freeze Laura with a glance.

"You're so lucky Amanda is here," he said.

"I think I recognize you from the magazine," Amanda said to Michael as he showed her the ingenious hideaway punishment furniture that the house's designer had built into the paneled walls.

"I've appeared in a couple of issues," Michael admitted.

"I'll bet you have girls lining up to play with you," Amanda observed, having quickly taken note of his V-shaped back, monumental quads and large hands.

"Well, I'm married," Michael said.

"To a lady in the scene, right?"

"Yes. You may have read some of her stories. She writes under the name Alma."

"I've read all her stories!" Amanda declared. "I hope I can meet her next time I visit."

"She'd love that, Amanda."

"Now I can see where she gets her inspiration," Amanda flirted.

"Look at this. It's a pull down spanking horse," Michael said, opening a cabinet and causing a leather-padded bench with support braces underneath to drop down.

"So, someone in the scene built this house for you?"

"Laura's ex-husband."

"Is he in the magazine?"

"Yes, he's been in a number of issues, going back to when your mother worked with Hugo."

"If he wears glasses, I know exactly who he is. There's a photoset of him spanking my mother and her sister. I'd love to meet him! Imagine, someone from this world who knew my mother before I was born!"

"So, you heard us playing when you walked up, did you?"

"What do you think?"

"You girls in the scene are all so impulsive. I hold myself blameless," he replied, patting the spanking bench. "Go ahead, try it out."

"What, you mean, bend over it?"

"Sure. You're curious, aren't you?"

"Are you suggesting that I let you spank me? Here and now? With Hugo and Laura in the other room?"

"Why not?"

"Well..." she looked at him, "okay!"

"Wait a minute," said Michael, positioning a cheval glass opposite them so Amanda could watch. Then he bent her over the spanking bench, so her tummy was flat against the leather. When she raised her eyes she saw her own face and above her and behind her, his. His large hand went around her waist to hold her in place while the other smoothed down her snug, woolen leggings. "Oh goddess of love, this is sexy," thought Amanda.

The next thing she knew, his big hand had come down on her bottom. Smack on one side, smack on the other. He let her savor the full-bodied sensation then increased the count to two per cheek. Then he went back to one, then two again. He left space between the medium strength swats, so the warmth and the impact could penetrate through the protective garments she wore.

"Do you think they'll be able to hear us?"

"Not from this room. It's virtually sound proof."

"So why weren't you playing in this room with Laura?"

"Hey, don't kibitz when you're in this position!" Michael warned, with a volley of admonitory swats. But Amanda was too fascinated by their reflection to notice the pain.

"With all this talent on hand," she suddenly said, turning to him, "why hasn't Hugo ever shot videos?"

"I guess he thinks it would be too much work," Michael replied at length.

"Maybe it will fall to me to take the company into the 21st century," she posited with some excitement.

"I see your mind is going all the time," Michael observed. "But that sort of interjection is very (swat!) very (swat!) rude (swat! swat! swat!) when someone is taking the time to show you around their equipment."

"Would you please show me around that equipment?" Amanda said, turning her head towards the rod-like object tenting his trousers.

"Fresh little girl, aren't you?" Michael responded by smacking her a good deal more vigorously and now, unremittingly, for a good two minutes, until a violent orgasm took her by surprise, leaving her tingling and breathless. She jumped up and rubbed her bottom through the wool trousers, which kept the heat in. It had been the combination of hard, fast, thoroughly penetrating spanking and looking up at that handsome and determined profile while it was happening that had triggered the throbbing, drenching response.

"Thank you," she said, throwing her arms around his neck and pressing her lips lightly against his but for a very long moment.

"I didn't do anything," he replied, squeezing her waist, burying his face in her hair and pressing his mouth against her silken throat. She trembled against him, electrified by the sensation of being kissed first softly and then hard by this extra tall and extra virile older man, the man even her father's fiancée had come to give herself to.

"Yes you did, you made me come, just by spanking me, through my clothes. I didn't even think that could happen."

"It must have had something to do with the way you were pressed against the bench."

"You were pressing me down. You really know what you're doing."

"If you came just like that you must be incredibly responsive."

"I hope we can do this again," said Amanda.

21

"Whenever you like," Michael promised. "You're just so cute, I want to eat you up," he said, kissing her on the mouth again. "But I shouldn't keep you in here any longer."

"Hugo, please don't jump to conclusions," said Laura, pouring and handing him a glass of Cognac with a none too steady hand.

"Novel way you have of thinking over a proposal," Hugo observed, sampling the amber Courvoisier.

"It was just something I had to get out of my system," Laura explained, a gust of defiance coming into her voice and demeanor.

"Well? Is it out?"

"No, because we got interrupted," she replied.

"I see!" Hugo slammed his glass down and she jumped. "You planned to go all the way."

"I did, but Michael didn't want to. He said it wasn't right, since you'd just proposed."

"Admirable. But I happen to know he has the morals of a rubber band. If we hadn't come along you would have consummated."

"Hugo, don't you understand, all my girlfriends have had him, my little sister's had him, her best friend's hand him, Marguerite, Damaris, Patricia, Carmen, Hope, Polyxena, Susan, Diana -- everyone's had him but me, and I've been looking at him all along. I'm curious!"

"You deserve to be strapped until you cry."

"I'm sorry!"

"Nothing is ever going to be easy with you and me, is it?"

"You're putting too much on this. View it as a sort of bachelorette party. For one."

"So, you're saying you'd decided you do want to get married?"

"Yes. I want to get married. I really do. You're the only one for me. Forever and ever."

"Really?" Hugo broke into a smile and took her in his arms.

"I love you completely," she murmured, her pulse returning to normal as she realized she'd either escaped or postponed a serious licking.

"But you're still determined to sleep with Michael!" Hugo thrust her away from him, his indignation returning at half strength.

"Just once."

"Okay, Laura, you get a free pass, just this once."

"Really?"

"Why not? I'm not unreasonable," Hugo said with sudden decision, realizing that he himself would be needing at least one free pass in the very near future.

Chapter Two

Amanda's Diary October

October 10th

Hugo warned me B&D support groups can be as exciting as standing in line at the bank and last night proved it. I couldn't help but doze during the orientation, except I could never really achieve a satisfyingly somnolent state because a rude young man sitting beside me appeared to delight in constantly exhorting me to, "Pay attention!" This David Byrne type was toothpick thin, with hair neither long nor short, horn rims and a silly watch full of dials. He also had a teasing smile (with good teeth), which I considered presumptuous to flash me, on such short acquaintance.

A lecture on knife play began and I decided to leave. I had to wriggle past a dozen pierced, tattooed, leather swathed or gothed out dudes on the way and one had the nerve to squeeze my bottom. I gave the closest pair of goons a scathing look and told them they weren't hot enough to get away with that. I glimpsed my annoying prodder grinning at my indignation.

So cosmically perfect that I was able to get Hugo to buy me the leather dress and fetish pumps instead of a lot of junk for my dorm room. It has long sleeves, a stand up collar plunging into a sweetheart neckline and a tight skirt that laces up the back. "You might want to be ambiguous about your orientation," he advised. "Let them think you're dominant, you'll get more respect." The shoes were 5" stack heeled black leather dream girl pumps. I want to make a good impression when I go places like that, one that people won't forget.

The annoying guy followed me outside and fast-talked me into having coffee with him. He was only just lucky that there was a cafe right alongside the punk club where the orientation meeting had been held. I never would have agreed to go anywhere that had required a cab or tram. He should have known he was wasting both our time but he was persistent.

He introduced himself as Marty Patmore, got my name out of me and started asking me impertinent questions as soon as we sat down, such as my orientation, whether I was married, belonged to someone, etc. I just looked at him, sipped my hot chocolate and pretended to be impressed by his watch, so I could see what time it was.

"Well, I have to go," I finally said.

"But, you haven't told me one thing."

"Because you're not my type," I explained, as nicely as you can say something like that.

"How do you know that? You don't even know what I do."

"Oh, are you out of school?" He looked to be early twenties, but he could have been a few years older.

"I am."

"And what is it that you do?"

"I design software to test products without using animals."

"That is admirable," I sincerely replied.

"Can't we just talk for a few minutes about our mutual interests?"

"No, that would only inflame you. You might decide to follow me home, stalk me, do any number things to attract my attention."

"You've been through this before?"

"No, but I couldn't help but notice how few girls my age were at the meeting." I knew I also stood out because I had on a demi cinch under the leather dress, which took my waist down to 22". (It was making me feel faint. I'm told it takes getting used to.)

"What type are you holding out for?" he presumed to ask me.

"Someone who knows how to dress and wear his hair. Someone hot and sexy. With a great look, to make my heart pound when I see him coming."

"So, you're looking for a rock star," he decided.

"Where's that ring from? MIT?"

"Yes. I graduated two years ago."

"Top of your class?" I asked. Something had given him the confidence to come on to me.

"Yes."

"I'm still not excited," I said regretfully. He did seem very well bred and well spoken, so perhaps I was being too harsh.

He sighed and seemed to accept that he'd gotten as far as he was going to get with me. He handed me a card with his phone number and email address, saying, "In case you ever need a friend in the scene."

"So, you're submissive, right?" I asked. He colored again.

"No!" He got up, seemed to want to add another comment, but decided against it and just left.

October 11th

Couldn't get to sleep last night thinking about how unkind I'd been to Mr. Patmore. Couldn't remember how many ways I'd insulted him until I read the above. So, first thing I shot him this email:

Dear Mr. Patmore,

I apologize for my unnecessary bluntness yesterday. (Though you did have it coming for following me out of the meeting.)

You seem nice. Calm. Coolheaded. You're obviously scientific, and therefore experimental. It gave me an idea. Maybe we could work some thing out. I'll get to the point, and you should understand where I'm coming from, having been yourself so recently an academic grind.

I'm a freshman at H. who has just discovered that she will have to work three times as hard now as she did in high school. So I won't have time for a conventional romance. I can allow myself maybe one night out a week. I think I'd like to spend the better part of that night in kinky sex. Which is where you might come in. And I'll be perfectly frank here. I'm not attracted to you, but if you're a good top, I may be interested in playing with you, once in a while, with no strings attached, going either way, just for kicks.

Sexually, I'm adventurous and therefore uninterested in an exclusive relationship. If I allow you to possess me more than once, this is not to be taken as a sign that I am yours, only that I enjoy playing with you now and then. You would have no claims on me, no right to my fidelity, no options on the rest of my spare time. Moreover, you would have to remain uninvested emotionally, okay with the fact that while you were doing me, I might be fantasizing about Antonio Banderas or some fascinating older man I might be going to play with at a future date. You would not be my only sexual partner or my only scene playmate. Even though I'm only 18, I am already well connected in the scene. My father is the publisher of a spanking magazine and I am going to appear on the cover in a few months. I plan to travel out to the Cape several times this season to play in Random Point, where there is a large concentration of hip enthusiasts.

If you like my idea, let me hear from you soon. I've already fucked all the hot boys on my dorm floor, but they turned out to be crème Brule. Which reminds me of a lyric from Rancid: "No way in hell am I going through life having vanilla sex."

> Best wishes,
> Amanda Sands

I hit send and went off to breakfast and classes, forgetting all about my impulsive proposition until I got back to my room after lunch. Mr. Patmore's return email read:

Dear Ms Sands,

Nothing could have surprised me more than your adorable letter. I absolutely love your proposition. In fact, let's do it fast, before you change your mind! At your service.

> Marty Patmore

Nice. So I set up a meet for Friday night. I have the key to Hugo's apartment on Boylston Street, so we won't have to do it in my dorm room or in whatever messy bachelor digs he inhabits. He's too young to be making much money yet and the way he dressed the other day belies any taste in decor. Hugo's place is ideal for a sophisticated rendezvous. I'll wear my black pvc hobble skirt, the fitted white blouse with the short collar and my patent leather 4" stack heeled ankle straps with seamed stockings and a gartered waist cinch, with frilled black nylon rumba panties.

October 14th

Imagine a first date on Friday the 13th. It turned out to be more than okay.

I walked into the bistro on the corner of Hugo's block and didn't see him at the bar. But he was there. He just looked tremendously different. It was as though some fabulous gay buddy of his had done a complete makeover on him in less than a week. The glasses were gone, the hair was cut short and geometric in back and on the sides but fell forward long and straight on his brow and it was a very striking shade of jet black, a fact which I had not taken note of before. His face was actually good. And his tall, thin body was just right for the really cool suit he had on, some sort of midnight blue silk, with a white shirt and no tie. Clooney couldn't have done better. So, no wonder I didn't know it was Marty. I kept standing inside the door, staring and staring. Finally this cute guy came over.

"Amanda?"

"Marty?"

He led me back to a small table, which had been reserved for us. I didn't want to go through the embarrassment of being carded so I just ordered grapefruit juice.

"What happened to you?" I asked.

"I just got a hair cut and put on a suit."

"Where's your glasses?"

"I'm wearing contacts."

"So, your reply to my note was brief."

"I meant to convey my approbation of your plan."

"Well, you did. But what other thoughts have you on the subject?"

Then the menus came and we picked out food. Finally he replied, "You seem to be a thrill seeker. As I understand it, if I perform satisfactorily and don't offend you in some other way, you may condescend to see me again, but otherwise I'm to have no expectations outside of the kinky sex."

"Your grasp of the situation is complete," I admitted, unable to stop staring at him, who didn't look nerdy anymore. He was looking more like Keanu by the second. I was getting turned on! But I kept wondering, will he have the guts to follow through, will he fumble, will he come in three seconds, will he be well endowed?

He asked me a lot of questions. What I'd tried, what I liked, how I liked it; we talked about positions, implements, safe sex, safe words, etc. I answered frankly. He gathered information, as a scientist will, and then planned his experiment. And that experiment was how many ways he could make me come in one night. (He found four.)

When we got up to the flat Marty said, "So who's this spanking magazine parent of yours?" When I told him he was properly impressed. And even more enchanted when I showed him what that meant, i.e., a luxurious apartment, painted in rich jewel tones with exquisite crown molding and gilt mirrors; equipped with a spanking bench, a toy chest, restraints, vintage wines, a stocked larder and some really good weed. Yeah, I had it all. Even a St. Andrew's cross concealed behind a panel in the master bedroom.

Meanwhile, he was starting to look even better to me. We were sitting on the sofa in front of the hearth and smoking Hugo's extraordinary weed when I noticed just how good he looked.

I think I may have even blurted out, "Gee, all of a sudden, you look good to me!" (I blame the wine, not the weed, for this candor.)

Marty didn't let this go to his head. Instead he rose and launched on a bit of a lecture. "So I hit the jackpot," he said, cool and incisive. "So maybe I don't deserve it." I could only shrug. "But let's remember one thing, young lady, I'm here on your invitation." That was true. I waited to see where he was going with this. He paced. "You're about the most conceited girl I've ever met," he declared, without rancor. "And the most controlling one as well."

"You've ever met other girls?" I said.

"Fresh too, huh? I'll take care of that."

"Really? You plan to?"

"That's why I'm here isn't it? So far you've controlled everything. You've circumscribed our relationship with micrometer precision, leaving me room to express my own personality in only one area: how I'm going to discipline you."

That sounded good to me. I wouldn't fight it. I facsimilated a Bardot pout and sat up quite straight on the sofa, perched on the edge, as a stiff Victorian waist cinch will make one do.

He rummaged in the toy chest and found a small pair of leather wristlets, then sat behind me and made me put my wrists behind my back. With my hands out of the way he began to take liberties, kissing me on the mouth and throat and squeezing my breasts through my blouse. When his hands went to my waist he realized I was cinched and gave me a look of deep satisfaction.

Pretty soon I found my wrists transferred to in front of me and myself over his lap, being spanked through my pvc skirt for a long time. Long enough for the heat to penetrate. I found the bony fingers weren't at all unbearable.

He doesn't ooze compliments, but he couldn't refrain from commenting on the aspect presented by my trim bottom so tightly girded in the incredibly shiny black pvc skirt with the zipper up the back.

When the skirt was unzipped and removed and the blouse was taken off, I was left in my sheer black bra, black waist cinch with garters attached, black frilled panties, hose and the patent leather shoes. I saw how I looked reflected in a mirror. His being fully dressed was an erotic contrast. Vanilla guys are always for just ripping their clothes off, but players know the power of fine pelts.

I spent a long time over his lap. He didn't lower my panties right away. He kept spanking me, then slipping his fingers into my panties, teasing me to insanity before he would actually do anything with them. Then, he did everything with them. Orgasm #1.

He rolled me over, took me in his arms and we kissed, Marty squeezing my breasts and going under my bra to pinch my nipples, just hard enough, while simultaneously biting my shoulders, throat and earlobes, just hard enough. Orgasm #2.

He slid back the St. Andrews Cross panel, made me stand facing it with my bottom positively thrust out, attached my wrists to the top of the X frame with the wristlets and boat hooks and my ankles to the bottom with similar leather restraints. Once I was generally positioned, he removed both my bra and panties, leaving me nude except for the waist cinch, seamed stockings and fetish shoes. He selected a deerskin flogger to begin with, but that merely made a lot of noise and almost no impression on me. He switched to a small cat-o-nine whip and demonstrated the accuracy of his aim and the control of his wrist as he touched me up smartly but not harshly for about ten minutes. Next he used a crop on my bottom, somewhat stingingly. I didn't mind. Everything was feeling great. But my feet were starting to hurt. I pretended to cry and he let me loose. I told him my feet were hurting me so he put me over the spanking bench, which allowed me to kneel on a lower tier while I bent over the top.

He forced my knees apart so that my legs were widespread and he could see, touch and admire everything of beauty I possess all at once. He used a small wooden paddle on my bottom until each cheek was solid magenta. I could see this reflected in a double mirror arrangement behind and before us as we played. He placed one hand in the small of my back while he decorated my bottom in this manner, pressing me down against the bench firmly. Orgasm #3.

Finally he got behind me and penetrated my oh-so-ready body with a big, beautiful, safely sheathed male member until my fourth orgasm triggered his first.

We took a little nap on the bed but I had an early class this morning so I wanted to be at school when I awoke. He dropped me off in his old but cherry Volvo, smiling, pleasant, but a little distant. No doubt guarding his feelings, in case I don't elect to see him again.

When I got back from class there were roses waiting for me with a small note: Call me!

October 21st

Just because I don't have time for dating - it doesn't mean I don't have time for sex. The thing is, you don't really have to make time for sex. You can just take it where you find it, on the spot, in between other things. Especially in a place that is utterly teeming with beautiful, intelligent men, as is this University.

This morning Alicia left early and said she wouldn't be back until late afternoon. The parade of callers dropping by to scribble messages on our door pad began at around nine. I didn't have to go to Spanish until twelve so I answered every knock.

The advantage of having a roommate who looks like Beyonce Knowles' even more attractive younger sister, is that vast quantities of fine young black men swarm around our door. But Alicia isn't interested in any of them, no matter how tall, muscular, doe-eyed and intellectual, no matter how earnest and politically correct, no matter how good a family or rough a background.

She considers them helpful in carrying laundry to the laundry room and occasionally she'll accept a ride across the city in one of their cars, otherwise she looks through them. Black boys, white boys, she draws no distinction, considering all men very nearly useless to her at the moment. She's a very serious student and I should strive to be more like her. I just started the semester and I feel as though my grades are already slipping because I'm spending too much time thinking about spanking and sex.

I asked her last week, "Do you mind if I make use of some of the men who come around to serve you? You hardly seem to use them at all, and never for their primary purpose, as far as I can see." She looked at me as though I were an adorable primitive, buying into the myth of the awesomely studly African American male.

"Don't you understand? All men are dogs," she informed me, though not unkindly. "But of course feel free to learn this for yourself."

Alicia is a pistol. I don't know if she's a dyke or just holding out for a tenured professor, but she's the hottest, most elusive girl I've ever seen. (She'd make a great mistress.) I think we were paired off as roommates because we're the exact same size and some thoughtful Dean of Residence was making sure we'd be able to lend each other wardrobe.

Anyway, the first interesting man to come by was Tommy Harrington. I'd been looking at him for a few weeks now. How could I help it? I've been a Snoop fan since I was twelve and he's got the braids, as well as an arresting way of dressing in monochromatic colors. Also, he has a sexy, pencil thin, black moustache and the handsomest ebony skin. So I said to him straight up, "Alicia won't be back until this afternoon. But I have an hour before class."

He looked at me for a second while my meaning penetrated. Then he stepped inside and locked the door. Of course, I had to tell him, "Yes, you are my first black man." (Adding a flirtatious, "How are you going to get me wet?")

He proposed giving me head, and I let him, but all the while I was thinking about spanking and how I could get him to spank me. Finally I asked, "Spank me?"

Being hip hop (and thus booty-oriented), Tommy understood pretty well what I meant. He bent me over the bed and while he was getting his dick positioned for penetration, he began smacking my bottom, not very hard, just kind of cutely.

"You're a bad little girl, aren't you?" he asked with some very real appreciation, I thought. Wow, did he ever have a big cock, really. But I haven't been with all that many guys so it's hard to objectively compare. (That adorable Marty Patmore was almost as big anyway, for all he's a skinny white boy.)

We had a very hard time at first. I told him he needed to spank me harder, like he meant it, if he wanted me relaxed enough take his whole cock. I saw him shrug in the mirror before he began spanking me again, this time a little harder. It was just right. Then he fastened his hands to my waist and started plunging in. I taught him the trick my darling Carlos always used to use to get me to come, placing his palm against my lower abdomen, just above my muff, and pressing it while he was drilling me. It worked! I came hard.

Tommy finished up and disposed of our protection. I thanked him, promising that if our paths met as fortuitously again, we might repeat the performance. (Why not? He was damn near perfect.) He walked out a little dazed but with a big smile on his handsome face. I never even asked him his major. I'm so bad.

Tommy did me so well that I only planned on interviewing the other interesting man who rapped on the door, looking for Alicia, before I left for Spanish. But he also turned out to be too interesting to let get away before test-driving as well. (What the hell got into me today? Oh, wait, I know, two cocks.)

Ronnie Van Horn, an earnest, bespectacled sophomore, dresses and talks like a Manhattan preppie. Alicia told me that he isn't here on scholarship, his parents have bucks. She's actually spoken somewhat favorably about him because he's serious and not as obvious a dog as the others. She is considering allowing him to take her to an afternoon concert and tea some day this winter.

Ronnie appeared very p.c. and was both shocked and seemingly offended by my offer of casual sex.

"I'm sorry Miss Amanda, but houseslave Ronnie is not available to service you today!" he scolded me indignantly.

I told him not to be so stuffy. He was a boy first and an enlightened African American intellectual second. I admitted that my initial attraction to him was probably based on his exoticness, but made no apologies for that.

He remained obdurate so I said, "Oh, never mind! You're obviously a prude or timid and I have no interest in that type of person, whatever the race."

I kicked him out and closed the door.

Two minutes later, he was back, knocking. When I opened the door he took me in his arms and kissed me. Not awkwardly, not half-heartedly, but like he'd been studying old Clark Gable movies. (I found out later he's a film historian and of course, a future independent film maker.)

He pulled me inside, locked the door and threw me down on the bed, actually saying, "You want me to make love to you?"

"Yes!" I replied, "But spank me first!"

This threw him and he seemed confounded. A large question mark quivered above his neatly crew cut cafe au lait head. His liquid brown eyes searched my face intensely. Did he hear correctly?

He got up, paced, looked at me, made double sure the door was locked, paced, and looked at me again. "Spanking! You deserve a paddling for how bad you are," he finally sputtered.

"Oh, you don't know the half," I assured him, looking straight into his devastatingly deep eyes.

"Maybe you picked the wrong person to joke with about such matters," he allowed judiciously.

"Maybe I picked the right one," I countered, rolling over on my stomach on the bed. I was wearing my short, fawn colored, wool pleated skirt and a brown velvet vest over a white shirt with cuffed, chestnut thigh high boots. No, it's not the supernaturally shapely booty of a black girl, but in its own quiet way, it juts.

He paced some more, unable to decide what to do. Perhaps this carefully brought up young man was afraid the freaky blonde slut would cry foul after encouraging an assault. I jumped up and grabbed my camera off the desk. "Look, we'll create proof of my complicity," I told him, placing it back on the desk in line with the bed and turning it on. "It'll do a two minute video."

I took him by the hand, led him to the bed and made him sit right in the middle, where I'd trained the camera. Then I stood to one side of him, defying him to turn me over his knee with a proud glance. He wasted a few seconds trying to consider whether this type of proof would help or hurt him should I turn psycho bitch and decide to lodge a complaint against him with the University. At last the greater imperative asserted itself and he yanked me face down across his corded thighs. He must either run or play some sport. Fantastic legs! He fastened his hand on my waist as though he'd been spanking girls all his life.

"What did you mean when you said I don't know the half?" he demanded.

"Oh, you really want to know?"

"Yes!"

"Well, then I'll have to admit, you're the not the first man I've seduced today."

"Oh? Really?" His hand came down hard on my bottom through the skirt five or six times.

"Yes, really! And the first one didn't hesitate. He gave me everything I wanted, all at once. And, oh yeah, he was also black."

"Oh my god, you're a slut!" Smack, smack, smack! Three, six, nine, twelve swats in a row. He knew what he was doing though, alternating cheeks, striking not too high, not too low, covering my

35

whole bottom, not just one spot. "I'll teach you to objectify black men!"

"I already know how," I replied, turning my face to look back at him, so the camera would catch my teasing expression.

"God, you're a fresh little brat!" More vigorous swats.

"Don't be so sensitive. You think Latin men squawk when white girls objectify them? No, they're profoundly grateful!"

Ronnie spanked me long past the two-minute video time on my camera, good and hard. Then he let me go and took me in his arms again. We kissed so long and hard that his glasses steamed up. Then we were all over each other on the bed. He didn't have protection, but I did and pretty soon, he was next in.

We made love face to face. I put my wrists above my head and he pinned them under one hand while unbuttoning my vest and blouse and unhooking my front closing lacy white bra to squeeze my bosom as he plunged his manly organ deep inside me. Gorgeous, lovable man!

Oh god, have I found my on campus-spanking boyfriend, so soon? If he is not a lifelong enthusiast for spanking, my name is not Amanda Sands.

Just before I left for class I got an email from Tommy Harrington. Which I quote below:

To the Fairest of the Fair, my Nymph, my Melisande,

When may I oh so delicately and carefully insert my throbbing engine of desire betwixt thy creamy, rosy orbs, that we may explore the deep mysteries of hardcore anal sex?

Your dusky knight awaits his lady's pleasure, bestowing hot kisses on her ravishing lips, eyelids and all.

Your most devoted Tommy

P.S. I'll bring chronic. Please be very bad in the meantime so I have many reasons to spank you again.

Gotta be an English major. And yes, I am charmed.

And now I have to watch the video I made of Ronnie Van Horn spanking me. For the twentieth time. It is delightful! My first spanking video, which I wrote, directed and starred in.

Still, I can't wait to get to Spanish. For there I'll glimpse again the one who may be more The One than any other. The aloof, aristocratic and possibly unobtainable, Castor Reyes.

October 22nd

This is very bad. I have a mountain of studying to do and all I can think about is boys, sex and spanking. I've spent almost the entire day emailing back and forth with Marty, Tommy and Ronnie. My famous ability to postpone pleasure seems to have evaporated into the Cambridge fog. I can't afford to waste any more time on this type of thing. Thank goodness Castor offered to tutor me and check over my exercises. Our duet will commence on a properly academic note. One must move very slowly with this type of male, allowing him to make every advance. (I mean, after the initial one of appearing to need a good deal of tutoring in Spanish.) When he's ready to possess me, it must seem to be all his idea. I should probably practice resisting in front of a mirror so it looks convincing when I try it out for real. I imagine there's a good deal of wistful head shaking involved and possibly extending one hand in a rebuffing gesture.

Once he knows he wants me, I will force him to woo me relentlessly possibly for weeks. And when I finally do give in, I will do so stingily, one concession at a time, starting with the right to nibble my earlobes and smother my throat with hot kisses.

I'll devastate Castor and ace my Spanish midterm.

Chapter Three

Amanda's Diary November

November 1st

"You can't be in love with your professor," Alicia remonstrated with me this morning, "it's a cliché."

But how can I help it when Mr. Keen is so adorable, so grave, so tall and lean and handsome? I am horribly in love. I write his name in the margins of my notebooks. I hang around after every class, with the cleverest questions I can think of, just to hear his voice and feel his gaze upon my face. I know he's onto me. His dark eyes mock me while he makes polite, concise, informative replies, punctuated with pleasant smiles and always a quick glance at his watch to let me know I'm on his time.

November 3rd

I think of Mr. Keen night and day and it is pleasant to do so. It is good to be in love. But can I have him? Is it in the realm of possibility? He's not married. He's only roughly twice my age, so it wouldn't be obscene. I've seen him play squash. He's fit and trim. It would not be an embarrassment to view his unclothed limbs. Oh why, why did I have to be given a teacher who so exactly resembles Richard Widmark?

I wonder if Mr. Keen has ever spanked a girl. Would it be awful if he weren't the slightest bit dominant? Would I fall instantly out of love? I think I would. I'm not sure why, but I think I would. I sometimes think I'm ready for a master. But suppose Mr. Keen is

38

unsophisticated? Suppose he fails to appreciate the gift the gods of love are handing him?

Then, obviously, I will cease to adore him. He will have proven unworthy. But I sense he is worthy! I feel he will know exactly what to do with me, and how.

November 4th

Hugo says the only way to make sure a man is fully dominant is to try to tempt him to go submissive to you. He says that men who are submissive or switchable can never resist the temptation to receive corporal punishment from a good-looking woman or girl. But a dominant man will always suggest the reverse, because that is his primary wish and we all do what we want to.

I said to him, "You don't think it would be wrong for me to try to get my most beloved professor to make love to me, do you?"

"That depends. Do you think the guy is cool enough to handle it, or could it make trouble for you in the long run? You can't jeopardize Harvard."

I said I didn't know if he was cool or not.

"Try to run into him after hours and get him to smoke pot. Then you'll know."

Easier said then done. I'd have to stalk the guy to find out where he spends his off hours. And that's not right. That could get me in trouble.

November 5th

The most wonderful thing has happened! Mr. Keen has invited his entire class over to his house for a wine and cheese party. I can see where and how he lives.

November 7th

Mr. Keen's wine party took place at his nice, old house in Cambridge, where he lives alone with a group of cats. I felt it was a place I'd enjoying visiting repeatedly. The sitting room has a lovely fireplace. We could see it begin to snow through the windows. I'm told it doesn't usually snow this early in the season, which portends a very cold winter.

I was the last to say goodbye to Mr. Keen at the door and since no one was looking except one of the cats, I seized the opportunity to lightly press my lips to his. He stared at me in confusion for a moment then finding his voice, lightly admonished me, "What's this all about? Are you being naughty? Go on, go home!" I was dismissed with a smack on my bottom!

November 8th

Hugo just called with advice to the effect that this whole thing could backfire on me severely. The love object could turn out to be a by-the-book philistine who might put me on report instead of receiving the proffered gift with untold gladness. Then he suggested I come out to Random Point for the weekend and he'd set me up with a good looking, local English teacher who was in the scene and could point out the error of my ways and maybe make me see reason. I decided to wait until I got to RP to confess that I'd already made my first move. Anyway, the schoolteacher sounds exciting!

I'm writing this in the train. Just like Oscar Wilde!!!

November 9th

Yesterday will go down in my short history as one of the best.

I'm writing this in the window seat of the Ball and Feather dining room where I am enjoying an enormous buttermilk biscuit, drenched in butter along with strong English tea. The snow is falling steadily outside and is about a foot deep at this point. Hugo's gone to chat with the innkeeper, so I can make this entry on my laptop.

Hugo met me at the station and took me directly to his shop, where Laura had been minding the counter. She made us all some coffee and produced some sandwiches for me that were lovely.

"So," Hugo said, "you want to meet Mr. Lawrence, the English teacher?"

"I do want to meet him!" I replied, "and have dressed accordingly." I had on my new black thigh high boots, textured tights, a short, grey pleated skirt and a black polo sweater.

"Well then, you can take my car and drive up the cove road to meet him. Here's the directions and the address," Hugo said, handing me the keys to his old Jag and a printout of the directions.

"David is very handsome," Laura told me when Hugo turned away to call my date and warn him of my imminent arrival.

"It's true," said Hugo, who had heard. "He's got lovesick teenagers throwing themselves at him every other day."

David Lawrence was waiting for me in the doorway of the little dollhouse he and his wife Hope live in, called Cobweb Cottage. They were right. The guy is A+ all the way, from face to form to dress to voice. I'll always think of him as "The Voice" because I've never heard one as smooth, mellifluous and well modulated.

He showed me around the cozy interior in a minute. It was not large but it was wonderful. Apparently the site has a long history of being home to scene couples, passing from one to another as a precious jewel set above the jagged coast.

"Let me tell you something, honey, I've been harassed and driven crazy by more youngsters than I can remember. It's not a pleasant sensation."

"Oh, bosh," I said. "Surely it's an ego stroke?"

"Not one that I need or want!" he insisted. I could see what he meant. He was married to a former video model in the scene, a breathtakingly beautiful blonde in her mid-twenties. She runs the coffee counter at Margaret Alexander's bookshop and she's magnetically attractive in body and spirit. David Lawrence doesn't need his students coming on to him to feel sexy.

"Being in the scene," I said, "haven't you felt tempted to spank them?"

"I have spanked two of them," he admitted ruefully.

"You let yourself go that far?"

"Somehow they found out I was in the scene. And they were too. But I merely spanked them. Well, pretty much so."

"I have no idea if the professor I like is in the scene."

"He probably isn't."

"He called me naughty when I kissed him the other day. And he gave me a parting swat."

"H'm."

"I know. It's intriguing."

"I don't think you should pursue this, Amanda."

"No?"

"I think it's putting your professor in an awful spot. He could get fired for playing around with his student."

I shrugged and protested, "I can't take back the kiss now."

"But you can resolve not to put the poor guy in this type of position."

"I could."

"I may help deepen that resolve."

I didn't let him grab me right away. I made him chase me around the little lodge-like sitting room. He's a smoker and he got irritated with this pretty quickly. Smokers in their 30's get winded fast. Finally he snagged me and put me over his knee. The cute part is that he spanked me through my tights. He never even tried to pull them down. Though they were sheer enough for the pink of my skin tone to show through the intricate charcoal knit. (I had omitted panties). I checked it out later in a mirror. It was a nice, good, long, hard spanking, with a slow, steady buildup and I blush to confess, an orgasmic climax. This occurred when he grabbed my wrist to prevent me putting my hand back to cover my belabored bottom and pinned it to my waist. Oh, that gesture. It slays me. Then he just kept going on and on, harder and harder and faster and faster. And I mini-came again.

He tried to make me stand in the corner but I didn't want to. He was adamant. I stamped my foot at him. He took off his belt.

Again, I made him chase me. After all that hard spanking, he must have been tired! I led him around and around the cottage and out the back door. He caught me on the back porch and bent me over the wooden railing. It was cold out there but after a few seconds I ceased to notice that. He was still clutching his belt and I soon felt it!

"I can't believe you would defy me after I went to all the time and trouble to counsel you today," he remarked, as though shocked.

I took about twelve hard licks with the strap before giving in. I'm building up an interesting tolerance but even it has its limits. I allowed myself to be marched indoors again and stood in the corner.

David Lawrence regarded me over folded arms, leaning back against a bookcase.

"Well?" he asked, "Are you going to cut your teacher a break and leave him the hell alone?"

I shrugged and thought to myself, "He did give me a swat. That demonstrates the right instinct."

"Save yourself the humiliation of being rejected and control your lust for your teacher!" was my new disciplinarian's final exhortation to me before taking me out of the corner and giving my hair a pat and my cheek an affectionate caress. I put my arms around his neck and pressed my lips to his lightly. His arms went around my waist.

"Now don't start tempting me, young lady," he warned. "I'm married!"

"Yes, I notice you didn't even lower my tights. Admirable control, Mr. Lawrence."

"That was out of respect of the fact that you're Hugo's daughter."

"But, he sent me to you for a thrill."

"You're awfully confident for a baby," said David, kissing me once behind each ear in a way that sent ripples through my tummy, then letting me go. "Thank you for the compliment, but I promised my wife I wouldn't have sex with any eighteen year olds this year."

I pulled away as I felt he wished me to do and kept my 1.5 spanking induced orgasms a secret from him, since he was so determined to behave well.

I asked him if I might email with him now and then and ask him questions about English literature and he gave me his address.

What a lovely man!

Chapter Four

Amanda's Diary December

December 1st

Met a most unusual and highly simpatico girl today as a direct result of Hugo's magazine (with me on the cover) coming out. I'd pretty much forgotten the little squib that Hugo inserted about me (with the stage name April Sebastian) looking to assemble a video cast in Boston for my freshman film project. Not that I'll even get into a film class until next year, but I can begin stockpiling material now. Hugo says that nothing I can do in this area will be wasted, for when a young girl into spanking creates spanking erotica, the result is always sure to be of interest to the spanking community at large.

I'm not sure I'll be able to get away with this, but if I work it right, I'll also be able to get an economics paper or perhaps even a thesis out of the idea, in due course. My plan is to start a small business from scratch, on the cheap, develop my own marketing strategy and whether it fails or succeeds, use the data gathered in the experiment for academic credit. (Of course, it will succeed. How could it fail with Hugo's mailing list behind me and an angle no one in the spanking biz has pursued so far - young, hip, and a little hip hop.)

Thalia Dunbar, a sophomore at B.U., saw the ad and called me. We met for lunch at The Grist Mill and is she cute! Wonderfully curvaceous, slim-waisted torso, baby-faced features, creamy complexion, blue eyes and chin length, straight brown hair. She told me she'd just started getting Hugo's magazine and couldn't believe how good it was, that she didn't really know if she was into spanking, but that the pix and stories were so hot that they turned her on.

She said she was a secret exhibitionist and had been a bad girl since age 14, so she was up for being in a video, either giving or receiving and that she was very interested in working with men of color, if they were beautiful. I showed her photos of Tommy and Ronnie on my camera and she agreed they were extremely good-looking. Not that Ronnie would ever agree to be in my video, but I'll bet I can get him to work the camera. I've already decided to offer both of them a financial partnership with me in lieu of compensation. Thalia told me she could find me other cast members because she ran into freaks all the time. I told her I'd give her a finder's fee for every one she found that I could use but she said what she really wanted was to meet Hugo. I told her nothing could be easier, as I have a standing invitation to visit whenever I want.

We agreed to take the train to Random Point this weekend to scout out locations for our first shoot. Maybe that nice Mr. Flagg will let us use his tavern after hours. I know I made a good impression on him.

December 2nd

Still reeling from the unsettling encounter with Castor Reyes in the quad this afternoon. I was returning from the library as a light snow began to fall. He marched up to me, brandishing the New Rod Quarterly (with me on the cover) in my face. Then he said, perfectly hatefully, "So, this is what my frosty virgin does in her spare time!" I could only stare at him dumbly, then mumble something like, "Where did you get that?"

"At the Globe."

"Just happened to catch your eye, did it?" I asked.

"Yes, I was looking for something erotic to read, as a substitute for sex, because my girlfriend doesn't put out. Except maybe for her father!"

"That's an ugly thing to say," I replied, trying to walk away, but he blocked me.

"Don't walk away from me. I want to know what kind of game you've been playing with me. Why have you been stringing me along for weeks, pretending to be pure and renunciant when all along you're planning to ..." he looked up my ad for the video cast and read aloud, "write, direct and star in your own spanking video this year!"

"Gee, you really read that thing from cover to cover, didn't you?" I marveled. "I'm surprised it held your interest to that degree."

"I'll tell you what really holds my interest, spanking the hell out of you for holding me in a state of suspended hard-on for over a month... for what? Fun? To see how long you could frustrate me before I went raving mad???"

I protested, "I thought you were old fashioned... a traditional Latin male, who would value me more highly if you had to woo me a bit."

"A bit? One kiss last week was as much as I've gotten from you. What kind of stereotype do you think you're dealing with? Some sort of Ramon Novarro mamma's boy, confessional-kneeling pansy? I was born in Manhattan in the 1980's, not Mexico City in the 1880's. You think I wanted you because you were pure?"

"Does this mean you aren't going to continue tutoring me?" I asked.

He looked at me for a moment before replying, then practically jumped down my throat with renewed indignation, "Oh, I'll tutor you all right. I'll goddamned drill you mercilessly. Be at my room tonight at nine!"

He turned to stomp away before hearing my reply. I called, "Castor!" The moment he turned to look at me I snapped him with my camera.

"What the hell are you doing?" he growled.

"I've never had a scolding from a college boy before," I told him, tucking the camera away, "I wanted to capture your face." He scowled and walked off. I studied the face on the way back to my dorm. Short, soft brown hair, wide-set hazel eyes, high brow, high cheek bones, pencil moustache tapering off to a sexy five o'clock shadow, strong chin, golden skin tone with an under flush now he was aroused - quite the most beautiful boy in all Boston. Oh goddess of love, let him be as potent as he looks!

December 3rd

Completely and most dreadfully in love, I write this first thing before class. Spent the night with Castor and ran back from his dorm just now in a freezing rain. The sky is like lead and it looks to rain all day. Only two hours before class and I'm starving, should shower and change, but let me just say....

I had knocked on his door on the second floor of Wigglett at ten p.m., dressed in a navy wool dress with a white linen collar and three quarter sleeves, sheer cream thigh high stockings and high, stack heeled, chestnut leather roll top knee high boots. He called for me to come in and was waiting for me, sitting on a chair with a riding crop between his hands. Dressed in black jeans, some kind of hot black boots and a tucked out grey cotton shirt. He sprang to his feet (as I started at the crop) and hastened to lock the door behind me, as if I might bolt if he didn't at once. It was a single with a window on the yard, with the hardwood floor and dark wood wainscoting that makes this dorm so desirable. Lightning struck, then thunder, then it started to rain and continued raining all night.

"Where the hell have you been? I thought I said nine." he demanded, taking the books out of my hands and tossing them on the desk. My eyes went to the neatly made single bed with its grey comforter and white linen. It looked inviting, like a page out of a Restoration Hardware catalog. It even coordinated with my navy outfit. The whole room was meticulously organized and uncluttered. God, he's anal.

"I had to read my assignments for tomorrow," I explained matter of factly. Being unprepared would be a hell of a lot more embarrassing than what he was about to do to me. "What are you doing with that crop?" I asked.

"What do you think I'm doing with it?"

"Are you saying that you're in the scene?"

"You think I found that magazine by accident?" he summarily turned me around and unzipped my dress down the back with adept confidence.

"What are you doing?" I turned in surprise. That was fast!

47

"Two months ago, I would have let you keep your clothes on for your ...spanking." (He pronounced the word with a certain savor.) "Now I want you naked. Immediately. Do you understand me?" He turned me back around and kissed me masterfully on the mouth. The next thing I knew, the dress was on the floor and he stared at me - taking in my fitted, cream lace décolleté teddy, hose and boots. A full-length mirror affixed to the wall opposite me reflected my ... I must admit, rather dainty image. (Note to self, insert photo of self in cream lace teddy and boots for reference.)

"Don't look at yourself!" he snapped at me, giving me the first slap on the bottom of the night with the palm of his hand. Then he deftly and confidently reached between my thighs, expertly unsnapped the teddy crotch and before I knew it, had it up over my head and off. Now I was in nothing but the stockings and boots. It was a little cold in the room and my nipples were standing up and very pink. He circled me and looked at me. I stood up straight and arrogantly thrust my bosom out at him. He didn't have to say anything, I could read his mind at that moment and he was thinking "they are even more perfect than I'd dreamed," as sure as my name is Amanda Sands.

"Get up on the bed," he ordered crisply, "On all fours. Right now!" He slapped the crop against his own flank for emphasis. I obeyed, but slowly. "Hurry up!" he snapped, shaking the crop at me. "Insolent little slut."

"You don't know that," I protested.

"Yes, I do, actually. I've been asking around ever since I found that magazine. Apparently you're already a legend in this dorm!" He came around to stand in front of me, tearing his gaze from mine to drink in the voluptuous effect of my breasts hanging down as I knelt, doggy style for his pleasure. I silently dared him to reach out and squeeze them and reading my challenge, he did, but gently, running his fingertips all across their velvet fullness, then fastening, lightly, but firmly around each erect nipple.

Then, quite deliberately, he took a small bottle of astroglide and several condoms out of his jeans pocket and tossed them on the bed right in front of me. "Well?" he demanded.

"...Okay," I replied, with girlish hesitation.

"I'm so relieved we didn't have to have our first quarrel over anal sex," said Castor, taking me around the waist with one arm, leaning up on the bed on one knee and bringing the spanker at the end of the crop down on my bottom in a shower of crisp smacks, evenly distributed from cheek to cheek and thigh to thigh, not unbearably hard but hard enough to make me catch my breath with every swat.

This set the pattern for the rest of the night. His style was a little dynamic, a little extreme. But I was ready for it. Then just when I was thinking, "He's a lot more B&D than he is spanking scene," he sat on the bed and pulled me down across his lap.

"Oh how I have wanted to do this!" he confided, bringing his hand down on my bottom hard and fast for less than a minute, but it was a very full minute. Then he lay me back on the bed and spread my legs, telling me that if I didn't have a wet pussy he would use the crop on it until it got wet. It was wet. He put two fingers in to test. I squeezed him hard to let him know what he had in store. I'm reading this back and it's getting fairly pornographic. Even though I was very, very wet, I urged him to do what he said with the crop, to get me even wetter. I have always wanted someone to crop me on my Venus Mound. He seemed enchanted that it wasn't shaved, but fleecy. I stopped the crop before it came down the first time and asked him to please go lighter now. He pretended to be annoyed but adhered to my request. I asked him to play Love Me Two Times, the original Doors arrangement. He actually had it. Then he had me, two times.

That's all I have time to write. Have to get to the dining hall or I'll perish. He is a hot head. I wonder if that's how he'll ruin this for himself.

Same day, afternoon

On reading this over, Castor comes across like a soulless meanie. Therefore let me hasten to add that we slept locked in each other's arms and kissed incessantly throughout the night and he gave me a gold ring with a small but blazing sapphire stone that he said had belonged to his late mother.

But I can't let him think he owns me now. I have to keep him hungry for me.

I'm going to ask Thalia if she wants to go to Random Point with me for the weekend. It'll get me out of Castor's reach and allow her to finally meet Hugo.

December 5th, Random Point, Cliff House

Susan Ross invited us to stay at Anthony Newton's house with her over the weekend. Thalia's mind is blown to get her own room overlooking the coast. Susan picked us up at the station, drove us up to the house and put herself at our disposal for the rest of the day. I had explained to Thalia that Susan met her famous lover, the composer Anthony Newton, through Hugo, about five years before and in addition to securing one of the best financial set ups on the planet, she loved the guy. Thalia said she too could use a sugar daddy as soon as possible. Her college loans were already mounting.

I told Thalia that if we made a good impression around Random Point we might get to shoot there when we started our project. So Thalia changed in the car from a cotton button down shirt to a ribbed woolen sweater that dramatically hugged her high, well-rounded bosom. I noted the improvement.

I decided to introduce Thalia to Hugo as a girl who wanted to do some modeling for the magazine, not the horny little sophomore who wanted to fuck him, which she was. Thalia thinks about and has more sex than I do, but she studies much less and smokes a lot more weed. I do like her!

Susan was the soul of hospitality, giving us the beautiful rooms and taking us out to a most elegant lunch in the village at the Ball And Feather Inn. A light, flaky snow was beginning to fall when we arrived at Hugo's shop in the late afternoon. Susan visited with her sister Laura in the front of shop where a fire was blazing in the hearth, while I brought Thalia into the back where Hugo's offices were. He was expecting us and ushered us into the lounge graciously, smiling at me while regarding Thalia with interest. In addition to the sage green sweater she had on, she wore a brown tweed skirt and calf high brown boots, all wrapping pinup girl proportions. Hugo seemed genuinely pleased that I had brought him a beautiful new model and praised her physical charms without reserve, knowing how much models like this type of thing. Thalia, who doesn't think she's especially pretty, only seemed to listen vaguely, unable to help staring at him in a moony fashion. At the first opportunity I took him aside to whisper, "She has a crush on you."

He looked harassed and replied, "Amanda, you're not setting me up with your friends!"

"Isn't that how the scene works?" I asked.

"In most cases," he replied, patiently enough, "but as you very well know, I'm still pressing my suit with Laura. Where do you get off throwing bosomy nineteen year olds at me in front of her?" (I admit, I hadn't thought of that. I must have gone very red in the face because he stared at me.) Then he said, "Yes, you may well blush for shame!" My heart raced as I tried to think of an excuse for objectifying my own biological parent.

"It was a reward for her consenting to be in my video," I lamely offered.

"You've got a lot of nerve. I should turn you over my knee right now," he threatened.

"I don't mind."

"Oh, you'll mind."

"Don't you like her for the magazine, though?"

"Yes, but what the hell is she expecting from me?"

"She will probably try to seduce you," I admitted, thinking it was best to forewarn him.

Hugo shook his head in amazement. "Here's what I don't understand," he said, "are you pimping your friends out to me or are you pimping me out to your friends?"

"I perceive I have been in error," I said, bowing my head.

"I'll ask Michael if we can shoot in his bar tomorrow morning. He can spank you friend and I'll take the pictures."

"Good idea!" I agreed happily. I love Michael Flagg!

It is disturbing how little I am missing Castor.

Hugo took us to the bookshop for coffee and gave most of his attention to me. This may have been to discourage Thalia. I noticed he never met her eyes. But he couldn't avoid laughing at some of the outrageous things she said. Nor did she scruple to shake him down for weed before we left the village. He gave us some and sent us on our way, telling us to meet him at Michael's tavern tomorrow morning at ten.

We went down to the tip of the village that is rimmed by a tiny strip of rocky shore. The snowflakes began to fall thicker and faster now and started to stick to the ground. We smoked the joint Hugo gave us and stared into the water. Then we walked over to the dress shop a friend of Hugo owns and bought a couple of fitted dresses with kick pleats to wear tomorrow. They were expensive but Hugo told me to have the bill sent to him as it was for his shoot and we could keep the dresses. The owner of the shop, Damaris, (who is married to Laura's ex husband William, who knew my mother), made a great fuss over me as Hugo's just-surfaced daughter. Then I found out that this dainty Damaris is also Michael Flagg's ex wife! Is it the spanking scene that is so incestuous or just this Random Point clique?

"I wonder if Hugo's fucked that hot little chili pepper," Thalia said to me as we stood outside the shop under the awning waiting for Susan to pick us up. The sun was going down and it was turning too frosty for comfort in our thin woolen coats.

"I'll ask Susan. She knows all the local dish," I told my new friend. I got Susan to talk plenty last night. We made a big fire in the library hearth and sat around it for hours drinking wine and nibbling on toothsome snacks from the pantry. After becoming moderately baked, Thalia admitted it might be thought a bit perverse, her being hot for her friend's dad, but she couldn't help it, she had developed a tendre for Hugo after reading his stories and looking at his photos in the magazine.

Susan told her not to feel constrained. It wasn't as though anyone here even knew about my existence until two months before. So even though he was technically my father, the whole thing seemed unreal. Except for our uncanny resemblance. "He belonged to the scene long before he belonged to Amanda. And he's had every woman in it, why should you be an exception?" Susan encouraged Thalia. Then Thalia wanted to know if Hugo had had her and Susan told us some very interesting things about Random Point, which had been a scene magnet ever since Hugo had bought the shop and settled there twenty years before.

"The summer before I started college I stayed with my sister Laura and her then-husband William here in Random Point," Susan explained. "William had answered Laura's personal ad in Hugo's magazine. He started courting her while Hugo was in Europe and by the time Hugo got back, they were already married. Hugo was somewhat resentful at having lost his opportunity with Laura and this made him irascible for some time. Laura brought me to see Hugo several times, since I was of age and just out in the scene. When he noticed that I found him fascinating, he used me without apology, to bring Laura to him. He was a lot more demanding in those days. One night when I was at his house with Laura, he took us down to his wine cellar and fucked me right in front of her, just to see if we both would put up with this, and we did."

Thalia demanded details and Susan replied, "He bent me over a trestle table and just pulled up my skirt and took me."

"Like in a porn?" Thalia pressed her.

"Exactly like."

"And he's fucked other women that you know?" she persisted.

"Almost every one," Susan replied with conviction. I was proud!

"But it was years before Hugo got my sister as a girlfriend. She was very hard won. Now he seems interested in marrying her."

"All the more reason to sew a few more wild oats first?" Thalia asked.

"Couldn't hurt," said Susan.

I felt compelled to relate the conversation I'd had with Hugo earlier, about how he wanted to stay focused on Laura and how peeved he had seemed at my throwing my nineteen-year-old friend in his path.

Thalia thought it cute that an inveterate slut like Hugo should suddenly become so romantic and go out of his way to avoid free teenaged pussy. Susan said it was proof he had evolved.

Thalia wanted to know if either Laura or I would be disturbed if she, Thalia made a successful play for him and got him to fuck her. Susan said that Laura would be in Boston all day and over night so she'd never know unless Hugo told her and he probably wouldn't. I assured her that I regarded Hugo as more of a glamorous legend than a blood relation and that I had no emotions invested in his sex life. Personally, I don't think she'll get anywhere at this point, but maybe I'm not giving her enough credit.

December 5th, Evening

I've definitely not been giving Thalia enough credit. She managed to accomplish her goal within an hour of arriving at Michael's bar. She had her outfit and makeup on perfectly when we arrived so she didn't have to go in the back like I did and fuss with anything. When I came out, properly dressed as well, Hugo was setting up lights and Michael picking out a bottle of expensive champagne to use as a prop for the photoset. Thalia was sitting on the bar swinging her shapely legs, punctuated by high heeled ankle strap closed toe, shiny black patent leather shoes. I noticed her staring at Hugo and now and then, he'd look up at her because he was lighting that area first. Then, rather unbelievably, I saw Thalia make an ok sign with the thumb and forefinger of her left hand and repeatedly begin to insert the index finger of her right hand into the circle it made while continuing to fix an intense gaze on Hugo's face. I looked at him and saw him blink in disbelief then shake his head at her with a grin. Thalia looked deadly serious as she tapped the dial of her watch, held up five fingers and then jerked her thumb towards the back of the bar, apparently confident that he'd understand what she wanted, when and where. He looked at her for a few seconds more, still shaking his head. Then he seemed to change his mind and shrugged quite casually before continuing to tinker with his c-stand for exactly five more minutes. At this point he straightened up and strolled towards the back rooms behind the bar. I looked up and saw Thalia was already gone.

I went to engage Michael in a conversation to distract him.

"How lucky for us you were available this morning," I told him.

"For me, you mean," he replied graciously.

"I hope we don't really have to drink that," I motioned to the bottle of Mum. "It's a bit early in the day."

"I wasn't going to open this, it's just for the set up. I was about to go find an empty bottle and fill it with ginger ale," he said helpfully. But that would mean him going in the back!

"Thalia loves champagne. And maybe it would loosen her up a little."

"But I'll bet you're both too young to drink, aren't you?"

Before I could think of any reason to prevent him from going to look for the empty Mum bottle, Hugo reappeared in the big room and went back to tinkering with his lights. Thalia followed a few seconds later, flushed like a peach and smoothing down her dress all around. When she caught my eye she gave me the thumbs up sign with a complete lack of self-consciousness.

As before, Hugo refused to take any bare bottom photos of me getting spanked, but encouraged Michael to get Thalia's panties down as soon as ever he liked. Thalia seemed a lot more sensitive to spanking than I am, or has a much lower pain tolerance because it seemed as thought the lightest swats of Michael's very large hand inspired the highest kicks I've ever seen. At one point it seemed as though she would start to cry at any moment and I expected Hugo to intervene and advise Michael to go a little lighter on the young bar patroness, who in the context of the photo set who could not manage to pay for the expensive champagne she had ordered and drunk a few glasses of very quickly. But Hugo simply appeared to be enjoying the performance and eventually, Thalia did start to cry. Without scruple, Hugo moved in for an extreme close up of her face, bedewed with real tears. I heard him whisper, "Poor baby," in the most blatantly insincere tone. But I saw him brush her face gently with his hand and make her smile as he added, "That's what you get for being so bad." She lifted her chin as much as to say, "I get what I want and damn the consequences!"

As soon as we were alone I asked her if she was furious at being spanked hard enough to make her cry the first time out. She told me it was fine as she was getting some extra hundreds of dollars for her discomfort and that on one level the entire experience was extremely arousing. Michael's cook arrived just as we were finishing up the shoot and we all had lunch before the bar opened. Then Hugo had to go and open his own shop so he dropped us off at the beach behind the woods at the end of Shadow Lane and told us to call him when we wanted to be taken back to the Cliff house.

As soon as we started walking on the beach Thalia told me how she and Hugo had achieved union in the powder room, with her bent over the sink and staring into both their faces in the mirror above. The entire operation had taken five minutes. "It was just right," Thalia confided, "I knew instinctively I wouldn't have to give him head. "And he talked all the while about how he was going to enjoy watching me get spanked really hard by the ex-cop," she added. "He also said if I wanted to get hired again I'd better cry real tears for him."

I should have been shocked and appalled but since it was Thalia, I wasn't. Still I had to ask, "But that was okay by you?"

"It was fucking hot," she replied.

I told her I wasn't surprised. He is a Scorpio.

Tuesday, December 8th

All of this reckless promiscuity may be beginning to back fire on me. I may be fooling around with too many men. And at the moment, half of them appear to be ...upset with me. Yesterday afternoon I ran into Ronnie at the library. He was working behind the reserve desk and I needed some books. He took my slip without even a smile so I knew something was wrong. When he brought back the books and stamped them I asked him what was up. It turned out he had just found out about me and Tommy and me and Castor and wanted to know if I was going for some kind of Wigglesworth record as sluttiest slut in the entire hall. I'm afraid I became rather rude and informed him in a low tone but as forcibly as possible that he was an asshole. Then I deliberately sat in the next room and read over my assignments right there where I could see him and see when his shift was over. As it turned out, he was off in fifteen. I jumped up and followed him out of the building into the cold, windy quad at dusk. A wet snow was falling and it was most unpleasant out.

"You have no right to be mad at me," I charged.

"I know," he countered, looking at me sternly as snowflakes fell on his beautiful, long eye lashes.

"I never said I'd be yours exclusively."

"That's so," he agreed, looking at me hard.

"Apologize for that remark!" I said, stamping my foot at him.

"I will not. What I said was true."

"Maybe it is, but the way that you said it was perfectly hateful!"

After saying this I impulsively scooped up a snowball of wet slush and crammed it into his sanctimonious face. He became furious and chased me through the quad, the both of us slipping and sliding. I skidded onto a bench and he fell onto the seat next to me. He pulled me over his lap and slapped me hard through my cords five or six times. He's got one hell of a hard hand, but maybe that was because he had so much (in his view) righteous indignation on his side. He pulled me up abruptly.

"Why did you stop?" I asked, breathless with excitement. He looked around. The quad was empty, all sensible people being inside next to a fire. Then he took me in his arms in that patented 1930's Hollywood-style, possessively protective, ultra-masculine clinch that had melted me so completely the first time he did it.

He let me go and said, "Why did you wait for me?"

"To tell you off."

"Well, consider me told off," he said, getting up and brushing snowflakes off his sweater. We were both just in jeans and sweaters but I didn't feel cold.

"But you're still mad at me," I said, rubbing my bottom as we walked back to the dorm.

"Just crazy with jealousy and insanely hungry for you," he admitted.

"Take me to your room and kiss me like that again and you can do anything you want with me," I said, taking his hand.

"And then share you with three or four or five other guys?"

"Well... why not?"

"I'm sorry, I just can't be that casual about you."

"Ronnie, even though I can't pledge my heart to any one person right now, I would consider you above anyone else as a permanent boyfriend."

"I guess I'm supposed to feel flattered by that?"

"I didn't mean to sound patronizing," I protested.

"No, you're being entirely judicious, Amanda. You're a goddess and therefore entitled to your whims. Someday I'm sure I'll feel honored to have been chosen as one of your toys. Right now though, thinking about you with anyone else is killing me."

We entered the dorm together but separated in the foyer, Ronnie going directly to his room without another word to me.

The encounter left me feeling hollow and guilty. Ronnie is a good man and I can't play with his emotions.

After dinner I went to the library to read for three hours. In the middle of this my phone rang. It was Castor, reminding me that I needed to come see him and cram for the next quiz. It wasn't too difficult to interpret his clumsy double entendre. How romantic! I felt a little peeved and delayed going to his room by stopping at the canteen for a cup of coffee with Alicia. She was rather unsympathetic about my quandary with regard to Ronnie and continues to maintain a no-man-is-a-good man attitude. When I wondered aloud whether I should admit to Castor that I really didn't need any help in studying for Spanish tests she heartily endorsed the move. "Why should he be allowed to think himself more important than he is?" she asked me indignantly. And scolded me for ever having had Castor tutor me in the first place. She was of the opinion that there was entirely too much protecting of male egos going around as it was. "Why do you spoil them so?" she demanded. Adding, "If you must use them, do so, but at least make them serve you, not the opposite!"

I can see her becoming a mistress some day, but not the type who wears leather and corsets. That would be objectifying and she'll have none of that.

My brain was nearly dead and I knew I could do no more work that night, yet I was restless and far too wound up to sleep, the half-pleasant half-unpleasant encounter with Ronnie going around and around in my head. I didn't think I was spoiling for trouble when I showed up at Castor's room, but I guess I really was.

His door was ajar and I walked in. He wasn't there but entered in a few minutes, fresh from the shower across the hall, with a towel wrapped around his slim waist. His black hair was still wet and gleaming and the v of his golden back flecked with drops of water.

"Amanda!" he cried, delighted at my appearance. Then he contrived to look severe and demanded to know why I hadn't called him all weekend. I explained about going out to the Cape with my new girlfriend and the photo shoot we had done. He was immediately jealous of another man having spanked me, even in the context of the shoot and became rather huffy with me. Things went from bad to worse when he locked the door and dropping the towel without further preamble, asked me to give him some head. Not that he needed any, mind you, what with that flagpole waving around!

"I'm sorry, I don't do that," I replied, looking at him steadily. Perhaps if he had been much, much more charming about the request or even have gotten me stoned first, but going from "Hi" to "Blow Me?" I'm not a porn star!

"What do you mean, you don't do that?" He seemed puzzled, as though I had suddenly started to speak in a language he didn't comprehend.

"I don't like to give head," I told him. "And, you're not even circumcised," I added to myself.

"I thought you were submissive," he protested.

"Why did you think that?"

"You let me spank you and sodomize you," he pointed out.

"Oh well, I do enjoy spanking and sodomy. But not oral. And after all, I'm not asking you to go down on me, am I?"

"I'd love to go down on you," he volunteered with a grin.

I covered a yawn with my hand. He stared at me.

"So you're saying you won't give me head?" he asked in disbelief, the flagpole drooping a bit at the revelation. He quickly pulled on a pair of jeans and a shirt.

"Don't you know that being a good lover is all about giving pleasure to others?" he lectured. "Are you a spoiled brat who just wants what you want and doesn't care about what anyone else wants?"

"I guess so," I replied. What an awful day so far!

"Maybe you need a good spanking before you do as you're told," he suggested, picking a small hairbrush up off his dresser top.

"You mean to try to force me to go down on you?" I bristled.

He stared at me hard, smacking the back of the brush against the palm of his hand.

"Luckily, I don't need a b.j. that badly," he said, "but you deserve something for sheer orneriness!"

With that he caught me by the arm and pulling me over to his desk, bent me over it. Then he administered six extremely stinging swats to the seat of my jeans with the little wooden brush.

Two pants warmings in one day - in retrospect - were not unstimulating. But I was in an emotional state when Castor put me over the desk and punished me and the spontaneous spanking really hurt! Suddenly awash with self-pity, I began to sob violently.

Amazed that such a brief spanking over corduroy pants could result in this type of reaction, Castor pulled me up and looked at me to see if I was kidding him. He was visibly shocked at my wet face and trembling lips and pulled me against his chest to comfort me.

"Oh, honey, I'm sorry," he murmured into my ear, kissing my wet cheeks and throat. "I didn't mean to bully you." As he pulled me against him I felt his renewed excitement, which I found quite annoying. How could he earnestly apologize for hurting me and yet unapologetically thrust at me a hard-on that had developed solely from my pain and tears?

I couldn't bear to let him see me at this extreme pitch of vulnerability any longer and tore out of the room with the briefest of farewells. I stumbled back to my own room, brushing the tears from my face and trying to ignore my own latent excitement at what had just happened.

Luckily Alicia was out when I got back to my room and I was able to get off against a pillow before drifting off to sleep. A most disturbing day!

Chapter Five

Blue China

It was a cold, wet, windy winter morning, but to mitigate the gloom, Hugo Sands was enjoying a hot breakfast of poached eggs, grilled tomatoes, fresh baked biscuits, sliced melons, sugared strawberries and espresso, with his fiancée, Laura Random and her younger sister, Susan Ross, in Susan's Victorian triple-decker, at the northernmost end of Shadow Lane.

Hugo had brought over the groceries, encouraged the girls to get out of bed and mildly reproached Laura for never being close at hand when he needed her. Ever since Anthony Newton had given Susan a house of her own to work in and spent one million dollars remodeling it for the artistic sisters' convenience, Laura had been spending an inordinate amount of time away from Hugo's own house in the woods and almost no time at all at his shop in the village.

"I need you to do me a favor," Hugo petitioned Laura, who was sleepily pouring out coffee for them, her long brown hair down on her shoulders, her slim body wrapped in a white brocade robe. Her sister Susan, who'd quickly dressed herself in jeans, a cream wool turtleneck and ankle boots, was twisting and tying her waist length honey blonde hair into a high ponytail as she came into the room. "I have to go into Boston for the afternoon and I'm expecting a very important call at the shop on my private line. Could you be there today to monitor my calls?"

"Yes," Laura replied, handing her sister a cup of coffee, with milk and sugar as she liked it. "But what's it all about?"

"A source of mine in London has located a blue china vase that once belonged to Oscar Wilde. Apparently, there's enough provenance to prove that the piece was seized from Wilde's house and sold off during the execution on his goods which followed his conviction."

"Not The Blue China?" Susan asked, in awe.

"Yes, The Blue China that Wilde always claimed it was harder and harder to live up to," Hugo replied with excitement. "If I can obtain the vase I'm sure a certain someone at this table's rich boyfriend will be wanting to buy it and endow it to his alma mater."

"And you'd get a nice commission," Laura reflected.

"Enough for us to close the shop for several weeks and take a proper honeymoon, in Italy."

"I'll stick by the phone like glue," Laura promised.

"Good girl!" Hugo said, lifting her hand to kiss the palm.

One hour later, having showered and dressed in a pair of brown cords, a wool polo shirt, walking shoes, a brown tweed coat, tam and gloves, Laura walked down graveyard hill and into the village of Random Point, against the wind all the way. Her umbrella blew inside out immediately and the raw cold stung her cheeks bright pink by the time she got to Hugo's shop.

The first thing she did after entering, turning up the heat and turning on all the lights was to light the hearth in the main room of the shop. Then she went back to Hugo's editorial and archival offices behind the shop and started a pot of coffee in the galley. While she was waiting for the coffee to brew she went out to the back garden, which faced the brook that ran alongside almost all of Shadow Lane, and smoked half a joint. Then she was ready to unlock the front door to the public and open the shop. Not that she expected any public off-season and on a morning like this.

Taking her coffee, Laura went to sit behind the large desk in the office where Hugo conducted his correspondence and phone interviews. Almost immediately she sat down, the phone rang.

"Hugo Sands' Antiques," Laura said brightly.

"Oh," said a disappointed female voice on the other end of the line. "Is Hugo there?"

"No, he isn't. May I take a message?"

"This is Francesca from Provincetown. He was supposed to call me this morning."

Laura remembered Hugo mentioning a young woman, one of his readers, who had recently begun to fixate on him because she lived less than five miles from Random Point. The tone of the caller's voice indicated that this was the person of whom Hugo had spoken. Her lover had many fans and had collected many hearts over the years he had been publishing the Northeast's most elegant spanking magazine. Some of these women were of such intelligence, charm and physical attractions as to have been invited out to pose for photo spreads, to be wined, dined, spanked and bedded by the man who had only captured Laura for himself within the last few years. (Though he had loved her for six.)

"I'm so sorry, he's gone to Boston for the day. I don't expect him back until early evening. Perhaps I could take your number?"

"Oh, he has my number," the woman, who sounded to be in her late twenties or early thirties, replied crossly.

"Well, I'll let him know that you called."

"Who am I speaking to?" the caller demanded.

"This is Laura."

"Do you work there in the office?"

"Uh, yes. I do drawings for the magazine."

"Oh! You're good," the woman said unhappily.

"Thank you."

"So, you've known Hugo a long time?"

"Yes, I have," Laura smiled.

"Are you his --"

"I'm his partner," Laura replied firmly, surprising herself.

"Oh. Well, please tell him I called," the woman said hastily and hung up.

That voice being as close as Provincetown made Laura uncomfortable. For the first time she realized that other women wanted her man. Not just to play with, as her Random Point girl friends sometimes did, but to keep. It was an odd sensation.

Laura strolled out to the main room with her coffee and sat on an upholstered stool by the hearth for several minutes, remembering the day, several years before, when Hugo had won her for good and all, though she didn't tell him so at the time.

It was a rapturously balmy early Spring evening, approximately eighteen months after the infamous caning incident, for which Laura had decided never to forgive Hugo, and approximately six months before she officially did forgive him and consent to be his lover. She had been conducting herself in his presence in a most guarded manner, not precisely unfriendly, but certainly not warm and of course, wholly inaccessible. She never came to see him at the shop, never met him for a meal or even stopped to chat in the street. When they met by accident she'd nod and faintly smile but not converse beyond a bland, "How are you?" and that without seeming to care about the answer. It was a way to punish Hugo for the insult of caning her too hard and it had worked wonderfully well. Her comportment towards Hugo pained him deeply. Not that he had given up the thought of eventually possessing her completely, but for a period, he knew he had to back away. After all, they lived in civilized times. He couldn't carry her kicking and screaming to his house and keep her locked in the attic. At least not for very long. So he bided his time.

But this particular early evening of an April day, they happened to cross paths at the grocery co-op on Brundle Street, where the mother of his recently surfaced, hitherto unknown daughter had once kept a large, splendid head shop and psychic emporium. Laura was in a white cotton a-line dress with cranberry trim and ankle strap platform heels of the same dark red. She was stuffing a string bag full of vegetables and fruit. Their eyes met over the first white peaches of Spring and this time he didn't let her turn away directly.

"Laura."

"Oh, hello," she said, blushing, and started to hurry away. The blush was new and Hugo noticed it at once. Was it that he caught her in a pretty dress for once instead of the perpetual woolen leggings of a New England winter?

"Laura," he repeated, touching the back of her bare arm with his hand. "Don't walk away. I want to talk to you." He didn't smile but held her gaze.

"Yes?" she felt compelled to stay and listen because he had looked irresistibly handsome.

"When we leave here you're getting in your car and following me home."

She paused and looked at him, a smile tugging at the corners of her wide, shapely mouth. "Why would I want to do that?"

"Because I've got something for you at my house," Hugo insisted.

"What?"

"Dinner," he said, indicating his hand basket, filled with steaks and mushrooms.

"Do I have to cook?" she asked cautiously.

"I'll cook," he replied.

"No. I don't think --"

"Don't think, just oblige me."

"If I come tonight --"

"You will."

"If I come tonight, the reconciliation is just for tonight."

Hugo shrugged, "Fine!"

And incredibly, she followed him to his house.

The moment he had her inside, he drew her to a sofa and took her in his arms, kissing her as though it might be the last chance he would ever have. She pulled away, saying, "What about the steaks? Don't you think we should get them out of the car?"

"That's the way you respond to the best romance I can throw at you?" Hugo demanded. Annoyed at her for not succumbing to his kisses, he rolled her over and swatted the back of her cotton skirt six times. "You used to be such a sweet, shy submissive. You had such good manners then," he reproved her, letting her up. "All right, go get the steaks. I'll open some wine."

"I can't help it if I'm hungry," Laura protested, rubbing her bottom as she exited the room.

Laura smiled, remembering the little scene. Then the phone rang again. She pounced on it, thinking this was at last Hugo's call about the blue china vase. But it was Francesca again. This time she said she had something important to tell Laura about her partner, something Laura would not know. Laura felt uneasy, not because she mistrusted

65

Hugo, but because she heard unhappiness, desperation and malice in the woman's voice. Francesca went on to reveal that not only had she played with Hugo but that he had possessed her. In fact, they were in a relationship. She felt Laura ought to know this. That was all. She hung up before Laura could organize a coherent reply.

Laura sighed, went out back and smoked a little more. While she was sitting on the low stone wall that overlooked the brook, her cell phone rang. It was Hugo, wanting to know if his contact had called. Laura told him about the phone calls from Francesca. There was a momentarily silence. Then Hugo said, "Yes, she's stalking me."

"You'd mentioned playing with her," Laura said, "but not sleeping with her."

"Well, I did that too. Unfortunately. Now she thinks...something."

"Why did you do that? She doesn't seem like your type," Laura pointed out, reasonably.

"She's not. Not by any means. But, you know how it is. She needed a complete scene. I never dreamed she'd fixate on me. I haven't seen her since and that was months ago."

"You mean it was a mercy scene?"

"Let me put it this way, within minutes of meeting her in person I didn't want to play with her, but I did anyway."

"Anyway, I was thinking about that night."

"What night?"

"The night you made me come back to your house for steaks."

"That was a real tease. Morning after, I thought I had it made. Then you decided to torture me for eight more months. How could you, Laura? Have I ever sufficiently beaten you for keeping me at bay for two years?"

"It was only six months more."

"My client's just arrived. I have to go. Call me if you hear from London, okay? And as for Francesca, just be polite and noncommittal. She lives close and may be crazy."

Laura closed the phone and went back inside, feeling worse for Francesca than before. She knew Hugo well enough by now to know that his heart was irrevocably her own. But here was an outside party, loving him to insanity and doomed to frustration.

Laura got on Hugo's New Rod Quarterly computer and brought up all the male personal ads from the New England region. There were about sixty. Surely one of these nice bachelors could take Francesca off Hugo's hands? Someone desperate enough to snap up a head case. Laura called Hugo back and asked how old Francesca was and if she was attractive.

"Why?"

"I'm going through the close-by ads to see if there's anyone we can hook her up with."

"Forget it. She's decided she only wants me."

"Really? That's worse than I thought," Laura replied with that same uneasy sensation.

"The only way we can settle this once and for is to get married, right away," Hugo suggested.

"That's not going to settle anything," Laura pointed out sensibly. "She only lives a few miles away."

Hugo signed off and Laura looked out the window. It had started to drizzle and she suddenly felt very hungry.

Grabbing her tweed coat and pulling it on, Laura put up the Out to Lunch sign, pulled the door closed behind her and locked it as she emerged onto windswept Shadow Lane. She ran across the cobbled street to the back entrance of Marguerite Alexander's bookshop, getting only a little wet.

Hope Spencer Lawrence was in her usual position behind the coffee counter, a slim Venus in blue jeans, a white shirt and red apron, her long blonde pony tail reaching nearly to her waist, her heart shaped face open and friendly.

"I'm so hungry," said Laura, sliding onto a counter seat.

"I have Tuscan Chicken soup," suggested Hope, letting Laura taste a spoon.

"That's great. And give me bread."

"I've got biscuits. Made this morning," Hope said, sliding a large one onto a dish for Laura and preparing the black tea Laura liked, in a small china pot. She then placed a small china cup and saucer with sugar and lemon in front of her friend.

"This girl keeps calling Hugo," said Laura, pouring out and blowing on her tea.

"Really?" Hope leaned towards Laura and whispered, "There's a girl in the shop right now who's been asking questions about Hugo."

Laura leaned back and waited for her soup with an accelerated heartbeat. Girl in the shop right now.

"Where's Sloan?" Laura asked casually, crumbling a piece of the large biscuit off and nibbling it, the taste of which was indescribably seductive. "Oh my god, these are good."

"I know. They don't even need butter. He's gone to Boston for the day."

"So has Hugo."

"That's her," whispered Hope, inclining her head towards the aisle where the person whom Laura believed to be Francesca was browsing. Laura was startled to behold a striking, auburn haired Amazon, perhaps six feet tall and beautifully proportioned, pretty and fair complected, with straight, shining shoulder length hair, a woman of 28 or 29, dressed in jeans, a sweater and boots and filling every inch of them magnificently. "No wonder she's confident," thought Laura. At that moment the tall girl's gaze met her own. Laura smiled as she would at any pleasant stranger she happened to encounter in the aisles of a charming bookshop. The girl returned a civil nod then made for a different aisle.

"Do you like being married, Hope?" Laura asked the mistress of the most popular cappuccino bar in a village filled with cappuccino bars.

"Truthfully, I do," Hope replied, "I feel the position carries with it the respect and respectability which was lacking in my life before David."

Laura remembered that Hope was a former B&D model and professional submissive who had been discovered at the Hollywood dungeon known as The Keep by her husband, when he was a teacher at Hollywood High, in the same neighborhood. They had come out to Random Point together so that he could improve his resume by a teaching stint at a Cape Cod prep school called Braemar. He was currently so well liked at that establishment that there was talk of his being made head of the English department by next semester. Meanwhile, Hope worked in the bookshop, mostly behind this counter, watching the world of Random Point go by and catching the cream of the tourists in her sugar spun web of mocha lattes, hot mulled cider, double espressos, drinking chocolate and spiced teas. One of her greatest marketing innovations at the bookshop was enabling the cozy visitor to make a meal of it while perusing their purchases, with various breads, bars, cakes, buns and muffins, along with rustic sandwiches sent over by the Inn. With her ravishing looks and an equally compelling menu, it was not surprising that Hope Spencer Lawrence took a significant amount of business away from all the other tea rooms and taverns in a three block radius, but even the other cafe owners forgave her, constantly drank her coffee and always brought her gossip tidbits first.

"She's good looking," Laura whispered across the coffee bar.

"I know!" Hope concurred.

"I'm surprised he doesn't want to put her in the magazine."

"Good idea. Maybe you can get her over to the shop and pay her for a photoset. Just some bend over shots. Might give her some face."

"She looks like she'd photograph very well," Laura mused. "I wonder why Hugo wants to brush her off so fast."

"You've obviously never been stalked."

"I think she just needs some attention," said Laura. "Maybe she thinks it has to be from Hugo, but maybe she's wrong."

"Got someone else in mind?"

"As a matter of fact, since she's so attractive, I think I do. But let me try the photo op gambit first."

"Well, take your time with the soup. She'll be working her way over to the shop in a bit. Fortify yourself for the coming episode," Hope said.

"If you weren't already married, would you have considered someone like Hugo?" Laura asked.

"Are you kidding? Hugo's got more magnetism than practically anyone. I'm madly in love with Hugo."

Laura stopped eating her soup, took out her phone and called her best friend Marguerite Alexander, now Mrs. Michael Flagg.

Marguerite was at home with her very small baby and answered immediately.

"Marguerite, do you know if Malcolm is seeing anyone at the moment?" Laura asked, leaving money on the counter for Hope and shrugging into her coat.

"I don't think he is, why?" said Marguerite. She was on somewhat friendly terms with her ex-husband, who owned and managed a climbing gym in the nearby village of Woodbridge.

"Do you think he'd be interested in meeting a tall, very arresting looking late 20's redhead in the scene?"

"He may be burnt out on tall redheads. Why, you know of one who's available?"

"She's one of Hugo's groupies. She's in your shop right now but she's getting ready to go over to Hugo's. I think she plans to confront me and ask me to give him up to her."

Marguerite chuckled. "If she's in love with Hugo, I don't know if Malcolm is going to cut it with her. Anyway, he's pretty prickly. He's not likely to go rushing over there to meet a woman just because she's in the scene."

"Really? What's he got going on that could be more interesting than that?"

"Honey, Malcolm just isn't that relaxed. But I just thought of someone who is. Remember that lovely boy I had last year, just before I got back with Michael?"

"Dru Baxter?" Laura asked, "isn't he at college?"

"He's in the village this week. I just saw him this morning."

"What's he like, nineteen now?"

"He's exactly nineteen. And I can tell you for a fact that he would be interested in running over to meet a tall redhead in the scene."

"Well, call him and tell him to wander into Hugo's shop in about twenty minutes, if he can. That might be as long as I can keep her there."

One hour later the phone rang in the shop and Laura jumped on it. It was Hugo again and she had much to tell him.

"Francesca has been and gone and Hugo, I made her very happy."

"What happened?"

"Well, Marguerite had a brainstorm to send that beautiful boy Dru over. Remember him, he crashed your party a few years ago when he and his little girlfriend from Braemar were way too young to be out in the scene?"

"Sure I do, nice kid."

"You're going to be so pleased with me. What do you think I did? I got them to pose for the magazine, with him spanking her!"

"But, she's so ...large," Hugo said, trying to visualize the image.

"Dru has shot up about three inches since we saw him. He's about 6'2" now and better looking than ever. I disarmed her right away by begging her to be in a shoot for the magazine and of course the kid was all over it. He probably sees he can turn Francesca into a dom in no time flat. Boy does she have the look. Anyway, the shoot went beautifully. By the way, that kid can spank. And Francesca didn't even need any make up. What skin. And what it did for her ego. Hugo, she forgot all about you. Dru escorted her out afterwards and I heard him inviting her to dinner at the Ball and Feather. I paid him in cash so he'll be able to get them a room at the inn if she consents, which I can't see her not doing. I could tell the posing turned her on."

"Laura! I'm extremely impressed," Hugo said without reserve.

"You're always so surprised when I do something right," she signed. "It almost hurts my feelings."

"Listen honey, it's apparent to me the blue china has slipped through my fingers so you don't have to sit on the phones anymore."

"Oh, I'm sorry! Are you getting on the road home soon?" Laura asked, finding that she missed him quite a bit that day and longing to lay her head on his shoulder that night.

"No dear, I'm going to stay in town a day or so more. I have some business to see to."

"Oh, really?" she couldn't conceal her disappointment. She was going to formally consent to marry him as soon as he got home and was looking forward to the pleasure this would surely give him.

"You almost sound as if you miss me!" he remarked with wonder.

"I always miss you when you're gone," she protested.

"You do?" he laughed.

Laura hung up, wondering if he even realized that she loved him. Just as she was closing up the shop the phone in Hugo's office rang. Laura ran to answer it and rejoiced to hear that Hugo's contact in London had obtained the blue china vase.

Laura tried in vain to reach Hugo on his cell phone, then attempted to find him at his Boston residence, the apartment in Back Bay. Since she knew that Hugo had given Amanda a set of keys and permission to use the lovely flat whenever she wished, Laura was not surprised when that young person answered the phone. What slightly did surprise Laura was Amanda's complete ignorance of the fact that Hugo was even in town. She would have thought he would have told Amanda that he would be needing the apartment that night. But Amanda replied that she had only stopped by to pick up some books she had left there a few days earlier and would not be there more than a few more minutes. She promised Laura to leave a note about the acquisition for Hugo to find as soon as he came in and wished her a good night. Laura shrugged off a vague sense of unease as she locked up the shop.

Chapter Six

Hugo Visits San Francisco

It was a clear, cool morning in mid December when Hugo landed in San Francisco on the Boston Red Eye. He took a cab directly to a boutique hotel on Geary Street, where he'd booked a suite. On the way he played his cell phone messages and was first pleased and then disconcerted to listen to several messages from Laura, the first merrily informing him of the successful acquisition of the blue china vase and the second wistfully wondering why he had not yet called her yet back. The messages were left eight hours apart. "She'll figure it out," Hugo thought, somewhat uncomfortably. Then he pushed the problem out of his head and determined to fully enjoy the day before him. "After all," he reasoned, "nine out of ten times, she pleases *herself*."

After showering, shaving and enjoying a light breakfast of coffee and rolls in the hotel café, he hailed a cab to Castro Street, telling the driver to take him to The Pearl, the largest combination psychic emporium and head shop in a city of psychic emporiums and head shops.

Hugo studied the windows before going in, just as he had done before a similarly named shop in Random Point, Massachusetts, twenty years before. The colorful arrays of carved statuary, polished brass pipes and incense burners, candles and incense were the same as ever, though there were many, many more books, requiring an entire bookstore annex to the main shop.

Before entering, Hugo noticed that the next storefront was that of a large yoga studio and day spa. One couldn't see inside however, the front window merely framing a large flower display and miniature waterfall.

Hugo went into The Pearl and looked around. There were a number of young employees behind the various glass cases and counters that ringed the main room, most of them multi pierced and inked, with blue-black or white-blonde dyed hair. Then he saw her, behind the furthermost counter, the one that held the golden amulets, so little changed it took his breath away and made his heart pound. She was ever the slender brunette, with her long hair still rippling to her slim waist. She was dressed in black pegged jeans, a white cotton shirt tucked out and leather ankle boots with sexy stacked heels. Her only jewelry was a few pieces of gold and her only make up was the dark red lipstick she had always worn for him. The closer he got to her counter the more clearly he could see how kindly the years had been to Cassandra. Perhaps she was right about the vegetarianism, or maybe it was the yoga. But she looked good to him, very good.

Not until he stood right in front of her counter did she raise her hazel eyes to his and instantly gave a most gratifying start, her small hands fluttering to smooth white cheeks that flushed deep pink at once.

"Hugo!" she breathed, evidently torn between astonishment, fear and boundless joy at his appearance. But he did not allow himself to smile, even at the knowledge that he too had aged slightly enough to be immediately recognizable. He merely folded his arms and looked at her so sternly that she fell back a pace.

"So you actually remember my name? You recall who I am?"

Cassandra blushed more deeply now, well aware of the very good reason for his sarcasm.

"You come to me later. You understand me, young lady?" he told her, handing her his card with his hotel and room number written on the back.

"What time?"

"Six," he replied, determining to sleep off his jet lag before dealing with Cassandra. Then he turned and strode out of the shop.

Cassandra ran after him and caught him on the street outside, flinging herself into his arms. He hugged her back as hard as she was hugging him and turned her face up to kiss her on the mouth.

"Do you want to meet him?" she nodded at the yoga studio beside her shop.

"Hell, no!" said Hugo. "Then I might feel badly about what I plan to do to you later. You'd better make up some lie about cleansing some sick friend's chi tonight. He never needs to know I've been here."

"My heart is beating so fast," she confided, her hand upon it.

"Mine too, honey." He kissed her once more then got back into the cab he'd left waiting for him. She stood leaning against her window, watching it drive off, her hand still on her heart.

"How the hell did you get out of the house in that outfit?" Hugo asked, opening the door of his suite to Cassandra at six-thirty. "You know you're late, don't you?" he scolded unconvincingly. She was ravishingly dressed in a gold brocade evening gown with a gauze fichu across the bosom, a fitted bodice and full skirt. A golden net evening coat and high heeled black velvet pumps finished the ensemble with elegant femininity and she carried a black velvet purse, from which she instantly extracted an antique gold cigarette case which he remembered giving her one Christmas.

"He had to leave for Los Angeles tonight anyway," she said, flipping open the case and offering him a joint.

"Oh, honey, you're so thoughtful!" he took and lit one.

"It's Humbolt."

"Of course. Let's go out on the balcony," he said, leading her onto a narrow walkway that overlooked Union Square. They smoked for a minute or two in silence.

"Okay," he said, "let's get this over with."

"What?"

"Let's get the unpleasantness out of the way," he said, taking another deep inhalation, then crushing the ember out in an ashtray and taking her by her slender wrist to lead her back into the luxurious suite, furnished and curtained in saturated tones of lilac and sage green.

Hugo looked around and found a wide divan to pull her towards. He pulled her down to sit beside him. Then he pushed her sheer evening coat from her shoulders and without hesitation pulled her face down across his lap. "No, no, no, this won't do," he said, pushing back the thick, protective layers of gold brocade skirt and white nylon crinoline sewn in underneath, to finally reveal, snugly encased in sheer, seamed black pantyhose, a small, well rounded bottom that had only benefited from eighteen additional years of careful diet and scientific exercise. Her thighs and legs looked equally attractive, as slim and well turned as he remembered them. "I guess you know why I'm..." he paused for the right word, "... upset with you."

"...yes," came the faint reply as Cassandra Campi hid her face in her hands.

Hugo sighed, holding her firmly against him with a hand thrown across her small waist. "I mean, we'll talk it all over in a while, but just now, I simply must communicate how I feel about what you did in an elemental way."

"You came a long way to do this, you might as well go ahead and do it," she murmured before burying her face in her arms.

Hugo hooked his thumbs under the waistband of her pantyhose and briskly yanked them down to the middle of her smooth, white thighs, completely exposing her pearly buttocks to his affectionate gaze.

"You probably haven't been spanked in a very long time."

"It's been years," she replied.

"Well, you'll really feel this then. I'm going to make sure you don't forget me this time," he told her, raising his hand. And yet, he still couldn't quite begin. He caressed her velvety skin. "Still so dainty and sweet," he told her, warmed by her compliance. He thought, why don't we have weed like this back East?

She arched up and looked at him beguilingly.

"No, why should I show mercy?" he replied to her unspoken question and gently pushed her head back down. "Better brace yourself," he warned. She gave a little sob of fear and remorse. The next instant the spanking had begun with an energetic volley of stinging smacks that took her breath away. Hugo had been giving all sorts of spankings for enough years to know how to mark a woman for one hour, one day, a week or more. In Cassandra's case, two minutes of hand spanking would leave her marked for five days. For two minutes of very hard spanking from a very large hand is no small thing, especially when one hasn't been spanked in years. Cassandra was crying real tears in less than ten swats. She couldn't help reflexively kicking her legs but bravely held her position, not attempting to wriggle away or cover her quickly pinkening bottom with her hand. She had done him a monumental wrong and he had clearly forgiven her but that didn't mean she might escape punishment.

He lifted her off his lap and sat her upright, handing her a handkerchief and advising her to compose herself, scarcely softened by her sobs and fixing her with a cynical eye. "So I'm in my shop a few months ago, proposing marriage to a woman for the first time in my life, she being Laura, the most treasured object of my affections for the last six years, and in the midst of her coyly demurring and teasing me to distraction instead of giving me a direct reply, who should walk in but...my daughter! Of course, I didn't know this right away. I thought she was the model from the agency, sent to do the spanking photo shoot. And she, being Amanda, thought this a fine joke and turning on a dime assured me that the model I'd engaged was suddenly ill, so the agency has sent her instead and was it all right?"

By now Cassandra had stopped sobbing and was delicately dabbing at her eyes and cheeks with the snowy handkerchief as her expression began to lighten and the corners of her lips curved upwards, envisioning a scene her daughter had told her of in detail long since, but enthralled to hear if Hugo would relate it in exactly the same way.

"Well, Laura is taking the photos it isn't long before she starts to notice the resemblance between Amanda and me. She gets hold of Amanda's ID on the pretext of taking a model release shot and we both notice that her last name is Sands. Then the real model from Boston calls from the station. I send Laura to pick her up and then I learn All."

Cassandra lowered her eyes and looked abashed.

"Honey," he said, taking her small hands and kissing each one. "Know one thing, you're not done being punished. But you took that... so well," he pulled her into his arms and held her close. Then he set her from him. "To continue my very interesting story about our very interesting daughter...did I mention that before I knew she was my daughter that I spanked her, pretty hard?"

77

"Amanda told me about the photo shoot. That you refused to lift her skirt," Cassandra grinned. "I quite agree, it would have been most improper to do so, under the circumstances."

"She didn't think so. Just a few weeks later she begged me to spank her in the woods. And I did it. Which scares the hell out of me. And strangely enough, we owe it all to you, who left my magazines where she could find them. It's one of the most perverse things I've ever heard of. I just want to know, what were you thinking, Cassandra?"

"Hugo, it wasn't like that. I didn't cold-bloodedly plan for her to become a spanking enthusiast. I figured when she was tall enough to reach the shelf with the sex books on it, she'd be old enough to appreciate them. But she was a lot more interested in the shelf above that one, the one with all your magazines. She devoured them with passionate devotion, praising their artistic content to me with a complete lack of self-consciousness. Of course she noticed those earliest photo sets of me and you and her aunt Carola and she started to ask questions and plot dates. It wasn't very long before she was confronting me about her paternity and I had to admit it was no coincidence her name was Sands, like yours. I felt it might be sensible to give her the name that properly belonged to her, on the off chance that if she ever applied to Harvard the alumni legacy might make a difference. As it happens, I think it did."

"You always did think of everything."

"By the way, thank you for picking up the college tab."

"It's the least I can do."

"I knew you'd feel that way."

"Of course you did, you know everything."

"Hugo, have no fears about Amanda. She adores you, but she isn't obsessed."

"You see, this is what I can't understand. If you were going to raise her like that anyway, why not have just stayed with me in the first place?"

"I was young and I had a very strong ego," Cassandra sighed. "I felt it would be crushed beyond recognition by your even stronger personality if I stayed within your influence. Perhaps I was wrong."

"I doubt it. You're almost never wrong," he sighed. "You and the Asian martinet did a much better job with the girl than might have been done with me around spoiling her."

"You see, that's what I thought. Now that her character is formed and she's neither lazy or immodest, you can lavish all the love on her you want without ruining her."

"Not immodest, she's a goddamned exhibitionist, Cassandra! She wants to model for Playboy."

"You'll talk her out of that, I'm sure," said Cassandra, taking his hand and rubbing it against her cheek. "At any rate, I'm sure you've noticed that other than that, she's a very good girl."

"Oh, I'm completely in love with her," he felt compelled to admit.

"She is easily distracted by shiny things," Cassandra pointed out in all fairness. "I got a note from her first grade teacher once complaining that Amanda was selling kisses to a little boy who had brought a bag of gold covered chocolate coins to school. She brought home that whole bag too."

"Tell me more."

"Well, she always needed two closets when she was little, one for her own clothes and one for her dolls' clothes."

"You're still so cute," he said, impulsively gathering her into his arms. "I have to have you," he said into her ear, taking the lobe between his teeth and softly biting it then pressing his lips to her throat.

"Shall I get out of all these clothes?" she whispered.

"You still look like this and you kept away from me all these years?" he marveled a few minutes later as she stood before him completely nude. He unbuckled his belt and pulled it free in one snap. "Over the edge of the sofa, young lady," he ordered, doubling the strap. "Remember what six of the best used to feel like?" He pressed his hand into the small of her back, admiring the small, rounded bottom arching up at him in the soft light of the exquisite suite.

"No," said Cassandra.

"How about twelve?"

She looked back at him with liquid brown eyes, mild and acquiescent, as much as to say, "I've also forgotten what foreplay is like."

Holding the doubled belt by the buckle end he applied the other to her upturned bottom in a measured and methodical style, taking perfect aim at the plumpest, mid-most portion of her small, firm cheeks, leaving neat red lines behind and eliciting a gasp or tiny pant with each successive stroke. "Twelve to begin with," he corrected his original estimate, "just as a warm up. Then several dozen more, don't you think?"

"Yes," she cried, drinking in the discipline as a pure aphrodisiac, remembering with exaltation how thrilling it had felt when he'd first treated her like this, so long ago and how exciting it now felt afresh. The tantric love making she'd been enjoying with her consort these many years was very fine in its way and perfectly balanced besides, but surrender of this sort was even more rare and deeply felt by that ardently free spirit.

"How dare you take it upon yourself, to decide, all by yourself, to deprive me of Amanda these many years?" Hugo demanded, underlining his disapproval with the fourth dozen sharp, stinging swats of the belt across Cassandra's fully exposed and by now, well striped backside.

"Truly, I meant well," she maintained steadfastly.

"What am I going to do with you?" he sighed, throwing the belt aside and yanking his own zipper down. "Don't move a muscle," he warned, fumbling a condom out of its foil. "I don't want another surprise showing up at my door in another eighteen years!"

Chapter Seven

Winter in Boston

Now that Amanda realized that she was no longer a princess, she began to wonder whether the charmed life she had led the first few months of the term had rendered her as selfish and self absorbed as Castor's scolding had implied. She was sitting in a local coffee bar, staring into the dark red depths of a cup of fragrant tea contemplating this when someone sat down opposite her in the small wooden booth. Looking up she saw with pleasure that it was Mr. Keen, the professor she had entertained so many fantasies about.

"Hello, Amanda," he said pleasantly, "May I join you?" he set his cup of chocolate down on the table and unbuttoned his tweed coat.

"Of course!" she sat up with a throbbing heart. The brisk weather outdoors had given his lean face a ruddy glow and his blue eyes looked merry that afternoon.

"Amanda, I could use a faculty assistant. Would you have time to do some work for me?"

"Oh, certainly," Amanda agreed at once, "I'm sure I would."

"It's just fact checking."

"I'd be delighted to do that Mr. Keen. When do I start?"

"Tonight, if you can," he said. "Do you have time pick up the list now?"

"Of course!" she agreed, thrilled at the prospect of a ten-minute walk across campus with him and then an additional perhaps five minutes alone with him in his office. But as it turned out, he'd left his paperwork at his home and as soon as they had finished their drinks, they walked there instead. It was a cold day with scudding, threatening clouds, but Amanda was on fire inside as she entered Mr. Keen's home for the second time.

Mr. Keen closed and locked the door, invited her to sit in the parlor and went to look for his notes. It occurred to Amanda while she waited that he might easily have emailed her the facts to look up. Which meant that he was genuinely interested in spending time with her. He came out with a folded piece of paper, which he handed to her. She looked it over briefly. "This won't take me long," she said, putting the assignment into her camel toggle coat pocket.

"Amanda, sit down for a second, won't you?"

"Sure."

Keen sat down beside her on a tufted brown leather sofa.

"That day you were here, Amanda, you kissed me."

"You slapped my bottom," she countered.

"Because you kissed me."

"Didn't you like it?"

"I did like it."

"Then why the smack?" she pressed him.

"Well, I saw you that night a few months ago at the B&D support group meeting. In your high heeled boots and leather hobble skirt. You looked fabulous by the way."

"You were there?" Amanda cried. More people in Boston were turning out to be in the scene than not!

"Yes. I was there. Now Amanda, that kiss was most disturbing."

"You handled it well," she commended him.

"Amanda, you're not getting a crush on me, are you?"

"Oh, there's no 'getting' about it," she laughed. "But I can't believe you were at that meeting and I didn't notice you," she marveled, visualizing that particular group of perhaps forty colorfully coifed, inked and pierced individuals crowded into that small, over-heated room. She was certain she'd scrutinized every person there as the orientation speech ran to forty minutes.

"I'm not surprised you didn't notice me. Your eyes were all for... the men."

Amanda stared at him, the only possible meaning of his statement penetrating to her quick, sexually sophisticated brain in less than three seconds.

"You were there... cross dressed?" she asked tentatively and very gently.

"My alter ego Marlene was sitting one row behind you. I did envy that boy you marched away with. How did that turn out?"

"Oh, very well, thank you. He's a lovely top."

"Ah, of course. The tops are always so much more interesting, aren't they?"

"Well..." Amanda hesitated as she groped for a non-exclusionary response, "...for now." She covered her confusion and embarrassment by commenting with what she hoped sounded like friendly, nonjudgmental interest, "So, you're a cross dresser?"

"You're disappointed, aren't you?"

"No. Not at all."

"You were wearing leather, you had the look of a mistress."

"And yet you slapped my bottom," Amanda reminded him.

"Well, I'm your typical schizophrenic switch. When I'm wearing pants, I'm dominant, and you have the most spankable bottom I've ever seen."

"Shall we talk it over?"

"I'll open a bottle of wine," said Mr. Keen, encouraged by the sympathetic tone of her response. "Maybe I shouldn't have told you but you seem like the coolest girl." He shrugged. "I've been sensing your interest in me lately and I figured you should know the truth."

"Do you ...have a photo of yourself cross dressed?" Amanda asked boldly, remembering hearing once that all cross dressers enjoyed being photographed in their outfits. "I'll bet you're a regular Miss High Heels."

"My God, you know that book?" Keen was dazzled. "Yes, I have photos, but ... some other time perhaps."

Amanda was greatly relieved.

"Come to think of it, Mr. Keen, if I drink wine now I'll never be able to read my assignments for tomorrow."

"I understand, Amanda," he grinned, "you'd probably better run along."

"Thank you for telling me your secret," she said.

"I know it's safe with you."

As she walked away from Mr. Keen's house in the cold, deepening dusk, she dredged an image from the back of her brain, of the second row behind her at the meeting, where a tall, thirty something blonde in heavy make up sat, dressed in a perfect copy of the black Yves St. Laurent afternoon dress worn by Catherine Deneuve as Belle de Jour on the afternoon she began work at the brothel. That must have been him, Amanda thought, shivering to the bone even in her sweater dress and woolen coat. She retrieved her cell phone from her deep pocket and hit a name on her call list.

Marty picked up on the second ring.

"I was wondering if I'd ever hear from you again," he said without reproach.

"I need to see you if you have time tonight."

"Of course. Why don't you come to my place this time?" He gave her an address which she jotted down on a pocket notepad and she made for the nearest train station to catch a local to Back Bay.

To Amanda's surprise, Marty Patmore's condo was high up in a graceful Beaux Arts building on Beacon Street. It was painted in rich, dark colors, off set by cream colored crown molding and furnished with expensive simplicity. It was a fresh, clean smelling environment with everything necessary to comfort: substantial chairs and sofas, sturdy tables, book-lined walls, ample mirrors, subtle lighting and an eccentric collection of clocks. The floors were of a dark wide planked hardwood and there was a splendid fireplace with a carved, cream-colored mantelpiece in the main room. Night had fallen and a few lights reflecting on the water was all that could be seen of the back bedroom view of the Charles. After receiving a tour of the apartment Marty prepared hot chocolate for them in the spotless and artfully designed modern kitchen.

"You seem to be pretty well off," Amanda observed as though nothing could have surprised her more.

"I made a mint off some software I designed a few years ago," he admitted. "But let's talk about you."

Amanda sighed. "I don't know, I feel like I've done wrong somehow lately."

"Tell me everything," he said, pouring the thick, cinnamon spiced chocolate into two dark red cups and offering her one.

"This is extremely good hot chocolate," she marveled. "What did you do, melt chocolate bars?"

"I bought it last summer in Italy," he told her. "I think it's what they're talking about when they say some chocolate is an aphrodisiac."

She grinned at him. "I've heard that about caning."

"Oh, you think you want a caning?"

"Maybe a small one."

"Let's go in the other room, it's more comfortable," he said, leading her into the living room.

"Can we have a fire?" she asked.

"Of course," he said and got a cheery blaze started at once.

She sat on a low, tufted leather bench a few feet from the hearth and began to unburden herself to Marty. She told him about scavenging among her beautiful black roommate Alicia's perpetually frustrated following of handsome African American admirers, picking out the two most interesting boys and getting them both to play with her and make love to her on the same day. She explained that while the one had gratefully accepted her erotic largesse as a gift from Venus, the other felt objectified and was now nursing monumentally hurt feelings over her careless usage of his wonderful body and fragile emotions. She then described how she had been willfully withholding her favors from an even hotter American Latino undergrad with the sole object of inflaming him beyond reason. Without really needing any help in Spanish, she had convinced the young man to tutor her almost daily, while granting him not the slightest favor, claiming that she took her love affairs too seriously to give in to an idle whim and allow him to even pet her, no less possess her. The most she ever allowed him was a slight pressure of the hand and finally, one or two chaste kisses in which tongues were not involved. But the boy's discovery of her photo spread in Hugo Sands' magazine, which showed her getting a spanking, (albeit over her well behaved navy wool suit skirt) and also contained the announcement that she was planning to soon begin producing and performing in spanking videos, had shattered her credibility as a puritan and inspired the hot blooded Harvard boy to order her to his room for punishment and penetration, and she had gone. Now having secured the affection of this long sought-after and fantasized about object, she had apparently managed to insult and alienate the perhaps slightly too macho junior master by refusing him oral sex. Amanda repeated Castor's analysis of her character as selfish and spoiled, comparing it to Ronnie's judgment of her sexual freedom as blameworthy promiscuity. Next, she admitted to having initially tricked her biological father, Hugo Sands, into spanking her before he had the slightest notion that they were in any way related, which she knew had thrown him into a great deal of confusion and then, subsequently teasing him into spanking her once more, in the woods of Random Point, which very nearly bordered on an incestuous pass on her part, though this spanking like the first had been administered over several layers of clothes and had not been accompanied by any other liberties. And finally, she revealed, with some embarrassment, the very large crush that she had nurtured for one of her teachers, which had led her to boldly and as she now realized, quite ill advisedly, planting a light kiss on that teacher's lips.

"In short," Amanda concluded, "I've gone a little wild these last few months and I'm feeling somewhat guilty about my behavior."

"You've been busy all right," said Marty.

"I...think about playing all the time," she confided. "And sex as well."

"What about your studies? Has all this activity distracted you from them?"

"No," she shook her blonde head firmly. "Not yet. But it's getting harder and harder to force myself to the library when I want to go to this boy or that one's room and surrender completely to lust."

"Well, Amanda," Marty said, "as I see it, you've done nothing wrong except to allow a couple of whiny and ungrateful young men to convince you that you should somehow feel guilty for bestowing your considerable favors upon them. The kissing of your teacher does seem a bit forward but I'm sure he was flattered and if you back off at this point there should be no harm done. Your relationship with your newly discovered father is decidedly unusual but certainly not lewd, so I wouldn't worry about that."

"So, you think I'm feeling guilty for no reason?"

"Oh, there's a reason all right. Two men told you off and you believed them. But don't worry. I'll help you get your head straight about this," Marty promised, flipping open a large, black wooden chest and drawing a thin rattan cane and a professionally fashioned and finished birch rod from its depths.

"What's that?" she asked, jumping up and looking at the birch. "I've never seen one before."

"It's a birch rod," he said, showing her the bunch of birch twigs, neatly bound up in a leather handle at one end and trimmed straight across at the other. "I'm told it produces a very interesting sensation. Want to try it?"

"Will it hurt?"

"It may."

"Well, that's all right. That's what I came here for."

"Just that?"

"Oh no, of course not, Marty," she said, kissing him shyly on his cheek. "I told you, I think about sex all the time. I'm so really hungry for it!"

"All right. Kneel on the floor and bend over the bench," he told her, putting her back over the leather divan on which she had been sitting. "And raise your skirt for me, Amanda." She reached back and pulled up the skirt of her cranberry wool polo dress to reveal a pair of matching cotton French cut briefs. Her long, smooth, shapely legs were bare from her thighs to the tops of her black knee boots, her athletic young body supple, firm and consummately graceful. Of course he had to take her face in his hands and kiss her cherry mouth before beginning. That astonishing face was the greatest miracle of all. She looked back at him with one warm, dynamic, unspoken assertion in her clear blue eyes. It said to him, "I yield to you without question and will continue to do so even though you make me cry."

"I'll let you feel it over your panties first," he told her, placing a hand in the small of her back and delivering six crisp, rapid swats with the birch twig rod. Swish-swat, swish-swat, the instrument's bewitching song resonated in the uncarpeted room, imparting an exhilarating sting. When he saw she barely rocked with each swat he laid on the next half dozen strokes slightly harder and more slowly. These birch lashes made her catch her breath and begin at last to move away.

"Hold your position," he warned her, pulling down her panties to expose her freshly pinkened, round, jutting, eighteen year old's bottom.

"May I ask you..." she raised her head hesitantly.

"Yes?"

"...to go fast? Just as you did before."

He inclined his head in acquiescence and pushed hers back down.

"But this time you're not to move away," he insisted.

"Very well," she agreed, steeling herself for the impending roller coaster ride.

Marty raised the rod and began again, hard, sharp and fast, administering several dozen strokes to the glamorously slender and leggy submissive in a style that induced an almost immediate state of erotic euphoria in that young lady that seemed to block out ninety percent of the pain. She heard herself pant and felt herself tremble and sway while knowing she was lubricating copiously and wondering if he would notice this. Shuddering with preorgasmic winks, she turned and stayed his hand. "Oh please, no more!" she begged, sitting back on her heels and gasping for breath. Her hand went back to her bottom. She knew she must be very red by now. She gave him a look that made him throw down the birch and take her in his arms. She herself wriggled out of her panties as they kissed, lay back on the leather divan and pulled her skirt up to her waist to show her soft downed Venus Mound and bedewed sex to him with her smooth white thighs spread as widely as possible. The usual minute of fumbling with a foil wrapped packet preceded the smoothest entry Marty had ever achieved of his sizable, lust engorged cock into a glove tight girl. Amanda's legs wrapped around his waist with extreme dexterity and he had to exercise all of his control in resisting the impulse to plunge in completely all at once. Experience had taught him to penetrate deeply but slowly, waiting for a girl to be completely ready before taking full possession of her. Even so, in a matter of seconds their groins were pressed flush against each other while he plumbed her to the depths of her wet velvety recesses.

"I should punish you severely for running after other men," he told her sternly, looking so seriously into her eyes that she gave a little sob of awakened emotion. The series of hard thrusts that followed brought her off in a matter of seconds and her subsequent throbs and wild contractions brought on his own climax almost simultaneously. After which they expired in each other's arms, rolled onto the floor and in a few minutes, fell fast asleep.

Chapter Eight

Further Misunderstandings

A few days after Hugo returned from San Francisco Laura was collecting clothes to drop off at the dry cleaners when she found an airline ticket stub in the pocket of a suit that bore faint traces of a perfume not her own. Recognizing the code SFO, Laura felt a stab of disquiet pierce her heart. The date on the ticket stub was five days past, when Hugo was supposed to have been in Boston. Cassandra Campi lived in San Francisco and Hugo had gone to see her. Another spasm shot through Laura's chest as she finished bundling up the dry cleaning in a mechanical fashion and threw it in the bottom of Hugo's biggest wardrobe. She suddenly felt limp. She really was dizzy with jealousy. No one in the world would have the kind of bond with Hugo that Cassandra had and that would only deepen as the golden Amanda became more a part of Hugo's life. Perhaps he had already decided to resume relations with the mother of his newfound daughter and was making plans for her to return to Random Point.

Laura pulled a taupe parka with a tawny hood on over her brown wool leggings and polo sweater, jumped into Hugo's old green jaguar and drove absently down Shadow Lane to the cul de sac where she used to live in the big house with her ex-husband, William Random. She thought about knocking on the door and visiting with Damaris and the baby but decided she couldn't face anyone at that moment and instead proceeded to the familiar path through the woods that led to the beach. It had neither rained nor snowed for a few days and the ground was hard packed and easy to walk on in her low collared hiking boots.

On the way she thought about the first time she had met Hugo face to face in that house. It was just the week after she returned from her honeymoon with William and a perfect summer day. William was at his construction company and Laura was still walking around the house in a daze, trying to get used to her new position as the wife of a businessman, when Hugo had knocked. She remembered all at once how attractive he had looked with his short, sandy hair, penetrating blue eyes and casually elegant suit. He always had worn perfect suits. That one he had taken to San Francisco was one of her favorites. That first summer day she recognized him immediately from his photos in the magazine and called him Mr. Sands. They had briefly corresponded about her placing an ad in the New Rod Quarterly and her doing illustrations to match the stories which her best friend Marguerite Alexander had begun to write for Hugo. Marguerite and Laura had been at Bennington together and had shared an interest in female submissive erotica, but it was only recently that Marguerite had come fully out in the scene, with Hugo Sands as her patron. Now she had brought Laura into the scene after her, unwittingly landing her an almost instantaneous husband. Laura's ad being squeezed into the publication on the day it went to press, it appeared in print almost at once, and while Hugo was away in Europe, Laura had swiftly met, been courted by, spanked by and proposed to by the dominantly virile William Random, whose unexpected affluence only added to his already considerable charm. There was no reason to even think that a romantically inclined submissive of her type could ever do better and William even lived in the same village as Marguerite, so that she could have her dream male and her best girlfriend near her at the same time. They were wed within two months of meeting, before Hugo ever had a chance to gaze into her limpid brown eyes and fall madly in love.

For years Hugo had stuck to the same story, that he had always known Laura was meant to be his, that he felt it when he read her first letter to him and gazed at the enclosed photograph. And he maintained that this intuition was confirmed on the first day that they met, the day she was recalling at that moment.

Walking between the winter bare trees under a cold, white sky, Laura remembered every detail of that first encounter with the man whom she had come to love so dearly over the intervening years.

She had invited him in, telling him that William wasn't home but expressing pleasure at finally meeting him in person, after having heard so much about him from Marguerite. She led him into the sitting room and offered to make him some coffee. He agreed, on the condition that he could accompany her to the kitchen. He knew the lay of the house better than she did, having been William's friend for years and seemed infinitely more comfortable than she did in navigating its halls. While she busied herself with the coffee preparations, Hugo complimented her on her drawings and offered to buy as many illustrations as she could give him for his quarterly magazine. Understanding that this visit was intended as a business meeting, Laura began to feel less embarrassed and more relaxed and gazed at him with greater interest, finding him extremely amiable.

They took their mugs back to the parlor and sat down together. Hugo seemed pleased with the coffee and already knowing a great deal about Laura's proclivities from grilling Marguerite, produced one of the fattest spliffs she had ever seen from a cigarette case and offered it to her. Instantly charmed, Laura confided that she would love to smoke but asked that they leave the house to do so, as William strongly disapproved of this habit and had made her promise to stop engaging in it.

Hugo had suggested walking in the woods and they immediately left the house. At first he hadn't spoken much, allowing the drug to work its peculiar magic on her brain. Then he idly began to question her about her new relationship. Was William not very controlling and judgmental? Laura admitted that he was. Very. Indeed, she was finding it a little hard to conform to his high standards of behavior. Emboldened by her frankness, Hugo wondered whether perhaps she had rushed into the marriage too quickly. She was obviously a free spirit and would quickly chaff under such unnatural restraints. Laura laughed and reminded him that she had met William through Hugo's publication, which seemed to strongly advocate male supremacy. Hugo said that was true, within limits, going on to point out that he'd never met a woman who could be controlled, no matter how hard she was slapped.

They walked on for a few minutes in silence, passing the joint between them. Laura remembered how beautiful and fresh and green these same pale, brittle woods were that summer's day. The next thing she knew, her back was up against a tree and Hugo was kissing her lips and throat, running both hands through her long, soft, silky brown hair and then fastening them to her small waist as he pulled her to him. He kissed her breathless before letting her go and she didn't even try to push him away. He told her then how he had felt they were meant to be together and that meeting her had convinced him of this inevitability. He said he still didn't understand how she could have slipped through his fingers so fast, before he'd even had a chance to meet her, but that nothing about what had happened felt correct. It was all due to circumstance and propinquity that she happened to fall across William's lap instead of his first. And it couldn't go on like this for long.

Laura finally broke away from him and they began to walk again, emerging at the beach a few minutes later. It was a small cove that took only five minutes to walk across. They walked up and down the beach for almost an hour, Laura protesting that fate had already decided for her which man she would belong to and Hugo contradicting everything she said.

To change the subject, Laura told Hugo about her younger sister Susan Ross, who would come to stay with them that summer before matriculating as a freshman at the Boston Art Institute. She tried to tempt Hugo with Susan, telling him that not only was she also in the scene and submissive but that she had artistic skills equal to Laura's own and would gladly supply more illustrations for Hugo along the same lines as Laura's. Hugo impatiently dismissed the idea of being interested in a lady that young and returned again to the concept of Laura's eventually leaving William. It felt very disloyal even to listen to such conversation and Laura begged Hugo not to pursue it anymore. He sighed and agreed, making a present of all the joints in his case to her before escorting her back to the house.

93

"You can come down to the beach and smoke them every day and think of me," he told her, patting her trim bottom through her dainty summer dress for the very first time. A shiver went through her and she shot him such a look that he couldn't help taking her in his arms again and kissing her deeply. Seized with a violent desire for her, he crushed her rounded, upthrust bosom under his hands and kissed her throat and earlobes until she squirmed against him. This time she became frightened that he would take possession of her, which would be sheer betrayal to William. She forcefully pushed him away and gave him to understand that she did not consent to be taken by him now. Perhaps some day, but not yet. Hugo shrugged, smiled and said, "I had to try."

That night when William came home, Laura told him about Hugo's call and the offer to have her draw for him regularly. Her new husband was far from pleased at his friend's spontaneous visit and questioned his bride closely about how long he had stayed and what they had done. He was even less happy to hear that they had walked in the woods and on the beach and asked her point blank whether she had flirted with Hugo or allowed Hugo to flirt with her. He knew Hugo pretty well and could guess how the fetish publisher would comport himself with a pretty submissive, be she ever so married. The manner in which Laura had flushed at these questions infuriated William who had without further conversation turned her over his knee and administered a stinging spanking and admonitory lecture, cautioning Laura to entertain Hugo Sands alone again at her extreme peril.

Laura emerged at the beach and began to walk up and down. It had been years before Hugo finally won her to his side. But all along he had hovered around the periphery of her world, snatching moments and hours with her whenever he could bring the planets into proper alignment. First she had had to go through the several rocky years of her marriage to William, during which her free spirit had indeed rebelled against his autocratic domestic rule. The first time she'd left him it was after discovering William's affair with his then secretary, Damaris Perez. After having a bit of a fling of her own with Marguerite in Manhattan, Laura had returned to William, less submissive, more assertive but still in the thrall of his muscular sexuality and skillful disciplinary techniques. In the back of her mind and her heart she was already more drawn to the decadent Hugo Sands than the sober William Random, but still unready to make a dramatic move in the publisher's direction. Then William had gone to the Andes for a climbing trip that had turned into a year away from home on a village engineering project. Laura was left to manage her husband's business in his absence and felt both rejected and abandoned by him. When he finally returned, William managed to seal her growing indifference to him by approaching her for sex before even shaving off his beard and getting into decent clothes again. Seeing his want of politeness as a deeper lack of respect, Laura told her wandering husband exactly what she thought of him and advised him not to count on a single favor from her. Outraged at being greeted with such icy distain after such a very long absence, William had asserted what he felt to be his ultimate right as a dominant male and had taken her across his lap and spanked her. He then bent her over and took what he wanted and believed to be his due as her loving if somewhat neglectful husband. It was the wrong thing to do.

Laura left William's home that day and immediately sued for divorce, charging William with the humiliating assault of an extremely non-consensual spanking and then near rape. Laura was serious about having her day in court and hearing her husband roundly rated by a judge. She wasn't out for William's blood, but she did expect a public apology and an uncontested divorce decree. She didn't want to see William arrested, but she did want him to be publicly embarrassed, designated a Neanderthal and made to understand that he had crossed a line that had nothing to do with playing as they knew it.

William was very sorry for the ill timed, clumsy, primitive ravishment of his wife and seemed to realize that he had destroyed the delicate balance of their relationship by pushing every part of it just a little too far. Laura refused a settlement and went to live with her sister Susan Ross in Anthony Newton's house on the cliff. Hugo had arranged for her little sister to come to the attention of the successful composer and the two had been a devoted couple ever since.

One would have thought that this would have been the exact moment for Hugo and Laura to unite, but Hugo had taken offence at

Laura's dragging the scene into the divorce court. He maintained that Laura could have had her divorce granted for any reason she chose and that there was no actual need to ever utter the word spanking in front of a judge. Since she didn't plan to bring a criminal prosecution against William over the non-consensual sex and spanking and she didn't even want a settlement, there didn't seem to Hugo to be any proper reason for introducing the domestic discipline motif into the hearing. Hugo saw Laura's action as a betrayal of the very scene that had nurtured her art and herself and landed her sister on deep, plush velvet for life. He had expressed his displeasure by giving Laura a public caning at a small local party that left her smarting a little too keenly for comfort. He had played the master and Laura had submitted because even then she knew that she loved him desperately. But she had become very proud in the year that William had left her in charge of his business and more liberated than she had ever thought possible. She was determined to hold her position, no matter how hard Hugo caned her. But Susan Ross, watching the entire exhibition in astonishment, had decided Hugo was out of control and had run out of the house to call William and report what was being done in his honor to his ex-wife. William had arrived within minutes to snatch Laura out of caning reach and bear her off into the night.

Laura had subsequently punished Hugo for misusing her that night by keeping well out of his grasp for nearly two more years. When she saw him in the village she greeted him in the manner of a bare acquaintance, with a faint, noncommittal smile and then moved on with only the most minimal conversation, as though her very words were too precious to bestow on the type of bully who would cane a girl like that. Initially he had paid little attention to her prolonged fit of pique, but when it began to stretch into years of no physical contact he began to seriously repent of his behavior on that fateful night and even made one or two overtures of formal apology. But Laura continued to appear uninterested and Hugo had no choice but to withdraw from the field, at least temporarily and console himself with casually dating a few of the pretty, playful women who came his way as models for or readers of his magazine.

Then one spring day the previous year, Laura had walked into his shop in a portrait collar sundress and essentially indicated to Hugo that she was ready to be his. Hugo could barely contain his joy while contriving to appear stern and aloof but she quickly broke down his reserve and four years after their first meeting, their true love affair finally began.

Everything had finally seemed just about right between them, when Amanda had walked into the shop two months before, on the day Hugo first proposed. Now Laura wondered if anything could ever be the same again. The way he had secretly gone off to see his child's mother filled Laura with misgivings. What had she, Laura, really been to him in comparison with Cassandra?

Laura walked back to the car, deciding to go and see Hugo at once. She drove directly to the shop in which a few browsers, with coats and scarves loosened, were examining old clocks and curios with Christmas presents in mind.

Hugo had just finished wringing up a sale at his back counter and was wrapping an old chess set in brown paper for his customer when Laura caught his eye. The customer departed and Hugo compulsively counted the cash in the old fashioned cash register before closing it and looking up to smile at Laura. Saying nothing she pulled the San Francisco International Airport ticket stub out of her pocket and tossed it on the counter.

"Where did you get that?" he asked.

"I found it in your pocket. What were you doing in San Francisco that you didn't want me to know about?"

Hugo could see that she was on the verge of tears and wished the few remaining customers would leave.

"Nothing honey, nothing at all."

"That's a lie. You went to see Cassandra, didn't you? You saw her and you made love to her. Don't bother to deny it, I can see it in your face!"

"I wasn't going to deny it," he replied with some dignity.

"Then why did you try to hide it?"

"I don't know," he gave a helpless shrug, as though it baffled even him. "It's not like me, is it?"

"Honestly, I have no idea. I realized today I barely know you."

"Laura, I understand you're surprised, but there's no need to be upset about this."

Laura folded her arms and turned away from him. Both were relieved to hear the outer door of the shop tinkle as the customers departed without making a purchase leaving Hugo and Laura completely alone in the shop. Hugo came around from behind the counter and tried to take her hand but she pulled away.

"You're still in love with her, aren't you? You went to ask her to come back to you, didn't you?"

"Of course not!" he protested, smiling at her supposition. "But I did have to see her."

"Why?"

"Well, for one thing, I wanted to hear from her own lips why she kept Amanda a secret all this time. And why after bothering to keep us apart, she apparently bred the girl up to be a creature of the scene."

"Well? Why did she?"

"Well, it turns out she didn't do it deliberately. The girl just found the magazines when she was twelve and became engrossed in them all on her own. Then she saw her mother's photo in them, started asking questions, found out that Cassandra had been my sweetheart and did the math. It was all exactly as Amanda had told me."

"And why did that mean you had to have her again? Why are you suddenly fucking around so much while supposedly wanting me to marry you?"

"Not so much," he protested in surprise.

"No? This week Cassandra, last week the statuesque groupie Francesca! Who else have you had lately?"

Hugo did not mention the recent encounter with Amanda's girlfriend Thalia in the bathroom at Michael's bar, but the memory did pop into his head and he wondered if Laura didn't have a point. He had been busy lately!

"No one, honey, no one," Hugo smiled, rather thrilled at this first sign of real jealousy that Laura had ever exhibited for him. He tried to catch her up in his arms but she pushed him away and folded her own arms in stubborn anger.

"Look, you have to understand," he explained, "suddenly discovering that I have a grown daughter has thrown me. And for her to be enough of a madcap to trick me into spanking her and photographing her before I even knew who she was and then to insist on posing for my magazine and bringing me models, it was all too crazy for words. I was starting to feel perverse. I mean more than normally so."

"Keep talking," Laura said, hearing much that was sensible in his words.

"I've never even had a daddy-daughter fantasy, though Amanda keeps trying to make one happen."

"What about that time with me?" Laura asked, remembering him once asking her to pretend to be six.

"Damn, you have a good memory. That was the exception that proves the rule."

"Well, go on," said Laura, "you were explaining your feelings and they do interest me."

"Well, I was only going to add that Cassandra was right, I never did want children. As it turned out, Amanda is no trouble at all. But the fact that she's so like me is disturbing. But I don't want to start living vicariously through my player-daughter's scene life. I want to keep living my own life."

"What does that have to do with having to see Cassandra again?" Laura demanded. Hugo paused, reluctant to admit to a renewed passion for his former love but unable to think of any other excuse for having made love to her again.

"I just needed to see her again, as a man, not as Amanda's dad."

Laura brooded over this, murmuring, "And I suppose she was just as pretty as ever?"

"She did look good," Hugo smiled, adding ingeniously, "of course, she's much older than you."

"Why are you smiling at me like that?" Laura cried.

"I just love that you're jealous," he admitted.

Laura glared at him before turning on her heel and marching down the aisle.

"Hey, where are you going? We haven't finished talking."

"I'll be at Susan's," Laura replied coldly. Hugo followed her and caught her by the arm before she could reach the front door.

"Oh no, I'm not letting you walk out in a pet," he insisted. "Now, give me a kiss and say you forgive me."

"No!"

"Come on, Laura, don't be a little brat."

Laura looked up at him from under her thick, dark eyelashes, absolutely challenging him.

"Oh, it's like that is it?" he asked, taking her by the wrist and pulling her over to the chair by the hearth in the front room of the shop.

"No, Hugo, don't!"

"I'm sorry honey, but you asked for this," he replied, pulling her parka off and tossing it on another chair, sitting down and pulling her over his lap.

"No!" she kicked her booted legs up so high he had to duck in order not to be brained. He pushed her feet back down and anchored one arm across her slim, sweater clad waist before bringing his other hand down on her well-rounded, corduroy covered bottom. Since he was spanking Laura through her thick jeans he started just as hard and fast as he had a mind to given her display of petulant rebelliousness. The succession of smacks that proceeded to fall sharply about both shapely, jutting cheeks momentarily deprived her of breath but subsequently provoked a symphony of squeaks, squeals and sobs. A very long, sound spanking followed, entirely over Laura's tight trousers, imparting a remarkable quantity of heat to her tantalizingly twitching and bucking nether regions. She stopped kicking her legs when stern swats were applied to the backs of her calves and thighs but continued trying to wriggle out of his grasp throughout the entire punishment.

"A small amount of jealousy is sweet," he interrupted the spanking at length to advise her, "but you know I don't like tantrums."

"Go to hell. I hate you!" she declared stubbornly.

Hugo sighed and resumed spanking her in such a manner as would be felt for days to come, even in spite of his not having pulled her pants down.

"That's a very naughty thing to say," he told her. "And what's more, it's a lie. You love me and you know it." Nevertheless, he was kind enough to conclude the lesson without forcing her to agree and stayed his hand the instant she began to really cry. She sprang from his lap, pressing her hands to her face and turning away from him in deep embarrassment. He knew her well enough by then to know that she didn't want to be hugged or kissed.

"Go home and wait for me," he told her coolly. Then he went to turn out the lights in the rest of the shop.

When he came out to the main room again she was gone. There was always a chance she'd disobey him and begin the old cycle of punishing him for punishing her by absenting herself from his realm, but he knew this was unlikely. After the type of emotion she'd displayed tonight, he knew he could count on her being at his house when he got home. To his delight, he found her waiting for him in bed.

Chapter Nine

Amanda's Diary Christmas

December 18th, Cliff House, Random Point, MA

Winter breaks lasts such a long time that I thought, why not get started on my (spankporn) start-up film project? I wrote to Hugo asking for advice and he replied most helpfully,

Dear Amanda,
Come out to R. Point next weekend and I'll introduce you to my friend A. Bartlett, who owns a department store. He's in the scene and maybe you can charm him into inviting you to shoot in his store while it's closed for Christmas Day. You may have to let him spank you.

From what you've told me about your friends and their capabilities, I would ask Ronnie to be your producer-director-cameraman. Tommy, Thalia, her friend Cameron and possibly one pro sub model from Boston - I know a cute black girl - could comprise your ensemble. You do the writing, casting and pr work but delegate everything else to others.

If Ambrose Bartlett okays the shoot, there's enough room at Anthony's house for everyone. He's out of town and won't care.

Affectionately,
Hugo

I saw Ronnie in the dining hall at breakfast the day after receiving the email and finding him alone with a virtuous bowl of granola and fruit before him, sat down and made my pitch. I said, "I know you're still mad at me but have you thought about being my partner in the video project?"

"You're not serious about doing that, are you?"

"Sure, why not? We could create something pretty adorable if we tried."

"That's what you call adorable, fetish porn?"

"Not porn, erotica. Haven't you ever wanted to do a sexy movie properly? With a clever, witty script and really attractive, engaged talent? We could achieve a John Waters-like insouciance but without the drag queens. Didn't Todd Haynes get his start with a tiny indie short called Dottie Gets Spanked? And didn't Spike Lee break with a comedy about a hot, sweet girl who fucks three men? Ronnie, what is more exquisitely artistic than a beautiful girl's bottom being spanked?"

"You're very persuasive," Ronnie agreed, munching cereal and gazing so deeply into my eyes that I felt a contraction in the pit of my stomach and an instant later a drop of hot liquid bead against my panty crotch. He has the most beautiful eyes in Boston and the black pencil moustache suits him so well.

I told him about the Xmas week suggestion that Hugo had made and that we could probably count on being able to film in a department store. But when he pressed me for details and it came out that I was going to be the bait for the department store owner, Ronnie's brow wrinkled in displeasure.

"And you really intend to appear in this artistic masterpiece, getting bare bottom spanked?" he demanded.

"Why does everyone put so much value on it being bare bottom or not? I have no inhibitions about posing fully nude. Why should I?"

"Because you might decide to have a legitimate career some day. In fact, one would think that was the whole idea behind going to Harvard. Who's going to take you seriously with bare bottom spanking photos of you floating around online?"

"Well, I really don't think it matters at all, but I find your concern for my future touching, it shows you really care for me."

"Of course I care for you!" he replied indignantly.

"All right, Ronnie, I promise only to get spanked over my clothes or panties in the video."

"And you won't sleep with this department store owner to get the location?"

"Oh, of course not!" I vowed, mentally crossing my fingers. If he's good looking and sexy, why shouldn't I sleep with him? Shakespeare said that youth is fleeting and everyone I know over the age of 30 has tended to back this up. Ronnie is a very prudish boy. And I think he loves me.

It was easy to line up Thalia and her new friend Cameron for Xmas week. Thalia doesn't like to go home to her parents and Cameron is too broke to leave Boston. I don't believe I've mentioned Cameron here before. He is a junior at B.U. who Thalia picked up at the last mixer. He's a graphic design major, very tall and slender, white skinned with a shock of jet-black hair. He has good clothes and wears them well and in general exudes an air of pampered metrosexuality. He has a good sense of humor, likes to party, loves movies, music and art. If he hadn't already fairly diddled Thalia I'd swear he was more gay than straight but she says that while she hasn't actually had sex with him yet, he knows a lot of tricks to get girls off fast and he treated her to one of them after giving her a really neat spanking in one of the bell towers at Radcliffe, where they went for afternoon tea last week. That's the most important part about Cameron, he's completely in the scene, with plenty of experience spanking girls and lots of personal toys that he almost fetishes, such as straps, paddles and floggers. I wonder if I should start my own collection of those things. I like hand best.

Cameron is somewhat shy but also a bit of a ham and he loves the idea of getting paid a few bucks to be in our movie. I haven't quite figured out where I'm going to get the money to pay people with yet. Maybe I'll get Marty Patmore to make an investment.

Today I'm going to meet Ambrose Bartlett. Hugo is picking me up and taking me to lunch with him at the restaurant in Bartlett's department store. I've been told to look as smart and professional as possible so I'll probably wear the navy pinstriped suit I bought to meet Hugo in with my high spectator pumps.

Same Day, Evening

The lunch went off like a dream. Mr. Bartlett is sexy and dangerous looking, in the manner of a Hugo Boss ad. His attitude was severe, aloof and arrogant, like a dom in a bad spanking story or a good gothic novel. I liked it! Of course, I didn't take it seriously. I could see how his eyes sparkled when he appraised me. At first he affected not to believe that I was really Hugo's daughter, as it seemed so improbable, but after a moment or two he began to see the resemblance and then seemed satisfied he wasn't being teased. The next thing I knew he was asking me to model in the Saturday morning fashion show next week. I protested that I'd never done that before and wouldn't know what to do. He told me he'd give me a video to watch and all I had to do was copy the way the girls walked. It was only an in-store fashion show to promote that week's designer line and no one but his clerks and lady shoppers would be watching so I needn't be perfect. I agreed at once, ready to oblige him in any reasonable request.

Seeing how well it was going, Hugo took it upon himself to explain my project and how I needed some great shoot locations and then he asked if I might be allowed to use the store. Mr. Bartlett raised his eyebrows in a 'That's rather a lot to ask on such short acquaintance, isn't it?' expression but let me make my own pitch before answering.

"I would be so grateful," I said, holding Mr. Bartlett's gaze until we both blinked.

A few minutes later, Hugo saw a friend across the café and excused himself to go and say hello.

"What was that look about?" Mr. Bartlett asked at once.

"Hugo said that if you did me this favor you might expect a favor in return."

"I wonder what he meant by that?" he seemed mystified.

"He said you might be interested in spanking me."

"He's that casual about his own daughter?" Mr. Bartlett said, genuinely taken aback.

"Well, I am in the scene. This spanking vid is my project. And I'm already playing with four or five doms regularly. If a casual tone has been set, I'm the one who's set it."

"You're pretty confident for a school girl. If it's really true that you are one."

"Of course it's true," I said, producing my student ID card for him to see.

"If you're going to Harvard why are you even thinking about frivolous stuff like spanking videos? You should be studying and making sure you make a high grade point average so you don't get thrown out."

"It's not going to be frivolous, Mr. Bartlett. It's to be a serious project for my economics thesis on niche industries. I plan to try to create a company from scratch, advertise and market my own product and see if I can turn it into a viable enterprise. Don't you think it will be interesting?"

"I think it's ridiculous and I can't believe Hugo is endorsing this craziness," said Mr. Bartlett with feeling.

I began to think that Mr. Bartlett was going to say no. The idea of my starting my own spanking video business seemed to be making him grouchy. He must have gone to some Ivy League school himself back in the 20th century and appeared to have a lot of emotion invested in preserving the dignity of this type of institution.

Hugo returned to us and I said, "I don't think Mr. Bartlett is too impressed with my idea."

But before Hugo could comment, Mr. Bartlett broke in with a conditional, "I haven't said no," and what passed for a smile with him. I wondered if this was the type of dom Castor was going to grow up to be, the type who can never see the funniness or silliness in the role they are constantly playing.

We spoke of other things for the rest of the meal, principally the subjects I was taking and how I was finding them. I found myself being grilled about how many hours a day I spent at the library and how many nights I stayed in and studied. Good thing this ball buster didn't turn out to be my secret daddy and I got Hugo instead.

Finally Mr. Bartlett looked at his watch and said he had to get back to work. Then he looked at me and said, "Come back at six thirty tonight and we'll talk about your shoot."

Hugo showed me around the store and together we picked out several areas that could be used as sets. As we passed by a boutique called Damaris, a tall, slender, elegant as hell twenty something brunette, stepped out into the aisle and hailed Hugo with a smile. Hugo introduced me to Pamela Crane and explained that she had once worked as his assistant at the shop. She was plainly amazed at my being Hugo's daughter and couldn't take her eyes off me the whole time we talked. When Hugo mentioned that Mr. Bartlett had hired me to model in next week's fashion show, she showed me her new Spring line, the dresses which were going to be featured. Damaris, she explained, was the name of her partner, the co-designer of the dresses in the shop. She worked half the week in Damaris' shop, in Random Point, the same shop where Thalia and I had gotten our dresses to wear in the shoot at Michael's bar.

The dresses for the next fashion show were marvelously retro, with features like fitted bodices, vests, peplums, princess jackets, and other daintily feminine trim. They came in tall sizes too, so I was very pleased with the idea of modeling some of them. I confided my lack of experience and Pamela assured me that she too would be modeling in the show and that I had only to follow her lead and do everything she did. Also, there would be a dress rehearsal an hour before the show, with only sales women in attendance, so I wasn't to worry. When she found out we'd been having lunch with Mr. Bartlett, she seemed disconcerted. As soon as we left her I asked Hugo if he'd noticed this.

"She's probably worried that Ambrose liked you too much. They're engaged but no date has been set so far and she's the kind of girl who really needs to be married before too much longer."

"What about you and her?" I made bold to ask.

"What about us?"

"She's in the scene, isn't she?"

"Yes, very much so. She was one of my customers before she worked for me."

"Well? Dish!"

We were in the shoe department now and Hugo pointed out how this would be the perfect environment for a scene. "Tell me about Pamela," I urged him.

"I shouldn't," he demurred, but only for a moment. "However, it is an interesting story." Then he told me about how he'd hired Pamela to tend his shop while he was on one of his European buying trips. She'd just finished years of secondary schooling in the apparel design field but couldn't face Manhattan yet and decided to hide in Random Point for six months to a year and gather her courage. While she was watching the shop and lonely, she began to be courted by Sloan Taylor, who then merely worked for Marguerite Alexander in the bookshop across from Hugo's Antiques shop, but is now her partner. Sloan, a handsome, sensitive and meticulous young man who shared Pamela's love of classic cinema, good literature and Tin Pan Alley, was, at great length, able to win her affections, in spite of his relative poverty, which had at first seemed a great objection to Pamela but gradually became less so.

Pamela had long counted on employing her exquisite looks and refined education to score a wealthy husband, like the girls in the movies that she so greatly admired. Moreover, she owed many thousands in college loans. So it was something of a disappointment to fall in love with a bookshop clerk, be he ever so charming. Like Pamela, Sloan had a degree from a very good school and like Pamela, he was lazily hibernating in Random Point rather than seeking his fortune in Boston or New York. But his natural charm finally overcame her prejudices, melting her into a compliant fiancée.

Then a glamour photographer came to Random Point and discovered Pamela. He took her on a world tour, photographing her extensively for a coffee table book, in which Pamela portrayed a number of fictional and historical figures, in the most evocative costumes imaginable. Sloan had let her go, full of kindliness and encouragement, but always with the stipulation that she come back to him as soon as she could. During the year she had been gone, Marguerite had hired another full time employee, Hope Spencer Lawrence, to run the new coffee and sandwich bar she had installed in the bookstore. Then Marguerite began to stay home more often, leaving the running of the shop entirely in the hands of Sloan and Hope. Hope Spencer Lawrence is so very beautiful, with a blonde ponytail to her 24" waist and the bluest eyes in the Commonwealth. Pamela nearly short circuited when she saw her and scarcely knew how to cope.

Pamela tried to pressure Hugo into offering Hope a job in *his* shop so that the bookstore position would be available to Pamela. Hugo liked Hope but found her impossibly loquacious. He also resented Pamela trying to tell him whom to hire for his shop. At any rate, there was nothing going on between Hope and Sloan. Sloan was still in love with Pamela, though she didn't seem to believe it.

Even Sloan complained to Hugo about Pamela's pushiness. Extroverted, cheerful, magnetic Hope was good for the bookshop in a way that introverted, moody and aloof Pamela Crane never would be and Sloan had no desire to hire Pamela in Hope's place. In fact, he was amazed at her even making the suggestion as forcefully as she was doing considering that she had been away for so long with so little intervening contact. She hadn't written or called much, just assuming Sloan would always be there, waiting patiently for her return. Which he had done, only with a lovely assistant who became a dear friend in the meanwhile.

Then Hugo got a bad idea, which was to distract Pamela from her jealousy of Hope by creating a much more challenging work environment for her at the antiques shop. He began to find fault with everything she did, to scold her severely for mistakes and finally, to give her a sound spanking every time he thought of it. In short, he became quite gothic toward the latently masochistic Pamela, with the inevitable result that she fell in love with him. (The way Hugo put it was, "She started to like me," but I could tell, even by the way she looked at him today when we ran into her, that it had been love.) The spanking, being hot, soon led to sex, which Hugo knew was highly irregular, Sloan being his friend, but which he saw no way to avoid, given that he'd initiated the foreplay sequence leading to it. Pamela, being of a generally cool nature with splashes of molten lava here and there for texture, became too engaged in the excitement of being Hugo's toy to forbear confessing to Sloan about what was going on.

Sloan was floored by the betrayal and broke the engagement off at once. Then Hugo too broke off relations with Pamela, realizing that he was only leading her on, as he had no intention of having anyone but Laura as his permanent sweetheart. Also, he fired her.

"Oh, you bastard," I said to myself but endeavored to look as nonjudgmental as possible as he concluded the unhappy history of Pamela and the men of Random Point. It surprised to me to realize that Hugo could err in so many ways relevant to one girl.

"I know," he said, as though he had he read my thoughts, "it was not my finest moment. But I did manage to get Pamela hooked up with Ambrose Bartlett and they're really a pretty good match. I think he'll marry her shortly and then all her worries will be over."

I was extremely glad he had told me the story as knowing that Mr. Bartlett has a lover will temper my behavior when we are alone later. This Pamela Crane seems to have endured much pain from the scene and I don't want to add to her sense of unease.

Late, the same night

When Hugo dropped me off at the house I found Susan Ross waiting for me and eager to hear how the day had gone. I explained all that had happened and that I was to see Mr. Bartlett that evening, perhaps to seal the deal. Susan has been so supportive of my idea about the video project and is indeed becoming my closest new girlfriend. When I told her that I was planning to ask Marty Patmore to lend me the money to pay my initial set of models she offered to do that herself, telling me that Anthony had okayed her investing some money in a quality spanking video production several years before but that she had never gotten around to setting anything up so far.

Susan told me that she and her friend Diana Stratton had gone out to the West Coast a few years ago boldly determined to film a video for one of the California companies. In the event, nothing had gone to their liking. They had chosen the wrong company to work with and the production was cheesy, sleazy and third rate B&D. They hated the end result so much that both Susan and Diana were grateful when Anthony Newton bought the master from the company, lest it be distributed to his darling's embarrassment. At that point he had told her that she should by all means do a video, but she should do it well and that he would help her when the time was right. Susan thought the present opportunity was ideal and enthusiastically offered me complete financial support.

We talked until sunset, when it began to rain and the wind to blow fiercely. I was suddenly feeling quite sleepy and wanted to do anything but go out again and be beaten by an implacably stern dom. Susan offered to come along as my chaperone and even share the penalty spanking I had obviously to pay up with before being allowed to shoot at Bartlett's.

"I don't like to think of you selling yourself for a shoot location," said Susan with concern. "I can't believe Hugo would want you to be put in this position." Then on second thought, she added, "On the other hand, it's just like him. He's always had the attitude that subs have to pay their dues to earn their place in the scene. But still, Amanda, you're only 18. I won't have you traumatized. I know what it's like to play with a mean dom and I get the sense that Mr. Bartlett is one of those."

I told her I was amazingly touched by her kindness and sisterly friendship but that I didn't dare change the mix without Mr. Bartlett's prior knowledge. She woke me up with some wonderfully rich coffee, mellowed me out with a superb joint and helped me dress in a cherry-red, wrap front, cap-sleeved, v-neck, jersey dress with a sash and my black boots, then she drove me over to Barlett's, and pulled into the parking lot behind the store. It was raining very hard and I was about to get out of the car when she stopped me saying, "Wait, Pamela's coming out. Let's not let her see you. She might figure out what's going on and get mad."

Pamela exited the employee's entrance in a very smart trench coat with a fur collar. She carried a briefcase and lit a cigarette as she walked to her car, a late model BMW. Her long, lustrous black hair hanging down her back looked well against her golden brown coat collar. Her gloves, boots and everything were quite perfect.

"If Mr. Bartlett has her, why does he need to play with anyone else?"

"We'll see if you call what he does playing afterwards," Susan chuckled.

She gave me an umbrella, saying, "Call me. I'll be over at the taproom at the Owl, if not closer."

I got out of the car and splashed through the rain showering down in sheets to the service entrance and went in. I told the valet sitting behind the package desk that I had an appointment with Mr. Bartlett and asked the fastest way to get to his office. The young man led me to the proper elevator, punched the correct floor number and told me exactly what path to follow when I got to the fifth floor.

Going up in the drab elevator, so different from the polished, gold trimmed, wood wainscoted, mirror-lined customer elevator, I felt a pang of regret at having so quickly agreed to this scheme, without having anything like a proper feel for the man whose hands I was putting myself into. It wasn't too late to hit the lobby button and run the hell out of there, but what would I tell Hugo after he'd gone to the trouble to set this up for me? That would be rather silly after all my bravado. "Daddy, don't let the bad man spank me!" It would be the last time Hugo would ever put himself out to help me with a project. I got out a small mirror and freshened my lipstick, shocked by the blush that suffused my cheeks and the heat that seemed to dance around my face. This felt wrong, wrong, wrong!

The elevator opened and in a dozen steps I was before Mr. Bartlett's door, timidly knocking on it while tucking my umbrella under my arm and flipping open the buttons on my over coat. He flung open the door, pulled me inside then locked it behind us.

"You're ten minutes late," he told me curtly. "That's not getting off to a good start with me."

"I'm sorry."

"Take off your coat," he bade me, sitting down behind his desk and motioning me to the chair opposite. "And just let me look at you."

I sat down obediently and found myself wanting to look anywhere but into his eyes. Besides, I had once heard that "masters" didn't like being looked in the eyes without leave.

"That's a most becoming dress," he said.

"Thank you," I murmured.

"What have you got on under it?" he asked conversationally.

"A black lace push up bra, sheer, lace trimmed black panties, a black lace garter belt and sheer black hose," I replied.

"Show me," he said, lacing his fingers behind his head and leaning back in his chair. He was quite a good-looking man, but possessed an impatience that did not seem to bode well for any submissive he honored with his attentions. I reminded myself that I had already played for years, that I have a substantial pain threshold and that my bare skin is nothing to be ashamed of, yet I felt unpleasantly objectified while pulling my dress over my head and allowing him to see me in my entirety. Without being told to do so, I slowly turned completely around, letting Mr. Bartlett assess my flip side for perhaps thirty seconds before facing him again. The outfit was extremely provocative but it also gave me power. Which is probably why he immediately told me to take it off.

"You want me nude?" I asked, startled. I was used to younger men pulling off every stitch of apparel as quickly as possible, but the several more mature men I'd had to do with of late seemed to savor the unwrapping. Mr. Bartlett wanted me to feel vulnerable and I suppose, he was rather a dog. I did not like his style and I promised myself that I would not let him have me this night, whatever else he did.

"Please!" he encouraged me briskly, pulling off his well-tailored jacket and tossing it on his desk, loosening his silk foulard tie and rolling up his white shirtsleeves to below the elbow.

"Very well," I agreed, sitting on a sofa to unzip and pull off my boots, which I set neatly side-by-side. Then, not looking at Mr. Bartlett, but at my legs, I carefully undid the garter buttons and rolled each stocking off, stacking the pair by the boots on the floor. Then I unhooked and removed the garter belt. Standing up again, very straight with my shoulders thrown back, I unhooked my front closing bra and freed my breasts, which, being high, full and cherry tipped, riveted Mr. Bartlett's gaze. Then I slipped my panties down and off and folded all my lingerie neatly, placing it on the sofa. I stood with my hands clasped behind my back, looking at him from under my lashes and waiting quietly for further instructions.

"Come here to me," he ordered, pushing his chair back. It was an armless chair, probably ordered expressly for this purpose, as what executive sits on an armless leather chair? As soon as I came to him he pulled me down across his lap.

"You've got a lot of confidence," he told me, positioning me to his satisfaction, one hand curling around my waist to hold me in place. "Whatever happened to youthful modesty?"

I didn't know if I was supposed to respond and so kept quiet.

"I don't care to spank playfully," Mr. Bartlett told me. "If it isn't real, it means nothing to me."

"I understand," I murmured, starting my deep breathing at that moment.

"You accept the terms of being allowed to shoot in my store?"

"I do."

"Good. Now, I'm only going to spank you for five minutes, but I promise you, you won't enjoy it."

God damned sadist.

"Okay," I agreed meekly.

"All right, here we go," he said and then he began. And he was right, I didn't enjoy anything about it. He was determined that I feel pure pain and plenty of, as fast as pain could ever be dispensed. My system was so shocked that in less than one minute I began to sob uncontrollably. But he held me fast and continued. Five minutes? I couldn't bear five more seconds of this brutality. But I gone so far, endured this much, if I stopped him now, would I be denied the shoot space? Would he make fun of me as a toy submissive and tattle on me to Hugo? I thrashed across his lap, gnawed my knuckle, twisted from side to side and finally began to kick. "Stop that," he told me sternly. "Put those legs down." I subsided in a perfect pool of tears, crying bitterly, despairingly. Nothing had ever hurt this much. Should I stop him now? Now? Should I cry mercy? Would Hugo really want me to take this much punishment from a total stranger who I didn't even like? Inside my head, I grew frantic. Was I really allowing myself to be abused, for a silly film project, me a Harvard girl, with all the valuable assets that would see me through the rest of my life? Then I thought, I've taken this much. If I can only hold out a little longer. He said five minutes. Five whole minutes. I increased my ujai breathing and tried to control my impulse to scream bloody murder just a little longer.

Then, all at once it was over and I was being told to get up. I popped off Mr. Bartlett's lap, still sobbing and dashing away tears.

"Go and stand with your face to the fireplace, hands on the mantelpiece," he told me. He actually had a working fireplace in his office, but it wasn't burning at that moment. I obeyed shakily and then heard the sound of a zipper coming down. I waited tensely, but nothing happened. I strained my ears to detect any sound and turned to see what he was up to. "Did I tell you to move?" he demanded, before I had a chance to see anything. I turned my face back to the hearth but by now had figured out that he was masturbating to the vision of my belabored backside.

At last I heard the zipper going up again.

"You did well, Amanda," he said in an almost friendly voice. "Why don't you go and wash your face now?" He handed me my clothes and pointed me towards his private bathroom. When I got in there (and it was gorgeous) I looked in the mirror at my bottom and recoiled with shock. I was terribly marked, just from his hard, bony hand. My tears had stopped flowing and I quickly dressed, wanting to get out of there as soon as I could.

When I came out, Mr. Bartlett was putting on his jacket and adjusting his tie. He turned to smile at me.

"You can have the store from seven pm on Christmas Eve to ten pm on Christmas Day. Shoot wherever you like but if you break anything or leave anything not as you found it, you'll be held fully responsible. Okay?"

"Thank you," I mumbled, unable to meet his eyes, the monster.

"By the way, my usual rental fee to film companies is $10,000 a day."

I assumed that this was supposed to make me feel less ill-used and thanked him again with the mildness of a lamb.

"Do you need a ride anywhere?" he asked.

"No, thank you," I replied. "Good night, Mr. Bartlett." And giving him one last respectful nod, I pretty much ran out of the office and found my way out of the building in a fog of fading pain and growing humiliation.

When I got outside the rain had slowed to a regular shower instead of torrents. I began to dial Susan's number when I saw a car waiting in the empty parking lot with its lights on. It was a big sedan and Hugo was at the wheel. As it pulled up to me I saw that Susan was in the back seat. I jumped into the front and slammed the door shut. Hugo took one look at my face and said, "Amanda, what the hell happened?"

I felt my eyes over spilling with tears and flung myself into his arms, burying my face in the smooth wool flannel lapels of his nice suit. "It was horrible!" I cried, clinging to him and feeling absolutely comfortable as he tightened his arms around me.

"Oh no," Hugo said, "this was all my fault!"

"Yep," Susan said from the back seat, "you did it again! And this time you set your own daughter up. You are one sick fuck."

"No," I protested, lifting my head in Susan's direction, "he couldn't know."

"Be yourself, Amanda, he always knows."

"I'm so sorry," Hugo said, dabbing at my cheeks with a snowy handkerchief. "I keep forgetting how young you are."

"I'm okay," I cheered up. Now that they felt sorry for me I stopped having to feel sorry for myself. The pain was beginning to disappear, except for a deep, muscular ache from having tensed so hard. Then I realized I was extremely hungry!

We stopped for a meal at an inn on the road between Woodbridge and Random Point, and it was a meal as only a New England inn can provide. After eating hugely of Christmas fare and drinking hot mulled cider, I was fully restored to my former optimism.

This was a hard day but not an unprofitable one. I landed my splendid and unique shooting space for my project. Then, on a scene level, I found out that some masters are assholes, that my new girlfriend, Susan Ross, really cares for me, and that my biological father is a joker. (But I love his voice and those wicked blue eyes.)

Chapter Ten

Ronnie Takes Barbara

It was a cold, white afternoon, just a few days into the new year and a powdery snow was beginning to fall on the Charles River as Amanda Sands, Alicia Bishop and Thalia Dunbar walked across the Harvard bridge from Boston back to Cambridge. Thalia had spent Christmas in Random Point, helping Amanda shoot scenes for her video project. Then Amanda had invited Alicia to come back to San Francisco with her for New Year's Eve. While Hugo was the proper parent to introduce the irreverent Thalia to, Alicia was better suited to her more politically correct California family and Amanda's mother Cassandra duly charmed her bewitchingly beautiful African American roommate.

Now Alicia was really beginning to warm up to Amanda and in doing so, seemed to relax her guard about sexual matters. It had been her wont to express the highest disapproval at Amanda's unembarrassed promiscuity and unaccountable fascination with what Alicia could only term sadomasochistic perversion. Nor had she ever seemed to tire of chiding Amanda for allowing herself to objectify and be objectified by the two handsome black students who originally began as Alicia's groupies. But as she listened to Amanda and Thalia discuss the problems and mishaps of the shoot in the minutest detail, Alicia began to realize how innocent and possibly even amusing, her tall, blonde roommate's scene might actually be.

"Ladies, I'm not insensible," Alicia said. "I can see the eroticism inherent in being swept off one's feet by a masterful male. In fact, it sounds like a great deal of fun. I've always taken control in my relationships, being fearful that my lovers would disappoint me if I didn't guide their every move."

"How interesting," said Thalia. "Maybe you're a dominant."

"Of course she's a dominant," said Amanda, laughing, then she suddenly went silent, seeing Castor Reyes approaching from the opposite side of the bridge, walking by himself, in jeans and a tweed overcoat. "Look, there's Castor," Amanda said, her heart fluttering.

"The male chauvinist fuckpig?" Thalia asked under her breath.

"Did I call him that?"

"He's so hot," breathed Thalia. "Can I have him when you're done with him?"

"Do you like to give head?"

"I don't mind," Thalia replied.

"He called me selfish because I wouldn't blow him," Amanda brooded.

"You let him have you. That should have been enough," Alicia weighed in.

"He got to have me both ways. And he got to slap me hard. He made me cry."

"Oooooooh, baby," said Thalia.

"He's noticed us," said Amanda.

In a minute Castor came level with the girls and greeted them with a pleasant smile. He took Amanda in his arms and gave her a New Year's kiss without an iota of self-consciousness, though their last encounter had been fraught with awkwardness, misunderstandings and hurt feelings.

"Young lady, why have you been such a stranger lately?" he scolded Amanda, then turning to her roommate said, "Hello Alicia, Happy New Year to you." Alicia inclined her head with a distant smile. After what she had just heard casually said about Castor, she was not disposed to like him.

"Castor, this is my friend Thalia from B.U.," said Amanda, after wriggling out of his grasp. "She's in the scene. In fact, she came home with me at Christmas and let me film her for my spanking video." Amanda waited a moment before speaking again, watching Castor take in her new friend's attributes, his expression revealing his thoughts.

He knew he could never hope to fascinate the icily judgmental Alicia, but had Amanda really just remarked that this peaches and cream beauty was in the scene?

"Oh, really? That's marvelous," said Castor, shaking Thalia's small, delicate hand. "Castor Reyes. I'm so happy to meet you." Then he turned to Amanda and sternly remonstrated, "You have no business wasting your time with that nonsense. You should be concentrating on your Spanish."

All of the students were mindful of their first semester grades coming out in a few days and all were suddenly quiet as they contemplated this awesome event.

"Oh shut up, you can't boss me around," Amanda said hotly, folding her arms and narrowing her eyes at him. Castor returned her gaze mildly, then sighed, as much as to say, "Okay, I get it, you're over me." Then he turned to Amanda's fair friend.

"Excuse me, Thalia. May I talk to you for a moment?" Castor took Thalia by the elbow of her long, faux fur trimmed, fitted cream parka and lead her a few dozen yards up the bridge. They stopped and looking over the side, began to talk.

Amanda and Alicia began walking again, but slowly, so that Thalia could catch up with them easily when she was free to do so.

"Gee, he works fast," said Alicia.

"He's pure predator," agreed Amanda, still smarting from the scolding, which seemed to hit home more forcefully today as she fretted about her upcoming grades. She knew she'd been fearfully distracted the entire semester, between all her different lovers, her luxuriantly decadent weekend trips to Random Point and the video project. Her plan of going out only once a week had proven untenable one week into the term. There were simply too many people she enjoyed spending time with and she'd never felt so much like having sex with beautiful young men.

"Look at that, she's nodding," said Alicia, "... so submissively."

"Oh, he's got her number all right," said Amanda, curiously not feeling any sort of jealousy.

"You'd better be careful the fuckpig doesn't expect you to jump into the mix," advised Alicia sagely. "All MCP's want two women at once."

"I wouldn't do that," said Amanda. "That's not my idea of romance."

"I'm so glad to hear it," said Alicia, linking arms with her roommate. Both young women were of the same reedy frame and their steps naturally fell into the same rhythm as they generated enough heat to warm them even though it was now under freezing out.

"Don't think they're all like him," Amanda launched into a defense of the men of her scene. "It's not all about assigning blame and administering punishments. A spanking scene can be highly seductive. And if the man knows what to say as well as what to do, he can make you want to give up control, to him and him alone."

"Well, I do have to admit, your friend Cameron intrigues me. He doesn't seem like the others. He's so cutely metrosexual. The way he brings you English breakfast tea and fruit and cookies and those beautiful museum cards he leaves notes on."

"Alicia, why don't you let Cameron initiate you into B&D, just to see what it's like?"

Before Alicia could reply, Thalia came running up to them breathlessly.

"We have a date for later tonight," she reported.

"I'm glad I could do that for him," Amanda said honestly, knowing that in spite of the initial thrill that seeing him had given her, her passion for Castor was spent. She saw him as a male who needed to be catered to and this was not agreeable. He was very handsome, but she had other handsome men in her life who weren't nearly as peevish nor half so demanding. It was best to break cleanly with him now and allow Thalia to annex Castor for their mutual pleasure. Thalia was an easy-going girl who didn't expect too much in the way of gallantry from her lovers and therefore would not be overly surprised or affronted by Castor's manners. But now she turned again to Alicia, whose sudden expressed interest in Cameron both astonished and delighted Amanda.

"Speaking of Cameron, Alicia, he told me he would be at The Museum of Fine Arts today looking at a visiting exhibit of 18th century portraiture. Why don't we go and run into him there?"

"Why not?" Alicia said at once, for no one could study the entire day and night.

Though unexcited by 18th century pictures, Thalia agreed to accompany them, in order to be able to grill Amanda more intensely about Castor. But Amanda would reveal no more, imagining her ex lover's indignation at being so discussed before being allowed to make his own first impression.

The girls managed to reach the museum an hour before closing and were in time to meet Cameron in the graceful second floor gallery, where they discovered him standing in awe before the most famous Reynolds portrait of Emma Hamilton, on loan from the Huntington.

"She's the most beautiful thing I've ever seen," Amanda commented to Thalia, who was just as forcibly struck by the young girl in the simple white dress.

"She started out as a prostitute," Thalia replied knowledgeably. "At maybe age 13." Thalia was English by birth and had such facts at her disposal.

"But obviously, a pampered one," Alicia observed, remarking on Emma's freshness and bloom.

Amanda invited the young man to join them for tea after their tour of the museum and he accepted with pleasure. They found a tearoom within a few blocks of the museum. Dusk had fallen and it had grown a little colder but less windy. Snow was falling lightly and the four new friends were grateful for small sandwiches, cake and strong, hot tea.

Alicia herself brought up the recent trip to Random Point the other three had made and asked several questions about the filming they had done there.

"I'm just curious. How can an apparently nice boy like you bring yourself to strike a woman?" Alicia asked Cameron, not aggressively but genuinely baffled.

Cameron glanced at Amanda before answering.

"Alicia isn't in the scene," Amanda explained, "but she's been listening to me go on about it."

"Oh," Cameron nodded, gulped his tea and tried to think of an intelligent answer that would sound both provocative and non-threatening. He generally thought long and hard before speaking, which often led people to believe he was a great deal deeper than he actually was. His circumspection, was, in fact, due to a fear of blurting out the wrong reply. "Well, that's a very interesting question, Alicia."

"Just say the first thing that pops into your head, Dude," Thalia interjected.

"Let me put it this way, Alicia," said Cameron, "There are brats, like this one here," he patted Thalia's velvety cheek, "and then there are ladies, like Amanda and you. Brats arouse one type of sensation in me and ladies, another. I'd envision a scene with a lady as sensual and romantic."

"Boring," Thalia said under her breath.

"She's going to be thrashed later," Amanda reassured Cameron, explaining about Thalia's appointment with Castor.

"Anyway, Alicia," Cameron said, filling Alicia's china cup from the tea pot, "don't judge from what you've heard us discussing about the video. Videos are hyper-real. They can't take their time being seductive, they have to be dynamic and really pack a wallop to engage the viewer. Real life spanking between consenting partners is often a lot more like foreplay and a lot less like discipline."

"Well said," Amanda grinned.

They parted outside, Thalia and Cameron proceeding back to the Boston University campus while Amanda and Alicia walked quickly towards the nearest train station to return to Cambridge. As they walked up to their door in the dorm they saw Ronnie Van Horn hurriedly ripping down the note he had just left on it.

"Ronnie, how nice to see you!" Amanda said at once, embracing him and wishing him a Happy New Year. Alicia smiled coolly and briefly at the handsome and unhappy looking young man before slipping inside the room. "I am so truly glad to see you," Amanda reiterated, locking her arms around his waist and pressing her head to his chest. The next instant his arms were locked around her and he was kissing her masterfully. She looked into his dark eyes and saw how much he'd missed her and how much he had tried to resist her. "I've been missing you so," she said, determined to make it easy for him.

Ronnie had gone to Random Point to shoot her video footage the previous week, but he had been noticeably cold during the frantic eighteen hours of filming they had done at Bartlett's department store. Together they had obtained hours of usable footage, but his attitude towards her and the rest of the cast had been fairly grim throughout. He had also nearly mutinied during one of the scenes she had insisted on performing in, a fantasy sequence where Amanda, playing a haughty customer in the designer shoe salon, fantasizes that her salesman, played by Tommy, is her pimp and that he spanks her for not bringing him enough money.

The scene was set in one of the plush dressing rooms in designer dresses and it was a challenging one, given the triple mirrors on one end of the room. But that was not what irritated Ronnie. It was the humiliating cliché and its implication that this was really what Amanda felt about the black men with whom she consorted. And, naturally, he hated seeing Amanda get spanked by another man, even if it was over her clothes. A long and heated argument ensued between Amanda, Ronnie and Tommy, with Amanda and Tommy defending the scene as cute and harmless and Ronnie raking them both over the coals for perpetrating a degrading and harmful stereotype. But Amanda had much of her father's stubbornness and a great deal of his vision as to spanking entertainment and she argued forcefully from the position that all spanking fantasies are politically incorrect stereotypes, with the goal not being the shoring up of a social conscience but giving people stiffies and wet pussies. Tommy also pointed out that he had spent a lot of time putting together his pimp suit and that he looked exceptionally attractive in it and really wanted to have this scene on film for his bachelor portfolio.

Tommy was all optimism and playfulness; regarding Amanda's project as an enormous joke on the straight world and basking in the future glory it would bring him as an all around joker. Ronnie was a perpetual pessimist, who still could not quite believe he had gotten into Harvard and who rationed his fun in teaspoons, lest he tempt fate to throw him back into the real world too soon.

In the end, Amanda had gotten her way. Even Ronnie had to respect the fact that the scene had been well written, fully memorized by the principals, blocked out ahead of time and magnificently wardrobed, therefore he finally yielded and shot it. The follow up scene took place in the shoe salon, with Amelia coming out of her fantasy, returning to the character of an obnoxious customer and being so rude to her well bred and polite, but not subservient salesman that he spanks her in reality.

Ronnie was wildly jealous of the ease with which Tommy took hold of Amanda and turned her over his immaculately trousered knee, in not one but both of the scenes. It was well that Amanda had insisted that her two scenes be shot first, so as to get them out of the way and allow her to concentrate on directing for the rest of the shoot. Ronnie had a chance to get over what he had seen, just a little. After that, Tommy only had one other spanking scene and in that one he spanked Thalia. Then Tommy became a helpful second cameraman and pointedly refrained from touching or flirting with Amanda in front of Ronnie for the rest of the trip.

And then there had been the additional, very welcome distraction of Barbara Johnson, aka Bootylicious, the exquisitely shapely, baby faced, twenty one year old, black agency model from Boston Hugo had recommended to round out Amanda's youthful cast. Barbara had initially entered Hugo's sphere as an enthralled reader of his magazine, then contacted him for modeling work. He'd had her out to Random Point several times to shoot photo sets and had always sent her back to Boston well spanked and in a state of heat. In the three years that Hugo had known her, she had graduated from fetish model to full blown hardcore actress, though she had nearly reached a saturation point in her triple x career and was about to abandon it entirely for nursing school.

Barbara had been one of the principal delights of the grueling, two day shoot, her joyful, ebullience keeping everyone around her energized, her glamorous good looks filling up the cameras with gold and her ingenuous, vivacious submissiveness giving them all manner

Eve Howard

of rarified thrills. She was a natural performer, an enthusiastic player and her genuine love of spanking made her a perfect pleasure to film. Besides this, she was the only one of them actually experienced in capturing this type of action on camera and managed to slice full hours off their production with a series of simple, though invaluable suggestions.

For example, she had troubled to read through the long and complex script several times on the train out to Random Point and her first suggestion was to shoot the hard spanking action before each complex dialog set up, arguing mildly but effectively that while this would upset the continuity for the performers, it would insure getting the vital action in the can while everyone was fresh and serve the dual purpose of relaxing the performers before they had to concentrate on their demanding lines. Amanda elected to follow Barbara's counsel and was extremely glad that she did.

In another instance, in the midst of one of the bare bottom spanking sequences, Amanda called cut to reposition Barbara and Cameron. They weren't getting the full on bottom shot that Amanda knew was needed and she thought it would be necessary to reangle the furniture and perhaps move a light. Barbara asked for a pause, exchanged a word or two with Cameron and then told Amanda and Tommy and Ronnie, both on cameras, "It's all right. We'll change the angle ourselves as soon as we get back in."

"Really?" Amanda had asked, skeptically.

"Don't worry," Barbara had replied with a grin, "I've been doing this for years. Nothing could be easier."

So Amanda called action and the spanking resumed. Within five seconds, Cameron had shifted Barbara on his lap, turned his body the correct number of degrees to point her lusciously jutting bare cocoa bottom directly at Tommy's camera while her sweet, heart shaped face came right into line with Ronnie's close up shot. The little porn expert had known exactly what she was doing and had saved them valuable minutes.

Naturally the presence of this female paragon had attracted the interest of all the men present, though Ronnie had seemed the least affected by her charms. Tommy fell madly in love with Barbara and knelt to her to kiss her hand after shooting her first scene. But to the worldly 21 year old, who had been all over the country shooting videos for three years, the college boys seemed very young. She was also rather tired of sex after doing so much of it lately, and knowing just how much sex eighteen and nineteen year old boys need, Barbara was initially disposed to hold herself somewhat aloof so as not to encourage any one of them to pursue her. She had no boyfriend at the moment, it was true, and did long for a lovable companion, but perhaps to merely kiss and hug for a couple of months, just until she got the three years of porn out of her system.

However, the less attention he paid to her, the more interesting Barbara began to find Ronnie. The fact that Ronnie had performed in none of the scenes with her, but only filmed them, mingled with his aura of authority as co-director and his own disinterested remoteness towards her, made the idea of going submissive to him very intriguing. He was also a tall, buff, handsome young man, with a most attractive and sensitive face and his intelligence was obvious. The offspring of teachers, and carefully educated from grade school up, he was well bred, polite and politically correct. She saw how it had pained him to film the pimp and 'ho scene and she loved him for that, though she thought the scene had been cute too.

As soon as they returned to Boston, Barbara called Ronnie and asked him to a New Year's Eve party as her date. Ronnie had never been to a rave before and had never done ecstasy, but he wanted to forget himself that night. All broken hearted leading men are entitled to one bender and Ronnie gave himself up to it without self-recrimination. As for Barbara, he hardly took her seriously. The idea of dating a porn starlet who hadn't completed even one term of college never entered his mind. This was to be a one-night stand and nothing more.

Then Barbara took him home to the apartment she shared with two other models. Both were out of town for the weekend and they had the flat to themselves. Barbara clearly stated that she was only available for spanking that night and nothing more, insisting he agree to these limits. She was wearing a smoky blue silk satin sheath dress and perhaps the highest heels he had ever seen a girl go out in. But she still only came up to his shoulder. Her proportions, however, were breathtaking. Ronnie was delighted by the invitation to spank Barbara and agreed to not molest her in any other way. Of course, they both knew that if he stepped over her threshold that night that he would not be leaving until morning and that he would surely possess her before doing so. He was 19, she was lovely and they had the apartment entirely to themselves.

While he had dreamt about spanking girls for years, he had really done very little spanking until he had met Amanda. In fact, the closest he had ever gotten to really spanking someone, prior to meeting Amanda, had been getting away with spanking his two slightly younger female cousins, who would come to visit his family each Christmas. From ages eight through eleven, he had contrived to spank them in the form of a penalty for losing games to him. He had tried, several times, to spank his high school girl friend, but she would have none of it. Which was a shame because she had a remarkably beautiful bottom. Now, for the first time, he had a compliant black girl ready to go over his knee, because she liked spanking and liked him.

They had spent the whole of New Year's Eve together and hadn't slept at all. Hours of spanking gave way to hours of the most exotic sex he had ever had in his life. Barbara made love suavely, receiving every attention he bestowed with unrestrained bliss and returning every favor she received with interest. Possessed of a full complement of highly developed amatory skills, no physical challenge was too great and she made everything she did appear easy. There was no need to ask for oral sex, she fastened her lips to his throbbing organ as a matter of course. And when he tentatively suggested that someday she might yield her bottom to him as well, she had the ideal lubricant at her fingertips before he'd even finished framing his delicate desire. She was, quite simply, the most complete seductress: passionate, voluptuous and sweetly wild. Barbara was the ultimate girl and Ronnie was predictably bowled over.

New Year's Eve blunted the jealousy Ronnie had felt about Amanda's apparently universal availability, restoring his ego and distracting his libido. But New Year's Day, with its inevitable emotional and physical hang over, brought him crashing back down to earth hard.

Barbara too awoke to a sobering dawn, when she could not but coolly reflect upon how inappropriate it would be for a mature, 21 year old working woman to spend time on a regular basis with a college boy. Ronnie had no money and so could never do anything for her. He would inevitably come to resent her modeling work and might also dislike her being around his university friends. The fact that she'd done hardcore would make her a dirty joke around the dorm where he lived and she would probably be subjected to insults if she were ever to visit him there. And really, nineteen was just too young. It would never, ever work. Sigh.

Ronnie was perceptive enough to read the signs of rejection at the simple fact of her not kissing him good morning or even offering him coffee before seeing him off.

Ronnie left and tried to forget about Barbara Johnson. "Last night was a gift," he told himself on the train back to Cambridge. "You don't get a gift every day."

But he didn't reckon with how much he had gotten under Barbara's skin, even in just one night. There were things about him she'd never found in other men, a certain sweetness in his nature, an undemanding tenderness that made her feel that she really didn't need to go into contortions to engage his interest. And the way he had topped her had pleased her tremendously. She had not had such a good and thorough spanking since her last visit to Hugo Sands, the first man who had ever spanked her well and the first man in the scene she had ever had a crush on. Ronnie was not only a handsome, virile, intelligent and gentlemanly black man, but he was a great spanker too. And Barbara wanted a spanking man in her life. She wanted a spanking man as her lover. And she wanted him to be of her own culture. By the evening of New Year's Day, it no longer seemed to matter to Barbara that she was not exactly Ronnie's female counterpart. His being younger and in school and as a consequence, broke, all seemed to fade into insignificance beside the warm, pulsating reality of his youthful ardor, strength and endless masculine appeal. She called him and invited him to dinner at her apartment that night, apologized for her coolness that morning, told him she had thought everything over and that there might be a way to see each other, frequently, without getting on each other's nerves or cramping each other's style. They would keep it to a few times a week and not crowd each other. But when they did meet, it would be as lovers. Ronnie could not but agree, mystified at what had changed her mind, but not arguing.

So he had come to see Amanda to tell her what had happened. But he found he couldn't speak of it at once. The way she threw her arms around him warmed him to the soul. She must like him a great deal, he suddenly though, she must really care. They went downstairs and found one of the parlors empty. Ronnie lit the log in the hearth and they sat on the rug in front of it to talk. Presently Ronnie brought out a halting and awkward apology for calling her a slut. Then he told her about Barbara and how his experiences over New Year's had made him realize that it was possible to be attracted to two people at the same time without loving either the less. It gave Amanda a little pang to realize that Ronnie was already in love with Barbara but she graciously murmured, "Barbara is divine. I'm awfully happy for you, Ronnie."

"You sound like a selfless second lead heroine in a pre-code melodrama. Margaret Lindsay perhaps," he observed.

"Oh, Ronnie," Amanda murmured affectionately, "I had a life in high school, so I don't know who that is, but I adore you," she said, planting the smallest kiss on his cheek then springing away. Their eyes met and suddenly Ronnie was on fire for Amanda.

"Ronnie, since you aren't mad at me any more, may I ask you to do something for me?" she asked, with a rush of enthusiasm.

"Yes, Amanda, anything but shoot another video. At least, not yet," Ronnie replied with feeling. The pressures of the two-day shoot in Random Point had taken their toll even on his young and resilient nerves.

"Oh, nothing like that. Well, it's just this. Report cards are coming out in a few days and I'd... like to show you mine," she said, significantly. It took a moment or two for her meaning to penetrate.

He warned her gravely, "You know I expect a lot from you, Amanda."

"I think it will be ... bad!" she cried, only half kidding.

"I wouldn't be surprised with all the crazy running around you've been doing," he observed, fixing her with his sternest gaze. Her cheeks suffused with pink, Amanda dropped her eyes.

Chapter Eleven

Frost on the Windowpane

Grades came out that Friday. And although Amanda had lightly attempted to eroticize the coming spectre by giving Ronnie to understand that he might play the role of disciplinarian should her marks fall below expectations, she was sick with dread at thought of actually receiving them.

Friday was also the day upon which she and Alicia relocated across the hall into their second semester room, which was really a suite, with a small sitting room flanked on either side with a tiny sliver of bedroom, each cubicle just large enough for the narrow wrought iron dorm bedstead, well rubbed wooden desk, chest of drawers and Windsor chair. The floors were of hard wood and the mullioned windows opened out and overlooked the quad. Alicia, who was raised in a tenement in the Bronx, walked around and around the parlor, absorbing every gracious element of the room's design, marveling at the crown molding, the mantled fireplace, and the window seats. Like every other Ivy League scholarship student who had grown up in a slum, the sheltered world of grace and luxury in which Alicia now dwelt seemed a very fairytale kingdom. Fear and want, peeling paint, mice and bugs, buildings on fire, gunshots in the night, were all far outside the university walls. Within was peace, warmth, pleasant good fellowship and an infinity of knowledge.

Amanda walked into the parlor holding her small, manila colored grades envelope, crest fallen, with the flush of embarrassment that had flooded her face at the mailbox in the lobby not yet faded from her cheeks.

"What's wrong?" Alicia cried. "Are those your grades? Are they up?"

"They just put them in the mailboxes."

Alicia darted out the door with excitement. Five minutes later the tall, slender girl strolled back into the room, smiling broadly. Amanda was sitting on a small slipper chair that Hugo had given her, gazing dumbly out the window.

"It's much worse than I expected," Amanda confessed, handing Alicia her report card.

Alicia studied the figures briefly, then sighed and handed her own grades to Amanda. In a flash of triumphant pride, Alicia cried, "In your face, party girl! Now you'll have to admit, I was right and you were wrong. I told you those stupid boys you waste all your time on are useless. Didn't I?"

"I can't live like you, I tried," Amanda protested, half smiling in spite of her devastated soul. She had never seen Alicia so animated with the pure joy of being Alicia.

"I told you, didn't I? I begged you to stay home and study. But no, you had to go fuck this black boy, or cocktease this Latin stud, or run out in the middle of the night to play B&D with some MIT dweeb or go shoot a spanking video or model in a fashion show or smoke dope! Didn't you? Didn't you?"

"Look," warned Amanda, "I know you're trying distract me from my pain and grief with idle banter, but keep it up and you'll find out all about B&D from me!"

"Oh really? You think you can handle me?" Alicia threw back her shoulders and planted her legs on either side of Amanda. Amanda slipped easily under her arm, spun Alicia around a quarter turn and stood eye to eye with her.

"Oh, in the mood I'm in, I could pound you to a jelly," Amanda promised, tweaking Alicia's velvety brown earlobe. Alicia wore her black hair very short, like a boy, to be taken more seriously and save time, but she had the profile of a goddess and her femininity needed no ornamentation. Amanda had always found her irresistibly attractive, but had never dreamed of making a pass at her. But now that her sanctimonious roommate had taken the liberty of scolding her, Amanda was of a mind to break down other barriers.

"Alicia, we're going out drinking tonight. And after we get back, I'm going to make you wish you'd never lectured me."

"Oh, and you think I'll just submit?"

"If you won't, I'll tie you up," threatened Amanda, with the smallest notion that if Alicia was into anything, it was or might be bondage.

"You know how to tie people up?" Alicia asked with extreme interest.

"I'm from San Francisco," Amanda replied, "so of course I do. You just wait. I'll teach you not to be so fresh!" Amanda promised, before going into her tiny, narrow bedroom to put away her clothes and set up her computer.

Hugo was alone in his office working on a column for his magazine, when Amanda called to deliver the news of her disappointing grades.

"Tell me," he responded with some trepidation, which he concealed. He was well aware of how distracted Amanda had been her first term and was honest enough to acknowledge that he himself had added to the temptations surrounding her.

She replied with deep self-recrimination, "I got a C+ in Economics."

"Oh? Well, that's a very challenging subject. If you plan to continue with it second semester, I recommend you get yourself a tutor. It's amazing how much you can get out of a few weeks with a tutor. What were you other grades?"

"B- in English, B in History and B+ in Spanish. Swimming was pass/fail. I passed."

"That's not so bad," said Hugo affably, extremely relieved that she hadn't failed anything. "Every scholar takes a dive in freshman year. I did myself," he lied with enthusiasm. "And you know, teachers are notoriously rough on freshman. You'll make it up this semester. Don't you think, dear?"

"You're very kind," she replied, "but I can't help but feel that after sticking you with these immense bills, I've let you down. I feel so guilty about that."

"Honey, don't give that a thought. That should be the least of your worries."

"You're so nice," she said, his warmth cheering her. "But, do you think I've let myself get too distracted, between all the boyfriends and the spanking stuff?"

"Amanda, you live life to the full. That's what you're supposed to do when you're young. You'll improve your grades as much as you need to and graduate from Harvard. And with a fluency in Spanish, you'll never want for employment. Do you really think that getting one C in your entire academic career is going to impact your future life?"

"What about the spanking stuff, the video and how much time it took?"

"Well, on the plus side, you now have a video product to market and a scene persona to exploit if you should ever wish to. I don't call that a waste of time."

"You've made me feel so much better," she told him, with pleasure.

"You're a good girl," he assured her. "Now don't worry. Take the night off and take a fresh look at everything tomorrow. And if you need extra allowance for the tutor, just let me know and I'll handle it."

"Thank you, Hugo. Oh, there's one more thing. May I use the apartment tonight? Alicia and I want to celebrate her grades and lament mine and we're too young to get served alcohol in town."

"Go right ahead, honey. She did well, did she?"

"She got all A's."

"She sounds like an inspiration," Hugo said, smiling.

"She is. She's inspiring me to kick her slim black butt for being such an arrogant little prig. I just found out what I've suspected for a while, that bondage is her secret fantasy."

Hugo looked at the phone receiver in surprise, then murmured, "Good for you, Amanda."

Amanda hadn't expected Hugo to scold her, he was too taken with her to be objective and she knew it. Ronnie wasn't nearly as sympathetic when she found him alone in his new room in Kirkland, unpacking his gear. He began reproaching her at once, faulting her for allowing herself to become distracted, which had resulted in Amanda obtaining only passable grades.

Amanda hung her fair head, as everything he accused her of was perfectly true. Ronnie droned on. Didn't she realize that she would have to work ten times as hard to get the sort of grades at Harvard as she had made at a California public high school? Ronnie returned to this point again and again during his general critique of her unimpressive first semester performance.

She had graduated high school with a 93% grade point average, roughly an A. Her SAT scores had been respectable, but not perfect. She had attracted attention at the admissions office with her personal essay, which was clever and graceful, her faculty recommendations, which had been glowing, and especially her accompanying photo. The fact that her father was a Harvard man had also helped. Perhaps most importantly, she was the kind of young woman admissions needed to pose for the recruitment catalog. Amanda had received early acceptance.

As Ronnie lectured her she wondered to herself whether she was really Harvard material and whether she could ever live up to its standards. She felt utterly downcast and the weather outside reflected her bleak mood. It was a bitterly cold day. A relentless wind battered the windowpanes and the sky was grayish white. Even running over to the dining hall and back for breakfast that morning had been painfully uncomfortable. She had never had to muffle her entire face in a scarf against the frigid sting of a biting five degrees and it took the heart out of her.

"These grades are terrible," he concluded with an awful finality. Then added, "So what do you think you deserve?"

Amanda had almost forgotten that this was going to be a game. But now she felt far too embarrassed, afraid and distressed to fall in with the plan she herself had suggested. She looked up at him so sadly that he sank down on the bed beside her and took her hands in his.

"Amanda?"

Hot tears began to spill from her eyes. "I feel so worthless," she mumbled against his shirt front as his strong arms closed around her.

"Amanda, you didn't take anything I just said seriously, did you?" he asked, stroking her silky hair. "I was just working up to an excuse to spank you. I mean, you don't get a real reason to spank a girl every day."

"I know. It was my idea to show you my grades," she murmured, sniffling into a pristine, embroidered handkerchief she pulled from her tweed skirt pocket. "But that was before I knew I was going to do quite so badly. Now I'm plunged into the depths of despair."

"Amanda, don't feel that way. You didn't distinguish yourself, that's true. But you didn't fail anything either. You'll improve this term and then you'll be fine."

"Do you really think so, Ronnie?"

"I'm positive."

"It's so cold outside," she shivered, pressing her head against his chest again. "I've never felt such cold."

"Me either," he replied, hugging her closer.

She looked up at him. "You're so handsome," she said, because she didn't think he knew this. He looked at her quizzically.

"Are your spirits quite recovered?" he asked.

"Getting better," she replied, putting her mouth up to be kissed. He kissed her in the way he knew she loved.

"Lock the door, Ronnie," she cried, springing from his arms and deliberately unbuttoning her sweater. Their clothes began flying off in all directions and in moments they were clasped in each other's arms on the narrow bed, kissing, squeezing, touching and finally merging with the boundless energy and effortless lubricity of teenagers in love. Amanda was quite unlike Barbara in her responses. She had no arts of love to draw on. She did not attempt to tease or please him. She simply allowed him to possess her. She was the object and the reward. Both of them knew this and neither of them questioned it.

Afternoon passed into evening quickly. Amanda put away all of her belongings, arranged her desk and made up her bed in her new, tiny sliver of a bedroom. As evening came on, a storm front blew in, the temperature rose and a wet, windy snow began to whirl around outside her windows. She checked in on Alicia, who had also squared away her small room and was deep in a book about Madame de Stael. They agreed that they were both very hungry, zipped themselves into long parkas with faux fur collars, over wool leggings, wool sweaters and high collared walking boots, and went out into the dreadful night. Wind gusts blew their hoods back and the girls were forced to secure them tightly with their knotted scarves. They half walked, half ran to the train station to catch a local to Back Bay. There was a welcoming bistro on the corner of the street where Hugo's building was situated. Marty had met her there for dinner there once and now Amanda led Alicia confidently inside. The smart little restaurant was perhaps a quarter full and they were seated at a window table at once. The waiter, who remembered Amanda from her first visit, promptly suggested two glasses of the house merlot. Amanda and Alicia looked at each other then said, "Sure!" He winked at them and hurried off to pour their drinks. As always, they planned to split the bill and chose two inexpensive, vegetarian pasta dishes with the lightest sauces. After their satisfying meal they felt deeply warm and able to face the cold again. They ran up the street to the building where Hugo kept an apartment and slipped into the lobby. Neither of them had ever been exposed to anything like this kind of cold and agreed that it had been depressing their spirits.

Once inside Hugo's apartment they stripped off their outer gear and Amanda set about getting a log lit in the sitting room fireplace. Alicia wandered around and looked at Hugo's beautiful things. She had never been in an apartment with tasteful and coordinated décor before. The richly painted jewel toned walls delighted her senses, while the comfortable disposal of rich, heavy, polished, carved and painted furniture seemed to promise extraordinarily luxurious modes of repose.

"So, he just lets you use this place whenever you like?" Alicia asked a moment later in the kitchen as she watched Amanda expertly uncork a bottle of Mendocino merlot.

"If he's not in the city."

"It's kind of incredible, isn't it, you just walk into someone's life who's never even heard of you before and he agrees to pay for your college and hands you everything else you ever wanted on a plate?" Alicia wondered. Over their wine with dinner the girls had opened up to each other about their backgrounds in interesting detail. Amanda had told Alicia the entire story of discovering that Hugo was her real father and the six-year build up to revealing her identity to him.

"Well, he was and still is very fond of my mother," Amanda explained modestly. "And all things being equal, had she told him she was carrying me and wanted to have me, he would have very likely persuaded her to stay in Random Point and marry him."

Alicia had revealed to Amanda that she had been the last child of much older parents, with all of her siblings almost fully grown when she was born. Her father was the manager of a discount shoe store in lower Manhattan and her mother had worked for the last twenty years as a counter clerk in the deli department of Macy's on Herald Square. Alicia was the first in her family to go to any college at all, no less Harvard and had led a fairly uneventful life of studying for tests and getting excellent grades from a very early age. In ninth grade she began dating the smartest boy in her class and they continued seeing each other exclusively through all four years of high school. He had gotten into Cornell. In tenth grade they had begun having safe sex and their romance continued through graduation. While everyone around them was smoking weed, doing ecstasy and going to all night raves, Alicia and her boyfriend were going to museums and art movie houses, biking and rowing in Central Park and constantly studying together. By senior year the passion they had known had pretty much burnt itself out and they'd settled into a pleasant but unexciting routine of academic companionship that neither found too heart breaking to sacrifice in order to attend the university of their choice.

"That's why I could never get interested in Ronnie Van Horn," Alicia explained, regarding her new glass of wine before taking a tentative sip, "he's much too much like my old high school boyfriend, Lawrence."

"Was your high school boyfriend black then?" Amanda asked.

"Oh yes. There were no white kids at my high school," Alicia explained.

"Have you ever been with a white boy?"

"No, I've never been with anyone besides Lawrence."

Amanda put on one of Hugo's old Cramps albums. He had wonderful music.

"I love this song," Amanda said, "it's a cover of the theme song from Faster Pussycat, Kill! Kill!"

As a lushly dangerous background of surf guitars filled the air, Lux Interior crooned, "It's that she doesn't see, what's wrong from right, she's running fast and free, child of the night."

"That's your problem, too much running fast and free and not enough studying," Alicia reverted to her favorite theme.

"Didn't I warn you what would happen if you continued to berate me for my miserable academic showing?" Amanda grinned.

"Look, I'll admit I'm B&D curious," Alicia protested, "but ...I'm not into girls."

"I'm not into girls either. I mean, do I look-slash-act like I'm into girls?"

"No, but..."

"Look, I don't want to eat your pussy and nor do I want you to eat mine."

"Okay," Alicia smiled, "so far we agree."

"You know what they say about B&D, it's not Sex, it's Sexy."

"Who says that?"

"Professional mistresses, when they're talking to possible undercover cops."

Alicia laughed. "How did you get so sophisticated?"

"I've been reading up on the subject of course and my boyfriend from high school and I used to play all the time."

They sipped their wine and looked at each other.

"You need to get high," Amanda decided, producing a joint and lighting it.

"Amanda, I told you, I don't want to start with that," Alicia protested firmly. "Look where all the partying got you," she added with a gentle but superior air.

"Don't you want to feel completely uninhibited?" Amanda tempted her roommate. When Alicia paused before replying Amanda knew she had struck just the right note.

"I am inhibited," Alicia admitted, taking the smallest drag on the joint.

"Hold it in," Amanda said. Alicia closed her eyes and a moment later exhaled a small wisp of smoke. "Take a longer pull this time," Amanda said, handing Alicia the cigarette a second time. Alicia blinked back at her slowly, with cat's eyes. "It's already doing something isn't it? How it makes your eyes shine." Alicia's second drag was large enough to make her cough uncontrollably. Her eyes instantly began to water as she caught her breath. She looked at Amanda and sighed.

"Now you've corrupted me. Are you satisfied?"

"I think we've made a good start," Amanda replied. "Are you feeling anything?"

Alicia stretched and looked around the handsome room then back at her extremely attractive friend.

"Yes, I feel happy and stupid all at once. And I think you're the prettiest thing I've ever seen."

"The feeling is completely mutual," Amanda confessed. "I don't know how they matched us up so well. At first I thought they only put us together because we're the same height and they figured we could share each other's clothes."

"And what we wound up doing was sharing each other's men," said Alicia.

"Is that what we're doing?"

"Well," Alicia smiled a rather secret smile, "I'll admit I met Cameron for coffee late the other night. And I let him ... touch me intimately."

Alicia got up and began to walk around the room, picking up objects and examining them. "Your father has such taste!" Alicia said appreciatively, of the glazed enamel box in her hands. "Gee, I'm beginning to see why people like this stuff," Alicia went on, sweeping the richly decorated room with her gaze. "Everything seems to be coming into sharper focus all of a sudden, and the colors are intense!"

"We should engage in a sensual activity," Amanda decided. "Come with me!"

Amanda conducted Alicia into the large bathroom connecting to the master bedroom. She pointed to the large oval bathtub, lined in gleaming white porcelain and set in milky green tile. "Bubble bath?"

Alicia looked around the luxurious bathroom with its walnut armoire and stacks of pale green Turkish towels. Amanda took two white terry robes out of the armoire and started the water running in the tub.

"Why not?" Alicia agreed, stripping off her clothes, folding them up neatly and slipping one of the robes over her pearly smooth cocoa colored skin. Amanda found a flagon of almond scented bubble bath and began adding large quantities of it to the hot water cascading into the tub.

While they waited for the tub to fill to the brim with creamy bubbles, they took a few more hits. Amanda took off her clothes and laughed at her own self-consciousness as she slipped into the tub and under the bubbles.

"It's perfect," she told Alicia, who dropped her robe and stepped into the opposite side and sunk under the bubbles as well.

"You are incredibly beautiful," Amanda said matter of factly. "I know I've told you that before but this is the first time I've seen you naked."

"Back at you, Amanda," Alicia grinned. "You are the babe of babes."

"Isn't this better than running around outside in the cold?" Amanda asked, lying back in the tub.

"I hate the cold," Alicia agreed. "It's so bleak and dreary. But this is wonderful."

They went on in this pleasant manner for a few minutes, concurring that the time, place and company they found themselves in could not be more agreeable. Then Amanda said decisively, "Well, I think we should fool around."

"I have no objection," said Alicia.

"In that case, I'll be the boy."

141

"Why do you get to be the boy? And for that matter, why do either of us have to be the boy? Can't we just be two women together?"

"I'm sorry, but I'm too het for that. Whenever I play games with another girl, I'm always the boy."

"You've played with a girl before?"

"My best friend in junior high school."

"Well, you certainly sound like you know more about things sexual than I do," Alicia sighed.

"Oh, I'm sure I do. I've been with ever so many dominant men this year!"

They got out of the tub, wrapped themselves in the thick terry robes and went into the bedroom. Amanda noticed that in the center of the ornately carved wooden headboard of the four-poster bed there was a bull's head in relief with a large brass ring through its nose. This gave her an idea and she reached for Alicia's waist summarily untying the sash of her roommate's robe and pulling it out of the loops.

"What?" Alicia asked, "So soon?"

"I need this," said Amanda, giving Alicia a gentle push down on the bed and pulling the robe entirely off her. A few drops of water still clung to Alicia's silky brown skin. Amanda pushed her down on her back on the thick green velvet counterpane. "Put your hands above your head," Amanda said, taking Alicia's slim wrists before Alicia could respond. Amanda looked down at Alicia's upthrust, full and well-rounded breasts, with their delicately shaped nipples erect and observed again that they were exactly the same breast size.

Amanda slipped the sash through the ring in the bull's nose, evened it and fastened it with a half hitch, then brought the matching lengths of the terry belt down to tie Alicia's wrists together in a lark's head knot. Once Alicia was fastened on her back, Amanda, still in her own robe, tightly knotted at her tiny waist, straddled Alicia and then stretched out her body over the length of her friend, took Alicia's face in her hands and kissed her on the mouth. "Just remember," Amanda said, "you are helpless and in my power." Alicia didn't smile, but gazed with intensity back into Amanda's slate blue eyes. A tiny shudder seemed to pass through the dark, slender girl as Amanda tugged on the sash rope to make sure it was secure.

Amanda worked her way down Alicia's body, gently squeezing her breasts, caressing her flat abdomen and finally entwining her fingertips in Alicia's silky pubic curls.

"I know I said I wasn't going down on you, but I think I really must," said Amanda.

"But you hate going down on people," Alicia pointed out, watching Amanda trace a straight line from her navel to the crest of her pubic mound with the pink tip of her tongue.

"I hate going down on boys," Amanda corrected. "But you're a sweet young girl."

Now Amanda delicately spread Alicia's labia, exposed the stiff pink button at its head and encircled it with her tongue. Slipping one middle finger up into Alicia's moist, clinging vagina and pressing gently down with the heel of her other hand on Alicia's lower abdomen, Amanda now began to mercilessly tongue lash her friend's rapidly swelling clitoris. Alicia's hips twitched and she squirmed helplessly, arching up towards Amanda's mouth in spite of herself. "Let yourself go," Amanda raised her head to exhort her friend. "No one will ever know."

"Fuck me harder," Alicia pleaded softly. Amanda inserted two more fingers into Alicia's slick pussy and plied them firmly in and out while sucking on Alicia's swollen clit and still pressing down on her g-spot with the palm of her hand. In moments it was all up for Alicia and Amanda heard the distinctive pant of a girlish climax issue from the lips of her overcome friend.

The girls lay against each other for a few moments before the one untied the other.

"Oh Amanda, that was divine," admitted Alicia, once she had been released.

"At least I did something right today," Amanda grinned, still chagrined over her lack luster grades but proud of her successful seduction of the elegant Alicia Bishop.

Chapter Twelve

Amanda's Diary January

January 11th

Sunday night of a hell of a weekend.

Yesterday was very good all day. Taught a morning yoga class and spent all afternoon in the library researching my history paper. At dinner Alicia told me about a house party in Cambridge that night and made me promise to meet her there. I passed by the TV room, arrested by the haunting theme music of a lush, Technicolor film from 1960, The Four Horsemen of the Apocalypse. I watched the whole thing and found it to be the most romantic and glamorous movie I have ever seen, more so than Funny Face.

With the movie still in my head and tears in my eyes from the conclusion, I went to shower and dress for the party. I decided on my black thigh high boots, the super short beige wool dress with the long sleeves and an open collar that I got at V.S., black tights and a wide black belt. Over the dress I threw the new black wool overcoat - Calvin Klein and gorgeously smart - that Mr. Bartlett sent me for no reason.

When I got outside and started walking off campus to the address a few blocks away I was sorry I hadn't worn my down parka instead as it was brutally cold, in the single digits and a bitter wind was whipping through the empty cobbled streets.

In ten minutes I arrived at my destination, a two story brick residence on Dunster and Winthrop, and found it crowded with people and extremely warm. All my muscles untensed and I felt good again. Metallica was pulsating through the entryway and living room, where boys were dispensing beer from a couple of kegs. I made my way from room to room, meeting a few kids I knew from classes and my dorm and refusing every offer of beer. Someone passed me a joint and I took a long hit, then drifted more slowly towards the back of the house where there was dancing in a large rec room. The room was packed with slim, nimble bodies, the kind you love to watch. A dj kept switching up the music from industrial house to vintage pogo punk to old school hip hop to classic disco. I saw Cameron and we danced to the house music set. Then when the punk came on, I danced with a geek, who offered to put my coat in the closet. It was nice and warm in the dancing room. Then an old New Wave song by the Motels came on. It was called Celia and I'd first heard it when I found some 80's cassettes at Hugo's apartment and had borrowed them. I was dancing to Celia myself when I saw that Ronnie was leaning against a table across the room watching me. An unmistakable spasm of excitement rippled through my belly and the song Celia seemed to fade and merge into the theme from Four Horsemen. For wasn't Ronnie my Glenn Ford, my Clark Gable and my Gary Cooper? I won't say my Johnny Depp, because as handsome as Mr. Depp is, he never appears in the slightest bit dominant. No, one needs an old, old movie star to find sexual dominance, no one more recent than say 1963.

Ronnie stood for a moment, looking back at me in the most penetrating way. Then he seemed to take a deep breath and came over to me. Without a word, he took me in his arms and we began to slow dance together. The song changed to Black Hole Sun and everyone else seemed to vanish from the room. I couldn't look away from his liquid, brown eyes, the most astonishingly beautiful eyes in Boston, and I have always said so. (Except for when I was saying the same thing about Castor.) After that song ended, a Siouxsie and the Banshees songs I don't know the name of came on, and we continued to dance and swim in each other's eyes. The final song I remember hearing at the mixer was Sweet Thing. We came together for the slow start and I leaned against him, putting my head on his shoulder. When I felt his lips brush my brow I pulled back and looked at him, for that lightest of kisses had given me the deepest of thrills. He pulled me against him again, taking me by the waist and planting his lips on my throat, then behind my ear. Then he took my earlobe between his teeth and gently bit it. I was destroyed. I looked at him and said, "You love me."

Then he countered, "You love me."

I told him, "You and I belong together and you know it."

"I know it," said Ronnie and clasped me to him, even though the song had progressed to the very fast cords. We clung to each other in the overheated room and breathed in each other's warmth.

We got our coats and practically ran back to campus. We had to, it was so cold. He took me back to Kirkland.

We couldn't get our clothes off fast enough, but then we had to jump directly under the covers because the heat had been reduced for the night. We made love several times and held each other close.

January 12th, Second Term

Day started out goofy. Sat next to Colby Hodge in Economics and remembered seeing an A+ on the top of one of his tests, first semester. So after class I stopped him on the way out and introduced myself. He looked me up and down in that utterly insolent way of his. As if to say, who was I to get between him and his mid morning donut? He's a jock but he seems to already be getting a little gut from beer guzzling and pretzel cramming. I guess he's not bad looking, tall, squared off shoulders, fair hair cropped pretty short. He always wears jeans and a tucked out button down shirt. When he and his buds are in any nearby café, they always make the most noise in the room. He's actually really pretty horrible but I need a tutor in Economics right now.

"I'm not getting this class," I explained. "I need someone to explain it to me."

"Are you asking me to tutor you?" he demanded in that rough, barking voice of his that's been strained to the limit from screaming at TV screens in sports bars. I guess he can pass for 21 or has fake id because I've never seen him out anywhere without full pitchers of beer being delivered to his table at five-minute intervals.

"Yes, I am."

"Well, that's okay with me but I charge for my services," he informed me coolly.

"I can't afford any more than ten dollars an hour," I replied judiciously. Privately I thought he had his nerve when he had to review for the class himself anyway.

"Minimum two hour cram sessions," he added, arbitrarily. I guess twenty bucks still buys a lot of beer.

"Oh, of course!"

"At least three times a week," he said, looking at my legs this time. (I had on textured tights and boots with a fairly short skirt and wool pea coat.)

"Sounds good. When should we begin?"

"Tonight at eight," he decided, writing down a room number in my dorm on a tiny piece of paper and handing it to me. "Bring cash," he advised me, giving my face one final glance, displaying the smallest of smiles and strolling off with his books under his arm.

Same day, after dinner, before tutoring with Neanderthal jock.

Want to cancel study session due to devastating news I got this afternoon, to wit, Ronnie is leaving for France tonight. A place suddenly opened up at the Sorbonne in the film school exchange program and Ronnie is to go for the Spring semester. He's packing now. We said our goodbyes after dinner, in the parlor downstairs. There's no time even to be together tonight. He has to be at the airport at seven. Poor Barbara. He won't have time to say goodbye to her properly either. I am very glad for him but I couldn't help but cry in his arms the whole time we were saying goodbye. He promised to email me daily and we agreed to meet in Europe this summer, somehow. But oh how cruel to lose one's dearest sweetheart the same week one realizes he *is* one's dearest sweetheart. And now I have to go and spend two hours with that lout Colby Hodge.

January 13th, morning

We were supposed to study in Colby's room but it was an appalling sty and I refused to remain five minutes in it, no less hours.

We went back to our suite. Hugo sent me furniture for our sitting room: a small sofa and two easy chairs in brown leather, dried out and cracked, but almost unused otherwise, plus a small reading table with a lamp and two chairs. Colby and I sat at the table, with our textbooks spread out and our laptops open for reference and notes. It had started to snow and I couldn't help looking out the window and sighing. Ronnie would be in the air by now, I thought, feeling sad again.

"Hey," Colby barked at me, "pay attention or I'll spank your ass."

Completely taken aback, ruffled and in high dudgeon I replied, "In your dreams, you vulgarian."

"Don't be haughty, you know you need a disciplinarian," he assured me.

"Please don't use language like that with me. I consider you a jockish goon," I replied blandly.

He absorbed and shrugged off my insult without further comment and we returned to the tedium of reading paragraphs aloud in our text book and then summarizing the ideas they expressed. He did all the summarizing, I made notes. He made me say back to him what he'd just told me without consulting my notes and in most cases, I seemed to retain about fifty percent of the information. So we spent the second hour reviewing what we'd gone over during the first hour. It was deadly boring but I felt as though I was understanding the concepts a lot better than right after class.

The session ended and I paid him in cash.

"Is this all I get?" he had the nerve to ask.

I just looked at him.

"Can't we fool around a little bit?" he asked, attempting to caress my cheek but winding up rather chucking me under the chin.

"Are you sexually harassing me?" I asked grimly. He gave a start.

"Why? Are you some sort of lesbian feminist?"

"Are you some kind of moron?" I asked, opening the door for him to leave.

"I'm sorry," he said quickly, gathering up his laptop and grabbing his jacket. "How could I not try, you're so hot."

"Get out," I advised him, pushing him out the door. Horrid, nasty piece of work that he is.

January 14th

Felt Colby staring at me in lecture hall, as though considering how he might advance his game with me tonight during our review session. I deliberately didn't meet his gaze.

Later in the afternoon I ran into him after my swimming class. I was hurrying back to the dorm in the high teens temps when he suddenly appeared beside me in sweats. He'd been doing laps around campus and was in a disgusting lather. He asked me if we were still on for later and I could not refrain from reminding him to shower beforehand. "Well see," he laughed and ran off.

I think I hate him.

January 15th

Study session highly productive. I'm really starting to get this, but I do need Colby badly.

It did seem as though he'd showered and appeared to be in clean jeans and his usual tucked out cotton shirt. Even though I had warned him about flirting with me, he started in on me right away, saying, "Better be good today or teacher spank."

I took a few seconds to think about how best to reply while noticing him looking at my legs in the black tights, knee boots and short camel skirt I had on.

"That's the second time you've mentioned spanking me before knowing anything about my disposition with regard to such matters. Don't you realize that's creepy?"

I could see that barb had hit home but he brushed it off with his usual arrogance.

"How can I help thinking about your butt when you twitch around in skirts that short?"

"Don't say butt. It's vulgar. Say bottom," I corrected him serenely. "You should know that, being into spanking," I couldn't resist adding.

"Who says I am?"

"You did. Didn't you?"

"I said you need a spanking, nothing more."

"Oh, you're into it. You've got a genuine spanking fetish. You probably fantasize spanking girls and women 24/7."

Colby put his chin on his hand and sighed, "You, anyway."

Then we proceeded to the lesson, for which I had thoughtfully supplied him with a six-pack, which gesture he seemed greatly touched by. So much so that he restrained himself at the close of the session and did not make a fresh pass at me.

January 16th

I was lingering over an extremely rich breakfast of butter soaked pancakes and sugared fruit when Colby slid into the empty seat opposite me with a cup of coffee and plate of sausage and eggs.

"I couldn't stop thinking about you last night, babe," he confided, cutting up his food with the precision of an obsessive compulsive economist, which surprised me, because hitherto I'd considered him somewhat haphazard.

"I stopped thinking of you the second you left. And don't call me babe."

"So, why don't you like me, again?" he asked.

"Because you're a coarse, ill mannered, beer swilling, sports screen shouting lout."

"Huh!" he grunted, filling his mouth with food.

"So stop coming onto me. You're not my type."

"And what is your type?"

"Metrosexual," I said off the top of my head. He snorted. Then he said, "Come see me play hockey tonight?"

"Why the hell would I want to do that?"

He shrugged off the brutal rejection lightly. This guy is great, I can say anything I want to him without worrying about hurting his feelings. In fact, I think I need to become increasingly more brutal with him as time goes by, just so there's no question in his mind as to his chances with me.

We agreed to meet for another review session on Sunday night. He was grinning to himself as I walked away with my tray. He's probably thinking that as long as I keep coming to him for tutoring, he's got endless chances to make endless plays for me.

January 17th

Ambrose Bartlett, that villain in a grey flannel suit, hasn't forgotten about me. He got me a job on a photo shoot that took place today for 6 hours @ $200 an hour. It was at the new Damaris shop on Newbury Street. Since I was supposed to get there at six am for makeup, I spent Friday night at Hugo's, which is only a three-block walk from the shop. I wanted to call Marty last night very badly. I haven't seen him in weeks and now that Ronnie is gone, I'm burning up for masculine attention. But I forced myself to read chapters and got to sleep very early so I could look fresh for today. Felt totally ahead of the game being able to eat a lovely breakfast with fresh ground coffee and then take a long, hot bath before going out into the terrible cold.

The only other model was Pamela, that young lady who is Damaris' partner and runs the Damaris boutique at Bartlett's part time. I don't know if she knows that I know that Hugo did her, so I avoided the subject of Hugo completely, so as not to betray my inside knowledge of their sticky affair. We were working with a photographer who has shot Pamela many times before, a very handsome man named Pascal Robbins. He worked fast with just a few lights and reflectors. Being outside at the crack of dawn, we didn't need much additional light. We had to pose outside the shop on the street, in the bus stop, and in a little café on the corner. We each had five outfits and in addition to the make up girl, there was a hairdresser to style our hair slightly differently for each set up. I was thrilled to do the café set up second because by that time I was ravenously hungry and took full advantage of the croissants and tea. Pamela hardly ate a thing and I saw her looking at her waist critically throughout the day.

Damaris was there to hand us the outfits but I'm overjoyed to say that Ambrose Bartlett was not. I found out from Pamela that he is backing this shop as an engagement present to her and she is now wearing his ring, a big one.

I went home with enough money to half pay for meeting Ronnie in Europe this summer. So it was a good use of my time, but it taught me that a career in modeling would be anything but enjoyable. I didn't like standing out on the corner in the seventeen-degree weather in spring outfits! That discomfort alone was worth two hundred bucks an hour. I'd rather teach a yoga class for twenty bucks an hour in a nice, warm studio. (I sound like a lazy, spoiled, ungrateful bitch.)

After the shoot I got a ride with Pascal Robbins back to Cambridge. He gave me his card and told me he'd be calling me again to work with him. He sure is one hot older man. I understand he's married to a beauty. Found myself looking at his profile in the car and envying the ease with which Thalia seems able to pick up near strangers. But I stopped myself from making a play. This was someone's husband, so what was I thinking? But the truth is, I need love.

January 18th

Third study session ended with predictable tussle. I could feel it coming. Maybe the problem was that I brought weed instead of beer this time. It got him way too relaxed. He barked and snorted less, which was nice. But we also got side tracked into political discussions, which wasn't helpful, though at least I now know he's a liberal. I told him I would only pay for study time and we reset the clock and got back to work. Colby may be an asshole in every other respect, but he has a way of distilling dense info that actually penetrates my brain.

Just as we were winding down he made his move, putting his hand on my knee under the table. I pushed it off. He put it back and squeezed me through my tights. I admit I'd worn a short skirt, boots and tights again. Damaris let me keep a couple of the outfits I modeled yesterday. I guess Mr. Bartlett has sufficiently made up for treating me so casually when we sessioned that time, though no amount of presents would ever induce me to go sub to him again.

I got up and said it was time for him to go.

"You know, you need a boyfriend," Colby told me as I pushed him out the door and slammed it after him.

January 20th

Econ 102 really coming into sharp focus. Had our fourth study session tonight. Colby has obviously decided to seriously court me. He brought me a small paper cup of remarkably rich hot chocolate that instantly heated my blood. And he seems to have started showering regularly. The two hours passed quickly. Then he suggested we go have a snack. I was ravenous so I agreed. We went to the Algiers Coffee House on Brattle St. and sat on the second floor terrace, looking down at the street. No one was really in the street, it was that cold. I had a delicious fried eggplant sandwich and some very good coffee. Colby had a lamb kabob and somehow got them to serve him beer. I have never enjoyed a meal more.

"I feel like I'm really getting somewhere with you," I confided, referring of course to my comprehension of Econ 102.

"I wish I could say the same."

"Well, as I explained -"

"I know, I know, I'm not your type. But I'm curious about something. You pegged me for a spanking fetishist just on some offhand remarks I made. How do you know about things like that?"

"It's the 21st century, everyone knows about fetishism. And I am from San Francisco."

"Really? I'm from Sausalito. We could visit each other over the summer." I didn't reply. He tried again, "You aren't seeing anyone, are you?"

I shrugged.

"What does that mean, are you or aren't you?"

"I'm not seeing anyone exclusively at the moment," I admitted.

"So what kind of fetishist are you?"

"I said everyone knows about fetishism, not everyone is a fetishist. I'm perfectly normal."

"Oh," he said, sounding disappointed.

"Go to the B&D support group that meets on Monday nights at that old theatre they turned into a punk club. You'll meet Goth girls and they'll let you spank them," I advised him knowledgeably. He quivered all over at the thought. I can see his point. If I were a guy I wouldn't want to kiss any girl wearing black lipstick.

"What would I have to do for you to let me spank you?" he made bold to ask.

"Colby, be yourself. Spanking is an intimate and possibly an exquisite act. I could never squander the divine gift of my submission on a lowly, uncivilized jock."

He sighed and ate his sandwich, knowing there was no arguing with my logic.

How much fun am I going to have with this charade? The joker is starting, ever so slightly, to get under my skin.

January 22nd

Fifth study session tonight ended with us both being hungry again. We bundled up and ran over to the Thai restaurant on Eliot Street. Split a veggie curry and a big pot of tea.

"So," I said, "did you go to the B&D support group yesterday and try to find some girls to spank?"

"I walked passed the door," he admitted.

"I know those girls aren't your exact type," I said, "but sometimes you have to compromise a little to get what you want."

"Is that what you do?"

"No. Obviously, I don't have to," I informed him patiently. He grinned the way he always does when I insult him, as though he were a large dog I'd just thumped vigorously.

"Want to go running with me at Walden Pond on Saturday morning?" he asked.

"Where is that?"

"In Concord. I can borrow my friend's car and drive us there. It's beautiful."

"Isn't it kind of cold for running?"

"I checked the weather. It'll be in the 30's on Saturday morning."

I agreed to do this with him. But he also tried to get me to commit to a movie between now and Saturday. I refused.

After our snack, we walked back to Wigglett as fast as we could. Our faces were numb by the time we got there. There were only a few people in the downstairs parlor and there was a nice fire going. Colby got me to sit with him for a few more minutes. I pretended I was doing it as a favor to him but I really wanted to be there. He tried to take my hand but I withdrew it immediately.

"Look, just because I had Thai food with you, don't start thinking things."

"You said yourself you don't have a boyfriend. Why don't you give me a chance?"

"I said I see a variety of people."

"For sex?" he demanded.

"For incredibly hot sex," I told him, staring deep into his rather nice blue eyes.

"Damn it, Amanda, you're driving me crazy!"

"I told you it wasn't going to happen with us," I reminded him. (I'm only being this cruel because of course it's going to happen. But he's going to have to work harder for this pussy than he's ever done in his life.)

"I'll break down your resistance," he announced confidently.

"No, you won't."

"Okay, let's put sex aside for a minute."

"Let's put it aside for all eternity," I returned.

"How about the spanking thing? You're curious about it. I can tell."

"How can you tell?"

"You sort of get a twinkle in your eyes when you talk about it."

"You're seeing what you want to see," I coolly shut him down. Then I said good night.

How long can I fend him off, I wonder? I see that after all, he doesn't really have a gut. He's just solidly built. His thighs seem formidable.

January 24th

Hugo seems impressed with the first edited clip from my amateur spanking movie, especially how fast it got thrown together. And he says the production standards are way higher than amateur. Tommy digitally sent the music he'd recorded and the titles he'd designed to Ronnie (in Paris - how I miss him!) who completed the edit and sent the finished clip back to me a few days ago. I forwarded it on to Hugo asking for advice. After I got those lackluster first semester grades, he had suggested that maybe I had better put off any more work on the movie until the summer. But after seeing the first scene edited so nicely and understanding that my work was essentially done, except for writing up the clip, he was all for promoting it to his customers online. He told me to go to the board of equalization next week and apply for a D.B.A. business license so we could get going on this for me. I wonder how many clips I'd have to sell to pay for a year at Harvard. Meanwhile, Ronnie, Tommy and I, via emails are trying to think of a name for the company. (And Tommy is now dating Barbara.)

About go to Walden Pond with Colby. Changed the run to a walk so I could wear my mocha wool turtleneck and short matching skirt with black tights and knee boots and my black cashmere coat. Am fairly sure he's never seen me in a snug wool sweater before so am mentally steeling myself for the most vigorous groping attempt yet.

Same day, evening

Was tempting fate wearing that sweater. It did send Colby all to pieces. He's sick with love and longing for me and can't master his emotions much longer.

"Just let me kiss you once," he said suddenly as we trod a path that was moist with melted snow. The pond was edged by both green trees and bare ones, with icicles dripping from their branches in the sudden thaw. The sky an unbelievably deep blue. It wasn't nearly as cold as it has been these past few weeks and the mildness of the day imbued me with an exquisite sensation of well-being.

"At least you said kiss and not spank," I replied. Oh, I am being bad and I know it, but he's going to wind up with a big prize at the end of his ordeals so they have to be severe. I freely admit to being on the verge of messing up Colby's head in the most diabolical manner imaginable. This is not like me. I've never played a prank in my life.

"Does that mean you consent to be kissed?" he asked, rather endearingly.

"Perhaps once, very lightly on the lips," I replied, standing still in the middle of the path, putting up my mouth and closing my eyes. He obeyed me to the letter, softly brushing his mouth against mine. I looked up at him (he's inches taller than me) and smiled. The next thing I knew he had swept me into his arms and was kissing me as though scoring the leading role in a silver screen romance depended on it. I pushed him away indignantly.

"I said once!"

"You said perhaps once."

We continued walking.

"You're very aggressive," I admonished him.

"I'm completely tame," he protested.

"How can I trust you not to date rape me?" I asked bluntly.

"Amanda, I would never do a thing like that. For one thing, I don't have access to the right drugs."

"You're very strong. And these sadomasochistic fantasies you live on. They frighten me!" I insisted.

"Honestly, you've entirely misunderstood me," he pleaded. "I'd never hurt a lady."

"But you want to spank them. I'll bet you want to make them cry. That's probably one of your hot buttons," I idly accused.

"No. Really," he protested again, but more weakly this time.

"How can I trust anyone who has those kind of fantasies and wants to possess me? How do I know that you won't tie me up in these woods and thrash me for fun?"

Colby looked at me with wonder, then laughed, "I like the way your mind works!"

"See?"

"Come on, Amanda, you know I'd never push what I'm into on you. I mean, since you're so obviously against it."

"No, this is happening too fast," I protested and the big sap accepted this statement as though it had some sort of validity. For a smart man he sure is easy to put one over on.

After a long walk around the pond we stopped in at Thoreau's cabin and speculated about his life therein, how cold it must have been for him inside it in the winter and what he might have eaten and drank.

Since Colby had the car for the rest of the afternoon he asked me what else I might want to do. I pretended I'd never been to Salem before and asked if we might drive there. Colby and never been and we proceeded there directly.

We stopped for lunch at the café in the House of the Seven Gables. I had a vegetarian panini and Colby had a cheeseburger. Then we went to the Witch Museum and took the little tour of the talking wax characters, which told the story of the Salem Witch Trials. I never stopped covertly watching Colby, while waiting for a certain moment in the narrative that I remembered from my first visit to the museum the previous year. Sure enough, about ten minutes into the presentation there came the spanking reference that had originally so startled me, as a stern village householder recommends that his hysterical young housemaid be spanked for accusing a neighbor of witchcraft. First I detected a small throb in the region of Colby's jeans' zipper, a moment later the entire area filled out with the outline of an impressive erection. (Note the power of a spontaneous spanking reference.)

I pretended not to notice anything and we continued on through the exhibit. But as soon as we got outside I began to rate him for his perversity. "I can't take you anywhere," I told him, while we walked a little into the village. He wanted to know what I meant. I just looked at him until he figured it out. He flushed.

"God damn, nothing gets by you, does it?" he demanded. (He noticed!)

"You've really got it bad," I observed. "I really think it's an integral part of your sexual makeup."

Colby groaned. "No, you've got me wrong, babe. I'm as normal as you."

"Then why did thinking about that poor little puritan girl getting spanked by her master give you a hard-on?" I drove my point home hard.

It was now about four thirty and the last little bit of sun had retreated behind some suddenly ominous clouds.

"It was standing so close to you that gave me the hard-on," he informed me confidently. "Nor do I regret it," he added serenely. "Because now you know that I have the goods to deliver."

"That is an important consideration in terms of intimacy," I tantalized him.

"Please, feel free to use me like a hard rubber thing," he offered gallantly.

"I suppose it gets painfully hard at night when you're thinking about me?" I asked sympathetically. But he didn't justify my comment with a response beyond an indignant "Humph!"

We're getting together tomorrow night for another study session. I don't think I can hold him at bay much longer sexually. But he's going to have to work to get me over his knee.

January 26th

Very close call last night. Tommy had come by to watch the final cut of the first scene of our movie and us both being in love with the footage, we reran it on my laptop three or four times. I didn't have the volume turned up too high, but still, the video clip produced unmistakable spanking and squeaky girl noises. Tommy lingered so long in our sitting room that he was still there when Colby knocked on the door. We shut down the computer right away and as Tommy was leaving, he said, "Tell Alicia I came by?" so Colby would think he'd been paying court to my roommate instead of me. I had clued Tommy in as to my new relationship with my economics tutor and how I was playing vanilla with him just to add one more obstacle to his inevitable conquest of me.

"What was that noise I just heard coming out of here?" Colby demanded as soon as he entered the parlor.

"Oh, you mean the audio from the spanking video I had on?"

"You had on a spanking video?" He seemed floored.

"Well, I felt I had to see what it was all about, seeing you're so into it and you're determined to try to date me."

"Well???? What did you think?"

"I'm just trying to figure out how anyone could find that much pain enjoyable," I replied. "I don't think I would find it so."

Colby looked at me somewhat helplessly, sighed and opened his laptop to our lesson. I could see his mind was fairly blown. He made no pass at me and after our session hurried off to watch a game and drink beer.

February 13th

Neither of us can stand much more of this. It's just a question of who is going to jump the shark first. I found myself thinking about sitting on his lap, winding my arms around his neck and kissing him after our last session. I know what kind of hard-on that would give him and it's been absolutely weeks since I've been touched by anyone. I've been studying every night at the library instead.

The last and only male I ever held at bay this long was Carlos, but that is reasonable with one's first boyfriend.

As horrifying as it sounds, I want Colby Hodge.

But I'm still not sure how! Should I be passive or aggressive or merely docile and reactive? How I behave the first time will set the tone for all the rest to follow. Do I get on top or let him? Should I regulate the progress of the seduction, allowing him a night of kissing only, then the next night add on petting, then the next, digital penetration, etc., emulating the patterns of a first high school romance? Or should I permit everything all at once as I normally do? Am I over thinking this? It's not like me.

I do know that I long to hear him call me beloved. Or some endearment other than "babe." I didn't crave a declaration of love or tokens of sentimental tenderness from Ronnie because our relationship began with me objectifying him and throwing myself at him. Plus there was the ever present under currant of race anxiety always making him cynical and suspicious. I would never expect him to say the word love to me. (Though he has in many emails this month and very sweetly.) But Colby is different. I've tormented him for weeks on end and watched his passion ...swell. I KNOW he thinks about me all the time and is being driven mad with longing to possess me, the subsidiary desire to turn me over his knee apart. So I feel fully justified in expecting an extremely sincere declaration of the deepest love and admiration to come tumbling from his very attractive mouth in accompaniment to his most assured upcoming conquest. The sick thing is that I love him back. I am in love with a big, coarse jock and tomorrow is Valentine's Day. If he asks me out and I say yes we pretty much know how it's going to turn out.

Late afternoon, same day

After class we went to lunch at the dining hall and I noticed immediately that Colby was barely eating as he tried to find the perfect words. Finally he muttered, "You don't have to pay me anymore."
"Really? Why?"
"I need the reviews as much as you do. It's time well spent."
"Okay!" I agreed enthusiastically.
"I came across some tickets to Morrisey for tomorrow night. Do you want to go?"
I stared at him, stunned.
"What made you think of that?"
"I just saw he was playing."
Which meant he'd been studying my CD collection when he came over to work. No way in hell was he a natural Morrisey fan. I was becoming impressed.
"Yes, I'd love to see Morrisey," I agreed without equivocation.
"Do you want to eat first?"
"Sure!"
We agreed to meet at six at the Thai place and proceed to the Agganis Arena at B.U. from there.

Chapter Thirteen

Valentine's Day

Unconsciously thinking with one mind, Colby and Amanda spent the day preparing for their date in almost the same way. Colby spent the morning playing hockey with friends on a frozen pond in a nearby suburb. Amanda taught a class that morning at the yoga center in Cambridge. Both ate a hearty lunch at the dining hall but did not meet. That afternoon, Colby got a haircut and bought new clothes. Amanda got a professional manicure and bought a new lipstick. She already had many new clothes, which she stared at in her closet for many minutes before deciding on which to wear that evening. Both felt butterflies throughout the day, contemplating from moment to moment, how the night would climax.

In spite of the way she had tormented him, Colby couldn't help but realize that she cared. There was no other reason on earth a girl as fine as she would consent to give him Valentine's Day. Amanda of course had known for sometime that Colby was not only mad to possess her but also to be her man. Thus they enjoyed, the entire day, the keenest excitement and most glowing happiness imaginable, anticipating the culmination of a passion excessively postponed by early 21st century standards.

The last thing Colby did before going back to his dorm that afternoon was to stop in at the Esprit shop and buy Amanda a smoky blue cashmere polo sweater for which he took great care in choosing the most luxurious wrapping paper and cloth ribbon he could find. The last thing Amanda did before returning to her dorm on that frosty white afternoon was to stop at the Abercrombie and Fitch shop and buy Colby a black leather belt, somewhere between wide and narrow.

Leaving the shop where he had purchased the gift-wrap, Colby was hurrying back to campus when the sight of a particular billboard caught his eye and caused his heart to contract in his chest. It was a large, glass-encased ad beside the train station entrance for a dress shop called Damaris. The girl in the ad was tall, slim, blonde and bore a remarkable resemblance to Amanda. Colby went closer to stare at the ad. Not only did the girl look exactly like Amanda, she was dressed in the same short sleeved, turtle neck, ribbed sweater dress that Amanda had worn the last time they'd had a study session. If the girl in the photo ad wasn't Amanda, then Amanda had a twin.

In spite of biting cold, Colby walked the rest of the way back to his dorm slowly, trying to digest what he had seen. When he got back to his room he took a long, hot shower and then carefully wrapped Amanda's present, still musing, in painful confusion on the implications of his discovery about the young woman who was not yet either his girlfriend or lover, but whom he had planned to complete the seduction of that night.

Meanwhile, Amanda also took a long, hot shower and then dressed in a short, black pleated wool skirt and white blouse under a pumpkin colored wool vest, with black ribbed tights and black walking boots. As usual, she wore her long, straight hair down and unfettered. Her only makeup was the new, cherry red lipstick and the cherry red manicure to match. A final spray of White Shoulders completed her preparations. And just in case her beloved to be should be careless in his own preparations, she tucked a few Rough Rider condoms into a secret inner pocket of her new, long, nicely fitted, faux fur collared black down coat. This coat had been a Christmas present from Hugo, who knew well the harshness of a Boston winter and cared deeply for the comfort of his newly found daughter.

On the way to the Thai restaurant, Colby paused once more in front of the train station ad, now absolutely certain that the girl in the photo could be no one but Amanda.

Having left campus at exactly the same time as Colby, Amanda found herself only a half block behind Colby as he proceeded to their rendezvous. She saw him pause in front of the train stop and stare at the ad behind it, which from this distance, Amanda couldn't make out.

She hung back looking in a shop window but covertly watching him until he finally pulled himself away from the train stop and continued on toward the restaurant. Amanda hurried forward and in a minute found herself before the large, glassed in ad of herself posing on Newberry Street in her new Damaris outfit. Now she herself couldn't help but stare. She had supposed that when she had accepted the modeling assignment that her image would eventually be published somewhere. She had thought perhaps it would show up in Lucky, the shopping magazine or possibly even Mademoiselle, but she had never anticipated being on a city street ad. As she examined the photo she could not help but inwardly thrill to how polished and attractive she appeared in it. Suddenly her former notion of posing nude for Playboy struck her in its full absurdity. How right Hugo had been. If she planned to make her good looks work for her, this was the way to go, not the other. This image had dignity and grace and could never become the butt of an indecent joke.

She proceeded on, shaking her head with a small smile, and remembering again how uncomfortable and tiring her modeling day had been. Now it seemed well worth the inconvenience. She would have this image for all time, to save in her scrapbook and remind her of her blooming youth.

Entering the restaurant she immediately joined Colby at a small table overlooking Harvard Square.

"Hello," she said gaily, first noticing the large, extravagantly wrapped package on the seat beside him and then the unhappy look in his pale blue eyes.

"So, you're a fashion model," Colby said flatly.

"That billboard was a surprise to me too," she replied lightly, then hastened to explain about her one photo modeling assignment that had come to her through a friend of her father's who owned a department store on the Cape.

"I see now why you've been holding out on me," he softly but indignantly declared. "Fashion models only do other fashion models, right?"

Amanda poured herself a tiny cup of hot, green tea and stared at him thoughtfully, wondering if she should relieve his anxiety by allowing him to reach into her inner jacket pocket and discover its contents. Instead she replied, "I don't know. Do they?"

"Why didn't you mention you're a model?"

"Because it was just a one time deal. I had to get up before dawn and freeze my butt off on a street corner for five hours. It's not something I'm looking to do very often. You know I'm committed to getting good grades."

"Huh!" he grunted, swallowing hot tea so fast that it burned his mouth and caused him to choke. Amanda grinned.

"Anyway," she said, "you're right out of the J. Crew catalog yourself so why should I discriminate against you?"

He brushed the compliment off with a snort.

"Happy Valentine's Day," he told her, handing her the large wrapped box. She in turn presented him with a smaller one.

"It's so beautiful. I hate to unwrap it."

"Let's wait until we get back to the dorm. We won't want to bring these to the concert anyway."

Amanda agreed and they ordered a few dishes to share from the pretty, petite waitress who came to serve them.

"Tell me honestly," he began half way through dinner, "are you seeing anyone else right now?"

"Honestly, I'm not. How about you?"

"You know damned well I'm not."

They looked at each other intently but said no more on the subject of seeing people and the meal was completed with the exchange of mild pleasantries and a lively political discussion. Colby was a hard news junkie and able to answer a full range of questions on almost any current event. Amanda had been enjoying mining his brain for factual knowledge and considered his ability to inform her with correct information on serious topics a valuable asset. It was the one trait he possessed that made him seem worthy of respect.

After their meal, which Colby insisted on paying for, they hurried back to Amanda's dorm suite to open their presents and get stoned for the concert. Neither of them smoked on a daily basis and the powerful strain of marijuana going around Boston that season immediately put them both into a sensual trance.

Amanda was stunned by the extravagance of Colby's present to her, figuring out that between the cashmere sweater and the Morrisey tickets, he'd probably spent everything she'd paid him for the eleven tutoring sessions he'd given her. There wasn't a doubt in her mind now that a very romantic relationship was about to commence.

Colby was even more surprised by his present. Naturally, no spanking man ever holds a belt in his hand in the presence of a pretty girl without thinking certain thoughts and Colby was a spanking man. But she was not, to his knowledge, a spanking girl, so why had she picked this object of all things to present him with.

"Are you being a wise guy?" he immediately demanded.

"What do you mean?" she appeared mystified.

"Never mind," he said, flipping the handsome belt over to check the size. "How did you know I have a 30" waist?"

"I didn't, but I was hoping," she admitted. Lately she had been studying his body covertly, very closely and had realized that he was trimmer than she had originally thought. He always wore his shirts tucked out, so it was hard to tell exactly how flat or round his waist was. But that evening, in his new, baggy salt and pepper tweed trousers and casually dressy black, button down knit shirt, it was obvious that he was as lean as she could have wished with extremely attractive shoulders and pecs, outlined by the soft shirt. His outfit was completed by black, lacing ankle high boots and a long black wool over coat.

"Should I try it on?" he asked.

"Well, what else would you do with it?" she replied.

Colby flushed at this remark and again wondered whether she was toying with him. She looked back at him deadpan. He tucked his shirt into his trousers and ran the belt through the loops, finding it a perfect fit.

"Nice!" she approved of his new silhouette, his broad shoulders and upper back tapering down to a V shape at his waist. "Should I try my present on too?" she asked.

"Would you?"

"Certainly!" she replied, going to get a small scissors to cut off the gift tag. Then she excused herself to retreat into her tiny bedroom to switch the blue grey sweater for the blouse and vest. The sweater was also a perfect fit, doing spectacular things to her voluptuous bosom. When she emerged in the sweater Colby could not restrain his impulse to take her in his arms.

She allowed him to kiss her and squeeze her breasts through the new sweater. It was the first time she'd felt his powerful hands on her body and she nearly swooned from the thrill.

"Let's go into your bedroom," he urged her.

"But what about the concert?"

"We'll miss the opening band, do you care?"

"Miss 10,000 Maniacs? I should say I do!" Amanda responded with a twinkle in her eyes. Tonight was going to be made easy for Colby, but not quite that easy.

The temperature was in the middle twenties with a whipping wind that very nearly sobered them completely as they walked briskly to the station, gloved hand in gloved hand, to catch the "B" train on the Red Line to Boston University. On the way they once again passed Amanda's fashion ad, this time both stopping to stare at it.

"You were already conceited," he mused, "I have to believe that this is going to wind up making you completely insufferable."

"Is that one of the items on your list of reasons to spank me?" Amanda teased. This time their faces were both so red from the cold to begin with that she couldn't tell if her words made him flush, but they did render him momentarily speechless. Finally he sputtered, "Yes!"

In the train she looked so fresh and lovely, her face framed by the tawny faux fur of her parka hood, that he had to kiss her red mouth. They kissed for one entire run between stations then realized that all the other people in the train car were looking at them. When they broke apart, several people clapped appreciatively. Amanda and Colby sprung apart, with burning cheeks. Then he pulled her by the hand into a different car. He didn't relinquish her hand until they were standing in front of Boston University.

"Wait," she said, "let's go finish that joint first."

They walked down the block until out of sight and after some difficulty succeeded in lighting the spliff in the wind. Then they passed it between them a few times until both their eyes began to water. Suddenly everything around them came into sharp relief, including the sky above them white with stars.

"Oh god, I love you so!" Colby exclaimed, drawing her into his arms for another long kiss.

"I love you too!" she replied at once and buried her head in his chest.

The concert passed in a dream of romance for Amanda, with Colby retaining possession of her hand or holding her around the waist the whole time. And when Morrisey sang, "I am human and I need to be loved just like everybody else," she felt her eyes go misty while an uneasy sensation of guilt rose in her breast. She hadn't treated Colby like a human who needed to be loved but rather a hard rubber thing (his words) to verbally pummel and then toss in a toy chest. She had called him a lowly jock, whereas he was in fact a grind and a scholar. And she had played havoc with his emotions with regard to his fetish, which he still had no notion that she robustly shared. Before "How Soon Is Now" was over, Amanda had resolved to grant him not only sexual but spanking liberties that weekend. Not that she intended to reveal her true nature all at once, but she suddenly realized that if they were going to have sex, there would have to be foreplay, and she preferred her foreplay to be over the knee. In fact, if she did not insist on a spanking, there might not be any foreplay at all, given the obvious urgency of Colby's need.

After the show let out they walked for a few blocks until they found an inviting café with interior walls of dark red and progressive alternative music similar to the kind they had just heard at the concert hall. They found a window table, which gave a view of the couples hurrying by out on Massachusetts Avenue. Colby sat and gave his attention all to her, his chin in his hand. She ordered mocha cappuccinos and grilled cheese sandwiches for them both, which were duly delivered and quickly consumed with extreme satisfaction.

While they were waiting for the bill she began hesitantly, "Look, I've been thinking about it and..."

"Yes?" Colby prompted her anxiously, unable to imagine was "it" referred to and fearing another postponement of the ultimate sexual conquest of his life to date.

"Well, darling," she said softly, "I was thinking about it and I've decided that I would be willing to submit to a ... very small spanking, before we made love."

Colby sat up with a start, as these were the last words he had expected to tumble from her beautiful red lips.

"What's this you're saying now, I can spank you tonight?"

"Yes, but just a little," she insisted.

"Really, honey?" he touched her smooth cheek and brushed back a tendril of ash blonde hair.

"Do you think you could spank me, just a little? I mean and not go overboard. Not really hurt me? Could you, Colby?"

"Of course, I could. If it's too hard, you just say mercy and I stop," he assured her.

"Really? Is that how it works?"

"Yes, it is!"

"And, could it be over my clothes?"

"I would LOVE to spank you over that cute little pleated skirt, Amanda."

"Why do you think you do?"

Colby shrugged. "I don't really know why. I just know I've always had an urge to spank girls. Going back to kindergarten."

"Alicia is going to be in tonight," Amanda said, "and I don't want her to hear that sort of thing. Those walls aren't very thick, even with the sitting room between our two bedrooms."

"My roommate is going to be in tonight too," Colby said. "But I can probably bribe him to go out for a few hours."

"That won't be necessary, dearest. My father has an apartment on Boylston Street that he only goes to once in a while. I have the keys and permission to use it whenever he isn't in town. And he isn't in town tonight."

169

Another short subway ride and a very chilly three block walk took them to the flat that had served Amanda's needs so well on a number of occasions since moving to Boston.

"So you had this make-out mansion all along?" Colby demanding, striding through the rooms with interest and delight. He paused in front of a wine rack in the kitchen and started pulling out bottles to examine labels.

"I'm not sure I have permission to drink all of those," Amanda said regretfully, "just the not very expensive ones."

"I'll have my parents send your dad a case of this," said Colby with a grin, brandishing a California merlot at her. "It's from their vineyard."

"Really? Well, in that case, by all means, open it!"

"I don't need any more intoxicants tonight, honey," he said, taking her in his arms and nuzzling her smooth neck with his lips.

"Would you like a cup of tea?" she asked, suddenly shy and reluctant to go back into the sitting room. She turned and filled a teakettle that looked like a red hen in the elaborately tiled blue and yellow kitchen. This was a beaux-arts building and the décor reached back a hundred years to a period of elegant crown molding and heavy casement windows with deep windowsills.

Amanda made the strong English tea in a tea ball in a china pot and then poured out the two cups.

"Want to smoke some more?" she asked, filling a pipe from a stash that Hugo gave her access to.

"Sure!"

"I guess I'm more nervous about tonight than I thought I would be," Amanda confessed.

"Why, because this is the longest you've ever put anyone off for?" Colby intuited with uncanny accuracy.

"That isn't true. I made my high school boyfriend wait a whole six months before I let him have me," Amanda protested.

"And how old were you then?"

"Fifteen."

"Damn it Amanda, you've been sexually active since age fifteen and you still played this hard to get with me? Why did I get singled out for torture?"

"I haven't treated you very nicely," she admitted. "Or spared your feelings in any way."

"Oh, well, how could you know even I had any feelings?" he said, sympathetically, taking her hand and kissing the palm. She withdrew it shyly, busying herself refilling the pipe, drawing on it and then passing it to him.

"You want to spank me," she said, "and the funny thing is that I've given you every reason to!" Under the influence of the powerful hypnotic, her circumspection was dissolving like a sugar cube in hot water. "That's the scary part," she added shyly.

"Amanda," Colby said soothingly, stroking the back of her hand, "you and I both know that that yoga trained butt of yours is going to hurt my hand."

She allowed him to pull her by the hand into the sitting room. He was about to take a seat on the long, elegantly upholstered sofa but Amanda instead pulled him toward a large, armless straight-backed throne chair placed adjacent to a cheval mirror.

"I want to watch my face while you're spanking me," she told him.

"Really?" he sat down on the wide velvet upholstered chair and gently pulled her facedown across his lap.

"I want to see if I look like the girl on the video clip I saw online."

Amanda had never stared directly into her own face while she was being spanked before and was agreeably surprised by the attractive double portrait of herself full face and Colby in profile above her reflected by the mirror. She both saw and felt him take her by the waist and smooth down her short skirt over her slim but remarkably jutting buttocks.

"I knew you had a beautiful... bottom," Colby said carefully, stroking her pert mounds under the pleated merino wool, "but it's more perfect than I realized."

"Do you like bottoms better than breasts?" she asked, turning her face up.

"I do," he replied. "But in point of fact, you're breasts are equally amazing."

"And you have very muscular thighs," she offered sincerely, because she was enjoying the way they felt firmly supporting her weight.

"I'm going to start now," he said. "But you tell me right away if it's too hard."

"I will," she promised, gazing deeply at their reflection in the mirror.

He began with six small alternating pats.

"You can go harder than that," she said eagerly, feasting her eyes with excitement on their image. He repeated the half dozen swats slightly harder.

"You can go harder than that," she repeated, feeling her heart contract as he tightened his grip on her waist. Six more times his palm fell across the seat of her little skirt, now somewhat crisply.

"You can go harder than that," she said again, settling down on his lap more firmly, and perfectly unconscious of how oddly imperative her requests for greater severity were beginning to sound. Colby turned his head and looked down at her face. She received another sharp thrill in the pit of her stomach at the curious look her gave her before shrugging and actually lifting his hand this time before bringing it down lustily on her skirted seat. After several dozen much harder, alternating swats to either cheek she gave a little wriggle, sighed and said, "You can go a little harder than that."

Again Colby looked at her. Again her stomach gripped. For the very first time she acknowledged his physical beauty. Now he began smacking her hard through her skirt, administering many dozens of swats and creating a tangible heat. Amanda fell into a state of physical rapture, greatly enhanced by the chronic she'd just smoked. The rhythm of the spanking was perfect, his lap felt divine and he looked monumentally handsome with his powerful, muscular arm coming down so forcefully.

He continued spanking her for a long time before finally pulling up her skirt and tugging down her tights and sheer black nylon panties.

Even in the low light of the sitting room he could see that his heavy palm had already stained her well shaped bottom cheeks dark red.

Folding her arm back and holding her wrist to her waist, Colby administered a dozen more smacks in rapid measure. A thrill went through Amanda when he pinned her arm, resolving itself into a small climax.

"Yes, that's good, so I can't get away," she breathed encouragingly. Colby paused and looked at her with even greater interest. She hadn't exactly been trying to get away and had barely even kicked her legs, though by any measure he'd been spanking her robustly.

"This isn't bothering you, is it?" he demanded, rolling her over on his lap to look into her mischievous eyes.

"It's hot and bothering me," she said, putting her arms around his neck and surrendering her mouth to his.

"Are you saying that you may be aroused?" he asked, as he squeezed her full bosom through her sweater.

"I've never been more aroused in my life. I want your cock now. Hard and fast, doggy style," said Amanda, jumping from his lap to strip off her clothes. Colby immediately did the same, fishing a condom out of a pocket and slipping it onto the big, circumcised, strapping, pink penis that jumped out of his pants the instant his zipper came down.

Amanda looked at him and said, "We'll need lube."

"I'll bet you're wet enough," he said, bending her over the arm of the grand sofa and inserting first one and then a second long finger into the lithe, nude blonde's tight, slick vagina.

"Turn me under your arm and spank me some more. That might get me wetter," she suggested. Colby gazed at her in shock and wonder but took her by the waist without question. The moment he pressed her down with a hand in the small of her silken white back she felt the same orgasmic ripples as before radiating from her heart center to the pit of her stomach to her clitoris and back. Now his hand came down rapidly on either upturned cheek, staining her satiny skin an even darker shade of crimson.

"Okay, good, I'm wet enough!" she cried at last, the sting finally beginning to penetrate through the haze of pure submissive sensation she'd been basking in.

Colby spread her carefully and penetrated her slowly, edging in and out by small degrees while using only nature's lubricant. Now she really was very wet and he took advantage of the slickness to plunge his rod inside her to the hilt, pulling her back against him by the waist and driving his point home again and again.

"Tell me how to get you off," he demanded.

"Just keep doing what you're doing," she replied, rocking back and forth with him as he took her. "And put your palm here," she added, applying the palm of his right hand underneath her lower abdomen to press it against her g-spot. He began to firmly knead her with his fingertips while continuing to drive into her from behind and was rewarded almost instantly by the sensation of her pussy convulsing in release around his cock, which machinations wrung his own climax from his lust engorged member only moments later.

"Simultaneous orgasm on our first time," Colby reflected when they finally broke apart to make their repairs. "Are you impressed?"

"How about that great spanking I took?" she asked, before scampering off to the bathroom.

"That's still blowing my mind," he admitted.

A few minutes later, Amanda led Colby into the bedroom and together they turned down the luxurious counterpane and got into bed. They'd put all the lights out but could see each other's soft smiles by the moonlight coming in through the window beside the bed. Colby took Amanda in his arms and they held each other tightly until a few moments later, both fell into blissful slumber.

Chapter Fourteen

President's Day Weekend

"Ian Astbury or Sebastian Bach?" Thalia asked Amanda as they sat in a window booth at The Ball and Feather Inn in Random Point one Friday afternoon soon after the commencement of Amanda's epic romance with Colby Hodge. The girls were snuggled in wool pants and fuzzy sweater outfits, their down coats hanging up on pegs beside the booth, contentedly watching the snow softly falling on the hedges surrounding the inn while sharing a large slice of Shepherd's Pie, garnished with cranberry orange relish and a pot of English breakfast tea. They had come out on the train from Boston just that hour and had walked from the station through the village to the inn to enjoy a meal before repairing to Susan Ross' house, where they had been invited to stay for President's weekend. Susan was out of town and Hugo had the keys to the large Victorian at the tip of the village and would shortly arrive to conduct them there.

Amanda replied, "Ian Astbury, since he identifies with Jim Morrison and that makes him inherently more perverse and hotter." The game was to name two persons fairly equal in either good or bad qualities and decide which one it would be preferable to sleep with. The girls were currently meandering in the meadow of alternative musicians from the era just before they were born.

"Geoff Tate or Anthony Kiedis?" asked Thalia, based on the music videos they'd stayed up late watching the previous night.

"Geoff Tate got a little chubby but he's still adorable."

"Alice Cooper or Iggy Pop?"

"Well, it's hard to choose since they both exploited S&M," said Amanda, stirring her dark, red tea. "I think Iggy Pop would be nastier in bed and he has an amazing body."

"And Alice Cooper apparently got born again," said Thalia.

"That's not sexy."

"Speaking of sexy, you can't believe how my heart is beating thinking about seeing Hugo any minute," Thalia confided.

"Really?" Amanda giggled. "That's so cute, you love my father."

"Has he mentioned I've been emailing him?"

"No. Have you?"

"Yes, I've been updating him daily on my sick, twisted, putting myself through college by being a call girl life."

"Wow, you don't really do that, do you?"

"What, make men pay for pussy? Yes. I do."

"Thalia, how could you?" Amanda was genuinely shocked, for at their tender age this seemed very wrong to her.

"I think it may be a compulsion. It doesn't bother me in the slightest. Though I'd probably stop doing it if I found a regular boyfriend."

"Isn't it working out with you and Castor?"

"He's a playboy, you know that."

"No, I didn't. But that makes sense. Anyway, he isn't really good enough for you. I do know that."

"The only reason Hugo has allowed me to stay in contact with him is because I'm a degenerate slut," Thalia explained.

"Yes, I'm sure he appreciates you on a John Waters level," Amanda agreed.

Hugo entered the pub and hung his overcoat on a hook, then looked around to locate the girls. Waving to them he stopped at the bar and ordered an Irish coffee from Connie.

"I love his suit," murmured Thalia to Amanda of dark herringbone that Hugo wore so comfortably.

"Me too," Amanda replied, almost as excited as Thalia to be around her amiable relation again. In a moment he was joining them, kissing first Amanda on the cheek and then Thalia very lightly and very quickly on the mouth. Thalia shifted into the middle of the curved booth, enabling Hugo sit to her left, facing Amanda. Compliments were exchanged and thanks tendered for setting up their accommodations.

They were both so pretty, sweet and fresh, Hugo didn't know which to look at first. He did quite enjoy entertaining his newly found daughter, who was disarmingly beautiful and utterly charming, but he was also forced to admit that her friend Thalia Dunbar was interesting in an entirely different way. When his eyes met Thalia's neither could help seriously staring as each remembered their encounter in the ladies' room at Michael's bar just a few months before, when she had beckoned him thither and then insisted he take her on the spot. Since Thalia was not only sexually precocious but physically pulchritudinous, with an English complexion and hourglass form, he found it impossible to resist her and had bent her over the sink and penetrated her from behind, holding her wrist to her waist and with his other hand shifting between pinching her earlobe and squeezing her bosom the entire time. Since everyone was waiting for them on the set to continue with their photo shoot, it was the fastest encounter on record for Hugo since his distant youth. He might have been content to leave the connection at that, filing it under: Wacky Aberrational Sexual Pickups, if it had not been for her delightful daily emails, detailing her colorful adventures in the Boston underground. She was his own girl's friend, she had already posed for his magazine and he had possessed her. All of these elements contributed to a high comfort level around Thalia, even in spite of the disparity in their ages.

"Laura's gone to New York for the weekend," Hugo announced, after calling for a second whiskey coffee. Thalia's heart jumped as their eyes met again. "So I'm at your disposal if you need rides anywhere, or anything else," he told them, then smiled at Thalia. It was no secret between them that she wanted to repeat the performance that had occurred at Michael's bar. She alluded to it in every fifth or sixth email, making sure to reiterate how much she had liked being held by the wrist to her waist, and the ear lobe pinching, etc. She made sure she told him about all her paid sessions with all the details, hoping that some day he would call her a little whore in some meaningful way, perhaps moments before a punishment-induced orgasm.

"If you would only be even more severe with me next time, I'm sure I could come even faster," she had written most recently, as a casual p.s. to a letter on entirely different subject.

Amanda went off to the restroom to leave them alone to make a plan. Hugo looked at Thalia until she squirmed.

"You're so bad," he said, reaching for her hand under the table and giving it a light squeeze. "Now tell me you're not really serious."

"About wanting you to fuck me again? I go to bed thinking about it every night."

"But why me?" he took away his hand and began his second drink. "You're surrounded by boys your own age who are teeming with sex."

"Young boys are good too," said Thalia. "But you fuel my fantasies."

"Well, you can come visit me later, if you like," he smiled, brushing back a tendril of her coppery brown hair.

"Will you devastate me?"

"Of course!"

"Amanda has to get up early anyway for the fashion shows at Bartlett's. The first one is for the employees at nine am, so she'll have to get there by eight-thirty. She'll want to be in bed by ten p.m. if I know her."

"What a sensible girl!"

"Oh that's right, I just remembered, sensible girl needs some good advice about that wolf Bartlett. Ask her to elaborate when she gets back."

Hugo drove them across to the other end of the village, where Susan's house sat on a gently sloping hill across from the graveyard and just a few blocks from the thin, rocky coastline that rimmed the tip of Random Point. It was a fine Victorian triple-decker that had recently been entirely remodeled to suit the needs of a Bohemian young lady and her friends. As a working playhouse, it contained an art studio, where Susan and her sister Laura worked on their graphic novels, along with a number of well furnished guest rooms. Laura had filled the larder before leaving for Manhattan that morning, providing everything two girls would need for breakfasts and snacks all weekend. The fireplaces were all well stocked with logs and Hugo made sure to light a fire for them in one of the upstairs bedrooms before he left them to unwind after their travels and comfortable lunch. He also provided them with excellent weed, which he helped them initiate before leaving them to their own devices. After they passed a joint around twice or three times Hugo asked Amanda what was going on with Ambrose Bartlett.

"I don't know, but I think part of the reason he asked me out to model in the show was to get another chance at playing with me," Amanda admitted freely.

"As I recall you didn't enjoy your first encounter with him very much," he pointed out.

"I didn't. And I don't want to play with him again."

"I didn't think you did," Hugo commented, still uncomfortable about having been the one who had set up that initial encounter between Amanda and Ambrose Bartlett. "You cried," he added.

"And even if it wasn't for my hating the way he played, I have a boyfriend now and I don't want any other man's hands on me!" Amanda cried.

"Oh honey, I'm delighted to hear that!" Hugo said. "Is it the boy whose been tutoring you in economics? The lowly jock?"

"Yes," Amanda grinned ruefully.

"And get this," said Thalia, "the poor dope is in the scene but so far Amanda has successfully hidden the fact that she's not only into spanking but that it runs in her blood."

"Is this true?" Hugo demanded.

"I've been leading him a merry dance. But he finally conquered me on Valentine's Day."

"You'll have to bring him out for Spring break," Hugo said.

"I will!"

"He's bound to learn your secret then though," Thalia pointed out.

"I know. He'll be furious too," Amanda agreed.

"So, you're saying you happened to accidentally acquire yet another boyfriend who is in the scene?"

"This one's really got it bad. He's been consciously into "spanking" since age five, and by 'into' I mean, the word 'spanking' in mixed company still makes him blush."

"But you haven't let him spank you?" Hugo asked.

"I have, but I made it seem like a concession, to prove my love."

"Why so perverse, young lady?" Hugo asked, noticing with some satisfaction, the eye-watering effect the hydroponically grown lesbian weed from Amherst was having upon both girls.

"At first it was a matter of pride. As you pointed out, I was used to holding Colby in contempt, as a lowly jock. His many sterling qualities were not readily apparent and I therefore undervalued him from the outset. I knew from our first session that he was one of us. But the idea of submitting to a beer-guzzling Neanderthal who said "ass" instead of "bottom" was repulsive to me. He earned my respect and admiration over time, in the manner of a Jane Austen hero. You know what I mean, reliable, sturdy, sexually unambiguous. But by then I'd already begun to amuse myself by calling him out as a spanking fetishist without admitting to being one myself. And when he did manage to successfully pull off a scene with me, I pretended to respond to those classic over the knee attentions in a purely sensual mode, as though merely reacting to the adept stimulation of a major erogenous zone."

"You have the boy completely snowed?" Hugo asked.

"He doesn't have a clue in hell as to what I am really about."

"Where did you come by this artfulness?" Hugo mused, but he didn't really wonder, remembering what a discreetly managing little woman her mother was.

"Maybe if I'm lucky, he'll never find out," Amanda said, sincerely dreading the notion of admitting playing such a long and drawn out joke on a hard spanking man.

Hugo left them alone for several hours, during which they enjoyed bubble baths in the private baths connected to their rooms. Thalia continued to marvel at Amanda's good fortune in suddenly discovering such a liberal and well-connected parent. Amanda admitted she had been born under a lucky star.

Hugo picked them up in the early evening and took them to dine at an inn with Hope Spencer Lawrence and her husband David, with whom Amanda had once played. He had spanked her for the real life infraction of coming to one of her teachers. As a high school teacher who found himself beset with lovesick teenaged girls from semester to semester, no matter where he taught, he had expressed a profoundly sincere form of indignation when he paddled Amanda for her own forward behavior with Mr. Keen. Amanda very much wanted to inform Mr. Lawrence that Mr. Keen had turned out to be a rather well tricked out trannie who longed to go submissive to her, but discretion forbade this type of disclosure. She merely reported that she had mastered her desire to go to bed with her teacher and had left him completely alone since her discussion with Mr. Lawrence on the subject.

The girls loved their sophisticated evening out at the inn with their engaging new scene friends. After dinner, Hope and David took Amanda back to their cottage on the cove and they all drank hot chocolate. Amanda thought them impossibly handsome, which only reminded her of Colby, whom she suddenly missed.

Meanwhile, Thalia went home with Hugo, who took her into his sitting room and lit a fire in his own hearth, for it was just the sort of night when one needed extra warmth.

He stood with his arms folded looking at her skeptically and said, "Tell me again why you want this?"

"I'm not perverse. I just like you," she insisted, coming up to him and laying her head against his chest. He locked his arms around her slender body.

"You are perverse. You love to break rules," he murmured into her floral scented smooth light brown hair.

"Because I know I won't get punished," she declared.

"Tonight you will."

Thalia demurely lowered her eyes. Hugo lifted her chin and kissed her.

"You said a lot of things in those emails," he reminded her. "How much of that did you really mean?"

"I can't remember what I wrote because I type them when I'm drunk, but if I said I wanted you to fuck me, that still holds. That's why I was so thrilled when Amanda asked me to join her this weekend. Should I take my clothes off now?"

Hugo told her to wait, banked the fire and took her up to his attic dungeon, which was furnished with leather covered play benches, cheval mirrors, wardrobes full of B&D accessories, chests full of paddles and straps, and a glamorously large box sofa, upholstered in cranberry red, royal blue and gold that appeared intriguingly versatile as a staging area for either discipline or romance.

"Now take your clothes off," he said, loosening his tie and taking off his jacket. He also turned up the thermostat to accommodate his guest's nudity. Thalia's clothes dropped quickly to the floor to reveal the body of a Grecian Venus, though with slightly fuller breasts, high and cherry tipped. The slight chill in the air caused her nipples to stand erect. Her waist was concave and her hips perhaps somewhat wider than was currently fashionable, girding a lushly plump bottom. Her thighs and calves were extremely shapely as well and smooth from regular running. She had slim ankles and feet and was creamy white and pink all over, the essence of dainty, womanly femininity. Her face was especially delightful to gaze upon with her wide-open eyes and wide red mouth so ready to laugh. Her fair complexion combined with the related Celtic trait of blushing often and deeply, imbued her face with a general rosiness that was not unbecoming. Her features were regular, her figure spectacular, with so small a natural waist that fellow fetishists took her for a corset enthusiast. But in the end, it was her quick intelligence and hearty sense of fun that piqued one's continued interest. She affected to be both wanton and mercenary, but she also made a joke of it, so he didn't know how many, if any, of her adventures to believe.

He drew a cream velvet robe piped with quilted satin from the teak clothing armoire and wrapped her in it. Then he gave her a joint to smoke. "You'd better smoke a lot of that. I plan to beat you very hard for all this nonsense about being a call girl," Hugo told her, situating her in the middle of the big, high backed sofa, with everything she needed to become fully relaxed, including a black raspberry cordial. Right on cue, Thalia blushed, but pretended not to be embarrassed.

"It's all right. I only do it for money," she assured him, looking at herself in one of the many mirrors wrapped in the luxurious robe. "Only you would think of handing me a robe," she said, impulsively throwing her arms around his neck and kissing him.

"Don't try to get around me. Yet," he said, putting her from him sternly. "I'm not through lecturing you. Now tell me the truth, are you really meeting strangers in hotels in Boston and giving them b.j.'s and letting them have you?"

"Yes, but I've only done it three times," she admitted. "I mean sex. All the other sessions I've done have been B&D."

"And how are these men finding you?" he demanded.

"I work for a madam," she replied without hesitation.

"Someone in our scene?"

"Yes, as a matter of fact."

"Young, wild and has good weed?" he continued to press her for details.

"Actually, yes," Thalia smiled.

"Don't tell me who she is, I don't want to know. (I think I know who she is.) Still, what you're doing is madness, especially at your age. Boston is a very conservative town when it comes to vice. I'm going to make sure Michael Flagg gives you an even more severe lecture tomorrow. He was a cop in Boston and he can give you the whole run down about what happens when you get busted for prostitution there."

Thalia pouted. "Don't jinx me, Mr. Sands."

"Then give me your word here and now that you're never going out on another such ... assignment." Hugo insisted.

"Is that the advice you're giving Amanda about Mr. Bartlett?"

"Why? Is he trying to bribe her to have sex with him?"

"Yes, I think he is doing just that. She said she got several emails from him last week intimating that he would be able to express his thanks in an extremely material way should she consent to grant him intimacies beyond what passed between them last time they met. He's sent her coats and dresses, fixed up that fashion shoot for her. She doesn't know what to think but she expects to be propositioned this weekend by him."

"I don't think she'd go for anything like that, but even if she did, a stranger is who she'd have to worry about, not a solid scene referral like Ambrose Bartlett. I don't want to have to come to Boston to bail you out of jail."

"You'd do that?"

"Of course," he said, taking a well trimmed, well bound birch rod out of another cabinet, "but allow me to demonstrate the sort of punishment you'd receive for putting me to that type of incon- venience."

He took away the liquor and ashtray and arranged her on the sofa, face down, with her arms pillowed under her head. Then he folded back the robe to expose her entirely bare bottom. The sofa seat was wide and he comfortably sat beside her, placing one hand in the small of her back, while raising the birch in the other and then lowering it across her upturned cheeks any number of times with full vigor and total ease of access. Faster and faster the bundle of closely wrapped birch twigs came down across her exposed pink bottom, swishing and whistling before impact and leaving the most stimulating sting in its wake. Bouquets of roses bloomed across both creamy orbs while her gleaming white thighs also came in for a brisk birching, leaving them similarly hued. She twitched and ground against the sofa seat, her bottom unconsciously rising to the birch. This went on for some time.

She stopped it herself, as she felt herself on the verge of something spectacular and wanted to save that for when he was inside her. Thalia turned over on her back and gave him the same look she had given him in Michael's bar when she'd signaled her availability. Hugo sighed, "You haven't been half punished yet," but readily shed his fine suit and everything that went with it. She looked sumptuous, half in and half out of the velvet and satin robe, completely nude beneath it, a close trimmed triangle of soft brown pubic curls surmounting the slick pinkness of her swollen labia. The birching had provoked an unprece- dented response, as far as she could tell, or perhaps she was simply in love. Meanwhile, Thalia was agreeably surprised by Hugo's trim muscularity. She knew he was lean but had no idea how much time he spent running, skating, biking and working out, to maintain the type of athletic physique that always pleased his lovers.

Hugo sat against the sofa back and handed Thalia a condom. Birching her and beholding her glamorous young charms had aroused him to a rampant state and all 7.5 inches of his clean, cut masculinity jumped to attention in her honor.

She continued to take his breath away by first placing the condom in her mouth and then artfully working it down over his cock with her lips. "Are you kidding me?" he asked, with open admiration. She shrugged, as much as to modestly admit, "Call girl."

Hugo had her mount him facing him, squeezing her large, luscious, stiff-nippled breasts in his hands and then pulling her down by her waist until she sat down hard in his lap, with every pulsating inch of his manhood deeply lodged her clinging, clenching vagina. He embraced and held her close, covering her throat and ears with kisses and taking her bottom cheeks in his hands while she worked her pussy up and down on his cock, her natural lubricity making the ride a delight. Once he had her bottom in his hands, he didn't let it go. He squeezed, patted, spanked and pinched her well-birched orbs and finally separated them to nudge one long, middle finger into her glove-tight bottom hole. Faster and faster she rode him, her light little body bouncing up and down frantically, her dainty muff grinding against his groin until her quickening pants announced the beginning of the end. Sealing the passionate encounter with the deepest French kisses imaginable, sex and romance merged into one phenomenally erotic and emotional experience that brought them off within moments of each other.

They drifted off in each other's arms, starting awake at almost the same moment less than a quarter of an hour later.

"We should go pick up Amanda," said Hugo, planting a final kiss behind one of her ears.

Thalia rose to dress. Hugo got up too but kept his eyes on his admirer while they busied themselves with buttons and belts.

Once they were back in their street clothes Hugo said, "I want to give you some allowance." He took some cash out of his billfold and stuck it in the back pocket of her tight blue jeans.

Thalia stared at him in surprise.

"You're paying me?"

"I can spoil you a little," Hugo said easily, not so much because he'd had her twice and knew she was used to getting paid for sex by older men, but because he wanted her to buy herself more sweaters, short tight skirts and boots.

"Thanks!" she grinned. "This almost cancels out the fact that I came on to you."

"Thalia, promise me you won't go out on any more sex calls?"

"But I started getting used to the money," she protested.

"You can make plenty of money just doing B&D sessions."

"Will you get me hooked up with some clients?"

"Of course I will. In fact, why don't you start with Ambrose Bartlett?"

"I'm game," Thalia agreed at once. She'd never met the department store owner but Amanda had shown her his photo online and aroused her with the story of his crude usage of herself in December. "At any rate, I'm content to be Amanda's cock blocker as regards Bartlett. That's what friends are for. And I got to see you."

"You're sweet. But if my beloved knew I was fucking my eighteen-year-old daughter's nineteen-year-old friend she might use it as an excuse to back out of our engagement. Laura just found out about me going to see Amanda's mother in San Francisco and it didn't sit well with her."

"Well, she'll never hear anything about it from Amanda or me."

"Oh, Amanda knows about what happened at Michael's bar?"

"She is my best friend," Thalia pointed out.

"That's lovely," Hugo smiled at her.

Hugo and Thalia drove over to Cobweb Cottage and picked up Amanda, then returned together to Susan's house. The girls insisted on Hugo coming in. He lit the fire in Amanda's bedroom and they sat chatting for another hour before Thalia's eyes began to involuntarily close. When Amanda walked him downstairs to let him out they embraced affectionately.

"Did Cassandra say anything about my visiting her?" Hugo asked while putting on his overcoat.

"She said you were as handsome as ever but rather severe," Amanda replied with a smile.

"When she came to my room she had on a ball gown made of gold tissue and gauze."

"She must have bought it especially for you."

"She looked like a dream. I was bowled over."

"I'm so glad!" Amanda hugged him again.

"Of course looking like that, she softened me up, so she didn't get nearly the beating she deserved for keeping you a secret for so long."

"I'll notate that technique for future reference," Amanda said appreciatively.

Even though it was very cold on that clear, starry night, Amanda grabbed her coat and walked Hugo out to his car, hanging on his arm the whole way.

On parting he said, "Try to discourage Thalia from the call girl madness, would you? I'm worried for her safety in Boston doing that."

"I will!"

"And as for you, young lady, don't be afraid to say no to Ambrose Bartlett."

"That's why I brought Thalia. I'm counting on one glimpse of her wasp waist to slay him."

But Amanda was less confident about her ability to repulse the advances of Ambrose Bartlett the following morning when Hope picked her up to drive her to the department store. Thalia was sleeping in, but had promised to meet her at Bartlett's and catch the second fashion show at eleven. It was a cold, snowy morning but intoxicatingly warm inside Hope's new luxury sedan. She had been saving for her own car for several years and had made sure to choose one large enough to transport several friends in extreme comfort. Amanda's bewitching blonde driver was clad in a long, blue-gray military style coat with faux fur lapels, frogged buttons and capacious pockets. She wore cuffed mahogany leather thigh high boots with gloves to match and a small, jaunty blue gray hat sat atop her head.

Under the coat she had on a matching skirt and vest the same color as the coat, over a white shirt. Hope was also to model apparel in the fashion shows that morning and brimmed over with excitement at the attention she would get and the free outfits she would bring home. Clothing mattered very much to both young women and they took these opportunities seriously. But Amanda was troubled by the prospect of confronting this first dominant she had ever done a professional session with a second time, especially in light of the emails he'd been sending her, suggesting they take the scene step further next time, with appropriate rewards.

"Should I have returned the coats and dresses he sent me?" Amanda asked Hope.

"Why? Do you feel they put you under some sort of obligation?"

"Yes!"

"May I ask what he paid you for the first session?"

"Nothing, but he let me shoot content for my video in his store."

"And what did the session consist of?"

"He spanked me nude, to tears and made me stand in the corner while he jacked off."

"Really?" Hope was amazed, having played with Bartlett a number of times without him ever unzipping his trousers. "And how many coats has he sent you?"

"Two coats, six dresses and two pair of boots. Good boots."

"That seems just about right considering you're only 18, gorgeous and ivy league. You don't owe him anything else. In fact, I'm a bit shocked he took that much advantage, you being Hugo's daughter," Hope said.

"I know. It seemed a bit much even to me," Amanda agreed. "Oh and I forgot, he got me a modeling gig in Boston at the new Damaris shop that just opened there. I got paid well and got to keep outfits."

"He knows you're into outfits and he has an endless supply, but that doesn't mean he gets to own you."

"What do you think of him?" Amanda asked as they drove the rainy coast road between Random Point and Woodbridge.

"I like him," said Hope. "And I'm into outfits too. But he's never j.o.ed in my presence. That's so Hollywood B&D dungeon."

"I know!" Amanda agreed.

"Does Hugo know about the jacking off bit?"

"No, I just told him Bartlett made me cry. He regretted setting up the gig for me because he could see I was upset afterwards, but he doesn't know how sleazy his old school buddy can get."

"That was good, Amanda, I mean your not telling all."

The girls had a few minutes to spare once they reached Woodbridge, so they took a side lane paralleling the street that Bartlett's dominated and smoked a joint.

"I don't think your idea of distracting Mr. Bartlett with Thalia is going to fly," said Hope. "He seems to be more partial to blondes."

"Why, is he nuts about you too?"

"Not just me. His ex-wife Paula Rohan was a natural blonde as well. And he's still in a monumentally bad mood about having let her slip through his fingers."

"But isn't his lover a stunning brunette?" Amanda asked, remembering the slender elegance of Pamela Crane at the Boston fashion shoot.

"Yes, but Mr. Bartlett honestly doesn't appreciate her. Pamela used to go out with Sloan Taylor, my boss at the shop. But first Hugo, then Mr. Bartlett seduced her away from him. Mr. Bartlett's then wife, Paula, found out about the affair between Mr. Bartlett and Pamela and went straight to Sloan with the information. Strangely enough, Paula and Sloan decided they were more compatible with each other than they were with Mr. Bartlett and Pamela, so right away, Paula left Mr. Bartlett. After divorcing Mr. Bartlett, Paula immediately married Sloan. Pamela remained at Bartlett's to run the Damaris boutique and became his official mistress. But he's still upset about having lost his creamy blonde wife and as a consequence, seems hesitant to add his initial to Pamela's monogram, though it would mean everything to her."

"Poor Pamela, she never seems to get what she wants, does she?"

"He did give her an engagement ring," Hope felt it only fair to add.

"How strange that an exquisite scene beauty should consider an asshole dom like Mr. Bartlett her last option," Amanda mused, with pity for Pamela.

Hope parked in the lot behind Bartlett's and the girls penetrated the fashion bastion via the employees' entrance. They took the employees' elevator upstairs to the second floor where the fashion show was to be held, in Designer Apparel. The service hall led them to a large dressing room where Pamela and three or four of the other most lissome clerks were already dressing in their first outfits. The in-house seamstress and half the staff of the juniors department, serving as dresser assistants, were readying all the subsequent outfits to be donned quickly. The employee fashion show was put on as a way to stimulate salesmen and women to better inform shoppers of the unique and luxurious contents of the Bartlett coffers. The second show, at eleven, was for discriminating customers who looked forward to this monthly event in the designer salon.

Ambrose Bartlett, polished and smart in a fine wool navy pin-striped suit with slim lapels, strolled through the dressing room at two minutes before the show was to begin, nodding and smiling at the amateur models, who in addition to earning extra pay bonuses for their trouble, enjoyed the prestige of representing the deluxe emporium. Even Bartlett's gift boxes were lined with blue velvet and trimmed with gold. But it was not for this reason that Amanda's heart began to pound the moment he stepped into her mirror space. She turned and awkwardly shook his hand.

"I'm so glad you could make it, Amanda," Bartlett said with the blandest of smiles, as Pamela's eye was upon him as she also adjusted her outfit in a mirror before leading off the show.

Amanda was last out and as Pamela was well out of eye and earshot, Bartlett said softly to Amanda, "I really am happy you're here."

"Thank you," Amanda stammered, feeling her face go red.

"What's the matter sweetheart?" he asked, noticing at once.

"Nothing, it's just warm in here," she murmured, hastening to join the others on the catwalk in the main salon. Bartlett went out to sit and watch the show, uncertain what to make of her confusion but finding her more bewitching than ever. He knew he had to have her, no matter how much that privilege cost. He also knew he was being willfully perverse, running after inappropriate girls and women who reminded him of his flaxen haired wife, but that didn't stop him wanting to possess them. Finally, he knew he was betraying Pamela, who had come to love him, in her high strung, obsessive compulsive way, and was prepared to throw her lot in with his, in spite of the fourteen year age difference and his bad temper. Pamela was almost everything he wanted in a lover and would make a show wife, the exact kind of spouse Paula never had the patience or inclination to be. But he mistrusted Pamela. He knew she'd been prepared to cheat on her fiancé, albeit with him. He'd caught her shoplifting. He suspected she took speed. Her character flaws were numerous. On the plus side, she was an educated beauty, an elegant designer and a sincere submissive who would never slip up into the double digit dress sizes, his one bone of contention with the otherwise peerless Paula Rohan. So why didn't he love Pamela more? He didn't know and had no time to care. He only knew that he wanted to dominate Amanda Sands again and as soon as possible.

Thalia came to the eleven o'clock show and sat with her coat open, so as to display the remarkable contours of her magnificently feminine body in her wool sweater, mini-skirt, tights and 4" high heeled calf high boots. After the show Amanda introduced her to Bartlett as "my friend, who starred in that video that we shot here over Christmas."

"Really!" Bartlett looked at Thalia again. "Very nice." Thalia lowered her eyes submissively.

"She's amazingly ...uninhibited."

"Is this true, Thalia?" Ambrose touched Thalia's shoulder lightly, causing her to look up at him with her wide, babyish blue eyes.

"Yes, I'm putting myself through college as a call girl," said Thalia without blushing, because Hugo had given her no specific admonition against engaging with Bartlett, and in fact seemed to wish her to draw Bartlett's fire away from Amanda.

Amanda looked at Thalia with shock, then looked around for Pamela. But Pamela had accompanied a few of the security men while they wheeled several racks of expensive furs back into the fur salon cold storage rooms.

"Where do you go to school?" Ambrose asked.

"B.U."

"I'm in Boston about once a week. We should have lunch," he said, handing her his card.

"I don't have any classes on Friday afternoons," she said helpfully.

"I'll remember that," he said pleasantly, then added, "Would you excuse us for moment, Thalia?"

"Oh yes, I was just going shopping anyway. Meet me in lingerie, Amanda," said Thalia, promptly abandoning Amanda to Ambrose. All around them discreet, well-groomed saleswomen assisted customers who wished to purchase the costumes they had seen during the fashion show.

"Come up to my office for a moment, Amanda, and I'll cut you a check."

Amanda's heart accelerated again as she quietly accompanied Mr. Bartlett to his richly furnished office, draped and upholstered in brown, cream and taupe, with a groomed and elegant view of quaint Woodbridge Street four stories below. Ambrose smiled at her only slightly less blandly than before and sat down to write her a one hundred dollar check for that morning's work in the fashion shows, as promised. Amanda had also been invited to select two outfits that she had worn to take home. But the envelope he had slipped the check into and subsequently handed her appeared to also contain a frighteningly large wad of hundred dollar bills.

"What's this?" Amanda asked with wonder.

"I want you to spend a few hours with me tonight at The Owl," said Ambrose, naming the largest inn at Woodbridge.

"What are you trying to buy, Mr. Bartlett, my soul?" Amanda said, looking up after noting that the envelope contained about fifty hundred-dollar bills.

He laughed, "No, but I want you, in every way."

"But I have a boyfriend now."

"Haven't you always had a boyfriend?"

"In a manner of speaking, but this time it's serious. And I'm in love," she claimed, appalled at how much her assertion sounded like a plea.

"Aw, that's nice. So use the money go to Europe with your boyfriend this summer," said Bartlett, reading her racing mind.

"No. I couldn't. It would be wrong on every level," she said, extracting the hundred-dollar check from the envelope and passing the cash back across the desk to him.

"Two hours of your time, Amanda. You're in Random Point anyway. And I promise it won't be anything like in December. I spanked you to tears then, I don't need to do that again."

"But what do you mean you want me in every way? You want to penetrate me anally?" she demanded.

"Yes! Exactly."

Amanda sighed, "You can do all of that with Thalia for a fraction of this," she gestured at the heavy envelope.

"Thanks for telling me that. I will! She's absolutely delicious. Haven't seen a body like that in I don't know how long. But she's not you."

"Hugo advised me not to do anything other than pure B&D while still in college."

"Sweetheart, you can trust to my discretion."

"But what about Pamela? She'd hate me if she ever found out."

"No one will tell Pamela."

"What if she happens to be strolling through The Owl when we're there?"

"She's going out of town tonight."

"That's convenient. But what about my conscience, my ethics, my morals? How can I face my new boyfriend if I give you everything? Including things he himself hasn't even had yet."

Logically these arguments should have drenched Bartlett's ardor in ice water but he only found himself more inflamed by her coolness and poise. He honestly didn't care that she wasn't attracted to him and was thinking up every possible reason to reject his tempting offer. He only knew that she was flawless and that he wished to possess her completely.

"You don't have to give me head or even kiss me. You can be completely passive, like a mannequin or doll, and just let me take you."

193

"Really?" She looked at him anew. "You want me to play dead?"

"Not exactly, but that would work."

"Mr. Bartlett, I'm only eighteen years old. This is too much for me, too soon."

"Listen Amanda, how about this, you meet me and we play pure B&D for a while. If you want to stop there, we can. You can keep whatever part of the allowance you think fair. But if I succeed in sending you into true subspace, you give me what I want."

"That's an interesting proposal. Let me think it over this afternoon. If I decide I'm up to this, I'll call you by five pm to confirm."

Amanda met Thalia in the lingerie department and they made purchases. Then they joined Hope in the chic café on the third floor of the store. The three young women sat in a booth, ravenously hungry after modeling and shopping all morning. Chicken and tuna salad sandwiches, accompanied by large stacks of perfect French fries and pots of brewed tea arrived shortly, making all three very happy. Lingering over shared slices of chocolate torte and cherry cobbler, Amanda voiced her many misgivings over meeting Mr. Bartlett at the Owl that night, though in very low tones, considering they were still in Barlett's store. Both Hope and Thalia advised Amanda to tell Hugo about the offer and ask his advice but Amanda was reluctant to even admit that she was considering such an adventure to her blood relation.

"He doesn't want to be put in a position where he has to tell me what to do, but if I'm honest about Mr. Bartlett's offer, how can he not try to dissuade me?"

"Hugo is practical. He's the best person to look at this proposition from every angle and decide whether it's proper or improper to pursue," said Hope.

Thalia snorted, "We all know it's improper to pursue."

"Which begs the question, is it going to fuck with your head?" asked Hope.

"Damn it, I know I should say no, but on some stupid level I can't explain, I don't want to insult Mr. Bartlett by refusing his offer."

"No one could accuse an eighteen year old girl of haughtiness for refusing to sell her body," said Hope.

"You don't think I should do it, do you?" Amanda asked Hope.

"I think you might feel badly afterwards," said Hope, who had only allowed her sessions to become overtly sexual with persons to whom she was otherwise extremely attracted.

"And you think I should do it, don't you?" Amanda asked Thalia, who nodded emphatically.

After lunch, Hope drove them back to Random Point, dropping them off at Polyxena Guzman's gym and European spa while she herself returned to work at the bookstore. Thalia used some of the allowance Hugo had given her to purchase a massage from Dieter Brandt while Amanda swam in the pool, then relaxed in the steam room, sauna and Jacuzzi, all the while trying to decide what to tell Mr. Bartlett when she called him at five. She thought back to December, when she had been going to meet Mr. Bartlett for the first time, recalling how she had even considered letting him make love to her, (if the session had gone well), as a new way of getting a thrill from the scene, through sex with a much older man. Her entire attitude at that juncture had been frivolous and light. But the harsh discipline he'd administered had completely extinguished any sensual curiosity she'd felt about the department store owner's sexual capabilities and she found herself repulsed by his predatory authoritarianism. Today he had seemed somewhat softer and more friendly, less demanding, more conciliating. Perhaps he would be nicer this time. He had looked very good in the navy wool suit.

Amanda's Diary
Sunday, February 22nd

Returning to Boston with Thalia, by train, with time to record the most tumultuous night of my life.

I'm not really sure what made me decide to go to Mr. Bartlett after all, but quite honestly, the five thousand dollars cinched the deal.

Thalia and Hope dropped me off at The Owl at six, then proceeded to Michael Flagg's bar where they planned to have dinner and visit with that tavern's amiable owner for several hours.

I was dressed in clothes I had mostly received from Mr. Bartlett, namely: a short, cream wool knit pencil skirt and matching cropped cardigan over a white shirt, with cuffed, 3" stack-heeled, café au lait suede knee boots and a matching shearling coat with a white notched collar and fine buffed suede finish. The coat was tailored, luxurious and a perfect fit. He seems to take great care in choosing my presents.

Mr. Bartlett had told me to take the elevator straight up to the third floor and knock on the door of suite 301. He let me in with a pleasant smile. He was still in the navy suit from that morning but I noticed he had a different shirt and tie on. He must have showered and changed before I got there. He's a meticulous man and would do that before this arranged seduction.

If I only had time to describe the ravishing suite appointments, suffice to say, I've seldom seen a prettier set of rooms. Mr. Bartlett had ordered pots of coffee and tea along with a tray of small sandwiches and petit fours for me, but my tummy was in absolute knots and I had only a small cup of red tea.

My host seemed much more relaxed and at leisure than the previous time we had been alone together, no doubt because Pamela was out of town.

He began by making me a few compliments, about how well I had looked in the fashion show that morning and how nicely I had photographed for the Damaris shop ads. I felt my face go hot as all I could think about was how soon he planned to start thrashing and violating my body.

"Why were you so reluctant to see me again?" he finally asked; "Was our first encounter that terrible?"

"Yes," I replied, staring down at the beautiful suede boots. "It hurt like hell and you treated me like a cheap session in a questionable dungeon."

"How do you know about dungeons?"

"I'm from San Francisco."

"Look Amanda, I'm sorry about that. It was coarse to objectify you like that. But I was in a bad mood due to it being the one-year anniversary of my wife having left me. And also, I didn't know what to think about this publicity stunt you have going on with your so-called father, Hugo Sands."

"It's not a publicity stunt," I sputtered.

"No?"

"Why do you doubt I'm Hugo's daughter?"

"Well, obviously, because he set up a session between us. And he put you on the cover of his magazine."

"Hugo didn't know I was his daughter when we did that photo shoot. I pretended to be a model from Boston and only confessed to my true identity half way through the shoot, when the real model called from the station. He wasn't going to print the photos but I promised that if he put me on the cover of the New Rod Quarterly I'd postpone my lifelong dream of posing for Playboy at least until after I turned 21."

"Unbelievable," said Mr. Bartlett, feeling for a cigarette case in his jacket pocket then seeming to realize that he had recently given up smoking.

"I'm sure you've been reading the magazine since its debut twenty years ago. My mother was Hugo's sweetheart. She was the first model ever to appear on a cover of the magazine and his first female editor. I only found out about all of this myself at age twelve, when I found the magazines on the top shelf of the bookcase. Mother left Hugo without him ever knowing about her pregnancy. The moment I learned the truth I wanted to meet him, but she convinced me to wait until I was an adult. And she was right."

"Does he know you're here tonight?" Mr. Bartlett asked, as though the idea troubled him.

"No. I never mentioned your outrageous proposal to me because I knew he'd be bound to tell me not to do this."

"Why do you say that? He's been fine with you doing everything else."

"I never told him any of the details of our first encounter. He only knows that you spanked me hard."

"I'm glad of that," Mr. Bartlett said.

"I only tell everything to my diary," I said. "And my best girlfriends."

"Would Hope Lawrence be one of those?"

"Yes. I completely adore her."

"Hope always insists on smoking the stinkiest skunk weed she can find before we play. Feel free to do the same if it will relax you. I always bribe the inn keeper not to put anyone else on this floor."

I took him at his word and filled a pipe. If I was going through with this I did need to be almost completely boneless. I had no sooner taken a hit then he extended his well-manicured hand for the pipe, saying, "I just quit smoking cigarettes and I want to smoke something." For a few minutes we smoked and stared at each other. I felt my shoulders relaxing first and then every other part of me. Then Mr. Keen popped into my head.

"You're such a control freak, Mr. Bartlett, are you sure you don't want ME to spank and fuck YOU?"

"Very sure, Amanda," he laughed. "But thank you for asking."

"That's good," I said, relieved to hear this as I wasn't actually prepared to follow through on the suggestion.

"Why do you even think that, girl?" he asked, smiling like a normal human being for once.

"Oh, a lot of things, your fussiness, your fixation with clothes and feminine perfection. You've got Preston Sturges syndrome to a very high degree. Though I haven't noticed you running after any sisters yet."

"Hope could be your sister," Mr. Bartlett pointed out, wandering just a little from the topic, as stoned people do.

"Hope likes you and I like Hope," I told him, "which give me hope that I might some day like you too."

"What the hell is Preston Sturges syndrome?"

"Haven't you ever seen a Sturges movie? The hero is always deluging the heroine with coat boxes and hatboxes and dress boxes, boxes of every kind, all containing luxe clothes and accessories. In fact, the shopping spree is a staple of every Sturges seduction."

"You amaze me, Amanda, when did you have time to watch old movies?"

"I took a film course one summer and Sturges was one of the directors we studied. What stood out the most to me was Sturges' playful, ultra feminized sexuality."

"You're right I'm a control freak but it's not a reverse D&S thing, it's just in my blood. I've been working at the store in one way or another since I was ten, I've been through every department as both employee and manager and I've learned that details are what matter. But you're dead on about one thing, my objective is to help stylish women achieve visual perfection. You are both my muse and my preferred customer, alluring in my apparel and unable to resist the allure of it yourself."

"About that, Mr. Bartlett, why do you keep sending me these fancy outfits and thus continually putting me under obligation to you?" I demanded, all my inhibitions dropping away. He seemed so different this time that I lost my fear of him.

"I was just trying to recompense you more fairly for that first time, Amanda. There's nothing average about you and in retrospect I felt that simply allowing you to shoot in my store was not adequate payment for the pain and humiliation you suffered at my hands."

"Well, I think you've done that pretty handsomely, Mr. Bartlett," I conceded. "I have the best wardrobe in Cambridge, bar none."

"That's nice, Amanda," he smiled again. "I love seeing you well dressed. In fact, I love looking at you." I believed him. I am ornamental and he loves ornaments. I pulled my shoulders back and let him look at me. He extended his hand and led me into the bedroom.

The bed was very high and wide and was covered with a crimson counterpane trimmed with gold. He carefully bent me over the edge and arranged me so my arms pillowed my head. Then he proceeded with a surprising amount of finesse to unwrap me like an expensive package, pushing up my skirt to my waist and fully appreciating my sheer backed white high cut briefs and white lace garter belt, attached to real beige nylons. Holding me in place pretty firmly, he used just his hand on my bottom through the filmy panties for a very long time, administering a really proper warm up. I let myself relax into the bed. (I was so stoned.)

Then I felt him pull my panties down to my thighs. Now he took his belt off and doubled it. I turned to see him do it.

"You're using a strap?" I gulped.

"You can say mercy any time," he told me.

"Okay," I meekly subsided and gripped the counterpane with both fists. But I needn't have feared. He eased into the strapping slowly, aimed carefully and let each swat sink in before laying on the next. I found myself breathing sighs (instead of screaming screams), just to encourage him to stick with this subtle new style of corporal punishment that was so superior to his jackhammer approach of old. I realized he was trying to seduce me and I didn't fight it. It was actually vital I enjoy this encounter, otherwise I really would be a whore and that's not me. I don't feel badly about what happened last night between Mr. Bartlett and me, except for having cheated on my beloved Colby and the aftermath of this misstep, which I will presently describe.

The strapping went on for some time, building very slowly in intensity. I was nowhere near the mercy zone when he finished, but I could see in the reflection of another mirror's reflection, that my cheeks were evenly stained dark rose. The surface of my skin was beginning to sting and feel hot but in a pleasant way. I was conscious of undulating my bottom at him, as I had begun to want to please him.

He placed a palm on each cheek and began to massage away the sting, then to spread me ever so slightly, especially down towards my pussy. He moved his long fingers down to my upper thighs and pushed them well apart. I kicked off my panties altogether. The more he spread me, the more I wanted to be spread and finally, to be probed. But he teased me for a few minutes, spanking me with his hand and making me forget the strapping. He'd spank me, then squeeze me, then spread me, but not attempt to penetrate me, not even with a fingertip. Then finally, he lay his whole palm against my pussy slit and felt how wet I'd become.

It must have been the power of suggestion that rendered me so pliant to his manipulations. He'd said he would send me to subspace directly and I was already there, floating, feeling and pulsating in response to said floating feelings.

I heard him say, "Take it one step further, Amanda?" And I heard myself murmur some sort of assent.

To make a long story short, he spread me and spanked me until I longed to be penetrated; then he finger fucked me until (I'm pretty sure) I really wanted his cock and finally he fucked me in just such a way that I was left panting for a sensation even more extreme and ended up yielding my bottom to him as well. He had good lube and the sheer slipperiness of it cinched my acquiescence. Before every new variation he'd ask me if I was up for it, giving me every opportunity to cry, "Stop, I've had enough." But it all felt fine and I stopped nothing. I let it all happen to me just as he wanted it to. And after it was over, I actually liked him.

I took my clothes into the lavishly appointed bathroom to quickly shower before dressing again. I had a text message on my phone from Colby. It read: "Playing pond hockey on Cape 2nite. Let's hookup?" My heart jumped into my throat. I'd actually forgotten about Colby's existence for the last hour and a half. My pleasure in the rich trappings of my surroundings vanished to be replaced by old-fashioned guilt. I hurried through my ablutions, regretting I would not have time to experience the super plush inn robes provided. I did use a large quantity of the almond moisturizing lotion that I found on the vanity though. In doing so I chanced to see my reflection in a full-length mirror. My bottom was dark red, the kind of red that would take hours to fade. I also detected a few distinct strap marks, well and evenly placed across the centermost portion of my bottom. Any eye used to the aftermath of corporal punishment would instantly identify those marks as having come from a belt or thin strap. If I got together with Colby later that night I could not let him see me undressed at any cost!

I dressed, combed out and quickly blew dry my hair and put on a little rose colored lipstick before rejoining Mr. Bartlett. He'd restored himself in the other bathroom and had also gotten dressed again. He seemed relaxed and satisfied. He had both worn a condom and achieved a rather enthusiast climax while deep inside the deepest part of me, so even though he'd gone against his nature and been nice instead of mean that night, I'm assuming he got what he wanted from me. When he pulled me against him in a hug, I neither resisted nor wished to resist. He had been charming that night, so I felt completely comfortable being hugged by him. Here, I felt, was the Mr. Bartlett Hope knew and admired. That other fellow I had met the first time must have been some aberration.

The last thing he did before we left the suite was to slip that big, fat envelope of cash into my shoulder bag. Then we went downstairs.

As we passed through the lobby, with its traditional inn fire blazing in the hearth, I happened to look into the dining room and then got a terrible shock. The room was crammed with college boys in fleece sweaters and wool leggings, perhaps a half dozen of them, ranged around one of the largest tables, and finishing off a large meal. The boys were ruddy, noisy and exuberant as only a group of hockey players with hip flasks on a twenty-degree night in New England can be. Among them was Colby, who saw me the moment I saw him.

"Mr. Bartlett," I said quickly, "I won't need that lift home after all. I just spotted my boyfriend in the other room and he saw me too."

"Amanda, get a hold of yourself. You've gone red as a beet," Mr. Bartlett softly recommended, shaking my hand goodbye in the blandest possible manner while audibly saying on Colby's approach, "Well, good night. I'll expect you for the Spring fashion show."

"I'll be there, Mr. Bartlett. Thank you."

The next thing I knew, Mr. Bartlett had disappeared into the taproom, where he joined Dieter Brandt, the masseur, who was sitting at the bar drinking. And then Colby was right in front of me.

'Babe! What luck running into you!" he said, embracing me warmly. I tried to concentrate every fiber of my being on restoring my color to something normal while looking as casual as I possibly could. "Amanda, what's wrong? You're flushing like crazy."

"I'm just excited to see you." And my heart really was pounding at a fantastic rate.

"Who was that, your dad?"

"No, Mr. Bartlett, the department store owner. I did some modeling at his store today."

"Hey, Amanda, let me dump these jokers and I can take you anywhere you want to go. I've got a car tonight."

I hesitated, checking my watch. It was only just eight. I wanted to be with him, but how could I keep him from seeing my marks, were we to become intimate, which we surely would the moment we were alone. I told him I had promised to go visit my father and he insisted on taking me there and meeting Hugo. I quickly called Hugo to clear this, out of earshot of Colby, while he kissed off his friends.

I rapidly explained the entire situation to Hugo without reserve, that I'd just done a big session with Mr. Bartlett, was marked and had just run into my new boyfriend, who had been playing pond hockey, and who knew nothing about me being in the scene, even though he was into it himself. Hugo advised me to bring Colby straight over, promising beer and sports talk in abundance. "After a couple of hours of that on top of playing hockey, he'll be sleepy enough for you to fend off until your marks fade," said Hugo, ever helpfully logical.

Hugo didn't have to do much to win Colby over. He was an old Harvard man, played hockey and didn't mind that Colby was fucking his daughter, so what was there for Colby not to like? Hugo entertained us in his den for a couple of hours, in exactly the way he'd described, which blessed time allowed me to completely decompress from my intense session, during which, I have to admit, I did climax. While Hugo and Colby chatted, I wandered behind their chairs looking at Hugo's books, but mentally reviewing what had happened to me that day in minute detail. The important thing was not to let Colby see my marks. I don't know why I need to keep up this charade of not being into spanking with my new boy, but since I've taken it this far, I'm curious to see how far I can actually go with it, just for the sake of a challenge.

At around ten I pleaded fatigue and asked Colby to take me home. He and Hugo parted fast friends and I felt I could reasonably beg off doing anything but going straight to sleep that night. But by the time he had driven me back to Susan's house, Colby was wide-awake again. He asked me quite politely whether he could spend the night with me in the guest residence to which I had the keys. I couldn't lie, I did want to spend the night with him, and I had no reason to believe that Susan Ross would dislike me allowing Colby to stay over. I assented with the stipulation that we go right to bed, because I felt extremely tired by this time, having started my day so early and done the fashion shows, etc. Colby agreed with alacrity and bounded up the stairs after me. I asked him to make up a fire in the bedroom that had been assigned to me. Thalia wasn't home from Michael Flagg's tavern yet. While Colby was tending to the fire I changed in the locked bathroom into a beautiful pair of ivory silk satin pajamas and a matching dressing gown that mother gave me over the holidays. With the lights turned down, in bed together, Colby would go insane rubbing against me. With any luck we could have sex, I could pull up my pajamas and get away with him not seeing my bottom at all that night or even the following morning. While I was changing I checked the marking. My bottom was still rosy all over, with a few faint strap marks besides. The overall color had started to fade, but it was far too richly saturated to appear normal in any way. I could not let him see my bottom that night!

When I came out he'd gotten the fire going cheerily and was sitting on a loveseat opposite it. He motioned for me to come sit on his lap, which I did at once. He immediately began to feel me through the heavenly silk satin fabric and a large erection came to life under me in seconds. We kissed and kissed. His hands kept going from my buttocks to my waist to my breasts while his lips traveled back and forth from my mouth to my throat to my ears.

I suppose with the crackling of the fire and our sheer concentration on kissing and squeezing each other, we didn't hear Thalia open the door downstairs or come up the stairs. But the next thing I knew, I heard her voice as she approached my bedroom door, which was slightly ajar, inquiring in her usual robustly cynical style, "Well, did we achieve full call girl status tonight with Mr. Bartlett?" The next moment she was in the room, gaping at Colby while he stared at her first and then me. I scrambled up off his lap, the ground disintegrating under me. What possible come back could I produce that would counteract the effect of those twelve fatal words?

"Amanda, what the hell is she talking about, call girl status?"

"Ignore her, she's just projecting. I ate an innocent meal with my boss tonight, that's all," I airily replied, but my burning cheeks belied my assertion. Colby looked at us.

"She's right. Ignore, me, I'm raving. I snuck a bunch of drinks tonight at that bar. I think I'll go take a bath," Thalia said, and escaped into her bedroom at the other end of the hall.

"Amanda?"

"What?"

"Did you let that old geezer pay you for sex?"

Before I could even answer, his eyes fell on my bag, which was full of cash. There was no way he could know that but I couldn't think of anything else. The pressure was too much. I'm not used to lying. I met his eyes and replied, "Yes."

"Amanda, I'm shocked," he actually almost staggered backwards.

"I know. Me too. But he paid me five thousand dollars so I found it hard to say no."

He absorbed this information with interest and in total silence for about a minute, just looking at me with a mixture of wonder and exasperation. Finally he sputtered, "So Little Miss Court Me For Five Weeks turns out to be a hooker? You know this is just the sort of situation where a good spanking would make perfect sense!"

"Oh no, I don't agree. Just because I let you spank me once, that doesn't mean I've gone lifestyle. If I let you spank me for this, you'll want to spank me for every little thing from now on. I'd be walking around permanently sore!"

"Every little thing? Selling your body is not a little thing."

"Fuck off Colby, I saw your eyebrows shoot up when I said five large. You know you're impressed."

I knew he was more fascinated than upset when he had to crack wise, "I didn't realize what a good tutor I was. You should get an A in economics for getting that much out of the old goat. Maybe I should manage you."

"Right, because pimps get to keep their 'ho's in line with corporal punishment, don't they?" Then, before he had a chance to recover from that thrust home, I finished him off with a neat, "Tell me you'd turn down that kind of offer from a good looking older woman, Colby."

He just looked at me with narrowed eyes, probably hating me for outsmarting him yet again. Evading the question he asked, "Do you do this often?"

"No. This was the first and last time," I sighed. Then I sat down and told him half of the truth about Ambrose Bartlett, the part about him becoming attracted to me after my modeling in the first fashion show and the parts about him sending me clothes and emails and setting up the modeling shoot in Boston, then how I'd felt somehow obligated to him for these considerations, which made it harder for me to resist his proposition without giving offence. "If I could take it back, I would. I didn't want to really do it. I just kept thinking about how I only wanted to be with you. But he suavely seduced me into agreeing to the plan. And I did it. I'm very sorry. I meant it when I said that I love you."

It was a lot to give him and I was eager to see what he would do with the gift, whether he'd be big or small about it. He paced around a bit then stopped in front of me.

"I won't be satisfied unless you let me spank you."

"No! It's too clichéd. I won't be objectified just because I committed an error of judgment. Did my behavior give you a disgust of me?"

"No."

"Do you consider me a slut?"

"Not really. More of a hypocrite. You played the prude with me forever, Amanda. And now I see how easy you are."

"You worked for what you got, but you got it for free," I pointed out.

"You're bad, you're really bad," he said, looking at me with wonder.

I drew back my shoulders and looked at him, as if coming to a decision. "I'll consider your request to spank me."

"You will?" his face broke into an involuntary smile.

"I'd like to think it over overnight. I don't want to start a precedent where you think you can turn me over you knee whenever you feel like it."

I saw his zipper front throb when I used that expression.

"Therefore, if you stay here with me tonight you have to give me your solemn word of honor that you won't attempt to ...punish me before I give you leave."

Smart enough to realize that I was simply postponing an inevitability, Colby bowed his head in acquiescence. He took my hand and swore that if I permitted him to stay the night with me and place his unworthy body beside my satin wrapped goddesshood that he would not so much as breathe a disrespectful word in my shell like ear, no less raise a hand to my divine person. I could see he sincerely wanted to get laid as soon as possible and put out the lights.

When we dove beneath the sumptuous down coverlet and thousand thread count sheets he was naked and I was in my satin jammies. I turned my back to him, let him slide the pants down and off in the dark and then I let him penetrate me from behind, while his nimble fingers located my clit and massaged my breasts. The urgency of his teenaged need for my tight pussy had completely tamed or subverted his jealousy into pure sexual energy. He pulled me back against him while plunging in deeply again and again, unerringly massaging my lower abdomen and stimulating my g-spot relentlessly until I orgasmed against his hand and all around his pulsating cock. Reminding him that he had forgotten to put a rubber on, I insisted he pull out before ejaculating and thus I probably owe Susan one set of thousand thread count sheets.

This morning I got up with the sun and showered while Colby slumbered, taking care to dress quickly and completely before he saw me. I checked in the mirror and although the redness had faded from my rear, there are still five or six faint strap marks in light pink against the normal creamy white of my skin. It will be at least another thirty-six hours before they disappear completely. I'll have to stay away from him until then and use the pretext of wanting to postpone the dreaded spanking.

To Colby's credit, he didn't look at me any differently this morning. Luckily, for me, his desire to give me regular spankings is far greater than the pull of any conventional morality on his soul or psyche. He slept lightly and quietly all night and awoke with a smile on his lips.

Before driving us to the station, Colby accompanied Thalia and I to Hope's coffee bar at the bookstore for breakfast. I'd informed Hope about the ongoing joke I was playing on Colby, pretending I wasn't in the scene so I trusted her not to make any offhand remarks that might give me away. Thalia was mortified at having revealed my secret life to Colby, but how could she have known he was going to be there? I didn't blame her in the slightest and had assured her of same, but she seemed sunk in disgrace all morning. And it didn't help that Colby started to rate her over our cappuccinos about turning me out. It was no secret to any of Thalia's friends that she was paying her college tuition as a professional escort. Thalia had the spirit to retort that she was proud to be a bad influence on me. She realized I was more comfortable with Colby thinking I was a whore than realizing how deeply in the scene his new girlfriend actually was. It's sure going to blow his mind when he finds out I'm really a submissive. He he.

Tuesday, February 24th

It being President's Day, there were no classes yesterday. I noticed by mid morning that Colby was not trying to get in touch with me nor did I see him in the dining hall. Obviously, he intended to teach me a lesson.

Curiously, he held out only until my 4 pm yoga class at the center. He'd never shown up to a class of mine before and I immediately saw where he was coming from with this display of muscular arm and thigh in gym shorts and tee. He still wanted me to take that spanking from him but didn't expect me to give it up for nothing. By coming to my class he was showing he was sporting and game, ready for any physical challenge I could pose, even if it tested him to the limit. If he passed muster, he would be that much more likely to command my respect. I did respect his nerve, but I didn't spare him. It was the hardest class I ever gave, with wall-to-wall warriors and chatarangas by the score. I was loving watching him try to keep up with these moves at the accelerated speed so popular these days, while keeping his gaze glued to my body. It looked to be his first yoga class and he'd never seen me in a tank top and yoga pants before. I couldn't help needling him mercilessly, calling out position corrections to him and in some cases coming over and adjusting his body, pushing down his knees or hips and really having fun with it. He was flushed and his eyes were sparkling with passion for me. He could not look angry for the life of him, though he really seemed to want to, because he was too fascinated. Whatever I'd done, it didn't matter, he was crazy for me and it was written all over him. This made things easy for me, like a game where I had all the winning pieces and cards. Had Colby been actually wounded or truly morally outraged by my admission my mood today would be completely distraught, filled with self-doubt and reproach, perhaps even genuine guilt. As it is, I don't know quite why I don't feel guilty about what I did Saturday night. Maybe because I definitely climaxed with Mr. Bartlett.

During shabasana, I came around to everyone, lightly aligned his or her shoulders on the floor and anointed each brow with a drop of lavender oil. I saved Colby for last. Of course his eyes shot open and he caught my wrist in his hand with an iron grip.

"Relax, yoga practitioner," I said soothingly, pushing him back down on his back and going through the usual ritual with pleasant detachment, still putting the class in the relaxation mode with breathing instructions and seashore imagery. Colby subsided but shot me such a look! I got a little flutter in my tummy. Since everyone else's eyes were shut, I impulsively leaned down and placed a very light kiss on Colby's lips. Now he returned me a very different look. Then I left him and prepared to conclude the class.

He waited until all the students had gone before approaching me.

"Well," he began without preamble, "did you think it over?"

"Yes."

"Well?"

"How did you like your first yoga class?"

"It was horrible."

"You appear to possess both the strength and balance necessary to execute advanced positions," I said encouragingly, for I had enjoyed his presence in class tremendously.

We exiting the yoga room and I headed towards the women's locker room.

"I'll wait for you," he said, heading towards the men's.

I took a long hot shower and made him wait quite a while as I dried and brushed out my hair. He had done the same and was steamed in three or four different ways by the time I joined him. As we left the over heated center and went out into the winter afternoon just turning dusk, a windy wave of sleet hit us in our faces. We ran under one umbrella to the nearest teashop, where it was cozy and found a wooden booth by the window. We ordered a pot of tea and shared a dish of the meat and cheese pasties the shop specializes in and another of jam tarts and lingered a long time in the window seat, watching the sun go down and the interesting looking young people hurrying and slipping along the cobbled street outside.

Colby was deliberately keeping his hands to himself and generally appeared to be trying to maintain his dignity. Normally, he'd be squeezing my knees and thighs under the table.

Finally he said, "I'm sorry but my honor demands that you submit to the punishment you deserve."

"What do you mean, your honor demands?" I cried.

"What kind of a man would I be if I didn't beat my girlfriend for cheating on me?"

"It wasn't cheating, Colby. I never pledged eternal fidelity to you."

"Eternal, we've only been seeing each for a week!"

"And it wasn't cheating. It was more in the way of a business arrangement."

"How could you do it, Amanda? Go from my arms to the arms of another man, just like that. I thought you were beginning to care for me."

"I do care for you!"

"So you're saying you only did it for the money."

"Not exactly, as I explained to you yesterday, Mr. Bartlett has thrown some excellent work my way, and I though grant you, it was wrong, I felt impelled to please him."

"How unlike you, Amanda, feeling impelled to please anyone."

"Colby, I gave myself to you last night in good faith that you weren't holding a grudge about what I did. You seemed willing to hug and kiss me all night. Now all of a sudden you're in a bad mood, which technically my yoga class should have sweated out of you."

"Your class kicked my ass," he acknowledged respectfully.

"Colby, do you want to break up with me over this?" I demanded.

"No, I just want to spank you for being so bad."

"No, I don't trust you. You'll go way overboard and probably make me cry. Then I'll have to break up with you." I predicted.

"You should be made to cry for your reprehensible behavior."

"Why should you be in a superior position over me?"

"Because I'm your tutor."

"That is not applicable to this situation."

"Because I know right from wrong."

"Do you? Then why couldn't you answer me directly when I asked you whether you would turn down that same amount of money from a cougar?"

"Never mind the hypothetical situations, we're talking about something you actually did."

"Look, I'll have to think about this some more before I consent to you laying hands on me in an admonitory manner," I stalled him.

Colby agreed and we decided to spend the night apart as we both had a lot of work to do. This was good because as of last night I still had a few faint marks remaining from the strapping on Saturday.

It snowed continuously all day. Still deciding whether to meet Colby for our usual Tuesday night study session or blow him off while I continue to ponder my inevitable punishment. Instinctively I feel I should make him work harder for the privilege of disciplining me. But how long could I string him out before he went a little insane and violated all his principals as a liberated male by laying hands on me against my will? How many times could I use genuine corporal punishment fan catch phrases before he would realize that I don't merely know all these scene nuances through the natural sophistication of having been brought up in San Francisco, but because I am myself an ardent enthusiast for the disciplinary arts, with impeccable lineage behind me? I always suspected him of being dense, apart from his academic acumen, but can he really be this utterly clueless? I let him spank me to orgasm on our first sex date. No, he really and truly buys the line I'm selling him, about me being condescending but empathetic towards perverts, which is ostensibly why I let him turn me over his knee, in classic style.

This is about to be history repeating itself, going back to Castor, whom I strung along for weeks at arm's length, until he stumbled on the magazine with me on the cover being spanked by Hugo Sands. It was all up when he read the blurb about me making spanking movies. He punished me severely that night. It was hot. But should things ever be allowed to get that hot between Colby and me? The Castor thing wore itself out pretty fast for me. Mostly because he's a male chauvinist asshole. I don't like that kind of bossiness in a man who isn't gay. I can't let Colby take me for granted. Our relationship is based on me being the superior one, except for my grasp of economics, which is much improved. However, I can't have a jock telling me what to do, and that's just what will start happening if I give him the natural right to turn me over his knee whenever he feels I've shown him disrespect or behaved not to his liking.

Of course this particular situation is different. I was very bad. Anyone would say so. If I had the nerve to tell Hugo what I did, he wouldn't say it, but he'd think it. He'd probably regret that I'd gone so far down the road to decadence at age 18. Mother I'm not sure about. She believes in using the power of sex at all times and if she did a card reading, whatever the outcome, she would claim that what I'd done was in perfect balance with the universe. In fact, I don't have to bother telling her, she probably intuitively knows. I mentioned Mr. Bartlett to her and the presents. That's more than enough for mother to project the inevitable outcome.

Should I spend Spring break in California with Colby? Or should I take him to Random Point with me? I have so many friends there now. But they're all in the scene. Could I even last one more day with Colby there without him finding out? Or is it time he found out? Maybe I should postpone letting him spank me again until he finds out I'm really into it. Wouldn't that make for about the hottest scene ever? All I have to do is take him to Random Point and it could happen anywhere we happened to go.

The special editions rooms in Hugo's shop would be a dead giveaway, with that illustrated 1903 first edition of Frank and I under glass. When we were at the bookstore, we were in a rush, and Colby was so busy looking at Hope run around behind the counter in her tight jeans that he didn't notice the legend at the front of the bookstore recommending the third floor gallery for connoisseur's erotica. Next time he visits the bookstore, he'll see the sign, go upstairs, find the treasure trove of spanking books and magazines and find Hugo's publications, including that most recent issue with me on the cover. Even if he mistook me for another model, he'd remember Hugo because he met him. Game up.

Or, he's staying with me at Susan Ross' house again, as I have an open invitation for the two of us and Susan shows him her studio and her artwork, including the graphic novel of the B&D girl's adventures that she collaborated with her sister on. Again, Colby would immediately start to ask questions and then he'd turn to look at me. I can almost feel my legs going out from under me at the thought, not to mention butterflies.

I guess during spring break, he finds out.

I cancelled our study date by email, but at the regular time he knocked on my door. I opened the door. He looked stern and said, "We need to study." My heart absolutely contracted in my chest because I was actually apprehensive of him grabbing me and spanking me just like that.

"You see, you have me afraid of you!" I sobbed, turning my back on him.

"Oh, honey," he pulled me into his arms. "I'm sorry, babe." I loved his arms around me and his Shetland sweater smell.

"So you won't reproach me any more about what I did?" I looked up at him and asked earnestly.

"Just tell me you're not going to sleep with him again."

"I will never sleep with Mr. Bartlett again," I promised in all good faith because that's something that never does have to be repeated, as well as it turned out in the end.

"Or see him again?"

"See him?"

"I heard him say something about a spring fashion show. Please don't tell me he's still going to be your boss."

"But I like that gig," I protested. "It's so much fun and I get an excuse to go to Random Point and visit Hugo. You know, we only just discovered each other in September. I'd never even met him once before then."

"Is that so?" Colby was momentarily distracted from the Bartlett issue, but got right back to it at once. "But do you really need to get into all that cat walking nonsense? Next thing you know you'll be starving yourself. You should be concentrating on your grades. You know that, Amanda."

"Colby, I'm only going to be 18 once. I might as well do things like that while I'm young." I refused to be argued out of modeling for Bartlett's in house fashion shows. The outdoor shoot at six am was one thing. I wouldn't rush to repeat that ordeal, but the department store exposure was extremely enjoyable. And I got to keep the outfits. He wouldn't understand. To a boy the only outfit they really want to see you in is none. "You know," I said, "you're really getting bossy, telling me what to do. Do you really think I'm going to put up with that?" I hoped the implication was clear. Girls like me don't drift without boyfriends for long.

Colby stared at me with narrowed eyes and opened his laptop at the table as usual. "Come on, sit your gorgeous butt down and let's study," he said in a tone completely devoid of heat. One thing about Colby, he knows when he's beat.

Chapter Fifteen

Spring Break

After helping Amanda to obtain an A- on her economics midterm, Colby felt confident that she would not refuse his invitation to spend at least a few days of Spring break at his family's home in Sausalito. Amanda agreed, with the provision that he spend a few days with her family in San Francisco and then accompany her back to Random Point for the remainder of their holiday.

Northern California was brisk and bracing in early March, with peek-through days of golden warm sunshine and temperatures soaring into the 60's, but this was never the case with Cape Cod at that time of year and Colby questioned why they were willingly returning to the biting winds and driving rains of the Massachusetts coast a moment before they had to. And yet he was not averse to the concept of staying with Amanda in the charmingly fitted up Victorian in that romantic little village, which possessed a frozen pond. He was going to take Amanda skating and then they would stay in all night by the fire. There were no two better prospects in the world to Colby.

Meanwhile, they began their holiday in Sausalito at Colby's family's vineyard. Colby's parents were out of town so he and Amanda had their splendid house, with a Pacific view, to themselves. There were long walks in the woods, inn dinners and wine every night and they felt amazingly grown up.

Colby was being so generally agreeable that on the second day of walking in the sun lit woods, Amanda presented him with an opportunity he would never have looked for from her. They were walking along a state park path, completely by themselves, when she saw a suitable log and took his breath away by suggesting, "I suppose you can't look at that fallen log with wanting to turn me over your knee?"

He just stared at her. "How do you know things like that?" he asked with a shiver.

"I know how the mind of the fetishist works. I did a paper on it once. The research was most entertaining."

"Well, since you brought the subject up, no, I can't."

"This does seem like a perfect spot for something like that," she said encouragingly. The next thing she knew, she was over his lap and he was pushing up the hem of her three quarters mocha parka with the faux fur hood. The jacket, along with the light colored riding pants and burgundy boots she had on accounted for one tenth of the total she'd earned during her extra naughty session with Mr. Bartlett. The pants molded to her bottom tightly and she felt Colby pass his hand over her cheeks, squeezing them momentarily.

"You're really going to let me do this?"

"You can spank me," she said mildly, as though she was not emotionally invested in the act, but rather was giving him a token award for good behavior on their vacation so far. He hadn't reproached her for her lapse lately and she appreciated his apparently new liberality on the subject of her sexual accessibility. "You can spank me hard," she added. "I'm ready for it now and this isn't a bad place."

He leaned down and lifting her silky hair, kissed the back of her neck briefly.

"So I can spank you hard, can I?" he patted her.

"You can, Colby. I consent. If you have any indignation left over that incident in Random Point that you inadvertently found out about, you may use this opportunity to express it."

A moment of relative silence followed, except for the sounds of the birds above them. Then Colby began to bring his palm down on her upturned seat somewhat slowly but extremely robustly with metronomic precision, allowing every solid smack to sink in fully before laying on the next, and obviously savoring the privilege as only a connoisseur will. Resounding in the woods that surrounded them, the spanking lasted many minutes and only came to an abrupt end when they heard the approach of other hikers, which unwelcome noise instantly propelled them to their feet as they hurried down the path away from the tree stump. Amanda's cheeks blazed with roses, not because she was embarrassed by Colby spanking her but because the unmistakably authentic spanking had very nearly been glimpsed by outsiders. Colby and Amanda had unconsciously joined hands as they rapidly penetrated the woods and when they were sure they were fairly far ahead of the unseen nature lovers, they fell into each other's arms and deeply embraced. "You're a darling," he told her.

Later that night, after dinner and a glass of wine that relaxed Amanda into an affectionate stupor, they made love in the loft that Colby inhabited in his parents' house. This long, wide room with a pitched ceiling of redwood beams and a heavy, polished planked wood floor, overlooked an ocean view the likes of which she had never before beheld. They left the window cracked the slightest bit in order to hear the ocean waves crashing below.

When Amanda mounted Colby she herself placed the palms of his hands on her bare bottom and crushing her full breasts against his well-molded pecs put her mouth beside his ear and murmured, "You can do things to my bottom if you want."

"Things?" he squeezed her cheeks lightly and ran his hands up and down her satiny back and thighs.

"You can pick up where we left off in the woods today," she invited him. "And probe me with your fingertip."

"I can continue spanking you?" he asked, his hands now fastened to her waist as she ground against his groin, his safely jacketed manhood lodged in her tight, creamy pussy to the hilt.

"I consent to the completion of today's activity in the woods," she assented, softly as before, against his ear, while pausing to take his earlobe between her teeth and gently nibble it.

Colby began to methodically smack her bottom and alternately penetrate it with first one and then a second finger, nor did he employ merely the tips. The harder he swatted her, the more enthusiastically she rode her young man, until there was no end in sight but a simultaneous orgasm for them both, to delight their hearts and justify their faith in spanking as the ultimate aphrodisiac. Though Colby again simply assumed that Amanda was being "nice" in allowing him these liberties, as any fun loving, sexually adventurous and not too politically correct new girlfriend might be with a companion she enjoyed.

In San Francisco, Colby was warmly welcomed by Cassandra, Amanda's lovely mother and her stepfather, a pleasant, modest yoga studio and health food storeowner. During the day Colby and Amanda visited local San Francisco attractions and at night went to clubs to hear alternative music. Colby did not spend enough time talking to Cassandra to learn anything of her more colorful past or her connection with Hugo's magazine.

The first day they were in San Francisco, while Amanda's step-father showed Colby his exercise studio, Amanda accompanied her mother to her enormous head shop and psychic emporium next door. Cassandra had a number of full time employees at work at the various stations and cash registers and she took Amanda back to her private office at once.

"Well Amanda," said Cassandra, "has Hugo Sands come through for you your first year at school?"

"He's come through for me in every possible way and he's the best man in the world. We're as comfortable with each other as can be and I know I don't bore him. But you were so right to keep us apart until now. He would have spoiled me so terribly. So far, he's refused me nothing, however unusual my requests have been," said Amanda, sitting in a consultation chair across from her mother at Cassandra's favorite card reading table, this one gorgeously tiled in garnet, gold and royal blue.

"When Hugo came to see me he told me you tricked him into playing with you and then demanded a second session from him. It seemed to bother him and he put it all on you," said Cassandra.

"That's correct," Amanda admitted. "I did get him to spank me twice, and it was such naughty good fun. I won't do it again though. I've no need to. I have Colby Hodge to spank me now."

Cassandra glowed with pleasure at the object of her affection.

"I knew you'd enchant him, of course," she said, without modesty, "but I wasn't sure whether he would be able to charm you as completely. After all, I hadn't seen him in such a very long time."

"Mother, we are so alike we can almost read each other's thoughts," Amanda reported with satisfaction.

"What about Laura? Are you getting along with her?"

"She leaves town whenever I'm about to show up," Amanda reported. "She thinks we want to be alone together, to catch up on eighteen years of not having one another."

"She likes you well enough though, doesn't she?" Cassandra asked with some concern, knowing how it important it was for Hugo to finally claim Laura as his wife.

"I think she likes me fine. But she seems fearful that Hugo still loves you."

"He does," Cassandra said with a grin. "But it won't affect his making Laura the best possible husband."

Amanda often wondered why, with his enormous fascination with spanking, Colby had not seen the New Rod Quarterly, but then she realized he'd been getting all of his spanking information online and had no need of magazines. She also wondered when he would happen to stumble onto her spanking clips, which were already posted on a download site and automatically depositing money into a bank account that Hugo had advised her set up for her experimental business project. Perhaps Colby had looked at a great deal of spanking material on line, but there was at this point, so very much of it to look at, that he simply hadn't gotten to her half dozen clips yet. At any rate, Amanda had gotten through the whole winter and half of Spring break without Colby drawing one iota closer to her secret life.

As soon as they arrived in Random Point, the fairly bright Harvard freshman finally seemed to notice something different about the ostensibly detached and analytical Amanda and her friends in the small coastal hamlet. The first remarkable event occurred upon their entry into Hugo Sands' Antiques, that cavernous emporium situated in the center of the village, opposite Marguerite Alexander's bookshop on one side and the frozen duck pond on the other. The bell tinkled upon them passing through the door and they gratefully plunged into the hearth warmed interior of the large and interesting shop. As they penetrated deeper into furniture and curio stuffed main room, enjoying the scent of cedar and cinnamon with which the air was perfumed, the tail end of an argument floated towards them, coming from the direction of the offices behind the shop.

"But I don't want to watch the shop two days in a row," they heard an attractive female voice softly complain. This was Laura, Amanda's father's fiancée.

"You never do, but I need you to do this for me while I'm in Boston next week," they heard Hugo rejoin firmly.

"When are you going to hire someone to help you as you've always done in the past?" Laura demanded, somewhat more aggressively. Amanda and Colby looked at each other, then paused to listen again.

"You know I'd like to do that but my expenses have risen this year," Hugo replied, making Amanda blush, for his taking on her college tuition and board was the only reason for this.

"H'm, that's true," Laura agreed, "but I still never signed on to be your permanent counter help. I want to be in my studio working on my book!"

"You're a selfish little brat. You're lucky I don't spank you!"

Now Colby blushed as Amanda suddenly affected to bump into a rack of vintage postcards so that she could create a bit of noise setting it to rights. The next moment, Hugo had emerged from the back with Laura shyly peeking around his shoulder.

"Amanda!" Hugo said with genuine pleasure. "We weren't expecting you until tomorrow. But this is great, Laura's finally around for a change."

Laura was introduced to Colby, who stared at her with fascination, entranced with the visual image of this attractive brunette being taken over the knee of the wholly excellent Hugo Sands. Then Hugo encouraged Laura to give Colby a tour of the shop so that he could have a word with Amanda. As soon as they were gone Amanda murmured, "I'll work in the shop for you this summer. I would love to!"

"I thought you were going to Europe this summer?"

"Only for three or four weeks of it. Oh please, Hugo, I would so love to be able to return something to you for your taking on my college expenses. I'll watch the shop while you're on your honeymoon with Laura!"

"Well, we'll see," he smiled at her, caressing her velvety cheek with his hand.

"By the way, Colby overheard you threatening to spank Laura."

"So he's still in the dark about you and us and the scene?"

"Yes."

"How long do you expect to keep that up?"

"Maybe through tomorrow night, but not the whole weekend at the rate I'm going now."

Hugo took Amanda back to his office and gave her the skates he had borrowed for her from Marguerite. "Here, these should keep you busy for a few hours. The pond across the street is perfect right now. Go and have a snack at the bookshop first. You can bring Colby over to the house for dinner later."

"You don't mind?"

"Silly. He's a nice kid and so are you," Hugo smiled.

"What's Special Collections?" Colby asked Laura as they passed through the hallway between the front of the store and the offices behind it.

"Rare books, mostly," Laura replied, opening the door for him to enter. "The door is kept closed so a constant temperature can be maintained inside."

Colby wandered around the medium sized room, which was lined on all walls by glass doored bookcases and bisected by a long display case down the middle with very old, illustrated books spread open beneath the glass, museum style. The room also contained two long reading desks with lamps with a number of wooden chairs behind them. Colby immediately noticed that everything spread open for inspection under glass was of an antique erotic nature. His eye was caught by several books that looked as though they'd been illustrated in the 1920's or 1930's, for they pictured what looked like flappers or schoolgirls with short bobs, being bent over for birchings, canings and enemas.

"They're for collectors," Laura explained in a manner detached enough to seemingly distance herself from the material so prettily arrayed for examination in her fiancé's shop. Laura noticed a flush instantly creep into Colby's fair face as he realized he now beheld vintage corporal punishment material for the first time in his life.

"Interesting!" he managed to remark in a normal tone of voice while passively allowing himself to be shepherded out of the special reading room.

A few minutes later he found himself being led across the street to the bookshop, where he had once before eaten a hurried breakfast and had barely had time to admire the considerable charms of the blonde Venus who presided over the coffee bar and appeared to be Amanda's newest and most intimate friend.

"That Special Collections room in your father's shop is pretty hot stuff," Colby remarked with excitement. "Can we go back there later? I really need to get a closer look at those books."

But before Amanda could reply, she was accosted by and looked up to see a pleasant looking man she'd never before met but seemed to vaguely recognize, smiling down at her. From behind the bar Hope Lawrence said, "Amanda, this gentleman would like to meet you."

The man, who looked perhaps a little younger than Hugo, with short, dark hair, glasses and a lithe, athletic body under outdoors clothes, stretched out his hand to shake hers.

"William Random. So this Amanda Sands I've been hearing about is not a myth?"

Amanda shook his hand. "I'm real!"

"I knew your mother when she lived here," said William, sliding onto a stool beside Amanda and reaching across her to shake Colby's hand when they were introduced.

"You knew my mother?" Amanda was delighted to hear this.

"Yes and you can tell her from me that she deserves a hairbrush spanking for keeping you a secret all these years!"

"I will," Amanda grinned, now remembering exactly where she had seen William before. "I've seen photos of you with my mother," she said. "You haven't changed much. She said you were the only other vegetarian in Random Point in those days."

"I dated your Aunt Carola too," he confided. "Does she still have that amazingly tiny waist?"

"Carola is still as glamorous as ever. She owns a beautiful corset shop in San Francisco now."

"Why did Cassandra keep you a secret all those years?" William asked. "She and Hugo seemed to get on so well together. Why did she just suddenly take off? None of us could figure it out."

"She didn't want Hugo to feel obligated to embrace family life."

"That's madness. He would have loved to have had you both with him all these years. Now he's stuck with my almost useless ex-wife," William smiled, showing that he still cherished a good deal of affection for Laura. "Well, I just wanted to introduce myself. If you ever need anything, call me," he said, handing Amanda his card, then tramping back out into the snow flurries on an increasingly gray afternoon.

Colby was still trying to digest hearing two spontaneous spanking references within an hour of entering the heart of the village.

"Amanda, are you having a joke at my expense?" he demanded, as soon as William departed and Hope set down their tea and sandwiches.

"What do you mean?"

"Why is everyone talking about spanking ladies all of a sudden? Did you tell all your friends here what I'm into?"

Amanda looked at him with a fascinated smile. "You're paranoid, aren't you?" she asked.

"Don't make sport of me, young lady," he said threateningly.

"They're old people, they use that figure of speech to indicate exasperation. That's all," Amanda explained, blithely biting into the crusty French roll with her even white teeth. She used her napkin delicately and smiled at him mildly while relishing the hot lamb sandwich and strong English tea.

"So, it's just a coincidence, all the spanking threats flying around on Shadow Lane."

"Oh, I should think so. I wouldn't set any store by idle words."

Hope came by with a fresh pot of tea for the pretty pair and said, "I saw the stunning billboard. Are you going to register with a modeling agency?"

"No. It would be too distracting. I already need constant tutoring just to keep up with my classes," Amanda admitted honestly. Colby nodded his approval, squeezing her thigh through her leggings. She trapped his hand between her legs and he let his fingers creep up to the crotch of her woolen pants. She squeezed his hand between her legs and he momentarily squeezed her back before taking his hand away in that public place. Hope saw a customer seat himself at the other end of the bar and went to take his order.

"Don't be so naughty in public," Colby whispered to Amanda.

"Why shouldn't I? I would give you the perfect excuse to spank me," she teased him.

"Like I don't have other reasons?"

They proceeded across the street to the duck pond, putting on their skates on a stone bench overlooking the frozen water.

The snow had thinned to a few swirling flakes but the sky appeared ever more leaden above them. And yet the temperature was rising. Perhaps the snow would turn to rain by evening. As soon as they went out onto the ice Colby realized that Amanda had skated before though she protested it had only been a few times as a child. Indeed she seemed a trifle wobbly at first but soon got her balance, as might be expected from a yoga mistress. Very shortly they were skating smartly, arm in arm, as a thin, pale sun attempted to shine through the clouds for at least a few minutes.

"You really are obsessed with spanking, aren't you?" Amanda continued to bait her new beloved. "You hear and see it everywhere."

"Wait a minute, Amanda, you're the one who's always suggesting that this would be a good place or a good time for a spanking."

"I'm only reading your mind," she admitted.

"I know, but I don't understand how you're doing it."

"I wonder if I've been too encouraging on the subject," Amanda mused. He tightened his grip on her waist and pressed his lips to her throat and then the back of her neck. Amanda was wearing both a stocking cap with a pompom on the end and faux fur earmuffs, but part of her smooth white neck was still available for nuzzling and Colby knew how to make her shiver in this manner.

"You have encouraged me," he agreed.

"Let's skate for a hour, then go back to the house and make love for the rest of the afternoon," Amanda suggested.

"Baby!" he kissed her lips and squeezed her waist again. They skated faster, becoming warm despite the high twenties temperatures and the breezes rippling across the ice and hitting them in their pink faces as they circled the small pond again and again, with only a few black birds in the bare trees above them for company.

They stayed out on the pond for about forty minutes, then the snow turned to rain and their jackets and leggings quickly became soaked. They hurried back into the bookshop for hot chocolate while they dried off by an old Swedish stove in the main room. It was there that Colby first noticed the sign pointing upward to the galleries, the third and highest of which was labeled Esoteric Erotica. Amanda had been up there before and knew that the shelves of this loft at the top of the spiral staircase contained a selection of her father's New Rod Quarterly magazines, with herself on the cover of the most recent issue.

"Look Amanda, this little berg appears to be a hotbed of high class pornography," said Colby. "If what they have upstairs is anything like what I saw in that Special Collections room at your father's shop, I want to make some purchases!"

"You still read your stroke books? Don't most boys take their laptops to bed these days?"

"There is something really sexy about a book or magazine," Colby admitted.

"I agree," Amanda said. "But by the same token, wouldn't you like to get right into that warm, cozy, big bed with me?"

They went right home and spent the rest of the afternoon in the cozy bed and Amanda put off the inevitable for one more day.

But Spring break lasts a long time. The young couple had three more days in Random Point and only part of that time had been set aside for studying. The next day it rained the entire day. Amanda was able to fill up the morning with breakfast in the village, a swim and spa visit at the gym and shopping for the groceries for an intimate dinner that they were to enjoy alone in the house, that night, once again playing grown up with impeccable style, thanks to the hospitality of her absent friend, Susan Ross. Amanda planned to keep the menu simple: melted Camembert on rosemary walnut bread, winter fruit, red wine and chocolate hazelnut truffles. Then much more sex while the rain pounded on the windowpanes. She was madly in love and a thrill went through her every time Colby fixed her with a penetrating look.

As there was no rush to get the groceries home, it being so cold in the streets of the village that wet and windswept March day, Colby once again suggested a visit to the third gallery of Marguerite Alexander's bookshop. Amanda's heart jumped in her chest but she cheerfully advised him to check it out while she stopped in across the street at Hugo's shop to say good morning and thank her father for dinner the previous night at his house. This dinner had been exceedingly pleasant, Laura having roasted several chickens, presenting them with a dish of Greek potatoes and a fresh tomato salad.

"I'm really glad you were able to bring Colby along last night," Hugo told Amanda while unwrapping a consignment of china that had just arrived. They were in the back of the shop, Hugo behind the long glass counter and Amanda leaning over it and looking at some cameos on blue velvet underneath it. "It seemed to put Laura at ease about you," he explained.

"Mother thinks it would be good if Laura consented to marry you."

"You talked about me with Cassandra?" Hugo smiled at the strangeness of that thought.

"She beamed with joy when I disclosed the many ways in which you have cosseted me since my arrival in your world."

"I still don't forgive her for keeping you a secret, but I'm touched that she's ready to entrust you to me now. We're still on the same wave length after all these years and that makes me feel less sad about losing her."

"You haven't lost her."

"That's the unsettling part. I've been thinking about her a lot since that visit."

"Not too much, I hope," Amanda said uneasily, for she adored her stepfather and was appalled at the idea of the more exciting Hugo Sands taking her mother away from him. Hugo saw her expression and hastened to assure her that he really only got out to California once a year, if that often.

"So you do plan to see her again!" Amanda said with wonder. "But if it was so easy for the two of you to get together, why did it take so long?" For one brief moment she began to question her mother's wisdom.

"You know how your mother decides things, Amanda. Star charts and card readings. It was the one thing that seemed to come between us, me being a rational human being. She probably did a reading before you were born and it told her that it behooved her to keep us apart for x amount of years, probably more than ten but less than eighteen. You found the magazines at twelve, I'm sure that fit right into Cassandra's forecast. If you had been a different kind of kid, I might have been stuck with a teenaged runaway, but somehow she was able to keep you on ice six more years. How was she able to do that? Most children are so willful. Didn't you insist on meeting me?"

"No. First of all, I was intimidated by the thought of you since I'd only met you as the editor of the NRQ. I believe your photo started showing up in the magazine with the third or forth issue, along with my mother's and my Aunt Carola and that nice Mr. Random we just ran into at the bookstore. He mentioned that mother should be spanked for keeping me a secret and you should have seen Colby blush. By the way, he now thinks the whole village is in a conspiracy to tease him for being into spanking. Did I mention that he managed to overhear you threatening to spank Laura earlier as well? It's no use, I have to tell him everything today."

"Why today?" Hugo asked.

"Because he's over at the bookstore now exploring the loft. He'll come back with an armful of NRQ's, doubtless including the most recent one with me and you on the cover."

"You don't have to worry about him getting that at the shop, I sold out of that issue the first week it was out."

"Really?"

"I should put you on every cover."

"So, Colby may find NRQ's, but just not mine."

"Exactly!"

"He'll recognize you though, in your editorial photo."

"Guys don't look at other guys in spanking magazines. Just don't say anything and I'll bet you he won't notice," Hugo suggested.

"No. I think it's time. He's going to be my true boyfriend. I don't want him finding these things out in bits and pieces."

"I'm still not sure why you kept all of this a secret from him in the first place but I was kind of glad he didn't know last night. I thought I was sophisticated but I honestly don't know if I would have felt comfortable talking scene talk with my daughter and her boyfriend sitting there. There's something just possibly a little creepy about that and I'm glad you didn't put me in that position. Later on, after Colby knows all, so to speak and proves worthy of your love, in other words, lasts until your next vacation here, he will approach me with the proper respect as the long time publisher of the NQR, which he is sure to love when he reads it."

"I understand," Amanda patted Hugo's hand, "you are still vibrating from the idea that you are actually someone's father. Especially as that word, father, has such a sleazy connotation in esoteric pornography. You cringe at the thought of anyone thinking you might get off on corporally punishing your own child. I agree, in theory it's a horribly squicky concept. Except I loved posing for the cover of the magazine and I forced you to play with me out of naughty curiosity. I'm a little pervert," Amanda said with a shrug.

"I like the current boyfriend," Hugo said, taking a cameo out of the case. "Take your chain off," he said. Then he took a plain gold box chain out of another case and attached it to the cameo of a 18th century girl's head in white ivory on a dark blue background, set in a golden oval. He put the small golden locket and gold chain that she usually wore into a jeweler's box for her, but not before popping the locket open and seeing the tiniest possible portrait of Cassandra.

"You're giving me a cameo?" Amanda asked, delightedly looking at herself in one of the many mirrors in Hugo's shop. "Thank you!" she cried, enjoying her reflection. "May I hug you?"

Hugo smiled fondly at her and accepted an over the counter hug.

Amanda met Colby at the front of the bookshop. He was carrying a sleek, frosted paper shopping bag heavy with books and magazines. It was now raining hard and Amanda borrowed an umbrella from Hugo for the dash to Colby's borrowed car.

"That shop is incredible," said Colby with excitement. His blue eyes were sparkling and he couldn't keep a wide smile from his face in contemplation of spending the cold, wet afternoon tucked snugly inside a fine house in front of a crackling fire, with what looked to be a world-class collection of B&D porn and the most beautiful young lady in the commonwealth ready to hand. "I found the best books and magazines in the world."

"You certainly bought a lot in a short amount of time," said Amanda, peeking into the shopping bag seeing a collection of Edwardian and Victorian paperback novels, all by Anonymous and at least a dozen back issues of The New Rod Quarterly.

"The owner of the shop waited on me, a beautiful redhead with glasses. She said she wrote some of the books I bought," said Colby. "She said her name is Marguerite but she writes under Alma. Can you believe that, just running into a famous fetish writer here in Random Point?"

"Did you turn amazingly red while you were talking to her?" Amanda teased, ruffling his short blond hair as he drove carefully through the almost blinding rain across the village and back to Susan's house.

"Not at all," Colby protested. "How could I be embarrassed when she was so natural about it? Then she asked me if I live here and I explained I was here with my girlfriend, whose father lives here. It turns out she's one of your father's best friends and was at Bennington with Laura. She invited us to her house for tea tomorrow afternoon. I told her I would ask you but I would love to go! I can't wait to read her books."

"Ah yes, the glamorous Marguerite Alexander. I've met her briefly once before. She's charming. I would love to know her better," said Amanda.

They quickly reached the house opposite the graveyard and rushed inside. Colby immediately started a fire in the downstairs sitting room while Amanda began a pot of coffee in the kitchen, her heart pounding as she mentally rehearsed her confession speech.

When she brought the coffee tray into the parlor Colby was sitting on the hearthrug with all the books and magazines stacked neatly around him in several piles.

He looked up and said, "You don't mind if I sort of take a bath in this stuff, do you? I've never seen so much high-class pornography together in my life. And it's just the sort I like!"

Amanda handed him a cup of coffee the way he liked it and then sat sipping her own perched on an ottoman near the fire.

"No, Colby, I don't mind. In fact, I have something to tell you relevant to the materials you've just purchased."

"Really?" he looked at her attentively.

"I've actually already read some of those books myself," she said.

"Really?" his voice was serious but his eyes merry, which Amanda attributed to his current euphoria at finding the cache of spanking books.

"I'm not sure where to begin but I feel as though I should tell you everything."

"Of course tell me everything!" he encouraged her.

"All right. But get ready for a big surprise."

"Okay."

"My father is the publisher of that magazine, The New Rod Quarterly," she said, reaching for a random copy, flipping it open to the editorial page and showing Colby Hugo's portrait shot.

"You're kidding!" he said, not meeting her eyes but studying the photo.

"No, and Laura has been doing spanking illustrations for him for the past six years. So has her little sister Susan, the girl who came by this splendid house as a direct result of being introduced to the composer Anthony Newton by Hugo. Newton, Laura, Susan, Marguerite, Hugo, the man you met at the coffee bar yesterday, William, as well as Hope Lawrence, Hope's husband and a number of other people who live here in the village, are all in the scene."

"All in the spanking scene?" Colby seemed genuinely amazed.

"Yes, and Hugo got my mother into it as well, twenty years ago when she lived here in Random Point. In fact, she was one of the first contributing female editors to The NRQ and if you were to obtain some of those rare issues from the first two years of publication, you would be able to see both Hugo and that man William Random, spanking both my mother and her sister Carola. They were some of his very first models."

"I'm floored," said Colby, "and utterly fascinated. Please tell me more!"

Amanda lit a joint, took a pull on it and passed it to her lover.

"Now comes the really interesting part as far as you're concerned," said Amanda, taking the joint back, taking another drag and then relinquishing it to him.

"Yes, I'm dying to hear about how you fit into this hotbed of perversity," Colby encouraged her.

"Well, naturally, I'm into it too," said Amanda. "I was into it even before I found the magazines when I was 12. I had fantasies as early as three. My stepfather did spank me when I was naughty up to about age five. Perhaps it all started there. At any rate, I always found conversations about spanking interesting and if I ever saw one, I was transfixed. I remember playing spanking games with my kindergarten friends in the playhouse. I looked up the word spanking in the dictionary. And I became riveted by an old movie channel my mother always left on in the shop. It ran a lot of movies from the 1930's and I noticed the lead men were always threatening to spank their saucy female co-stars. And then I found those magazines, whose editor had the same last name as me, Sands.

"I always knew my stepfather was not my real father. He arrived on the scene when I was a toddler and served as father to me since then, and a fine one he has been, but with my mother's photos all over the magazines with Hugo Sands, it didn't take me longer than ten minutes to figure out he was my real father. Our physical resemblance alone was a dead giveaway. I asked my mother what was going on, why had she broken up with this handsome, lovely man with his delightful magazine? And why, furthermore, had she kept us apart all these years? She simply felt it was the right thing to do at the time. Naturally I was all for writing to Hugo immediately, but my apparent affinity for the spanking material caused my mother some alarm. Not that she was against my being a deviant, but I was still so young. She didn't forbid me to contact Hugo, but suggested it might be more fun to wait until I was over eighteen before penetrating his very adult world of spanking publications and photo sessions. She's so smart, because how would a pain in the butt, sexually precocious preteen fit into Hugo's world?"

By now the joint was half gone and both their eyes were watering with the strength of the THC.

"My god, that's an amazing story. I'm utterly entranced. I met a spanking princess!" said Colby, impulsively taking her hand and kissing it on the back. She stared at him.

"You? Being courtly? You must be stoned."

"So, then what happened?" Colby asked.

"You want my full spanking history?"

"Well, yes, of course I do!" Colby replied with the avidity of a tabloid journalist.

"It includes other boys and men," she warned him. "But I think I do want you to know everything, all at once, so nothing will pop up to surprise you later."

"By all means, don't leave out a detail."

"I turned my high school boyfriend Carlos onto spanking. He's Spanish so he's naturally inclined to be into it, but he really took to it on top of that. We played all through high school, going all the way by the Spring of Sophomore year. We had toys too, leather and wood and some restraints. Carlos spanked me into sub space once a week. He spanked me all the time. He did it for foreplay. I got used to it and I can take a lot. Then freshman year came and we broke up. He's at Cornell.

"I came out to Random Point before the term started to meet Hugo for the first time. I was all over him to spank me, just for the crazy thrill of it, but it freaked him out, me being his blood daughter. He agreed to pay my Harvard tuition and board and palmed me off on a few friends of his in Random Point, to take the edge off my ravening desire to play. I wound up getting spanked by Hope's husband, a local English teacher and the husband of that beautiful bookseller Marguerite. His name is Flagg and he owns a tavern called The Dutch. I hope you can handle tea at Marguerite's house knowing her husband spanked me but since I don't know whether she knows that he did, please don't mention anything about that in front of her."

"Don't worry, I'll dummy up on that issue," Colby promised faithfully, more fascinated than ever by the milieu into which he had luckily stumbled. He couldn't help wonder whether he'd ever get a chance to spank the amazing bottom of the redheaded bookstore seller who wrote the spanking romances. Her voice had been like velvet as she praised his selections one by one, a small flush coming into her fair face when she came to the stack of her own books that he was buying.

Amanda continued with her colorful confession, "Okay, I'm not proud of this, but my first month in Cambridge I probably fucked every cute boy on my floor in the dorm."

"Oh my god, you little slut," said Colby with admiration.

"And then I started to go after my roommate's admirers, hot black men. I snagged two of them and made them both spank me. I also attended a B&D support group meeting and picked up a young man who I saw for a while for play sessions at his loft in Back Bay. Finally, you're not the first tutor I've had this year. I let a boy named Castor tutor me in Spanish. He turned out to be a dom and for a very short while I let him have me, but he was way too bossy and wanted blow jobs." Amanda paused. "You don't want blow jobs, do you?"

"No!" Colby replied cheerfully.

"Truly?"

"Even if I did, I wouldn't expect them from a spoiled brat like you. Pray continue with your narration," Colby said.

"I will do so for we are almost at the end. I began to fall in love with Ronnie Van Horn, one of the hot black men I mentioned before. Ronnie was also latently into spanking and we were starting to enjoy a rather interesting relationship when he got picked for a year at the Sorbonne and suddenly took off for Paris. I haven't seen anyone else since I started, uh, being tutored by you, who are, by the way, a much better tutor than Castor.

"Oh and that whole thing with Mr. Bartlett didn't start as sex but spanking. I saw him once before for a spanking session and this second time, he added in sex. But it was always primarily about the spanking."

"You do spanking play sessions?" Colby let that sink in as he said it.

"No, just those two times with Mr. Bartlett. And it only happened because he had access to me while I was modeling at his store and he saw what a whore I am for clothing."

"Is that it?" Colby asked.

"Yes, I think that's everyone," she said, trying hard to remember whether she'd left anyone out.

"These are stunning revelations, my Amanda," Colby said, "but are you sure you haven't left anything out? Any little morsel of interest?"

"I don't think so," she said slowly.

"What about this?" Colby reached into the backpack he had not taken with him that morning but tossed into the corner of a sofa, pulling out what looked to be the most recent issue of The NRQ, the one with Amanda on the cover.

"What?" she grabbed it and looked up at him. "How long have you had this, Hodge?"

"Since the week before you accosted me and asked me to tutor you," he said. The impact of this statement took but a moment to penetrate Amanda's brain.

"So then, when you said..." she began.

"...I'll spank your ass..." he picked up her thread, "yes, I was trying to flirt with you. I'd bought the magazine at the Globe and had been reading and rereading it, trying to place the girl on the cover. Then, the next class we had together I realized it was you. Oh my god, how I wracked my feeble brain trying to think up brilliant introduction lines, anything at all, just so you come and have coffee with me or even just walk back to the quad together. Then, while I'm still trying to formulate a plan, you walk up to me and ask me to tutor you."

"Oh Colby, if you only knew how badly you screwed up with that one crass line about spanking my ass. It was at that precise moment that I decide to fuck with you."

"And so you have."

"Even now I'm not exactly sure why I've kept the secret for so long."

"You mistrust raucous jocks, it's highly understandable, someone of your exquisite sensibilities. Now, when may I have my satisfaction?"

"What do you mean?"

"You don't think this joke is going unpunished, do you?"

"Oh? You plan to play the big, bad dominant disciplinarian?" she felt her heart accelerate as she looked up at him.

"Oh Sands, you have no idea. What you put me through?"

"What?" Amanda squared her shoulders and looked at him fearlessly.

"I challenge you to get through MY yoga class."

A few minutes later they climbed to the third floor, where there were two long rooms, one on either side of the corridor. The room overlooking the cemetery was Susan and Laura's art studio and the walls were lined with their framed erotic drawings and comic strips. Both sisters had been illustrating Hugo's magazine for years and had recently brought out several graphic novels of their own. Amanda encouraged Colby to take his time exploring the room, eager to postpone her ordeal as long as possible. Usually he wore contacts, but today he had proper glasses on and she loved the gravity they gave his face as he examined each framed graphic with rapt attention.

"So the girl who owns this house and her sister did all of these? And your dad is about to marry one of them?"

"If you're moderate in your behavior and don't try to take advantage of me, you may get to meet them some day," Amanda said.

"So, are you're afraid I'll spank you as hard as you deserve for turning me into your puppet?" Colby asked, refocusing all his attention on Amanda.

"Well, yes. I'm a spanking enthusiast not a masochist."

"You are a Spanking Princess," Colby said seriously. "And being you, I wouldn't be surprised if you insisted on postponing your discipline for days or weeks. That seems to be your style."

"No, I won't," Amanda said. "I've prepared myself for this and I can face it. You do deserve satisfaction and I suppose I do deserve a good licking for doing that insane thing I did with Mr. Bartlett."

"By the way, speaking of that old roué, you're not going to see him again, are you?"

"Just to be in his fashion shows Colby. I promise."

"Somehow I'm not jealous of any of the others but that image seems to get on my nerves," he admitted.

"How about you, Colby, have you played with any other girls?"

"Played with? You mean spanked? My high school girlfriend let me spank her every birthday after I gave her a substantial present. Then, my first week in Cambridge I went straight to the combat zone and did a bunch of sessions in a club there. I think I spanked two girls a night for about five nights in a row. I blew through all the money I made at my summer job, but it was worth it. I felt like I was tasting life for the first time. Then I saw you in Econ 1 and it was over. You were all I could think about. I had a huge crush on you, that's the only way to put it. Then you walked up to me and asked me to be your tutor. I thought I was dreaming."

"Colby whatever made you make that clumsy remark so fast?"

"I'm young and dumb, why else?"

"That one remark set you back months," she said sadly.

"Rub it in, girl. While you can," he said smoothly.

Amanda led him across the hall to the studio playroom, the central focal point of which was a large mahogany leather divan, seven feet square. The room had a heavy planked wooden floor and beamed ceiling with windows looking out on a woods. The other furniture was all designed with a view to presenting girls for corporal punishment and included spanking horses and trestle benches as well as a couple of whipping posts and an X frame on one wall. There were armoires full of fetish gear and costumes and trunks full of toys. Mirrors lined the walls and candle sconces promised an even softer intimacy at night. And as it happened, dusk was falling. Amanda lit the candles.

It was the best-equipped dungeon he'd ever seen, including any room in the B&D salon he'd visited that first week in Boston.

Amanda turned up the heat because she sensed his first command would be to divest herself of every stitch. How else to conduct a disciplinary lesson?

Colby went routing in a trunk and found it to contain nothing but wooden implements of correction. He came up with a wide backed ebony hairbrush and a medium sized oak paddle shaped like a heart and painted dark red. Then he went into the leather trunk and found a heavy razor strop very much to his liking. Finally he searched inside the standing armoires until he found a drawer full of canes, birches and switches. He took out a thin rattan cane with a straight handle and a small birch rod of thin green twigs wrapped together at one end with suede felt to form a handle. All of these he placed on the leather divan. Then he sat down and motioned her to him.

"I want to undress you myself. May I?" he asked, looking up at her, his hands on her waist.

"Yes," she said, covering her face with her hands, suddenly immensely embarrassed. He made her sit down beside him and shifting her long legs to his lap, slipped her boots off. When he took one of her feet in his hands she pulled it away. "No, I can't bear tickling!" she protested.

"Really?" he grinned but didn't pursue the slender foot in its white wool sock. Amanda suddenly noticed the stereo component system across the room and sprang up. "I want to see if Susan has any good music," she said. "Oh boy," she said, going through a row of CD's, "Psychedelic Furs, They May Be Giants, Public Image, Adam Ant…"

"Stack them up and put them on," said Colby, looking around the fantastically well-equipped room as he tried to figure out what he wanted to do first.

"You know, there is no actual reason to punish me," Amanda said, having second thoughts as she watched him swish the cane through the air. "I mean, since you knew all along that I was in the scene. You were playing with me as much as I was playing with you."

"I didn't know you were in the scene until just a minute ago when you confessed."

"But you had the magazine."

"I had a magazine you had modeled for. For all I knew, you were a purely disinterested fetish model. And the way you talked about fetishism seemed to bear that out. Your attitude was nonjudgmental but detached, as though this were just a bit of knowledge you happened to pick up from books and magazines and living in the modern era. You snowed me and you know it," Colby said as the unpleasant voice of John Lydon singing the jerky and neurotic ballad Solitaire filled the room.

"I love this song," said Amanda.

"It does have a good beat," said Colby, capturing her, bringing her back to the divan and pulling her sweater over her head. Immediately confronted by her full, creamy, upstanding bosom, breathtakingly presented in a white point d'esprit pushup bra, he paid homage to her beauty with his hands that gently squeezed her breasts and his lips which kissed them adoringly through the lace bra. "Absolutely gorgeous," he sighed, looking up at her, then with a smile he began to unbuckle her belt and take off her wool leggings, under which she wore French cut briefs of the same material as the bra. Then he drew her down across his lap where he sat and spanked her through her panties with his hand.

"There is one thing you haven't mentioned yet," he said, pausing to roll the panties down to her knees.

"Oh?"

"The video."

"The video? What video?"

"The spanking video the magazine said you were planning on making. Do you still intend to do that?"

"I already have."

"You already have?"

"Sure, there are six clips online you can download."

Colby stopped stroking her slightly pinkened bare bottom and spanked her with some irritation. How had he missed those?

"Do you work under a different name?" he asked.

"Yes, Hugo thought I should have a stage name. It's April Sebastian."

He smacked her bottom six times in rapid succession. "And how did it turn out?"

"It turned out well," she said, over her shoulder.

"It's a crazy idea, you doing videos," he scolded, spanking her harder. "No wonder you found it hard to concentrate on economics. You can't spread yourself that thin and get through Harvard."

"I know. That's why I've put the video project on hold until the summer. Then maybe you can help me and be in some clips."

"Are you crazy? I haven't even decided between teaching and journalism yet. I can't have a porn video hanging around in my background and I'm amazed you've gone and done this now."

He paused to let the lecture sink in, while rubbing away the sting left by his palm on either satiny cheek.

"I'm going to be an entrepreneur and work for myself so it doesn't matter what I'm in now or ever," she declared haughtily, inspiring him to continue with the spanking with greater vigor.

"Oh is that so? You don't think you'll ever go for a job with a company?"

"I thought I wanted to. But when I ran that video shoot I got a taste of what being in control was like. It was hard and stressful, but I got to do something I wanted to do in exactly the way I wanted to do it. There's a lot to be said for that."

"Don't you dare speak so sensibly while I'm spanking you," he ordered, now selecting the heart shaped wooden paddle to lay into her with.

"Ow! That's wood!" she cried.

"You're damned right, it's wood."

"But what about the yoga positions?" she asked quickly, sorely in need of a break. "And me nude in them?" she added temptingly.

"All right then," he said, unhooking her bra and lifting it away from her then pulling her upright. She kicked her panties entirely off and pulled off her socks. Then stood looking at each other, she entirely naked, he in his blue jeans, walking boots and a tucked out putty colored corduroy shirt. She was five feet eight inches tall and he six two. She liked that she had to look up to him a little. He kissed her briefly, then looked serious.

"I love you with your glasses on," she told him.

"Don't try to butter me up," he told her, picking up the birch. "Just get into a forward fold," he added, pulling her back to a large, oak framed mirror positioned between two elaborately mullioned windows upon which a heavy rain was now beating and washing down the outside of in sheets. Amanda straightened her back and placed her palms on the floor in front of her bare, neatly manicured toes. She saw that if she looked between her calves she would be able see herself in the mirror being birched, with Colby off to one side.

"Oh no, this is too embarrassing!" she protested weakly, for her nudity in this position was absolutely complete. Her pink pussy, her bottom crease, even a fuzz of blonde pubic curls were visible when she bent over in this fashion.

"It's all right," Colby assured her. "In a second the pain will drive every thought of embarrassment out of your head."

"I feel so exposed. Can't I do Ardha instead of Uttanasana?"

"What's Ardha?"

Amanda lifted her torso and brought her palms to rest on her shins, jutting her bottom out more but affording her a bit more modesty.

"Sure, I'll be magnanimous, but keep in mind, right after this, you're getting into plough," Colby told her cheerfully.

"You bastard," Amanda murmured.

"So tell me about this phenomenon subspace," he said, swishing the birch in the air. "How does someone get you there?"

"Start light, build slowly, spend a long time getting there, end up hard and fast," Amanda succinctly replied.

Colby followed her instructions to the letter, tapping the birch across both her cheeks with increasing force and speed but by the most subtle incremental degrees, observing every corresponding impulse rippling through her and listening closely for every variation in her breathing, every small sigh or excited pant of appreciation. Harder and faster, Colby plied the birch across the centermost portion of her buttocks as well as just above and just below, never going higher than the crest of her hips or lower than the juncture between her bottom and the tops of her thighs. In the wake of the neatly trimmed birch twigs, roses blossomed in Amanda's cheeks, delicately staining her entire bottom a luscious shade of red.

"Harder!" Amanda suddenly cried, shooting him a passionate look over one bare shoulder. Colby placed his hand on the small of her back and began to apply the birch rod afresh and now quite severely to her sensuously swaying behind. She was rocking with every swat of the multi twigged tool of correction and Colby could see her dewy essence gleaming on her blonde pubic curls as they provocatively peeked out below. The birching lasted about five minutes, at the end of which time Amanda found herself deeply immersed in the highly exhilarating top layer of subspace, the excitement layer, to the accompaniment of a series of clitoral winks, sensations something akin to miniature orgasms, along with the well known butterflies, that tantalizingly brief manifestation of exquisite arousal blended with romantic adoration which has encouraged love making since the beginning of sex.

Colby saw the effect he had had upon Amanda and paused to take her in his arms.

"So you want me in the plough?" she finally said, looking up at him with a naughty smile.

"I know you do a beautiful plough. How long do you think you could hold that position?"

"Oh, I can hold that position indefinitely," she claimed, lying on her back in the middle of the large divan, raising her legs straight up above her, then bringing them slowly down towards her head and then over her head, until her knees were on the leather couch on either side

241

of her head, her shins and feet down on the sofa and her entire buttocks and vagina completely upturned and well spread. Colby looked at the implements and decided to reject them all in favor of using only the palm of his hand on her entirely exposed cheeks. He spanked her and then paused to divide her pink labia with his fingers. He spanked her and then began to dart his fingers into her continuously lubricating pussy. He reddened each buttock even more completely, slapping her soundly with the palm of his hand. Again and again he alternately spanked and masturbated her until she was crying, "Ow!" and "Oooooh!" with equal enthusiasm. Amanda's fair skinned backside got warmer and redder as her pussy got wetter and began to visibly throb as well as copiously lubricate.

Colby sensed the time was right to unwind Amanda from the position and take her. He placed her on her back, unzipped his jeans and produced a condom. Amanda took it from him and looking up at him as he straddled her, carefully unrolled it down on his fully erect engine of desire.

"You have a beautiful cock," she said, completing her task and helpfully arching up to meet his first thrust.

"You have a beautiful everything," he said burying his face against her throat and gently biting her ear lobes around the tiny gold studs she always wore. She gasped in excitement under these ministrations and locked her long, slim, muscular legs around his waist, pulling him as deeply inside her as she could. He filled her even more completely after taking her bottom in his hands and pulling her up against him even harder. The divan was large enough for them to roll over completely without falling off and Amanda wound up on top half way through the engagement. This position worked even better, because Colby could massage her well-spanked cheeks as she rode him. After playing so intensely, with Amanda grinding her clit against his own blond furred groin and Colby never taking his strong kneading, caressing hands from her bottom, finally finding her tiny anus and fingering it as deeply as possible, their mutual orgasms did not take very long to arrive. They were learning each other's rhythms and were ecstatically in love.

"There's a super sexy shower in the master suite," said Amanda, taking Colby there. This was Susan's bedroom and it was the most richly appointed room in the house. The bathroom was a wonder of modern of hygienic luxury, tiled in milky green and rose. The shower was double sized, and even more elaborately tiled within, with six showerheads, two above and two on each facing side and there were also facing seats on each side. It was their first shower together and it naturally included another round of exuberant teenaged sex, this time with Amanda bending over with her hands on one of the stone seats and Colby behind her, his hands fastened tightly to her small waist, while warm water hit them from every direction the entire time. Half way through, Colby sat on one of the seats, took her on his lap facing away from him and pulled her back down, lodging his cock deeply inside her. In this position, a strong jet of water hit Amanda's Venus mound directly while Colby bounced her up and down on his lap. Direct clitoral stimulation by a strong stream of water was a pastime she had long enjoyed in the privacy of her own shower, but Amanda had never experienced it in concert with full vaginal penetration. The confluence of sensations brought her off again, even though she had only come minutes before in the dungeon. Colby wisely withdrew before his own climax and ejaculated harmlessly into the steamy air. They rinsed off and got out to wrap themselves in thick Turkish towels and rush back to their own bedroom, where they climbed under the duvet covered down comforter and clasped their arms around each other, hugging as if they were the world's first lovers.

"You're my favorite spanker ever," Amanda purred in Colby's ear.

Chapter Sixteen

Rainy Days

On the first Monday of April Laura awoke to rain beating on the windowpanes of Anthony Newton's Greenwich Village town house. She had spent the night in the guest room beside her sister Susan's master suite on the third floor of the smart, trim residence, which had been renovated many times within since its erection in the 1920's. Laura had come into the city over the weekend to join her sister for a book signing of their second graphic novel, which was held in the bookshop just around the corner from Anthony's house. The event had taken place the previous night and Laura's neck felt stiff from looking up to talk to each person who passed by the table set up in the little, over crowded shop. They had sold ninety copies of the new book, which was rather an impressive amount considering the esoteric nature of its contents. Their books would never be on sale at Wal-Mart, but would rather show up in comic book stores and independent book shops as well as online. But here in Manhattan, the graphically illustrated adventures of Susan and Laura's characters barely raised an eyebrow. In fact, some of the longest going dungeons and sex clubs in the city had been thriving just one subway stop further downtown for upwards of forty years. If there was anyplace on earth one could feel at home being into B&D, it was Gotham. The nickname said it all, the Goth vibe was alive in New York and always would be.

Laura slipped out of bed, pulled on a rose colored satin quilted robe and went to the window to look down on the rain soaked cobble stoned street below. It would be a good morning to take a long, hot bubble bath and simply stay indoors. Laura went downstairs and started a pot of coffee. Two youthful cleaning ladies were busily working around the kitchen. The little team came every Monday and spent all day going over the house from top to bottom. The only full time employee who lived in the house was Dennis, Anthony's driver. He had a small apartment in the back of the house, over looking the garden on the third floor. Both Anthony and Dennis were currently in London and the only other resident in the house was Laura's sister Susan, who had already left for work uptown. Anthony's secretary, Paige, had just resumed working for Newton after an almost two year maternity leave. She occupied a tiny office on the first floor of the house and Laura assumed she was there most of the day, but had no desire to distract the pleasant young woman from her work.

Laura broke off a hunk of crusty French bread she found well wrapped in a breadbox, grabbed her coffee and an ambrosia apple and took the tray upstairs. She wandered into Susan's room and sipping her coffee, sat down at Susan's computer to read the New York Times. As soon as Laura stroked the keyboard the flying toasters on the Mac monitor were plastered over with open emails to Susan from her many friends.

"My email program does the same thing," Laura thought, systematically closing all the emails one by one and wishing she knew the universal command for doing closing them all at once. Then jumping out of the ocean of words flashing in front of her eyes, she saw the word Hugo. She should have closed the email directly as she had done with all the others, but she hesitated. She looked at the signature to the email: Thalia. Then she looked up at the extra-ordinarily terse message to which it was attached. It read: "Hi Susan. You have to help me think of some way to get invited back to Random Point. I must, I absolutely must fuck Hugo Sands again!"

Laura's heart seemed to contract in her chest as she now hastened to close the appalling email. Knocked back in the chair by a wave of adrenalin pumped emotion, she steadied herself, feeling sick to her stomach and faint. Hugo was doing his own daughter's nineteen-year-old friend. And here was the full bosomed slut staking her claim to him through her own sister. Which meant that Susan knew about this for as long as it had been going on. Which, knowing Hugo as she knew him, probably dated from Thalia Dunbar's first visit to Random

Point back around Christmas, when the girls had shot that photoset in Michael's bar. "Hugo has been fucking a nineteen-year-old for months and I never guessed a thing."

Laura took a small bite of the bread then put it down, barely able to swallow even that much. She drank some coffee and stared at Susan's computer screen, which now revealed the front page of the New York Times.

"He's been fucking Thalia," Laura thought. "And that's not all. He went to San Francisco to fuck Amanda's mother. He fucked that leggy redhead, his groupie, that Francesca from Provincetown. And last year he fucked Pamela right out of her engagement to Sloan."

It was insupportable. And he wanted her to marry him? Laura gave up on her breakfast and went to take a hot shower. The jealous tears that washed down her face felt hotter than the water that drenched her. Visions of the nineteen-year-old pinup girl kept filling her mind. Laura looked down at her own well-shaped breasts. In her mid thirties, she was still slim and lithe, and looking at herself did not upset her. But Thalia was an Aphrodite and how can a mortal engage with a dewy goddess? Thalia gleamed with the high gloss of youth and the glamour of novelty. Of course Hugo would prefer her bouncing, adoring company to that of his cool and willful long time companion Laura.

More hurt than angry, Laura spent most of the morning moping around the upper floor of the townhouse in tears. As soon as the cleaning ladies broke for lunch, Laura slipped outside in jeans, a trench coat and boots and walked under an umbrella through the village for a couple of hours, looking in shop windows, going in and out of stores and boutiques in a desultory fashion, and finally stopping in a small café for tea and a sandwich. But she still had no appetite and abandoned her repast after a couple of bites. Laura wandered home and spent the rest of the afternoon sitting in a window seat in her bedroom looking out at the rain. Hugo called a couple of times during the afternoon to see how the book signing had gone and ask Laura when he might expect her home. She returned none of the calls but sent him a brief email explaining that she was going to stay on in New York a few more days to do some shopping. When Hugo got Laura's email he was immediately surprised by the emotionless tone of her message, which she had only signed off with her name and without any of the usual accompanying triple x of kisses. Then when she failed to return his several subsequent phone calls he began to wonder if she was upset about something.

Hugo called Susan at work and asked her if anything was up with Laura. Susan told him she hadn't noticed anything but would check it out right after work and get back to him directly. All afternoon Susan kept looking up from her drawing board in the studio in Chipper Knight's print advertising department with a nagging sensation about something to do with Laura. It wasn't until she was swinging on a subway strap on the way home that she remembered that last email she'd gotten from Thalia the previous night. She could have sworn she'd closed the file and deleted it, as she normally did with non essential correspondence every night, but then she remembered something annoying, about her email program automatically opening the last ten letters she'd received when the computer woke up. She'd been meaning to ask Anthony how to defeat that function just yesterday. Now she figured out exactly what Laura had seen the moment she'd stroked Susan's computer on that morning.

The moment she walked into the house and saw Laura's face she knew she'd guessed correctly. Susan said, "You saw that stupid email from Thalia, didn't you?"

"I'm sorry I read your email. I was closing all the open windows and that one caught my eye because of Hugo's name. I couldn't help reading it." And with that Laura once again burst into tears.

The sisters sat together on the bottom steps of the staircase and Laura sobbed out all of her jealous anxiety onto Susan's shoulder. Nor would any amount of reassurances on Susan's part, as to Hugo's complete devotion to her sister assuage the brunette's grief.

"But Thalia's just a slut and you know that Hugo loves you," Susan reasoned.

"If he loves me so much than why does he keep having affairs with all these other women?"

"They throw themselves at him. He can't brush them off. It would hurt their feelings."

"You mean it would hurt his insufferable male ego to have one or two fewer notches on his belt," Laura corrected her sister cynically.

"How can you take any of this seriously? Hugo's love for you has stood the test of time and beat all the odds. And if you're even thinking of walking out on him again, over something as trivial as this, I'll beat the hell out of you myself!" Susan threatened, feeling like crying with frustration herself. Laura smiled weakly at Susan's jest.

"You didn't always stand up for the men," Laura reminded her sister, who had long been an active crusader for the taming of out of control masters into reasonably tractable dominant lovers.

"I just don't think it's fair of you to hold Hugo to some impossibly high moral standard that you don't even subscribe to yourself, depending on your mood, your opportunities and the day of the week."

"That's not true, I haven't been with anyone but Hugo in what seems like years."

"That's only because Michael Flagg won't fuck you since he found out you're officially engaged to Hugo. You know damned well you'd do it with him on a dime if he just gave you the nod."

"Oh Susan, don't even joke about things like that now. My heart is broken, don't you see?"

"Okay, you're jealous, I get that. But don't you think what you're feeling now proves beyond a shadow of a doubt that you should link up with Hugo in a permanent way, namely by marrying him like he's been asking you to for I don't know how long?"

"I've already been married to one wolf. You think it's fun finding out your husband cheats on you? William did that to me with Damaris. You know how it upset me."

"More like it liberated you. I remember you having the time of your life in New York with Marguerite getting over it and you came back to Random Point a new person."

"I just remember the pain of finding out I'd been betrayed."

Susan sighed. Nothing would make Laura happy that day. "Hugo knows something is up with you. He called me at work. He'll be calling again shortly. What should I tell him?"

"Tell him I'm going to stay here, if I may, for a period of time as yet undetermined."

"Seriously? You're not even going to talk to him on the phone?"

"I don't want to talk to him on the phone or anywhere else. At this moment, I am not a fan of Hugo Sands."

Hugo took Susan's call in the back of his shop and the news she began to rapidly report made his heart skip more than one beat. "Damn," he breathed, "this is not a good development."

"I'll work on her," Susan promised, "but you'd better let her be for a couple of days. Otherwise you'll just have to listen to a big tell off."

"Thanks, honey," Hugo said with genuine relief. He felt like he needed a couple of days just to think about what he was going to say to Laura to make this go away.

"For now though, what should I tell her?" Susan asked.

"Tell her I'm sorry and I'll make it up to her," Hugo replied with his usual optimism.

"Thalia is a slut," said Susan helpfully. "That makes a big difference in the equation, you never having been able to resist one."

"Yes, you should know," Hugo replied pleasantly.

Susan hung up and immediately told Laura that she had bought her a few days. Laura sighed, crawled into bed and spent the rest of the night listening to the rain beating on the windows and roof.

The next day Laura got an email from a new admirer, a man named Norman Teasdale who had come to the book signing two days before and introduced himself as Susan and Laura's biggest fan. She remembered him immediately because they had spoken for a long time together after the signing and he'd referenced numerous obscure details from Laura's body of work as a scene illustrator, showing how closely he'd been following her since her first fetish illustration had appeared almost ten years before, when she had free lanced her very first drawing to several underground newspapers and the few remaining monthly B&D magazines. After their discussion he had passed her his card, which proclaimed him a partner at a Manhattan law firm and asked her if he might email her with any other questions he might think of. She had assented and handed him her own card.

During their long conversation she'd had ample time to assess her admirer. He was a tall, stocky, powerfully built young man, perhaps thirty six or eight at most, with dark brown hair cut short and spiky, warm brown eyes and one of the most engaging smiles she had ever seen. He exuded affability and a modest desire to please without spilling over with treacle or seeming the slightest bit forward. He conveyed the impression that he was the type of man who would be there when one needed him. He had also seemed almost deviancy-free during their first conversation, despite his apparently deep historical interest in B&D art, so the extremely adult content of Norman's first email rather took Laura aback, reading:

Dear Laura,

It was such a pleasure meeting you. I'm still in a trance from the experience. I know you're busy so I'll get right to the point. Long ago when you first appeared in spanking magazines, you indicated you sometimes sessioned with players. I would LOVE to session with you while you're here in NY. I'm free any afternoon this week and always play at Isabel Bruno's dungeon. She knows me well and can give me a reference.

What I would be interested in would be a one hour session where I would get to tie you up, corporally punish and tease you and then I would like you to consent to participate in one additional really perverse activity with me, like letting me watch you douche or letting me shave you. As Isabel will tell you, I fall into the sensual category, with the discipline being more of the stimulating than severe variety. I'd like to feel that you are submitting to me, but I will not hurt you and if I do, you can call the session right away. I will not take my clothes off and no sexual favors from you to me will be expected.

I've always loved the way you look in your photos and even your characters have that far away, intrigued look in their eyes, dreaming their way through their various ordeals. I like that. I want to make you dream.

I don't know what all of this is worth to you but I was thinking a grand.

Best wishes,
Norman Teasdale

Laura looked up Isabel Bruno's dungeon on line and immediately dialed the number of the famous B&D salon located in the neighborhood of Columbia University. It was the early afternoon and Isabel herself answered the phone.

"Hello, Isabel?"

"Yes, this is she."

"This is Laura, from Random Point. We've met at some of Hugo's parties, I'm his girlfriend..." Laura let her sentence trail off while Isabel mentally pictured her.

"Oh, yes, Laura. How are you?" Isabel asked warmly.

"Very well, thank you. The reason I'm calling is that one of your regulars proposed I meet him at your dungeon for a session and advised me to get a reference from you. His name is Norman Teasdale. Says he's an attorney..."

"Oh yes, Norman. Lovely man. I've known him for years," Isabel replied at once.

"Well, what kind of scene does he do?"

"Norman? Easy as pie, Laura. B&D with training wheels. I give him to my newest newbies to gently break them in, the college girls, not the street kids. He'll do wrist cuffs, a leg spreader bar, the whipping post, bondage bed, spanking horse and as I recall he either likes to watch a girl pee or douche. He's a big tease. Medium spanker, but he likes to use every implement in the house. You can trust him though, he'll never try to nail you. Let him whip your breasts and pussy, he's totally light handed with delicate parts. I go sub to him myself when I really want to relax."

"Sounds nice. How come this paragon doesn't have a girlie of his own?" Laura asked.

"For all I know he's married with five kids. I don't like to ask. It spoils the fantasy."

"Right. Well, thank you, Isabel. I'll probably be coming in one afternoon this week to meet Mr. Teasdale."

Laura put down the phone, surprised at how quickly she had made up her mind. But she needed some sort of distraction or she'd just sit and brood about nineteen-year-old sluts.

Dear Norman,
    How about this afternoon at four?
                Laura

Laura only had to wait three minutes for a reply.

Dear Laura,
    It's a date!
                Norman

Now it was done. It was raining again as Laura went out in her raincoat and boots to buy an outfit for the afternoon's tryst. She had not brought any sexy clothes with her to New York and her sister was one size smaller than herself, so her sexy clothing would not work.

There was a boutique on the next block and Laura stood in front of the window for a long time before going in. She finally went in and went straight to the rack that held the pvc. She quickly picked out a black zip bustier, a black mini skirt and a long matching coat, all in shiny vinyl, size small. A pair of black patent leather thigh high boots with a four and three quarter inch heel on a one-inch platform caught her eye. They had them in a seven. All the items were placed in a cedar lined fitting room for Laura while she lingered over the leather skirts. She finally selected a gun metal blue leather pencil skirt with a matching pair of snub nosed four inch stack heeled pumps, also on a one inch platform, thinking how they were just the sort of shoes Hugo really liked and how he really disliked pointy toed shoes. In fact the only thing he disliked more was bell-bottoms and she had never dared to buy a pair of either all the while she'd been seeing him. Not that she really wanted bell-bottoms or pointy toed shoes, she thought with a sigh. The truth was that she shared Hugo's tastes almost completely. For example, the double breasted, cropped white leather vest with chunky buttons that she spotted at the last minute was just the sort of top he liked and would look sharp as hi def when paired with the blue leather skirt.

She went into the fitting room and tried everything on. All of the items fit her handsomely, accentuating her slender curves to the greatest possible advantage and she handed the clerk her credit card without hesitation. Then she added elbow gloves to match the skirt and shoes. Her shopping spree had cost her more than she planned to collect from Mr. Teasdale that afternoon, but now she possessed a New York fetish wardrobe that would get her through the entire spring, if she decided to stay on. At the very least, through the week-end, which was to feature a spanking night at Club Paddles.

Laura knew it was undignified to continue feeling sorry for herself and had decided that filling the next week with sensual distractions might prove a speedy cure for her blues. She was classically, violently, sick-makingly jealous of the nineteen-year-old fox Hugo had had at least twice that winter. Once on her first visit to Random Point, once on her second. With Thalia's amusing personality and Hugo's readiness to be charmed by any promiscuous girl with the slightest hint of poise, there was not a doubt in Laura's mind that he had even tried to resist. He'd possibly even met the girl once more on a trip to Boston. Perhaps he fit it into that lost weekend escapade in San Francisco, where he had gone specifically seeking a sexual assignation with Amanda's mother. Like a forlorn little trolley car in the world's smallest village, Laura's mind kept going back to the same dismal theme, which was all the attractive women her supposed fiancé was playing with on a regular basis.

Laura stopped in at a small café on the way home and forced herself to eat most of a salad and a French roll, trying to keep the session in the front of her mind, so as to crowd out unwelcome thoughts of Thalia and her nineteen-year-old bosom and radiantly rosy skin. Laura had edited the photos from the shoot at Michael's tavern, when he'd taken Thalia across his magnificent lap and spanked her for the camera. She remembered that Thalia had no problem crying real tears, which guaranteed that young lady an instant following in the scene. Now Laura realized why Thalia had tried so hard to make such a good impression. The little slut was love struck. And Hugo had made sure she had not gone home disappointed. Laura quickly paid her bill and rushed home with her purchases, determined to stop dwelling on Hugo and his sluts for the rest of the afternoon.

Smoking her first joint in days, she ran a hot bath and tried to focus on Norman Teasdale and his famously sensual B&D. She couldn't actually remember ever experiencing sensual B&D, with the possible exception of those few sessions she'd joined Marguerite Alexander in, where she had played sub to Marguerite's dom, to titillate Marguerite's clients, going back to her earliest days in the scene. In point of fact, she'd not done more than seven sessions in her entire life, all of them either accompanying Marguerite or by Marguerite's arrangement. Perhaps four of the sessions had involved clients who were dominant or switchable spanking enthusiasts, in which case, Laura would submit to corporal punishment from them instead of or in addition to from Marguerite during the course of the play. None of this had ever been unpleasant.

The only truly unpleasant session Laura had ever endured was one she'd not been paid for but had given up as a forfeit to Hugo's friend and client Victor Kesselring, after Laura had done Victor something of a mischief several years before. That had been the worst play scene of her life, far worse than the one when Hugo caned her, after which she had sulked for two years.

Submitting to Victor had been a point of honor for Laura. Victor had arrived with a young submissive from a club called The Keep in L.A. He had promised the pretty blonde a luxurious trip back east at peak foliage with visits to historic sites. Instead he was beating the hell out of her every half hour and making her shiver on her knees in skimpy California clothes with only limited bathroom privileges. Naturally observing this travesty of the romance of discipline, the sensitive Laura was impelled to rescue Aurora, which was what the twenty-two-year-old traveling submissive had been called, plucking her from Victor's ghastly grasp and depositing her safely into Marguerite's secure and warm nearby home in the village. But one doesn't liberate a slave from a self-important master like Victor without paying a price. The price was that Laura had to take Aurora's place that night, and please Victor with her own submission. Naturally this was not easily done. Laura recalled again how this had been by far her worst experience playing, if you could even call it that, ever.

Laura shook off the memory of Victor, wondering why such an unpleasant memory should linger so vividly in her mind. Again she had to stop the monotonous trolley of negativity and consciously refocus on the pleasant hour in the dungeon awaiting her. She didn't dress in her fine fetish apparel for the cab ride uptown, but wore jeans and a white button down shirt with clogs, with a light khaki raincoat. She carried a museum of art umbrella with a Van Gogh design and a large, shiny, round patent leather bandbox with her special wardrobe packed carefully inside. She made sure to leave herself enough time to arrive a full half hour early, hoping for a private interview with Isabel Bruno.

It was a very quiet afternoon and Isabel herself opened the door to Laura and immediately invited her back to her pantry for a cup of tea. Leaving a smart young hostess in charge behind the semi circular polished wood reception desk, Isabel conducted Laura down a hall and into a state of the art kitchen, with wine racks alongside an enormous refrigerator, which Isabel kept stocked with snacks for her girls and her guests. Customers paid a premium to visit the exclusive salon, which was said to be staffed almost exclusively by Barnard and Columbia women (the schools were virtually across the street) but in fact only had one Barnard girl on staff and she was merely the weekend bartender and never sessioned, and yet Isabel's club had an éclat that could be boasted of by no other B&D salon in Manhattan. Isabel herself was 70% of the draw, versatile as both mistress and submissive and ever enchanting to behold, her own personal sessions alone would have paid her overhead. But there were only so many hours in the day and she couldn't see everyone herself. She kept girls on staff to sprinkle sessions on. Her reputation as a lovely person had been garnering the best new talent in New York to her parlor for years. Women knew they could trust Isabel to watch out for them. That didn't mean she didn't cater for the occasional sadist, but when she did find herself entertaining that stripe of player, she never handed him any individual other than a true masochist to match him limit for limit.

In fact, Isabel was an artist at matching up doms with subs, and her reward was that everyone spoke well of her in the scene.

Laura showed Isabel her new leather and pvc. The mistress beamed with approval and suggested Laura devastate Norman Teasdale with the PVC outfit. Laura obediently stripped off her jeans and shirt, then exchanged her white cotton bra and panties for a black lace push up bra and sheer backed black lace French cut briefs. Next she donned a black lace garter belt and a pair of black fishnet stockings with seams up the back. Now she sat on a heavy, carved wooden kitchen chair to pull on the thigh high pvc boots. The black patent leather mini skirt simply zipped up the back and was on in an instant, though once on, glove tight. The matching bustier zipped up the front and was donned with similar ease. Finally, she slipped into the long pvc coat, with its notched lapels, cuffs and tailored detail. The coat came down to mid calf while the mini skirt ended at mid thigh, the juxtaposition of good and bad behavior dramatic and whimsical all at once. The high stack heeled boots finished the look to polished perfection. Isabel was visibly excited. She was also in love with Laura and Susan's new book, which Laura had brought her as a present. Just as Laura was suggesting that they could introduce a new character in the ongoing series based on Isabel, the doorbell rang. Norman Teasdale had arrived.

Right from the outset, Laura knew it was going to be a perfect session. He was something of a stocky young man but his gray wool business suit fit him well and he smelled clean and fresh without a trace of aftershave about him. His white nylon rope bondage was quick, symmetrical and pretty as he set her up in beautiful positions, against the whipping post or prone on the bondage bed. With every new position, an article of Laura's outfit was removed, beginning with the coat and ending with her black lingerie. Once she was in a new position, she would be caressed and teased, lightly flogged, squeezed and pinched, then slapped open handed, just a little harder. Special attentions were paid to her well-rounded, upstanding breasts and gently swelling labia, the last of her charms to be fully revealed. Pussy spanking was a particular passion of her new client and he approached her pretty sex with care and restraint, beginning with the smallest and lightest of floggers and ending with firm, resounding spanking with the palm of his hand. He noted how she moved towards and away from him and made minute adjustments in the speed and force he was exerting accordingly. He did not speak, but gave his entire concentration to the play at hand.

During the second half of the session, after he had gotten Laura fully nude, he began to bind her more provocatively, with her legs well spread, on her back, on her stomach, on all fours and finally, in the knee to elbow position, with her head bowed low. Now the spanking got harder, tinting her entire bottom a deep shade of magenta. Laura's well-spanked pussy was also as pink as it had ever been, the rosy skin of her Venus mound radiant beneath her soft brown pubic curls.

Just before proposing the ultimate naughtiness to Laura, he inserted a joint between her lips and commanded her to take a few hits. Now everything was vibrating for Laura, from her swollen pussy lips to her fully activated submissive imagination. Then he showed her a pink, pint sized plain water douche with a long white nozzle.

"May I?" he asked politely. She nodded, unable to speak. Norman pulled her up to a squatting position, which was enhanced to the full by the only raiment she still had on, the shiny, high-heeled pvc boots, and slipped a silver basin under her bottom. Her client gently separated her labia with his fingers and inserted the long white plastic nozzle up into her lubricating vaginal canal. When the pink rubber bulb full of warm water was flush with her pussy and bottom, he placed one of her own hands on the bulb and instructed her to squeeze. Laura obeyed and began to flush herself out with the warm water, which spilled down and out into the basin immediately. She had rarely if ever douched in her entire life, never seeing any need to do so, but found that the sensation was not unpleasant. In fact, it was extremely sexy. She did not turn her head to look at her client, well aware that this was the most important moment of the scene for him, the kinkiest one and the one during which he must have felt that he was exerting the most control over his pampered toy.

Once all the water had been diffused from the douche into Laura's body and then flowed out again, Teasdale took away the basin and patted her dry with a white towel.

"Have you ever smothered anyone?" he asked, lying back on the bondage bed and gently coaxing her into the proper position for enacting this rarified variation of bottom worship. Laura straddled his head with her knees on the bondage bed on either side of it but only lowered her body down far enough for him to stretch his tongue up to her pussy and lick at it's damp surface. "Come down lower," he urged her.

"I'll crush you," she protested.

"Come on, send me to heaven," he beseeched her, pulling her down hard to literally sit on his face. She pulled back up but he yanked her back down. "It's okay," he assured her, cupping one of her cheeks in each hand. "I want to feel your weight."

"I can't!"

"Yes, you can. Do it, girl!" he positioned her just as he wanted her, his darting tongue gaining full access to her increasingly creamy slit and his nose buried in her bottom.

"Don't you want to take your clothes off at this point, Mr. Teasdale?" Laura asked.

"Lean forward and unzip my pants," Teasdale urged her. When she complied his penis popped out with the thick resiliency of a pink rubber Doc Johnson joystick.

"Oooooh," Laura couldn't help but remarking, tentatively touching it and almost giggling when it rebounded back at her with a life all its own. "Damn, you are big!"

"Just grab onto it lightly," he encouraged her before diving back between her pussy lips and bottom cheeks and while supporting her twin hemispheres in the palms of his hands. Laura had only just lightly encircled Teasdale's remarkably robust penis with her soft little hands when he started to spurt a predictably copious liquid tribute to her considerable allure as a dainty bondage heroine. She kept pumping him lightly with her cherry red manicured finger tips until every luminous white drop had been extracted from her fan's impressive cock, knowing that she crossed the dungeon sex line beyond redemption but not minding very much because Mr. Teasdale had been so sweet and was far too much of a B&D connoisseur to turn out an undercover cop.

They quickly set themselves to rights and Laura began to tidy up the dungeon. Norman pressed the promised thousand dollars along with a large tip into her hand before kissing her lightly on the cheek, making her some courtly compliments and then discreetly slipping off into the spring evening. Laura went out into the lobby to make sure that Norman had paid Isabel for the dungeon rental, noticing out of the corner of her eye that there was at least one gentleman in the side parlor, being attended to by one of Isabel's house subs, a slender girl with a northern European complexion, smooth light red curls meandering down her back, and a lean torso tightly laced into a white brocade Victorian corset, sans bra. Laura had a fleeting impression of a saucy, rosy tipped bosom and a pair of cherry red lips as she quickly walked by the open door, but no more than that as she immediately addressed herself to Isabel, who was once more behind the semi circular console reception desk.

"Did he give you money?" Laura asked, quickly thumbing through the wad of hundred dollar bills Teasdale had handed her. "Oh my god, he gave me a 50% tip!"

"Good for you! Yes, he paid me. You're all set."

"Here, because you've been so sweet," said Laura, handing Isabel two hundreds.

"Oh, how nice you are!" said Isabel, not arguing but putting the money into her under the counter purse.

"I don't remember her being so nice," said a masculine voice with a European accent from behind Laura. She turned towards the parlor and was taken aback to see the dreaded and abhorred Victor Kessel-ring standing in the door before her. "So many things she doesn't do," he added, crossing to her in a few strides. Laura stared at him, speechless with shock that she had just thought of him two hours past and here he was, curling in the mist like a foul Belgian miasma on her very doorstep. Actually, he was as tall, lean and upright and as well groomed and well favored as ever. He was turning fifty, turning gray, but still attractive, if one cared for that sort of harsh, chiseled face. She for one did not care for it even slightly, much preferring faces that broke into spontaneous smiles every hour of the day.

Suppressing a shudder and pretending not to be horrified to see him, Laura murmured a bland, robotic greeting and then returned to the dungeon to get her wardrobe case and change back into her street clothes, her heart pounding with anxiety and resentment, because she knew the beast would never take the hint and let her alone. She knew this because first, Victor had glimpsed her in the dramatic pvc costume, topped off by the impossibly elegant patent leather coat. Secondly, her skin held a seductive freshly spanked glow that hovered like a pink, shimmering heat about her lovely face. Thirdly, she was Hugo Sands' private submissive from Random Point, an artist and a pampered ivy league brat, therefore much more exotic to Victor than any other girl currently tottering about on five inch heels and/or swaying from side to side in a breathtaking corset under the lavishly tiled ceilings of the club. Finally, he had formerly had her for free and free was a very good price. She had to cross the lobby again to get back to Isabel's changing rooms and Victor pounced on her the moment she emerged.

"Laura, come in here and we'll talk," he said, taking her by the elbow and leading her into the second parlor, which was empty.

She pulled back from him and lifted her chin saying, "I don't want to talk to you."

Taken aback by her vehemence, Victor stared at her.

"I don't like you," she declared, glaring into his cold blue eyes. Victor recoiled as if struck but after a moment smiled thinly at her.

"Should I call Hugo and ask if we can play?" Victor asked, flipping open a cell phone.

"I don't belong to Hugo anymore. We broke up."

"What do you mean, you broke up. He's your master, isn't he?"

"No. Why do you think that? It was never like that between Hugo and me."

"He gave you to me that night. You obeyed him."

"Yes and you beat the hell out of me."

"Your doe eyes inflamed me, so perhaps I got carried away. Anyway, it was your own fault. You took that girl away from me."

"You can't even remember her name, can you?" Laura demanded.

"I can, it was Aurora. I was very fond of her. She was the perfect submissive until you ruined her and spoiled her. Then you took her away from me. So I punished you. The deal was fair. You agreed to it. Now you're whining about it."

Laura shrugged, "Fine. The deal was fair and you're a B&D god. Now get the fuck out of my way, I'm going home."

She tried to push past him but he caught her by the arm, "Laura wait, I want to talk to you. I have to play with you tonight. You looking maddeningly good in that outfit."

Laura stared at him uncomprehendingly. Had she or had she not just cursed at him? Why wasn't he reacting with masterful indignation? "Are you saying you want to pay me for a session Victor?" she asked emphatically. "Before you answer be aware that these days I only do *dominant* sessions with euro trash masters like you." She didn't wait for his reply but pushed past him and back out into the lobby, where Isabel was waiting curiously to see what would be decided between her two volatile visitors. Victor marched resolutely after her.

"Laura wait, let's get a dungeon," the jaded player insisted, irresistibly drawn to the bitchy new Laura.

"Did you hear what I said, Victor? If I go into a dungeon with you, you'll be the one bowing down to me."

"I understand," he said.

"And do you understand that I hate and despise you and that I've been nursing a grudge against you since that disgusting night when you treated me like some sort of Castle Roissy slut out of the Story of O?"

"You think I did you a wrong, I'm offering you the opportunity to take revenge."

"You mean punish you?"

Victor was silent.

"And how much did you plan to bribe me with?" Laura inquired with unabashed curiosity.

"Whatever amount you say," Victor replied affably enough.

"Let's say, three times whatever you were going to pay the club girl you were about to engage."

Victor nodded his assent.

"Very well," said Laura, "give Isabel the money, book the room and meet me in the gallery in ten minutes." The gallery was a long, narrow room, painted jewel tone blue and lined with curious bondage portraits in glossy carved wood and gold gilt frames. At one end was a low stocks, at the other, a St. Andrews Cross, with a whipping post and a bondage bed down the middle. The floor was of a dark, planked wood and the ceiling colorfully lined with brick red inset tiles. It was a beautiful room to play in, far too nice for the likes of Victor K, thought Laura as she exchanged the black pvc outfit she'd worn for Norman Teasdale for the blue leather skirt and white leather halter vest outfit with the blue fetish pumps and matching leather elbow gloves. Now that she gazed at her image in Isabel's mirror, she realized that it was the gloves that truly made the outfit, along with the square gun metal buckle self belt that adorned the trim pencil skirt and so becomingly emphasized her slender waist. She pulled her long brown hair back into a blue leather barrette that she placed at the nape of her neck. Then she touched up her lipstick, dark red, trying not to think about what she was doing beyond the fact that it was distracting her from her jealousy of Thalia Dunbar. Also, it would be good to get even with Victor for that night of horrors with him, to get the rancor out of her system once and for all. She realized it had been eating away at her and coloring her view of all European dominants, of which she was now inherently suspicious one hundred percent of the time, exceptions made for the dorkily endearing English ones.

Laura strolled into the dungeon with a tall, formidably built but shapely and graceful young woman clad in a white leather warrior tunic with lacing sandals to match, each garment well trimmed with brass studs. The girl looked about nineteen and had pretty, thick, long, straight sandy blonde hair and a truly golden tan. Laura remembered they had just passed spring break and assumed this enterprising college coed had been down in Florida the previous week. Victor was taken aback at the young girl's appearance but Laura informed him with a careless, "She's going to do the bondage for me." Then she suppressed a yawn and lit a joint as Xena went to work on stripping Victor to his boxers and binding him facing the St. Andrews Cross with his back and buttocks outwards. Laura smoked indolently as she watched Xena intent on her work. She was a strong girl and used to tying big men up and down.

"Thank you, Xena. Leave us for a few minutes now. I'll call you when it is time to change the position."

Xena left, enchanted with her new playmate, as Laura had booked her for an hour and had promised her an extra bonus.

Laura allowed Victor one puff of her cigarette before extinguishing it. "You see, I'm kinder to you than you were to me right from the start," she pointed out. "So oblige me by telling me why would you want to session with a woman who just told you that she hates you?"

"Emotions are interesting. I have hardly any myself. Love, hate, all are interesting."

"You're full of crap, Victor. You're a fucking sadomasochist. Just admit it."

"Sure I admit it. Why wouldn't I? Aren't you?"

"No. I am absolutely nothing like you!" she cried indignantly. "I hate that master slave bullshit. It fucking makes me sick. Do you understand me?" Laura took up a riding crop, ripped down Victor's shorts and began laying into his not extremely well padded nether regions with a rage that she had been ignoring for years.

"Yes, Yes, I understand!" Victor gasped a few minutes later, as Laura cropped him until her arm ached. Then she threw the crop aside and grabbed up a strop. Wielding this article of heavy harness leather with both hands, she brought it down across his buttocks several dozen times. It made a loud noise when it connected and left large swatches of purple red in its wake. But Laura soon exchanged this for a long, one-inch thick oak paddle with a sturdy handle. Again, she took up the implement with both hands and aiming carefully at first and then, quite as carelessly as she chose, she lambasted his already well-belabored backside with the heavy and punishing wood. Apart from the occasional grunt and intake of breath, he made hardly a sound.

Laura called Xena back in and ordered her to bind Victor on the bondage bed with his arms well out of the way and everything exposed. Victor lost the remnant of modesty his shorts had afforded as they came off as well. Xena made Victor kneel on all fours and bound his wrists and ankles to the table using buckling leather straps and o-rings.

"Thank you, Xena. Now take one of those long oak paddles, about equal in weight to this one here and get on the other side of Victor. We'll take turns paddling his bottom with our large wooden paddles. We can even move around and switch positions half way through. The important thing is to keep smacking him, no matter how much he wriggles or how much he whines. Okay?"

"Yes, Mistress!" Xena replied gratifyingly.

After punishing Victor in this fashion for ten minutes, Laura called a halt and warned, "He's starting to numb out. He won't feel a thing soon. Best put him in a hogtie while I think what to do next!"

Laura stood with her arm folded across her pert bosom, her back against one of the whipping posts in the beautifully equipped playroom, watching Xena quickly and neatly truss Victor up on his stomach in the center of the bondage bed. The strong, tall, plump club girl used white nylon rope cut in short equal lengths to affix their victim's wrists to his ankles.

"You can rock back and forth on your penis while you're waiting," Laura suggested, starting him off with a push on his thigh, as though she were starting a cradle or swing. He obediently began to grind against the bondage bed, with an extremely erect penis underneath him. Laura took Xena from the room to confer with her again out of Victor's earshot and returned a moment later, alone. She stilled Victor's motion with a hand on his head. She pulled his head up by his hair and made him look into his own reflection in a mirror opposite them. She stood beside him and forced his head up to regard her entire image, from her smoothly coifed head, with her luxuriant ponytail creeping around over one shoulder, to her slender, well molded torso in the white leather buttoned vest, her slim arms in the blue leather elbow gloves, her small waist emphasized by the large metallic blue buckle of her skirt belt, her slim, girlish hips outlined by the blue leather skirt, and her well-turned, slim-ankled legs displayed to maximum advantage by the high heeled, semi-platform pumps.

"Look at me," she commanded. The world-class fetish apparel fit her charming body exactly as an expensive, well designed and exquisitely coordinated leather outfit should, to perfection.

"Very nice," he murmured.

"Thank you, but I didn't invite you to chatter at me," Laura said, selecting a cane from a circular basket full of implements of correction. Just then Xena returned, her arms full of cellophane wrapped objects, which she dumped in a heap on the bondage bed behind Victor.

"First thing, Xena, gag him. I loathe the sound of his voice," said Laura. Xena began to tear open one of the cellophane bags but Laura stopped her, "No, not the ball gag, the penis gag." Victor picked up his head and looked at Laura but did not bother to protest. Xena took a ball gag with a penis shaped rubber dildo attached to the interior side and forced Victor to open his mouth for it. "It's okay, I'm sure he's had bigger dicks than that down his throat, he's such a slut," said Laura with a complete lack of concern as Victor initially gagged, then accepted his new 6" throat lozenge, which Xena affixed firmly into Victor's mouth by means of a strap around his head.

"You know what my problem with you is, Victor?" Laura asked, walking around him and helping Xena to free him from the hogtie. Victor shook his head. "It's that I want you to feel pain and suffer, but I don't have it in me to be that cruel." In spite of the uncomfortable gag he wore, Victor managed to throw her a quizzical stare. "That's why Xena is here," said Laura. "She has absolutely no problem being harsh with useless men. And she's over the moon at the chance of bringing a pompous master to his knees. Right Xena?"

"You bet, Mistress!" Xena replied with enthusiasm, as they pulled off the last ropes of the hogtie and helped their captive up to his feet, only to make him bend over and grab his ankles.

"Xena, rub a bit of cinnamon lube over that big chrome dildo you have there," said Laura, placing her hand in the small of Victor's back and pulling back with her choice of standard straight handled cane. "It's okay, Victor, relax, you won't truly get made our bitch until your sorry ass is fully on fire from this cane." Then she began the caning, forcing herself to omit any sort of regular warm up. "I shouldn't even aim, considering who I'm doing this to, but that's me," Laura admitted and did scrupulously take aim before allowing each successive slash of the rattan fall across her erstwhile persecutor's flattish backside, the thin skinned vista of which was soon stained dark red and purple, with lighter white welts rising above. Laura caned Victor until her arm began to feel tired, striping him from the bottom of his hips to the mid point of his thighs. He never made a sound but to occasionally grunt or catch his breath. Finally she handed the cane to Xena, nodding at the punishment device her young assistant had prepared and set to one side on a clean towel. Xena tucked the cane under one arm, cheerfully took up the seven and a half inch chrome phallus, spread Victor's cheeks with the confidence of a nurse and slid the large dildo into his rectum. He moaned into the gag but did not protest further.

Laura stepped in front of Victor, turned her back to him, slowly hiked her tight skirt up to her hips and revealed her creamy pink and white bottom, girded by a white garter belt and clad in white silk French cut briefs, the full seat wrapping her satiny cheeks like a wedding present. She leaned over and positioned herself so that his nose nestled in her panty clad bottom crack then she nodded over her shoulder at Xena to begin the caning again. If either of the women noticed Victor covertly capture his own penis in one of his hands while he bent over and breathed in Laura's essence through her panties and got his final caning while metal butt-plugged, they didn't comment. Everyone knew what the objective was and that it should take no longer than three to five minutes to achieve. They got it in two.

When Laura returned to the townhouse, she found an email from Norman Teasdale effusive with praise and gratitude for their adventure in the dungeon several hours before. She had other emails from friends but there was nothing from Hugo. After speaking with Susan, Hugo now knew exactly why Laura was brooding so far out of reach, but hadn't decided how to respond. "Always so circumspect," Laura thought huffily.

Susan had just gotten home from work and the sisters walked out into the rainy April night under an umbrella until they came to an Indian restaurant they both liked and went in. Laura did not hesitate to report everything that had happened to her since she had seen her sister that morning and Susan was suitably impressed. They ate spicy salads and awaited other savory dishes while looking out the window onto the black, glistening, rain drenched Village Street.

"So where did you leave it with Victor?" Susan asked. "I mean, did you hug him?"

"I just walked out of the dungeon and let Xena get rid of that freak," Laura replied without embarrassment.

"So how much did he wind up paying?"

"Nine. Isabel, Xena and I each got a third."

"And you got fifteen hundred from Norman?"

"Yes."

"Did Teasdale want to see me too?" Susan wondered idly, having also met their fan at the book signing.

"Susan, be yourself, everyone knows you're Anthony's protégé."

"Have you spoken to Hugo yet?" Susan asked, sipping a glass of merlot while nibbling at a papadum.

"No," Laura replied.

"Laura you're being really bad."

Laura shrugged and stared into her wine glass. The pain was much less today but it was still too soon to speak to him and far too soon to return to him. The sessions had distracted her. They had helped. Especially paying back Victor in his own coin for that abominable scene, which she had suffered at his hands that had left her feeling ill-used for years. She had told an asshole master off and had gotten away with it. The code of the scene required that she never reveal what had happened in the dungeon that day between herself and Victor to Hugo, though for some reason, that code didn't apply to her sister or any other woman who might cross Victor's path and need forewarning that he was a nightmare as a dominant but as docile and compliant as one might wish as a submissive.

"I think I'll stay through Friday night and go to that party in Chelsea," said Laura decisively.

"Great idea!" said Susan with real enthusiasm. When Laura excused herself to visit the rest room, Susan texted Hugo, "We'll be at Paddles Friday night."

Chapter Seventeen

April Night

Laura spent the rest of the week taking cabs and walks around Manhattan, meeting friends for lunch, receiving spa treatments, visiting museums with her sketch book and doing a great deal more shopping. By Friday she was beginning to feel more lonely for Hugo than jealous of Thalia and was on the verge of calling him several times. However each time she stopped herself, still not entirely ready to put the incident behind her. She felt rather proud of herself for having avoided a confrontation with Hugo earlier in the week, while her emotions were running so high. And yet even by week's end, the hurt and anger still lingered, far too much to seem to make any type of normal conversation possible between them.

Susan and Laura ate a late dinner out at a neighborhood café, passed by the bookshop to see how their book was selling, were delighted to take a reorder from the shop owner and returned to the townhouse to dress for the club in a leisurely manner. Laura chose the softest possible look, donning a full-skirted, sheer white cotton shirt waist dress, with an embroidered hem, waist darts and round buttons, accented by a narrow notched collar, short sleeve cuffs and belt in pale grey. Her shoes were multi-buckled, round toed, black patent leather 4" stack heeled platforms with a high vamp. She wore very little make up, dark red lipstick and nail polish and her long dark hair hung down her back without restraint. The rain that had lasted all week stopped at dusk that night and a warm, unnaturally balmy wind blew the streets of the city bone dry before dark completely fell. Laura carried a sheer grey tulle evening coat over her arm.

Susan played butch to Laura's femme, dressing herself in a high collared leather cat suit and sensible 3" high-heeled knee boots. She didn't know if she would even play that evening, but whatever side she decided to land on, she was perfectly attired for action. If she chose to be dominant, her front zipping leather jump suit would lend her all the polished authority she needed to cause any male submissive to kneel before her gleaming thighs. If she decided to yield to a crop or paddle in the hands of an attractive male top, she had packaged one of the cutest size 5 bottoms in Manhattan in the snuggest, most supple black leather fetish couture she could find and the effect was most agreeably seductive.

The young women took a cab to 26th Street between 7th and 8th Avenues and entered the club at ten p.m. At exactly ten minutes after ten, Laura saw Hugo enter the main room. At the sight of him her face went blazing pink and her knees seem to go out under her. She leaned against the soft drink bar and stared at him, reeling with the impact of seeing him again. He looked extremely good to her in a single-breasted taupe suit and white shirt. She didn't recognize the suit but liked it very much. He had entered the room with a pleasant smile but as soon as he turned to see her that bland look was replaced by a stern glance. He folded his arms and stared back at her, communicating across the large room, already half filled with fetish-clad celebrants, how displeased he was with her. He seemed content to gaze at her in this manner almost indefinitely and she felt her eyes hypnotically engaged by his, until the connection was rudely broken by a small, well rounded young lady, who accosted Hugo, demanded hugs and began to barrage him with excited chatter. In another moment, several other young women had discovered the magazine publisher in their midst and surrounded him with questions, enthusiastic greetings, teasing and requests to play with him as soon as he could give them the time. Laura watched his usual easy smile replace the penetrating gaze he had reserved for her edification as he bantered with the set of girls.

Laura turned towards the bar and requested a coke from the club girl dispensing iced drinks in waxed paper cups. Looking up and noticing there was a long mirror above the bar, Laura realized she could keep an eye on Hugo and his entourage without even turning her head. How tall he was and well he looked, she thought. She saw someone hand him a long wooden paddle and watched him examine it. At last he seemed to decide he would have to do something with it and turned the small, plump, blonde girl who had first addressed him under his arm and swung the sorority paddle against the seat of her snug gray leggings perhaps a dozen times before she finally popped out of his grasp, both hands clasped to her spanked bottom. Laura couldn't help staring and noting as she did that it was the very youngest of his group of fans he had chosen to shower his attentions on. Tears prickled the backs of her eyes as she envisioned Hugo with Thalia locked in his arms for the thousandth time.

"Mistress, may I serve you?" asked a timid voice at Laura's elbow. She turned to regard a short, lithe, muscular, young man clad in black jeans and a black t-shirt. He had short, black, geometrically cut hair and wore thick, black-rimmed eyeglasses, which together conveyed the effect of a somewhat hip geek.

"No thank you," said Laura, with a polite but disinterested smile, her gaze drawn inexorably back to the mirror, where she now observed Hugo chatting with their friend Patricia Fairservis, whose blonde hair caressed her slim shoulders and whose slender body was tightly encased in a sweetheart cut pvc sheath. Laura remembered with a start of anxiety that Hugo and Patricia had once been lovers when the aggressive and attractive P.R. woman had lived for at time in the luxuriously renovated lighthouse at Random Point. Laura knew that Hugo had not seen Patricia in some time and would now be fully engaged in telling her his news of the century, the story he would dine out on for the rest of his life, about the sudden emergence of his hitherto unknown daughter not only in his life but in the scene itself. It was a good story so how could he not tell it to as intimate an old friend as Patricia, but it would take some time to tell. Laura looked at the very eager to please young man beside her again. He took her light glance as encouragement and gathering his courage, asked, "Mistress, would you spank me?"

"Don't grown men get caned?" she asked in an offhand way.

"I would LOVE to be caned by you," he replied, flushing with excitement.

"You're crazy. I'm not even a mistress and I am in a very bad mood."

"Why are you angry?" the boy asked with interest. "Is it because of some man?"

"Yes, you're very astute for a male submissive. Most ones I've met are completely wrapped up in themselves."

"Isn't everyone? But you're so beautiful. If I found you a cane in the next five minutes, would you cane me as hard as you can?"

"You don't know what you're saying. I don't even know what I'm doing with a cane. I could really hurt you," Laura warned him, but to no avail. The young man had gone in search of the most serious cane he could find. She thought, "Why am I suddenly topping all these men? This isn't me. Why do men force women to top them?" The next instant, the young man was before her with a straight rattan cane.

"Let's go in there," Laura nodded towards an inner room, taking the cane from his hand and waiting for him to precede her. This room was smaller than the main hall with some interesting spanking and bondage furniture arrayed for the amusement of guests. Laura paused before a trestle bench and looked at her new submissive. "Bend over," she told him, taking care that he was facing a mirror. She walked behind him and examined the appearance of the target area, snugly clad in black jeans.

"I suppose it would be pointless to start over these?" she asked.

"Yes, Mistress," her calm victim brightly replied.

"Or bother with a warm up?" Laura asked.

"Totally unnecessary, Mistress," said the young man, helpfully unzipping his jeans and shorts and tugging them down to his knees before bending back over the bench.

"What are you doing?" Susan Ross asked, entering the room, which was otherwise empty. "Did you know that Hugo's here? Who is this?" Susan walked in front of the young man and lifted his chin to look at his face.

"Yes, who are you?" Laura asked, swishing the cane through the air behind him.

"Ryan," the boy answered, looking up at Susan's in wonder, for she was even more sensational looking than Laura and a lot more dominant to boot, in her skin tight black leather cat suit. The mirror before them reflected the entire backside of the petite siren, complete with naturally blonde ponytail to a provocatively tiny waist, flaring down into cute hips and a classic sweetheart shaped bottom; the package was well balanced from the small, high, well rounded bosom straining against the front-zipped black leather cat suit, to her little feet so elegant and powerful in the sexy high heeled boots. But best of all was her smiling face, as fresh as April itself. One could see at once that she was a pleasant girl who liked to enjoy life. Ryan's eyes could not but go back to the firm little buttocks encased in black leather reflected in the mirror before him, while Susan distractedly ran her gloved hand through his short hair.

"Beautiful, muscular body Ryan has," Susan remarked, leaning over to inspect Laura's as yet unmarked target, snowy white and sculpted in the manner of a Greek statue. "Now this is more like it," Laura thought approvingly, contrasting the masculine beauty she now beheld with the scrawny withers of Victor. "He's small and perfectly formed for a girl to control. And he must be quite young with that skin tone."

"How old are you Ryan?" Laura asked.

"26, Mistress," he replied readily.

"Laura, what are you getting into here? Don't you want to go and talk to Hugo?"

"He'll find me eventually," said Laura, applying the first stroke of the cane evenly across the centermost portion of Ryan's bottom. "Anyway, Ryan wants a caning. He asked me for one and I said I would deliver."

Laura took careful aim and applied two more strokes, one above and one below the initial cut. Three red marks appeared on the otherwise unblemished cream canvas. Susan, finding Ryan appealing, stood quite close to him and pressed his head against her thigh, keeping her hand wound in his hair. "Can you smell the leather of this outfit?" Susan murmured to him.

"Yes, Mistress," he sighed, in another world of contentment.

"You will receive a total of one dozen strokes with the cane and then my sister will find us some matching sized wooden paddles and we will demonstrate their use to you," Laura decided, noticing that the last cane stroke she had administered was beginning to leave a pink weal. Ryan barely noticed.

"You're sisters?" he gasped, thinking he must be dreaming.

"It's true," said Susan, finding some paddles on a bench not too far from where they played. "And we never do this."

"So, we'll each take a side?" suggested Laura, examining the long, black leather paddle Susan had handed her. Susan had chosen the same sized implement in hard wood for herself.

"Don't you think straight across the middle with these?" Susan asked, laying the long, thick blade of her wooden paddle across Ryan's buttocks.

"Perhaps you're right, in any case, I'll go first."

Laura was fond of sets of six and began one with her leather paddle. She felt more comfortable wielding it than a dangerous cane, though this boy was an obvious pain slut. Then Susan took her turn from the opposite side, with her wooden paddle. When the thwacks became audible, they began to attract a small audience of onlookers. The intimacy shattered, Laura and Susan wound up the scene in a matter of minutes, each, however, taking care to lay on several dozen swats with her implement of choice. After which, the girls helped Ryan put himself back together and each bestowed a hug on their enchanted new fan. It was only a little later in the evening that someone told Ryan he had been entertained by two of the most interesting cartoonists in the scene and advised him to go and buy their books that night. Meanwhile, he was very well pleased with his encounter. His bottom stung agreeably and he would cherish the image and sensation of the playful and generous sisters, in their contrasting outfits, the blonde one smelling like leather, the dark one like Chanel No. 5, for all time. But he was a true submissive and once he sensed the scene was fully over, he gracefully withdrew to the outer room and did not accost either Susan or Laura again that night.

Once the demonstration was over, the little crowd that had entered the room began to thin, with several familiar faces materializing before the girls to claim their undivided attention. One belonged to their beloved Sherman Cooper, who had in turn dated each of them in years gone by and the other was a tall, good looking young man Laura remembered from somewhere but couldn't quite place.

"This is Monty Powell, he works at CK," Susan explained, "But he's a complete bondager."

"Have you seen this new bondage bed they just installed" asked Sherman, after exchanging hugs with both girls. "It's got a post built into either end so two girls can be bound kneeling opposite each other."

"It's got attached leather cuffs," added Monty, which meant the bondage heroine could be fastened in place in seconds.

"Come on, we'll show you," they said, taking Susan and Laura into a connecting room, which did indeed boast a new bondage bed, with posts on either end.

"No, this is not a good outfit for that. I'll just watch," said Susan.

"No, I'm not getting on that either," Laura shook her head vigorously, "it's too rude!"

"If you didn't want to be tied to a whipping post, why wear that dress?" Monty Powell asked reasonably. "Look, let me just show you how easy this is, young lady, get up on the table here. Right now."

Laura looked at Monty with deep suspicion. "No!"

"Come on, Laura," said Sherman Cooper with the propriety of a former sweetheart. "He's right. You're obviously asking for it wearing a Sweet Gwendolyn dress to this club. Now just get up on your knees and straddle the whipping post and I'll pin your skirt up to your waist."

Somehow Laura found herself on the new bondage bed, facing the leather upholstered whipping post, on her knees, with her wrists being bound to the other side of the post above her head.

"Spanked by two men at once? No, I plead sensory overload," she protested.

"I'm not going to spank you in the slightest," Monty promised, standing in front of her and merely fingering one velvety ear lobe. "I'll just make sure you can't get free the whole time," he added, tweaking one of her nipples through the layers of bra and dress that protected it.

Electrified by Monty's forwardness, Laura responded with character-istic passivity, closing her eyes and melting against the whipping post in a state of modified abandon. She could only imagine how she might look from behind, with her white skirt and petticoat pinned up, her bottom encased in sheer white nylon panties, her nude, seamed stockings held up by a matching garter belt, her obscenely little girlish demi Mary Jane fetish pumps, of such shiny patent leather and so naughtily leading up to the innocent white underpinnings of her pure white dress, skin all golden white and perhaps after Sherman spanked her bottom, somewhat tinged with pink.

Once her skirt was pinned up, the attractive, fair-haired Manhattan attorney wasted no time in reacquainting himself with the curves of Laura's backside. The see-through French cut briefs were so thin as to allow the first blush of pink to immediately gleam through the fabric as he spanked some color into her cheeks. It had been several years since they had played and Laura knew he was all but engaged to Patricia Fairservis, but she cherished fond memories of her several nights with Sherman Cooper, a good player and easy companion. Laura regarded Sherman's fair, smartly groomed, clean-cut, well-suited profile reflected in the mirror before her. Yes, it WAS much easier to give in to beautiful people, whatever they asked. Like that boy a few minutes ago.

But two men at once? "No," Laura cried, lifting her head and tossing her long, smooth mane of dark silky hair. "It's too much! I'll die of embarrassment," she claimed. Monty, Sherman and Susan all laughed. Sherman continued to apply the open palm of his hand to Laura's panty clad bottom while she knelt, partially straddling the whipping post to which her wrists were attached. Monty arranged her hair behind one shoulder and turned Laura's face towards Susan momentarily.

"You poor thing," Susan said mechanically, mesmerized by the sight of two of her favorite men artfully molesting her sister.

With Sherman vigorously spanking her and Monty cupping her bosom in his large, powerful hands, Laura experienced a rare strain of erotic euphoria. She knew there were limits to what could happen at Paddles and she trusted Sherman Cooper not to cross unchartered boundaries. Then she remembered that Hugo was loose in the club. Did she really want his first glimpse of her to be red bottomed between two men?

"I have to get down," she told Monty at length, feeling her bottom radiant with warmth under the tight nylon of her panties.

"Okay," he said affably, unfastening her wrists from the leather cuffs at once. Sherman unfolded Laura's skirt and let it drop back into place then helped her off the table. They hugged closely for several minutes.

"That was so hot," she whispered in his ear, "but I didn't want Hugo to see that."

"I know," Sherman said, kissing her lightly and letting her go. "I'm glad Patricia didn't come in while we were doing that too!"

Laura turned to smile at Monty then gave him a long hug.

"Thank you," she said, completely at ease with her new friend.

"We should pick this up at a later date," Monty suggested.

"Okay," Laura agreed softly, then wandered back out into the main room to see what had become of Hugo and nearly walked into him as he came to find her.

"Oh, there you are," he said, catching both her hands and regarding her at length with all the severity he could muster while succumbing to the allure of Laura in the daintiest white dress he had ever seen. "Though it's been so long since I've seen you, it's a wonder I recognized you straight off," he admonished her. Laura looked down at her shiny, high heeled, triple bucked Mary Janes and Hugo followed her gaze, taking in this last touch to her marvelous outfit with approval. "Let's find somewhere we can be alone," he told her, retaining one of her hands and leading her back to yet another room, fitted out with more bondage furniture and mirrors. It wasn't entirely empty, but the few couples hanging out in its corners were quietly engaging in bondage or teasing activities and paid no attention to Hugo and Laura as they entered.

He looked around, pulled her over to a whipping post, placed her with back her against it and kissed her on the lips. Laura's eyes filled with tears at his gentleness, which recalled to her the earliest days of their courtship, when she was still another man's wife and constrained to repulse him at every turn.

Hugo found a bench and made her sit beside him.

"You haven't returned any of my phone calls or emails and you've stayed away a whole week," Hugo reminded her unnecessarily. "Is that a nice way to behave?"

Laura dashed away the few tears that had fallen on her face, hoping he hadn't seen them but gazed back at him with some defiance.

"Oh, and I suppose you always behave nicely?" she demanded.

Hugo's sighed, "I take it you're referring to my playing with Thalia?'

"That's what you call it, playing?"

"Why, what do you call it?"

"Obviously, you've been having an affair!"

"No, we haven't. An affair implies love and romance. I'm not in love with Thalia and we're not having a romance. We've only been together twice and both times you had gone out of town, which I sincerely wish you would stop doing so much."

"Tell me about the first time," she demanded, though she knew it would pain her bitterly to hear the details. "How did it even begin?"

"She dared me do her in the bathroom at Michael's bar during that photo shoot she came down for with Amanda. It was some sort of whim she just got in her head after reading the magazine for a couple of nights in a row."

"So since she came onto you, it's okay, you're held harmless?"

"Yes!" Hugo replied enthusiastically, adding reasonably, "Have you seen that girl? She's a force of nature."

"You're not even sorry you did it, are you?" Laura marveled, her anger and jealousy fully refreshed.

"I am sorry, because it's upset you. I give you my word I'll never touch Thalia again."

Laura sat brooding, her arms folded across her bosom, swinging her beautifully shod feet under the bench like an angry cat thumping its tail.

"It's not just that little college slut. You have so many women!" Laura finally cried.

"Me? No, I don't!" said Hugo with genuine surprise.

"No? What about Francesca? You had to fuck her, so as not to disappoint her, as your dedicated groupie. And Pamela; even though she was engaged to Sloan at the time, you had to fuck her because she was working for you and you fuck all your female employees. And then most recently there was Cassandra. You didn't even tell me you were going to see her, but that entire trip was about rekindling your creakingly ancient romance with the mother of your child! Wasn't it?"

Hugo was taken aback by her vehemence. He shook his head in protest, "No, you've got me wrong. You've always been the one, the only one."

Laura continued to pout.

"Especially in those adorable shoes," he added, taking her by the wrist and pulling her across his lap.

"No!" she tried to break his hold but he locked his arm to her waist.

"Oh? You think I bothered to come all the way to this club tonight not to spank you? After how you acted all week?" He smoothed her skirt down over her curvaceous bottom. But Laura was remembering how red her bottom must already be from the attentions paid to it by Sherman Cooper and was loathe to have the evidence of these salutations glimpsed by Hugo after she had just been so self righteous about his recent lapses of propriety.

"Oh, all right!" she cried, bit her knuckle and did not have long to wait before the first round swat fell and another ten or twelve smacks besides.

"What have you been up to out here all week by yourself anyway?" Hugo demanded, folding one arm back to her waist and pinning it there before taking her breath away with another dozen hard smacks.

"Nothing."

"How long were you planning on staying away?" he asked. When she didn't respond, he administered another dozen ringing swats to her skirted seat, then paused to push the skirt and sewn in white petticoat up to her waist.

"I don't know," she cried, wriggling on his lap but remaining firmly pinned by the wrist.

"What were you thinking when you chose this dress?" Hugo asked, smoothing her sheer white nylon panties down over her well-spanked cheeks. "To me it says, wedding dress."

Laura didn't reply but turned to look at him over her shoulder.

"Don't give me that look. I first proposed to you in September. You've been stalling for eight months," Hugo reminded her, carefully but briskly yanking down her panties to completely bare her bottom to the room, the pretty, rosy sight arousing the interest of the several other couples present. It was unusual to see men in suits and girls in cotton batiste party dresses in that particular club so the scene appeared particularly novel to the onlookers. "What's it going to take for you to take me seriously?" he asked. Without waiting for an answer he continued with the spanking, now gratified to feel her warm, firm flesh rebounding under his palm.

"I'm taking you seriously!" Laura hastened to reply, eager to escape further punishment and suddenly unable to block out the curious onlookers who seemed to have multiplied in the last few seconds and were approaching ever nearer to their corner of the room. "Get away, you B&D zombies," Laura thought, feeling suffocated and overly warm. Besides, her bottom, which had now been spanked by two hard hands in a row, had begun to blaze with heat and ache with pain.

Noticing the group of voyeurs now encircling them at a distance of but five or six feet, Hugo considered taking pity Laura, restoring her modesty and letting her up. But he decided to continue spanking her instead, for how much understanding or kindness had she shown *him* that week?

"Hold still, I'm not done with you yet," Hugo told her, anchoring her firmly across his lap and slapping either cheek a dozen times. "You need a lesson in returning phone calls and emails." Again and again his hard hand came down until the sting began to numb and Laura began to float, now only vaguely aware of anyone looking at her. Only when a solid field of dark red swathed her glowing cheeks from hip to thigh did he begin to think of releasing her.

"Apologize for your unconscionable rudeness," he ordered.

"Not unless you apologize for having to fuck every woman and girl you cross paths with!"

"Oh, Laura, I do not!" he cried, pulling her up and giving her a shake. Laura looked stubborn as she tugged her sheer white panties back up and allowed the graceful folds of the Elie Tahari tea dress to fall back into place.

"Did you just get in this evening?" she asked.

"Yes, I've only been in town long enough to check into my hotel."

"Isn't it getting too warm in here?" Laura asked pointedly.

"It's terribly warm. We should leave now before more people find us," he said, resisting the urge to blow on his hand, that was practically smoking from repeated stern application to Laura's firm, gym trained buttocks. She seemed no worse for her correction and her flush began to fade within seconds of exiting the club onto the street, which smelled heavily of spring.

"I have something with me," said Laura, opening a tiny black velvet purse on a cord she had worn over her shoulder all night and showing Hugo a fat joint and a lighter.

"That's the first friendly thing you've said to me in a week," he grinned, hailing a cab for Battery Park. The traffic was light that evening and they arrived within a few minutes at the tip of Manhattan, paid off the taxi and began to stroll along the embankment, pausing at the most deserted length of railing they could find. For a couple of minutes they smoked in silence, mesmerized by the neon lights beaming from the Jersey shore reflected in the inky waters of the Hudson. The evening's sudden balminess imbued them both with a sense of well-being. It had been a long, cold New England winter.

"You know," said Hugo, "I don't think it's Thalia you've been jealous of, I think you've been jealous of Amanda."

Laura didn't reply at once.

"It's true, isn't it?"

"Yes," she replied at length. "Because she's perfect and you adore her."

"That's because against all odds, she wound up in the scene," Hugo explained.

"Against no odds. Cassandra planned it that way. She created, then deployed her own personal Cupid to recapture your heart."

"That's fanciful. It's her stepfather's fault that Amanda's in the scene. He spanked her when she was three."

"It's great how you can sort everything out so neatly in your head. But I'm curious about one thing, how you can possibly justify turning your own daughter out?"

"I did no such thing."

"Yes, you did. Susan told me that session you arranged for Amanda to trade Mr. Bartlett for permission to shoot at the store concluded with him objectifying her most crudely."

"Really? I had no idea," Hugo replied, with a sinking sensation.

"As if all of your dealings with Amanda haven't been entirely inappropriate!" Laura accused.

"At least I stopped her from posing nude for Playboy," he said in his own defense.

"But now she's all over the internet getting spanked!"

"But only over her clothes."

"Hugo, she's just a college freshman."

"But she wanted to do it."

"You see, you can't say no to her. It's a wonder she didn't go completely off the rails with all the Faustian temptations you threw at her freshman year."

"I know!" he agreed.

"I mean, you're paying her damned tuition. It would have been the most reasonable thing in the world for you to advise her to wait until after she graduated college before getting involved in the adult industry or doing half the other crazy things she's apparently done. I mean, who ever heard of an eighteen year old owning a fetish wardrobe?"

"That's true," he conceded. "It just didn't occur to me to dampen her enthusiasm."

"As I recall you didn't even let my sister come to one of your parties until she was nineteen."

"I know, but Amanda is, well, taller."

"You haven't even tried to make her behave."

"But that would be so clichéd. Or maybe just creepy."

"Really? What about turning her out?"

"Laura, please stop using that appalling expression!"

"Why? It's accurate. Bartlett paid her five thousand dollars to let him have sex with her the last time they played."

"How do you know that?" Hugo asked, again feeling a painful twinge of remorse at having made the initial introduction between the department store owner and his young daughter.

"Amanda told Thalia, Thalia told Susan and Susan told me," Laura admitted, already sorry she had betrayed Amanda's one guilty secret. Hugo was silent for some time, thinking about how many mistakes he had made in his dealings with his daughter.

"It never occurred to me he'd push it that far," said Hugo. "Or that she'd go there."

"His approach was masterful, we all give him that. He undermined her ethics with lavish gifts, then proceeded to take classic advantage of her submissiveness," reported Laura. "But none of that ever would have happened if you hadn't simply handed her to him."

"I agree that my influence on Amanda this year has been questionable at best," said Hugo.

"You spanked her in the woods."

"That was wrong."

"You passed her on to Michael and David."

"That was to distract her."

"You gave her the keys to your apartment to use as a make out pad."

"Because I'm hardly ever there."

"You're spoiling her rotten."

"You're a lot more spoiled than Amanda," Hugo said pointedly, deciding it was time to refocus the conversation onto his beloved. "I don't think you've done an honest day's work since I introduced your sister to Anthony Newton."

"All right, point taken," Laura replied.

"The problem with you is that you have too many options due to the endless amount of houses Anthony owns. You have a room here, a room there, a room everywhere. If you'd stayed home with me more often, you'd find far less to give you unease."

"You're right," Laura said, feeling she had been away from home too long and suddenly eager to hasten their return.

"You'll feel a lot more settled and happy once you're married again. Your first husband was severe. But I'm just right for you. You know that."

"All right," she said meekly, for it had been the most emotional week of her life and she felt exhausted.

"Let's go get a bite," he suggested. "I know a café a few blocks from here that stays open late." They strolled New York's oldest streets slowly, intoxicated by the freshness of the night and being together again. Presently they came upon the tiny bistro Hugo had remembered and went in. Halfway between a restaurant and a sandwich bar, the small room was furnished with checkered tables and a limited but agreeable selection of foods and wines. A young couple sat at a corner table; otherwise the café was empty except for one post punk waitress and whoever was in the kitchen. Hugo ordered a bottle of shiraz and baguette sandwiches, promising Laura the best Italian scrambled eggs she had ever tasted.

While they were sampling the wine and awaiting the meal Hugo flipped open his phone. "Look, I just got a message from Marguerite," he said, showing Laura the tiny screen across the table. Laura took the phone and read: "See you in Vegas Monday!" Laura looked at Hugo in surprise.

"You're going to meet Marguerite in Vegas on Monday?"

"Marguerite and Michael are meeting us there. They're going to be our witnesses. Or, my reinforcements in case you try to wriggle out of marrying me."

Laura felt her face go red in the semi dark cafe, unaccountably embarrassed at the though of taking ritualistic vows with a dominant man a second time. The rite was a primitive one and after its enactment, everything changed.

As if reading her mind, Hugo said, "It's time for a major change in our relationship, dear. So you'll never feel the way you did this week again."

"The way I acted wasn't right," Laura admitted, downing the last of her second glass of wine some thirty minutes later, at the conclusion of a most delicious repast. "Because I do really love you."

Hugo called a cab to spare her any more walking on the high heels. It arrived as he paid the check and they got in the cab to return to Anthony's house and collect Laura's luggage. Susan was not home yet so Laura left her a note as to where she was going that night. What with all that had gone on, the playing, weed, food, drink and emotionality, it was very difficult for Laura to focus on packing so Hugo helped her. He looked at her questioningly as he came to the expensive new pvc ensemble of skirt, vest, long coat and boots with which she had captivated Norman Teasdale. "I found a cute shop in the village," Laura explained inadequately. Then he came to the new blue leather skirt, shoes, gloves and white top that she had worn to jellify Victor.

"You went on a leather shopping spree?" he asked, examining a blue leather pump with interest.

"I must have had an intuition I was going to Vegas," she replied, arranging her several soft valises open on the bed. Hugo lay all the leather and pvc in a neat pile then loosely rolled it up and lightly placed it in one of the bags. The fetish shoes and boots went into the sides and the bag was zipped closed.

"Come on," he urged her, "gather up the rest of your clothes or whatever you think you'll need for the next three days." Then he saw her eye the bed longingly with a sleepy look in her soft brown eyes. "Don't even think of crawling into that bed, young lady. You're going to finish packing so we can go back to my hotel and leave from there first thing tomorrow."

"Just for a second," she said moving towards the bed with its down counterpane wrapped in purest white Danish muslin.

"I didn't want to have to do this again tonight," said Hugo, bending her over the bed and smacking her awake.

"All right, all right, I'm awake!" she cried, far more sensitive to his hard hand now, after the comfortable dinner and infusion of red wine than she had been when primed by other handsome men that she liked at the spanking club. She felt every spank and the pain and sting were not pleasant at this point in the evening.

As always, spanking Laura aroused Hugo and he realized she was in the perfect position to be possessed. He pushed the skirt and petticoat of the delicate white dress up to her waist and tugged her sheer white panties down. Laura heard his zipper come down and turned her head to look at him.

"I'm not tired," he said, his cock nodding agreement at her. She arched up a bit and straddling the floor in her high heels, spread her legs. Her smooth, oval cheeks still held a faint pink tinge from her earlier spankings, now overlaid by a darker red blush from his hand a moment before. She was wet and open to him. He sheathed his cock and did not hesitate to penetrate her pussy to the hilt. Slipping one hand under her flat belly and placing his fingers unerringly against the tiny, invisible spot on her lower abdomen that always made her climax, he took her with characteristically powerful thrusts and manipulated her with deft finger tips until she was seized by a series of inner spasms that wrung an echoing response from him in a couple of seconds.

"The wedding dress has served its purpose," said Hugo, after a few minutes on the bed with Laura in his arms. "Leave it here for next time you visit. Now change your clothes and finish packing and I'll tell about something nice you can look forward to on Monday."

"You mean, our wedding day?" Laura smiled shyly at Hugo.

"Yes, and the day of your bachelorette party as well."

"Oh no, Hugo, no, I could never sit there and stick dollars in a male stripper's jock," Laura protested with horror. She did not tell him that she had already enjoyed a private bachelorette party with the two handsome men who had ravished her with bondage, spanking and kisses at Paddles earlier that night. She didn't have to tell him. He was the person who had suggested to Sherman Cooper and Monty Powell that they overtake Laura and soften her up for him.

"Who said anything about that? Didn't I tell you Michael Flagg was going to be there with Marguerite? He'll give you your bachelorette party, just as you've always wanted all these years while I take Marguerite out gambling. Don't bother protesting. It's all settled and you'll like it."

"It sounds like you've thought of everything."

"I'm glad you finally noticed!"

About the Author

In *Random Point*, everything is linked to spanking and this is true for the author of the Shadow Lane novels as well. Eve Howard has been writing and producing spanking erotica since the 1980's, when she began freelancing for one of California's largest fetish magazine publishers. While editing *Spank Hard* magazine (as Lizzie Bennett) in 1985, she was discovered by the video producer Nu-West and offered a chance to perform in spanking videos. In 1986 she published the first Shadow Lane story and the following year formed the video production company Shadow Lane with her partner Tony Elka. The Shadow Lane novel series, originally published by Eve in serial form in her magazine *Stand Corrected*, was brought out in paperback volumes by Blue Moon books beginning in 1992. There are ten titles in the Shadow Lane series and Eve is currently working on a pictorial publication called *Shadow Lane's Art of Spanking*.

Since 1988, Eve has written, directed and produced over 150 spanking videos, the vast majority featuring the same male-spanks-female dynamic portrayed in her novels. Female-friendly and designed to make people feel good, rather than guilty, about being into spanking, Eve suggests an irreverent alternative to the all or nothing B&D subculture portrayed in such beloved classics as *The Story of O*. Many spanking fans have discovered the real life spanking scene by following the same patterns of social networking as described in the Shadow Lane novels. And for almost twenty years, Eve's company Shadow Lane has been one of the primary social organs of the real life spanking scene. She lives with her husband Tony Elka and their cats in Las Vegas.

Reader Reviews about the Shadow Lane Series

"I've become addicted to the "Random Point" series so much that I can't wait until the next chapter. I've ordered the first two Shadow Lane volumes and have re-read them over and over. I never tire of them. Eve is the only person I know who can make an enema sexy."

"I discovered Shadow Lane about a month ago via AOL. Prior to that time I thought I could write excellent spanking erotica. Then I ordered, "The Problem with Laura." This is just a note to commend Eve Howard's spectacular talent and to say thanks for an incredible erotic experience."

"I have just completed "Return to Random Point" and decided that I had to write about how much I enjoyed it. I have not been so aroused since reading my first discipline novel many years ago, about a girl raised in England and "coming of age" as I believe they put it. More recently I have enjoyed reading Grant Andrews' My Darling Dominatrix and Ann Rice's "Beauty" series. It seems that women, though, have the right touch when it comes to writing about this subject. Eve, especially, knows how to touch that erotic nerve and bring it to a pure, raw sensuality until one feels that he/she is near bursting with lust."

"I, for one, have always loved (and by loved I mean devoured... breathlessly) Eve Howard's novelettes. To read them... especially when I was just 'coming out'... was to feel completely validated. I truly identified with each and every heroine; the feisty, sassy ones, the shy, demure ultra 'subby' ones... the young ones, and the more mature. I loved the gentle yet firm "taken in hand" nature of the romantic variety of spanking D's that Eve always incorporated into the stories. I loved that the plots were not complicated... but, feasible nonetheless. I loved the depictions of sexual escapades after many of the spanking interludes. I appreciated that the girls were cherished and adored by the affably rogue-ish gents... that the submitting was willing and desired... that it wasn't like 'rape.'

I like the settings... having grown up in New England and living here almost my whole life. I LOVED the idea of the bookstore (which I always find sexy). Then and now. I could cite many passages too, but I fear I've rambled enough. Eve was/is always my favorite spanking author."

www.ingramcontent.com/pod-product-compliance
Lightning Source LLC
Chambersburg PA
CBHW021957010726

47494CB00003B/780